PRAISE FOR *EVERY MOVE YOU MAKE*

"C.L. Taylor knocks it out of the pa[...]
Make is a compulsive page-turner yo[...]
Clare Macki[...]

"*Every Move You Make* takes your worst fear about letting the
wrong person into your life, multiplies it by four and then hits you
round the head with a totally brilliant twist that I for one did not
see coming. I absolutely loved it!"
Lisa Jewell

"You'll need your wits about you to track the truth in this terrifying
thriller about victims who turn the tables on their stalkers. I read it
with my heart in my mouth – exhilarating stuff."
Louise Candlish

"Wow this was exceptional! *Every Move You Make* is a breathless,
chilling one-sitting read with twist after brilliant twist. Clever,
original and filled with tension, this is a story I won't ever forget.
C.L. Taylor's best yet."
Claire Douglas

"Spine-chilling at every turn! *Every Move You Make* will grab you in
the first few pages and not give you a moment's rest until the very
end! Brilliant characters, a devilish premise and an evocative voice
make this one of the best thrillers of the year."
Jeffery Deaver

"I absolutely love C.L. Taylor's writing."
Liz Nugent

"A tense, twisty thrill-ride of stalking, obsession and revenge."
TM Logan

"Just when you think C.L. Taylor couldn't possibly get any better,
she does just that. *Every Move You Make* is an exceedingly clever,
tense, surprising and satisfying rollercoaster of a book – I devoured
it in one sitting."
Andrea Mara

"Full of surprises and intriguing characters. I was GRIPPED."
Marian Keyes

"A C.L. Taylor novel has style, speed, and more hooks than a tackle
shop. By-the-throat suspense, unfussy and unmissable."
A.J. Finn

PRAISE FOR C.L. TAYLOR

"From the moment I picked this book up, I resented every minute I couldn't spend between its pages. *The Guilty Couple* is a one-breath rollercoaster ride, with twists, turns, ups and downs . . . then just when you think it's over, there's another loop ahead! A proper, classy thriller."
Janice Hallett

"I loved *The Guilty Couple* so much I was up until 2 am finishing it. Twisty and compelling, tense and fast-paced and thoroughly unputdownable."
Angela Marsons

"Twisty and gripping – another brilliant book from C.L. Taylor."
Jane Fallon

"With high stakes and a killer premise, *The Guilty Couple* takes the reader on a thrill ride of a journey. A perfectly paced and propulsive read, told with C.L. Taylor's trademark instinct for edge-of-your-seat reveals."
Lucy Clarke

"Pacy, surprising and with some brilliant twists – C.L. Taylor's best yet. Brilliant."
Catherine Cooper

"Compelling. Compulsive. Crafted. Cleverly calculated."
Jane Corry

"C.L. Taylor has done it again. A fast paced, thrilling read that I couldn't put down – with a twist I didn't see coming. I loved it!"
Heidi Perks

"Wow, *The Guilty Couple* doesn't let up for a moment – you're in for ride!"
Sarah Pinborough

"Wow, *The Guilty Couple* was everything I needed it to be and more. I raced through it, hardly coming up for air. It's twisty, taut, unbearably tense and a masterclass in nerve-shredding storytelling. Brava, C.L. Taylor, you've done it again!"
Emma Stonex

"A brilliantly written, fast-paced and very clever thriller – I couldn't put it down!"
Susi Holliday

C.L. Taylor is a *Sunday Times* bestselling author. Her psychological thrillers have sold over two million copies in the UK alone, been translated into over twenty languages, and optioned for television. Her 2019 novel, *Sleep*, and her 2022 novel *The Guilty Couple* were both Richard and Judy picks. C.L. Taylor lives in Bristol with her partner and son.

By the same author:

C.L.TAYLOR
EVERY
MOVE
YOU
MAKE

avon.

Published by AVON
A division of HarperCollins*Publishers* Ltd
1 London Bridge Street
London SE1 9GF

www.harpercollins.co.uk

HarperCollins*Publishers*
Macken House, 39/40 Mayor Street Upper,
Dublin 1, D01 C9W8
Ireland

This paperback edition 2024

24 25 26 27 28 LBC 5 4 3 2 1

First published in Great Britain by HarperCollins*Publishers* 2024

ISBN: 978-0-00-866693-4

Typeset in Sabon Lt Std by Palimpsest Book Production Limited,
Falkirk, Stirlingshire
Printed and bound in the United States of America

To my sister Rebecca Taylor

Thank you for rescuing me when I needed you most.

Chapter 1

Natalie

Natalie Beare has forgotten how it feels to be normal. She can't remember how it feels to leave work without a tight, thick knot in her stomach; to raise a hand in goodbye, to stride out of the building and sigh with relief as the door closes behind her. She has forgotten how to stroll to the tube, barely aware of the commuters streaming around her. She has forgotten how pleasurable it is to grab a seat and lose herself in a book.

The moment Jamie regained his freedom she lost hers.

She stands at the window that runs the length of her office, watching as her colleagues drift out of the building, chatting and laughing or glued to their phones. Her gaze flicks to the street beyond, to the restaurant opposite, to the waterway, to the trees, to the cars driving past. She's looking for anyone who doesn't fit the scene, someone who isn't heading home from work. Someone still; who shouldn't be there: a shadow in the driving seat of a car, a dark shape resting against a lamppost; a solitary figure

1

watching the building, looking for her, waiting for her to leave.

Her phone bleeps in her hand: a WhatsApp from the group.

Alexandra: Be careful. If you so much as catch a glimpse of him run into a shop or get someone to walk with you. Do not let him confront you alone.

River: Ring the police if you see him!

Her phone bleeps again, twice, before she can respond.

River: Want me to come and meet you at work?

Lucy: We're all here for you. Message us as soon as you get home.

When she was told that Jamie was being released from prison on licence her family had tried their best to dull her fear: 'He won't go anywhere near you', 'Things are different now', 'If he comes within a hundred metres of you, he'll be sent back to jail.'

'You don't understand what he's like.' She'd repeated the same phrase over and over.

She had told her Family Liaison Officer how afraid she was. She had begged him to help and, in turn, was told to change her name and telephone number, to move house and get a new job.

'It won't make a difference. He'll find me. He always does.'

She had searched the internet for help and stumbled upon a closed forum for the survivors of stalking. There was no 'join' button; instead, she had to ring a number and talk to one of the administrators. She cried as she explained what she'd been through, then cried some more when she was told she'd been approved to join. She read dozens of posts but found herself gravitating towards the other Brits in the group; their stories and experiences mirrored hers. When one of the London-based women decided to take things offline and create a WhatsApp group, Natalie was invited to join them.

'You ready to go, Nat?' Across the grey-carpeted room her workmate Claire pushes her chair away from her desk. She's not a close friend, but they've fallen into a routine of walking to Canary Wharf station together (a routine initiated by Nat).

'Yep.' Natalie taps out a quick reply to her group:

Thanks all. River, that's really kind but I'll be walking to the tube with Claire again. I'll message when I'm safely home. Everyone stay safe. Chat soon. x

'Oi! Nat!' Claire shouts from the other side of the office where she's holding open the door. 'Come on. Some of us want to go home.'

Natalie does her best to pay attention to what Claire's saying as they walk from the Barclays building to Canary Wharf underground station, a nip to the September air that makes her wish she'd brought a coat, but the most she can manage by way of conversation is the occasional grunt or 'uh huh'. She's scanning the faces of every man she sees: the men in suits who overtake her, their expensive shoes clacking against the pavement, the workers in neon jackets and the commuters wearing trainers and carrying backpacks.

It would be almost impossible for Jamie to track her down here. She's changed jobs twice since he was sent to prison. Her Facebook account is under a different name, her Instagram is private, and she doesn't go anywhere near

TikTok or Twitter. But 'almost impossible' doesn't reassure her; she still feels sick with fear.

'See you tomorrow then, yeah?' Claire's voice draws her gaze away from the man in the black coat who's just sprinted past them in the direction of the Elizabeth Line.

They're inside the station, standing a couple of feet from the escalator, in the no-man's land between the Elizabeth Line and the Jubilee Line. Claire shifts her weight and adjusts the shoulder strap of her bag. Natalie smiles uncertainly. They haven't reached the hugging goodbye stage of friendship yet and there's an awkward beat before Claire raises her hand and says, 'See you tomorrow then. Have a good night.'

Natalie raises her hand too and heads towards the Elizabeth Line. She takes two steps onto the platform and scans the throng of commuters. She moves towards the left, where it's busier, weaving her way through the tired, warm bodies. Musty air wraps itself around her as a train rumbles closer. The crowd contracts as the train pulls up to the platform, then surges as the doors open. Natalie moves with them, but something makes her falter. An invisible thread yanks her gaze towards the square archway she walked through minutes before.

She turns her head.

She's imagined this moment for three years. She's always thought she'd scream, that she'd run. Instead, she draws thick, fusty air deep into her lungs as fear snatches her out of her body. She is floating, suspended inches above the solid, grey platform: hollowed out, helium filled, weightless.

Run! screams the voice in her head but she cannot wrench her gaze away.

Run! Run!

Beep! Beep! Beep! Beep!

The frantic trill of the train doors, heralding their closure, pulls her back onto the platform and she trembles back into herself, heart pounding, skin prickling, breath choked in her throat. Just one step – into the train – will separate her from Jamie. He's barely moved from the archway, but the carriage is full. Commuters are packed together, elbows into sides, shoulders touching shoulders, chins craned upward. There's no space left.

Jamie is watching her, waiting for her to make her next move.

Beep! Beep! Beep! Beep!

Natalie leaps, throwing herself against the wall of bodies, as the doors close around her. She pushes herself into the non-existent space between a man in a suit and a young woman with pink streaks in her hair.

'Sorry,' she breathes as the doors seal everyone inside. She wriggles for space, her cheek pressed against the window as the train pulls away.

She seeks out the archway as the train moves past it. Jamie is gone.

By the time the train pulls into Tottenham Court Road, Natalie has convinced herself that Jamie didn't make it on. She was less than a foot away from a carriage and had struggled to board. Even if the carriage nearest him hadn't been packed like hers there's no way he could have made it there before the train left, even at a sprint. If he had, he'd have squeezed his way through the standing passengers, and moved through the carriages. He'd be beside her now, an arm locked around her shoulders, his hot breath whispering warning words into her ear. For the last five minutes she hasn't taken her eyes off the connecting door.

As the train grinds to a stop and the doors open, a new thought hits her. What if he made it onto the train but stayed in his seat because he didn't want to risk a scene in public? She steps out onto the platform and looks to her left, towards the carriage where Jamie may have got on. Should she continue her normal route, taking the Northern Line to Camden Town, and then walk home? Or jump back on the train and go somewhere else?

If Jamie knows where she works, he might know where she lives.

There aren't any London Underground staff on the platform. She could go up to the ticket office, try and find someone there. But what would they do? Take her to a back office maybe, assuming they believe her. She's read dozens of stories about women trying to get help in train stations, shopping malls and pubs, only for over-worked and stressed staff to shrug them off, telling them they can't help and to call the police.

Even if she is listened to and given refuge in a back room, she'll have to wait hours for the police to turn up. And then what? They'll take her to a station, and she'll wait for another hour or so before a detective is available to take her statement. Then they'll tell her to call someone who can accompany her home. The alternative would be to exit Tottenham Court Road and get a black cab, but it'll take forever to flag one down on Oxford Street in the rain, and Jamie might catch her up.

An impatient commuter shoulder-barges her, forcing her to step away from the train. She glances around, searching the platform for any sign of Jamie, and makes a snap decision.

6

She'll get the tube to Camden Town and when she's safely in her flat she'll call her Family Liaison Officer, Jessica, who she trusts. Home is where Nat feels the safest, with two locks and a safety chain on the door and double glazing at the windows. Home. She heads off towards the Northern Line, sticking close to the other commuters heading in the same direction. She just wants to get home.

The sun is low and pink as Natalie exits Camden tube, but the streets are buzzing with people. She feels less anxious here, surrounded by the bars and restaurants, the familiar and the predictable. She isn't afraid of drunks or dealers or the musicians and artists who possess a kind of effortless cool she'll never have. But she weaves her keys through her fingers anyway, hastening her pace down the street and under the bridge. She approaches the park, skeletal trees waving in the wind – all angles and stark spiky branches against a soft palette of orange, yellow and red. Her mobile pings as she reaches her street, but she doesn't bother to fish her phone out of her bag. It'll be the WhatsApp group, asking if she's home safely.

The group was originally called The Stalking Survival Group, but Alex said they shouldn't be defined by their experiences and suggested, 'Fuck you stalker twats' instead (later abbreviated to FYST by Lucy). The name stuck.

A male shout cuts through the air like a whip crack as Natalie reaches the steps that lead to her basement flat. She turns sharply. A group of lads, their arms around each other's shoulders, is leaving the park. They sway down the street, laughing and joshing as they head towards the nightlife and bars. That was her once, with her female friends, laughing and singing, not a care in the world.

7

She descends the concrete stairs to her flat, the light fading with each step. Her landlord needs to fit a security light: she's been asking him for one ever since she moved in six months ago. The stairs are uneven and crumbled but she's at the bottom now, beside her front door, her keys in her hand. Her phone bleeps again and something, some instinct she can't name, nags at her to look at it.

The screen flashes with a new notification, then another, and another. An unknown number is bombarding her with texts.

Think you're too good for me do you?

Too good to even say hello?

After everything you did.

Why would you run from me?

I told you what would happen.

You don't get to pretend I don't exist, Nat.

I fucking told you what would happen.

She is still staring at the phone, her back to the street, as Jamie silently descends the steps.

Chapter 2

WhatsApp group: FYST

18.22
Lucy: Nat, are you home yet?

Alexandra: It's saying she hasn't logged onto WhatsApp since a quarter to six. I'll ring her

18.23
Alexandra: She's not picking up.

Lucy: Oh god.

Bridget: She's probably on the tube

River: This late? She's normally home by this time.

Bridget: Let's try not to panic. Maybe she's gone out.

River: And risk running into her ex? No way. She wouldn't do that.

9

Alexandra: I'm going to check her Facebook

River: I thought she deactivated that?

Alexandra: She's got one under a fake name.

River: She didn't tell me about that :(Did the rest of you know?

18.27
River: I take it from the silence that's a yes.

Lucy: Bridget, how's your day been? River, I'm sure it's nothing personal. She probably just forgot to add you.

Bridget: Weirdly quiet since my stalker sent me a tweet saying she knows where I work, and that worries me because it means she's planning something.

Lucy: I know what you mean. It's the not knowing that's so scary.

Alexandra: River, you weren't even added to this chat until we'd seen your face on Zoom.

River: Oh. Right. So because I'm a bloke I'm automatically a threat am I?

Alexandra: Oh my god. It wasn't about whether you were a bloke or not.

River: You sure about that? Did you have to show your face on Zoom?

Alexandra: I started the group

River: Bridget? Lucy? Did you?

Alexandra: Nat hasn't updated FB in days

Bridget: Ring again.

18.45
River: No reply to my question from Lucy and Bridget. So I was right. Thanks a lot. Really supportive.

21.53
Alexandra: Anyone know where Nat lives? Maybe one of us should go round? @River are you still sulking?

Bridget: Camden I think. Not sure where though.

Alexandra: Yeah, it's definitely Camden but I don't know her address either. We can't call the police if we don't know where she lives.

Bridget: I imagine her mum's ringing them.

Lucy: I feel sick. I really hope she's okay.

07.23
River: Anyone heard anything? I can't stand this. She hasn't logged on to WhatsApp since quarter past six yesterday. That's not like her.

Lucy: I'm really hoping that someone stole her phone and that's why we can't get in touch with her. Going to school now but keep me updated. Can't have my phone on when teaching but I'll look when I can.

River: Will do.

11.25

Alexandra: Oh god. Someone just posted to Natalie's FB page. Please tell me it isn't true.

Chapter 3

Alexandra

Murder: it's the one word the vicar won't say. Alexandra's heels, tucked beneath the pew, tap out a silent plea – Say it, just say it. But he won't say it. He's been swerving the word since he stepped up to the pulpit, his bassy, reverential tones filling the small chapel, showering the congregation with anodyne phrases like, 'lost her life', 'taken too soon' and 'cruelly snatched away.'

Natalie Beare was murdered. Her ex-boyfriend harassed her, threatened her, stalked her and then stabbed her to death on her own doorstep. And yet it doesn't feel real.

'A beloved daughter, sister, colleague and friend. As a child Natalie attended . . .'

Photos appear on a screen to the vicar's left: Natalie as a baby in a soft white blanket. Natalie as a toddler, jumping over waves. Natalie on her first day of school, and her last.

Alex didn't know any of those Natalies – she never even

13

met her in person – but she knew her stalking story, about Jamie and how scared she was. She's scrolled back through Natalie's group messages and it's like reversing time, skipping from 'Just leaving work' to 'He'll kill me when he gets out of prison' to 'My ex-boyfriend has been bombarding me with messages and I just want him to stop.'

Theirs is a group no one wants to be part of, and everyone wants to leave. But not the way that Natalie did.

She tears her eyes away from the screen, each image as heartbreaking as the last, and looks for the others. When she arrived at the church thirty minutes earlier she didn't dawdle outside. She hurried inside and chose a seat on the right of the chapel. Sitting by the wall would reduce the chance of her stalker sitting beside her by one.

Not that she knows what they look like.

Her stalker is a shadow and a ghoul – faceless, ageless, genderless – but she's read enough of their messages to recognise their venomous tone. They know everything about her: where she lives and works, who she loves, and what she fears. As an actress in the public eye her life, and her past, has been laid bare in the press and she's been trolled on social media for years – for leaving a popular soap, for an unflattering outfit, for a minor popstar boyfriend – but she's never experienced anything like this. Her stalker is relentless, bombarding her with tweets, photos, silent phone calls, flowers and 'gifts'.

Even now, as she scans the church for Lucy, Bridget and River, she can feel her phone vibrating in her bag. More vile messages, undoubtedly, telling her she's a vacuous, untalented waste of space and how she'll pay for what she has done.

A man in the centre of the church catches her eye: tall,

thin, late twenties with wild, bird's-nest hair and black-framed glasses over a generous nose. He raises a hand in hello and his mouth twitches into a self-conscious smile. For a terrible second, she thinks it's her stalker then her brain connects the three-dimensional head with the face she's seen on her laptop screen. It's River Scott-Tyler, the only man in her stalking support group. He gestures towards the other side of the church where Lucy is sitting, her blonde hair tied back, her face blanched with grief.

Organ music swells and the coffin is lifted onto the shoulders of men that Alex doesn't know. Natalie's tear-stained family follow her out of the stifling darkness of the chapel and into the soft light of an unusually warm October day.

As the congregation files out behind them, Alex gestures to River to head over to Lucy, then makes her own way through the pews to the other side of the church. Up close she can see tear tracks in Lucy's foundation and dark mascara smudges beneath her eyes. Gone is her CBeebies presenter vibe – the bright, vibrant colours she normally wears – replaced by a plain black dress, cardigan and sensible shoes. As Lucy stands and joins them, Bridget steps out of the shadows at the back of the church. In her late fifties she's the oldest of the group. She's short and heavy set, her black suit jacket too short in the arms and too tight across the chest. She moves tentatively towards them, as though she mistrusts the sturdiness of the floorboards under her feet.

'Hi guys.' River breaks the silence as they gather into an awkward, shifting square. 'It's so nice to see you all in person. I wish it was under different circumstances.' He turns towards Lucy and opens his arms for a hug. She recoils, shying away.

15

'Sorry. God.' His throat flushes red. 'Was that inappropriate? I feel like I know you all so well; but maybe—'

'I'll hug you.' Bridget lunges towards him and pulls him into an embrace so heartfelt and enthusiastic that he gasps in surprise.

'I'm so sorry, River,' Lucy says as Bridget releases him, 'I was just a bit caught off—'

'It's fine, honestly.' He looks so unbearably awkward that Alex turns away. 'I'm just glad we could all be here, for Natalie.'

A weighty silence falls, and Alex's gaze drops to the uneven wooden flooring beneath her feet, to the planks scuffed and worn from hundreds of weddings, baptisms and funerals. She thinks of all the hopes and dreams that must have filled the small chapel over the years, all the broken hearts and the tears. She hasn't been in a church for a very long time, but it feels the same – cold and damp, smelling of fading flowers and musty kneelers. She can almost hear the echo of a guttural grief-filled groan, as powerful as a roar – but she tunes it out. Memories can't bloom if you nip them in the bud.

'It's never going to stop, is it?' The tremor in Lucy's voice shakes her back into the present.

'Lucy—'

'No. Don't! Don't tell me it'll get better because it won't. I've moved house twice. I've changed my job. I can't do it again. I won't. It's not fair on the students. Why is it me that has to—'

'Lucy,' River says softly. 'If you go to the police—'

'No.' She turns to him, cheeks flushed. 'I've told you. No police.'

16

'But—' Bridget begins, but Lucy talks over her.

'I can't live like this, not knowing what he's going to do next. I can't do this any more. Earlier I . . .' her gaze flicks towards the empty pulpit. 'There was a moment when I wished it was me in the coffin. Not Nat.'

Alexandra jolts as though stung. 'Lucy, don't say that. Please never say that.'

'If you tell the police, they'll find him,' River says. 'He'll be arrested and sent to jail—'

'He won't stop!' Lucy's shrill cry echoes off the cold, stone walls. 'Just like Jamie didn't stop. Nat went to the police; she testified in court; she did everything right and he still killed her. He still—'

Bridget coughs loudly. They're being watched. The vicar and two middle-aged women have come out of the vestry, but Lucy is still in full flow.

'This won't end until one of us is dead.'

'Well if that's the choice . . .' Alex lowers her voice, '. . . then it needs to be—' She stops abruptly. A blonde woman in her early seventies is heading down the aisle towards them, a wreath in her hands. As she draws closer, she thrusts the flowers at Bridget who shakes her head sharply.

'I'm not family. They're outside.'

'I know,' the woman says. 'I was heading to my car when someone gave this to me: dark-haired woman, nose ring, and a neck tattoo. She had quite a strong foreign accent. I couldn't really understand her, but she gestured inside the church as though she wanted me to give it to one of you.'

'It'll be for Nat.' River leans across her and plucks a small rectangular piece of card from the arrangement of white

17

roses, jasmine and foliage. 'There we go. Rest in Peace, and the date.'

'I'll take it to the family.' The woman gives them a small tight nod and heads back down the aisle, the wreath in her hands.

'Hang on!' River holds the card aloft, but the woman's already disappeared outside. 'I got it wrong. This isn't today's date. It says the twentieth of October, not the tenth.'

'Let me see that.' Bridget whips the card out of his fingers. 'It's a mistake, obviously. A typo. Happens all the time, especially when customers order flowers through the website. A two instead of a one, easily done.'

Alex touches a hand to the cold wood of a pew. 'The twentieth is the first night of my play.' She looks at the others. 'Is it a significant date for anyone else?'

River looks thoughtful then shakes his head.

'That's my parents' fortieth wedding anniversary. I'm going out for a meal with them,' Lucy says, 'but it has to be a typo though, doesn't it, Bridget? It's a coincidence that Alex and I both have something special happening that day.'

Bridget doesn't respond. She's staring past Lucy, a haunted look in her eyes.

'Are you okay, Bridge?' Alex asks.

'I'm sure it doesn't mean anything.' She gives herself a little shake as though settling herself back into her skin. 'At least I didn't give it much thought at the time but, on my last day of my last job, at the florist I worked at, my boss hugged me and said she'd see me at my birthday party and Charlotte said, "If it happens" under her breath.'

'When's your birthday?' Alex looks towards the exit and

18

the bright sunshine outside. But she doesn't move. She doesn't want to believe that it's real.

'Guys,' River holds up his hands, palms out, 'let's not freak out. It's a typo. That's all.'

'When's your birthday?' Alex asks again.

Bridget gently places the card on a prayer book on the back of a pew.

'It's the twentieth, isn't it?' Lucy says.

Bridget turns to look at her.

And she nods.

Chapter 4

Bridget

Nine days until someone dies . . .

It's the day after Natalie's funeral, 5.30 a.m. on a chilly London morning, and Bridget slows her pace as she approaches the back door of the flower shop, keys in hand, her senses tingling. Someone's watching her. She can feel it as powerfully as if they'd reached out and stroked the back of her head. They're not directly behind her. She can't smell them, hear them or sense them but they are watching; of that she's sure. She steadies herself, drawing in deep lungfuls of air – in through her nose, and out through her mouth – and turns slowly. She looks for sudden movements, for someone ducking behind a skip or darting out onto the street, then scans the row of windows that overlook the alley. There's no one there; no one she can see anyway. Whoever was watching her has used the darkness as a cloak.

20

'If you're following me then you'd better think twice!' she shouts, but her words are eclipsed by the peal of an ambulance. 'This needs to end,' she says, more softly, as she fits the keys into the lock and opens the door.

It's a little after eleven o'clock in the morning, the wholesaler fresh flower delivery has arrived, the stems are soaking up water in their buckets, several arrangements are made up, and Bridget's colleague Mark is selecting flowers for a bouquet while she inputs an order into the computer behind the counter. It's not *her* flower shop, much as she'd love it to be, and she's enjoying the sense of responsibility whilst the owner Stella is on holiday.

Yawning, she reaches for her coffee. She barely slept last night; scenes from Natalie's funeral played over and over in her mind: the coffin, the singing, the tears, the vicar's relentless drone. It didn't feel real. It didn't make sense that Natalie's lifeless body was in that wicker casket, that WhatsApp was still announcing that she hadn't used the app for over six weeks. It all felt like some terrible, wicked joke, or a staged funeral as a last, desperate attempt to get Jamie to leave her alone. But it wasn't a joke, was it? Natalie was dead and Jamie was back in jail, this time for life. Poor, poor girl. She hadn't done anything wrong.

Her mobile rings as she mentally calculates how many rolls of cellophane wrap they're going to get through in the next week. She jots a number on the pad beside the laptop before she picks up her phone.

'River?' There's surprise in her voice. River's never rung her before; none of them have: they communicate solely through messages.

21

'Oh god, sorry,' She can hear the awkwardness in River's response. 'I'm not sure what I did there. I was trying to message you and the phone fell off my desk. I must have hit the call button when I picked it up. I didn't want to hang up in case you got worried.'

Mark, on the other side of the shop, sings along to the radio as he reaches for a spray of gypsophila. He couldn't be more different from River, who is the jitteriest person that Bridget's ever met. At Natalie's funeral he had danced from foot to foot, wringing his hands, his eyes flitting this way and that. He was even nervier than Lucy. They were all worried about their stalkers turning up; Bridget had glanced around several times herself, but River was a bundle of unrestrained energy. It was why she'd hugged him: to try and absorb the excess.

'It's fine, it's not a problem, River.' She uses the soft sympathetic voice she uses with bereaved customers when they call to order wreaths.

Wreaths.

She shivers, remembering the delivery the day before. They had left the church as a group in search of the florist's van, but if there had been one, it was long gone. Instead, they tracked down the older lady who'd brought them the flowers, but all she could tell them about the florist was that she was a dark-haired woman, medium height and in her thirties or forties. With nothing else to go on, Bridget had promised the others that she'd ring round as many florists in London as she could once she got back to work. She warned the others not to get their hopes up, that the chances of her tracking down the right florist in London was tiny; a quick Google had thrown up one hundred and ten results.

'How are you anyway?' she asks River. She's not exactly sure what kinds of products he designs, but she knows he works alone in the small second bedroom of the flat he shares with his girlfriend Meg.

'Oh you know,' he sighs heavily. 'I've been thinking a lot about Natalie, and I'm always worried about what Vanessa will do next. Did I tell you she followed Meg to the hairdresser's once and—'

The bell tinkles above the door of the flower shop as a short, slender woman with a blonde bob and black-rimmed glasses bursts into the shop.

'Shit,' Bridget breathes.

'What was—' River says into her ear, but the rest is lost as Charlotte storms up to the counter screaming obscenities at Bridget.

Bridget backs away, heart pounding, stumbling as her heel catches on a cardboard box. She tries to steady herself and smacks her hand against the corner of a shelf. Pain leaps up her arm.

'Hey!' Mark bounds over to the counter, the bouquet still clutched in one hand. 'What the hell do you think you're doing?'

'Get her out!' Bridget shouts, her back pressed up against the wall. Her body is quivering, and the palm of the hand still clutching her mobile to her ear is slick with sweat. On the other end of the line River is becoming increasingly frantic, but Bridget's brain has muted him. She's entirely focused on the screaming woman on the other side of the counter: her staring eyes, the flush of rage across her chest, her wildly gesticulating hands; and the scissors on the counter, within her reach.

23

Bridget is still staring at the scissors as Mark bundles the woman out of the shop. As he flips the 'Open' sign to 'Closed' and turns the latch on the door, she slowly exhales and slides down the wall.

Chapter 5

Lucy

Nine days until someone dies . . .

Lucy is on duty, hugging her cardigan tightly across her body as a cold wind sweeps across the playground, lifting the hair of the departing students. The girls are squealing and clamping their hands to their skirts whilst the boys nudge each other and laugh. She can remember being that age; the horror at the prospect of humiliation in front of your peers, the desperate need to fit in, and the collective smothered groan when the most despised teacher in the school walks in to cover a lesson.

She's scanning the crowd for one particular student: Jada Arnold, Year Nine. Her gaze flicks from the teeming mass of bodies to the edge of the crowd and she finds her: head bowed, eyes downcast, sleeves pulled over her hands; a solitary student, walking alone. Jada hates school but Lucy hates watching her walk out of the gates at the end of the day. She knows what she's going home to. She knows about the dad that's in prison, the mum with mental health issues who's shacked up with an abusive and controlling man. She knows about the younger brothers and sisters, his children, who get all the attention while Jada is left to fend for herself. At school Jada is safe, she's cared for, and she's fed; Lucy makes sure of that by slipping her a breakfast bar and an apple when she pops into her room. It's been four months since Lucy started at Thames View Academy and it's taken her that long to get Jada to talk instead of grunting and shrugging in reply. She wants to do more but she isn't sure how.

As Jada slips through the gates and disappears, Lucy turns her attention to the gaggle of Year Sevens still hanging around on the pavement, waiting for a parent or older sibling to pick them up. In a few weeks they'll probably make their own way but for now they're still being shepherded home. They look so little in their oversized uniforms, their faces still soft and round.

'Excuse me!' a dark-haired woman touches her on the arm, making her jump.

'Sorry, I was miles away. You must be . . .' she tails off. She's got no chance if this is one of the Year Seven mums. She's only just learnt all the children's names.

'Julie,' the woman says, 'Kai Harrison's mum. Dave normally collects him but he's got a stomach bug and doesn't want to leave the house, so I've had to leave work early, and . . .' she takes a breath, 'anyway . . . one of the dads just gave me this to give to you. He said he was in a hurry – although aren't we all?' She hands a folded piece of paper

26

to Lucy. 'Don't ask me his name. I wouldn't have the first clue. Actually, come to think of it, he looked a bit on the young side to be a dad. Maybe he was an older brother, who knows. Anyway, got to dash.'

Lucy feels breathless herself as the woman rushes off. She unfolds the note as the woman extricates her child from the group at the gate, then glances down at the piece of paper in her hands. She's expecting to see a request to take a child out of school for a dentist appointment or to arrange a meeting, but the note says neither of those things. Her grip on it tightens as the wind pulls at the paper, threatening to rip it from her hands as she re-reads the words, scrawled in black biro:

Come back to me, Lucy. I love you and I always will, and I'd do anything to fix what went wrong. Please let me do that. I'll look after you, the way you looked after me. You're the love of my life and I'm yours. We were meant for each other. What was it you told me? Soulmates don't just give up. I'm going nowhere.

M xx

PS I'd appreciate it if you'd give up the pretence that you're going to report me to the police. We both know why you can't do that, and if you come back to me, I'll never tell.

Someone's watching her; she can feel the weight of their gaze, the way it sweeps over her body making the hairs on the nape of her neck stand up. Heat rises to her cheeks and her breathing quickens as she raises her eyes, still clutching

27

the note in her trembling hand. Marcus is standing outside the gates staring at her from between the bars, a long grey coat falling from his wide shoulders, his face unshaven, a black beanie covering his long fair hair. Their eyes meet for a second, two, three as he puffs on his cigarette. Lucy knows that she should run. That she should tell him to go. That she should return to the safety of the staffroom. But she can't break the spell. She can't move. It's like the first time he looked at her, properly looked at her. It was wrong. Everything about it was wrong. She should have looked away. She could have saved herself, and him.

A child's sharp cry – of pain, distress or danger – sends a jolt through her that makes her turn, in search of the sound. Two year seven boys are grappling with each other just metres away, backpacks swinging wildly as they throw whirling punches that don't connect.

'It's all right Miss Newton, I've got it!' Craig Fergusson, one of the Year Seven tutors, speeds past her. 'Oi! Lennon! Max! Break it up!'

Lucy heads after him, heart pounding a guilty beat as she crumples the note into a ball and buries it deep in her pocket. How could she have missed that? How long had they been fighting while she stood there, failing to react? She glances back at the gates, anger flaring, blazing through the guilt. It's Marcus's fault she screwed up. If he hadn't sent the note; if he hadn't turned up . . . but Marcus is gone.

28

Chapter 6

Alexandra

Nine days until someone dies . . .

Alexandra is dead; sprawled on the ground, her cheek against the cold, wooden floor, one arm stretched above her head, the other wrapped around her body, her eyes closed, her lips parted. Moments earlier she'd been sitting at the piano in the drawing room, bare-legged, her white silk negligee riding up her thighs, when her husband had grabbed her by the hair and pulled her off the stool. He had strode out of the room then, leaving her alone. She'd dragged herself to her feet, checked on their guests, who were going through a manuscript in her front room, and excused herself, saying she was going to bed. No one came after her as she ascended the stairs to her bedroom and no one stopped her as she opened the top drawer of her vanity unit, took out a gun, raised it to her temple, and slowly pulled the trigger.

29

'Bravo!' a voice calls from the darkness. 'Alex, Conrad, that was much better. Much, much better.'

Alex opens her eyes, peels herself off the stage and runs a hand over her face. Her palm is red and sticky with the tomato juice Conrad spat at her earlier in the scene. She's covered in the stuff: it's on her slip, her neck, her legs. Her co-star darts onto the stage from the wings, offers her a hand and helps her up. She smells booze on his breath as he hisses in her ear, 'Less of the melodrama next time, darling. You're not a soap star any more.'

'All right everyone,' Liz, the director, calls from the stalls. 'Let's break for ten minutes while Alex cleans herself up then we'll meet back here for a quick debrief before we call it a day.'

Alex hands the gun to the stagehand as she leaves the stage then heads for her dressing room. She's emotionally spent from throwing herself around the stage for the last ten hours, and so tired that she just wants to curl up in a ball and sleep. She's thirty-five but she feels twenty years older.

'Oh!' She presses a hand to her heart as she opens the door to the room and discovers Bex, the wardrobe mistress, spinning in a chair in front of the lightbulb-framed mirror. 'You made me jump!'

'Sorry.' Bex gets to her feet and runs a hand over her blue cropped hair. 'I thought I'd wait to get that off you.' She points at Alex's stained slip.

'No worries.' She pulls it over her head and hands it to her. 'Hope you can get it out.'

Bex fishes a plastic bag out of the back pocket of her jeans and opens it so Alex can drop the slip inside. 'So do I. I've ordered six more for the run.'

30

When *Hedda Gabler* opens on the West End in nine days' time, Alex will be soaked in tomato juice once a night from Monday to Friday and twice on a Saturday.

'Cheers Bex.' She flashes the wardrobe mistress a smile then, dressed only in a tiny skin-coloured G-string, heads into the adjoining bathroom and steps into the world's smallest shower. She washes the sweat, tears and tomato juice from her face and body then opens the door a crack to let the steam out as she dries herself. She can hear her phone repeatedly vibrating on the table as new notifications arrive. It's probably just messages from the WhatsApp group but the constant *bzz bzz bzz* sets her teeth on edge. She muted Twitter notifications weeks ago and rarely bothers to check her replies after she posts about the show, but she can't change her email address or phone number without informing every contact she's made in the last fifteen years. Her stalker uses email to send her photos they've surreptitiously taken of her doing her shopping, seeing friends and attending events, and each time she blocks an address they create a new one. It's never-bloody-ending. What kind of abuse is awaiting her now? Criticism of her acting skills? More moaning about the fact she left *Southern Lights*? Comments about the mole on her left cheek? Photos of her going to the corner shop? Or coming out of the theatre? More bullshit about being her biggest fan?

She wraps the thin towel around her body then kicks at the bathroom door with her foot. As it swings open, she catches a glimpse of the door to her dressing room slowly closing and the handle turning as it's pulled shut with a soft click. Strange. Was Bex hanging around the whole time she was showering, waiting for her to finish, but then gave up

31

at the exact moment she came out? Alex heads for the door, intending to shout down the corridor, but as she passes the mirror she freezes. Lying next to her phone is an uncapped red lipstick and on the glass of the mirror someone has scrawled *It was your fault*.

She stares at the words, heart racing, then rushes out of the room, clutching the towel to her chest. The corridor outside is empty apart from Conrad, who's opening the door to his dressing room, a glass of whisky in one hand.

'Conrad!' His top lip curls as she approaches, her damp feet slapping on the cold wooden boards, and he sighs dismissively.

'Yes?' He lounges against the wall and raises the whisky to his lips, languid and bored.

'Did you see anyone coming out of my room just now?'

'No, but I certainly heard you.'

'You're sure? You're quite sure?' She can hear herself getting posher, her vowels more clipped. It's something she's always done subconsciously: matched her accent to the person she's talking to. Sam says it's because she's trying to form a bond with that person, or she's sharpening her dialogue skills. She thinks it's because she doesn't really know who she is.

'Yes, Alexandra, I'm quite sure.'

He doesn't ask what's wrong or why she's concerned. Instead, he takes another sip of his drink, opens the door to his dressing room, slips inside, then closes the door in her face. She dithers beside it, unsure whether to continue on down the corridor to see if there's anyone else around or go back to her room. If she asks the rest of the cast and crew if they saw anyone, they'll only ask questions and that's not something she wants to invite.

She hurries back to her dressing room, puts a chair against the door, soaks a paper towel in water and rubs at the mirror until the words disappear and lipstick runs like blood over her hands, wrists and arms.

Chapter 7

WhatsApp group: FYST

19.06
Lucy: I'm still so upset about Natalie. I've been thinking about her all day.

River: Me too. It still doesn't feel real.

Lucy: Marcus is getting braver. He sent me a note at school, gave it to a PARENT to give to me then watched from the gates as I read it.

River: Creep. He's pushing your buttons. Ignore.

Bridget: Still so desperately upset about Natalie and sorry you had such a terrible day, Lucy. Mine was awful too. Charlotte came into the shop and screamed obscenities at me. Mark had to throw her out. I haven't stopped shaking all day. Last week she forwarded a Macmillan Nurses email to me from a new email address she'd created. She typed 'For when you get cancer and die' at the top.

River: She came into the shop, Bridget?!! Have you got CCTV? The police will want to see that. I hate to say it, but Vanessa's upped her game too. She sent Meg naked pictures of me, and old texts where I'd said how much I loved her. If the police don't arrest her soon Meg will leave me, but no one knows where the hell she is.

Bridget: Have you tried her friends?

River: They've blocked me. She told them I'm a narcissist who coerced and controlled her. WHEN THE OPPOSITE IS TRUE!

Alexandra: Sorry you've all had such shit days. Any luck tracking down the wreath sender with the florists, B?

Bridget: I phoned around a dozen earlier. No luck. I was told that customer orders are confidential, data protection etc. Suspected as much.

Alexandra: I wish we could take a machine gun to the lot of them. Our stalkers, not florists, obviously. Talking of which – my own personal psychopath scrawled something vile on my dressing room mirror. And no one saw anything. I'm starting to think they're a fucking ghost.

Lucy: Oh god, Alex. I'm so sorry.

Bridget: Alex, that's awful. What did they write? Did anyone see who did it? Is there anyone you suspect?

Bridget: River, yes, have told the police. No sound on the

35

CCTV footage though which is annoying because you can't hear the threats she made. I'm not going in tomorrow. I'll have to hand in my notice and get a new job. Again.

Lucy: I'm so sorry it's come to that, Bridget. I'm not sure how much longer I can stay at Thames View either.

River: Don't you think it's weird that ALL our stalkers were active today?

Alexandra: Psychic fuckwittery. No one saw anything, btw. It's a theatre, there's no CCTV, no security guards. In theory anyone could just wander in from the street.

River: Maybe it's time to lure them out of the shadows. I don't want to scare anyone but the date on the wreath is in nine days' time . . .

Lucy: River don't. I barely sleep as it is.

Alexandra: He's got a point. We need to do something. And yes River, something that doesn't involve the police . . .

River: Actually, I might have an idea . . .

Lucy: WHAT?

Bridget: Go on . . .

Alexandra: Spill! Right now. River! Don't you dare log off.

River: I'll tell you all soon. There's something I need to buy first.

Alexandra: If it's not a machine gun I'm going to be very disappointed.

Chapter 8

River

Seven days until someone dies . . .

River Scott-Tyler is stalking his girlfriend. More accurately, he's stalking his girlfriend while he adds a gradient to the marketing banner he's spent the last hour working on. He squints his eyes critically, then deletes it. It's the bane of his life – clients who see an advert online that they like and demand he applies a similar roundel, border or gradient to the agreed design. It's always at the last minute, just before he's about to deliver and start something new. He tries not to moan to Meg about it, but it winds him up – the lack of respect for his time and his skill.

Meg. He glances at his phone. There's a new update, a ping that he missed because he had his headphones on. He takes them off then rolls back his shoulders, moves his head from side to side to loosen his neck. According to the app,

Meg arrived at the Royal Free Hospital seven minutes ago. He checks WhatsApp to make sure it's accurate, and yep, there's a text from her:

Just arrived on the ward. Did it work?

It feels wrong, stalking his own girlfriend with a GPS tracker, but it's not as though she doesn't know about it. They'd had an in-depth conversation about it the night before, after he'd returned from a trip to a spyware shop near Walthamstow with a black plastic bag in his hand.

Meg had been coating fish in flour and breadcrumbs and there had been a strong smell of cumin in the air.

'Basa curry. Should be ready in about ten mins. The rice is already cooked.' She hadn't looked up from her task as River had perched on a chair at the kitchen bar.

'I bought something.' He'd reached into the bag and removed four little black cardboard boxes with *Earth Search* embossed on each one in white text.

'Let me guess. Another PlayStation game?' There had been a weariness in her voice. If they weren't arguing about Vanessa, they were quarrelling about the amount of time he spent gaming.

'Trackers.'

She'd turned to look at him, holding her flour-encrusted fingers away from her body. 'What kind of trackers?'

'This kind.' He'd removed one from the box and cradled the small black disc in his hand. 'I read about them in a *New York Times* article the other day. They run on GPS so unlike some of the others on the market you're not constrained by Bluetooth, and you won't get an alert on your phone telling you that a tracker has been placed on you.'

38

Meg had run a hand over the back of her neck and River had noticed, again, how long her hair had become. Without multiple clips in it for work, her pixie cut had become a mullet, with flaps of hair hanging over her ears and a fringe she had to push out of her eyes. She'd refused to return to her hairdressers since Vanessa had turned up, taken the seat next to her and spent the whole hour either glaring at her, or telling the hairdresser what a shit her ex-boyfriend was and what a fool the woman was that he'd left her for. 'Is that even legal?'

'No.' He'd put the tracker down, feeling deflated. He'd wanted her to feel as hopeful, as optimistic as he did but she'd jumped straight to the biggest sticking point of his plan. 'It's illegal to place a tracker on someone, in their belongings or in their car, without their knowledge, but no one's been taken to court for it yet.'

'*Yet.* River . . .' She shook her head, her sentence unfinished but her disapproval written all over her face.

He didn't want to break the law. None of them would. But what was the alternative? Natalie was dead and one of them was going to be next unless they acted, and they acted *fast*. Being arrested was infinitely preferable to the alternative.

'And it sounds dangerous,' Meg added. 'You realise how close you'll have to get, to put that on her.' She jabbed at the tracker with her finger, leaving a floury fingerprint on its smooth black surface.

River had shaken his head. 'I won't be going anywhere near her. We're not planting the trackers on our own stalkers. We're . . . swapping.'

'Great.' Meg had taken a slug of her wine. 'So what? You go after some psychopathic man and try and slip that into his pocket? And someone else goes on a wild goose chase to find your ex? A woman the actual police can't find to arrest?'

River had breathed in deeply through his nose and out through his mouth. Showing his irritation wouldn't help either of them. Meg's negativity was because she was scared.

'I've got a plan,' he'd started. 'I've given it a lot of—'

'What if one of the stalkers finds the tracker and takes it to the police? Will you be arrested because you bought it? That's assuming the stalker doesn't go absolutely batshit crazy and kill you first. What if someone else dies? What if they're killed because of you?'

'Meg, please.' He'd slipped off his stool, joined her on the other side of the counter, draped an arm across her shoulders and pulled her close, feeling her body quiver against him. Natalie's death had shaken her up so much he almost didn't go to the funeral. Meg didn't know Nat, just what he'd told her about her, but her death made danger seem closer, and Vanessa more terrifying. Meg was never this nervy, never this scared. She was so joyful, so vibrant, so courageous when they met. Vanessa was certain that there was an overlap, that he'd cheated on her with Meg, but that wasn't true. Their relationship was over, and he was looking for somewhere to live, when he met Meg at a cookery class. As the only singles in the group, they were paired up and sent out to Portobello Market to choose their ingredients for an Italian feast. Normally he'd have felt inordinately awkward, being coupled with a stranger – and an attractive stranger at that – but Meg was so warm and smiley that, as they sniffed plump tomatoes and leafy basil plants, he couldn't help but relax. They chatted about life in London, food, music and art. They discussed why an aubergine became a rude emoji rather than a courgette or a carrot, and expressed their love for *Succession*. They discovered that they were both left-handed, had both been to the same London Grammar gig the month before, and were equally as desperate to visit Vietnam one day. They searched for more similarities – laughing in delight when they discovered that they were both only children, had been forced to play the violin at primary school and had both failed their driving tests three times. They reacted in mock horror when they found differences (Meg wasn't a fan of French cinema, River thought Eurovision was silly), and resolved to change each other's minds. They'd only just met and, already, they were talking as though they were going to become a part of each other's lives. River couldn't decide whether the stars had aligned or if someone was playing a cruel joke on him. How could this small, beautiful human make him feel so alive?

'No one's going to die.' He'd squeezed her tighter and nuzzled his face in her hair. Even after eight months together – sharing a flat for six – he was still incredulous that she was his. 'You know me, I never do anything without creating a detailed spreadsheet.' He paused, waiting for a laugh that didn't come, then filled in the silence. 'The slightest hint of danger and we stop. I'm not putting anyone in harm's way. Quite the opposite. I've even worked out how we can get a tracker on V.'

Meg had shuddered. They never mentioned Vanessa by name – she was always 'the ex', 'you know who' and 'our stalker'. Even her initials were banned.

'Sorry, sorry.' He had looked longingly at the wine. Maybe Meg had the right idea. The thought of getting so paralytic he passed out was increasingly appealing. But he had to stay strong. There was too much to lose.

'River.' Meg had wriggled from beneath his arm, his body cooling as she moved away. 'I'm not going to pretend that I haven't got a bad feeling about this. I do. But I can tell you're set on doing it. I just hope that if she finds the tracker, she won't make our life even more of a nightmare than it already is. I'm not sure how much I can take.'

'She won't find it. I promise you, Meg. This is going to get her out of our lives.'

Behind his back River had wrapped the middle finger of his right hand over his index finger and squeezed.

Chapter 9

Alexandra

Seven days until someone dies . . .

Samuel casts a lazy look in Alex's direction as she slips off the bed. 'Where are you going?'

'Living room. I've got a Zoom.'

Her boyfriend twists his wrist to look at his watch. 'At this time of night?'

'I know.' She sighs, twists her hair into a bun at the back of her head then reaches for the dressing gown on the back of the bedroom door. 'Can you pause that?' She points at the TV at the end of their bed. 'I want to watch the ending together, or you'll only spoil it.' She waits until her boyfriend reaches for the remote control and the room falls silent then adds, 'River's got a masterplan. Apparently.'

Samuel props himself up on an elbow, his eyes searching her face. 'You don't look or sound convinced.'

43

'I'm not.' She opens the door then glances back at him. 'Don't turn it back on the minute I leave the room or you're dead.'

His finger twitches against the remote control and the sound of a fight scene fills the room.

'Oi!' She swipes a mug from the dressing table and holds it aloft, as though preparing to throw it. 'You know I'll do it.'

The TV goes quiet again and Samuel's soft laughter follows her out of the room.

Alex shuts the living room door and checks her phone. Five new messages have arrived since she and Sam settled down in the bedroom to watch TV: one from her agent, one from Liz (which was unexpected), two from friends and . . . she sighs loudly . . . her stalker's got themselves a new number.

Boyfriend over for the night is he? You dirty whore.

She jabs at the message – block and delete – then walks over to the window. If her stalker's out there, hiding in the darkness, she hopes they see this.

'Fuck you!' she mouths, then pulls the curtains closed.

It's pure bravado and she's still shaking as she settles herself onto the sofa with a blanket over her legs and pulls the laptop onto her knees. It's ridiculous of River, getting them all to log onto Zoom so late at night. Why couldn't he tell them his brilliant plan on WhatsApp instead of acting so bloody cloak-and-dagger about it? Now she's got to spend a precious hour between rehearsals and sleep listening to him waffle on in that strangely nasal monotone voice of his.

Alex gets it – the anxiety, the paranoia, the anticipation and the fear; but, whilst she finds comfort and support in the group (it was her idea after all) the daily influx of emotion and neuroticism can be overwhelming, especially when she's had a tough day at work. She shifts the sofa cushions around behind her, trying to get comfortable, and feels a flood of warmth – and a pang of remorse – as three familiar faces appear on the screen. It's not River's fault she's pissed off. Conrad was being an arsehole and their rehearsal was strained. They'd had an argument backstage before Liz's debrief; a hissed debate about who'd messed up the blocking in an earlier scene. Alex had insisted that Liz had changed it the day before, whilst Conrad was convinced it had been abandoned after they'd given it a try. His final comment, muttered under his breath as the others filed past them, 'And that's why soap stars should never do theatre,' had made her want to swing for his head.

She'd never planned on revealing her true identity to the group. She'd disclosed her real name to the moderator but used a pseudonym on the forum – as most of the members did – to protect her privacy. It was only when she decided to establish the WhatsApp group – and vet the members via Zoom – that she realised she'd have to reveal her true identity. She wasn't sure how to approach it. 'You might recognise me,' sounded wanky and pretentious. 'Just to let you know that I'm a TV soap actress,' sounded boastful. In the end she decided to hold the Zoom without pre-warning her new friends and deal with any reactions there and then.

She needn't have worried. Lucy had asked if they'd met before, then realised that Alex was in her mum's favourite soap and River had no idea who she was. Only Bridget had responded with a gasp, clearly recognising her. Alex couldn't tell if Bridget was naturally awkward anyway, or if it was her 'fame' that made the other woman go pale and stutter. Either way, by their third or fourth Zoom Bridget had regained her composure.

'Hi Alex!' a miniaturised Lucy waves at her from the screen but before Alex can reply River takes charge.

'Okay everyone, now we're all here I'll keep this as brief as I can as I know there are things we'd all rather be doing.'

Lucy takes a sip of red wine; Bridget pushes her glasses further up her nose and Alex bites her lip. They're all too eager to hear what he has to say to make the obvious joke, that they'd rather do *anything* else.

'So,' River continues, holding a circular black *something*, about the third of the height of a mobile phone, up to the screen. 'This is a GPS tracker, and it's going to help us regain control of our lives.'

Alex moves closer to the screen to get a better look at it. Lucy looks similarly impressed, but Bridget shakes her head.

'If that's an Apple AirTag it's no good. If the stalker's got an iPhone it'll alert them.'

'It's not an AirTag.' River turns the tracker over in his hands. 'This little beauty uses satellite technology which means the stalker can never be out of range. And, as long as they don't find it, they'll never know they're being tracked. I tested it earlier today on Meg, and I was able to . . .'

Alex eyes Lucy's glass of wine enviously as River continues to drone on about tracking his girlfriend during her journey to work and on to Tesco afterwards.

'There is a three-minute delay,' River says, loud enough to suggest he's realised he's lost her attention, 'so it's not live per se, but the closest we can get.'

'When you say *we*,' Alex shifts against the cushions. 'Are

you suggesting we plant one on our stalkers? Because that's going to be pretty bloody—'

'No. No, no. That would be far too dangerous. My suggestion would be that we target each other's stalkers. They don't know us so—'

Bridget raises her hand. 'That's not strictly true. If a stalker took the wreath to Nat's funeral, he or she has seen all four of us.'

River's jubilant expression fades. 'I hadn't thought of that.'

'Although,' Bridget pauses dramatically, 'it does make more sense that a florist delivered the wreath.'

'Sorry,' Lucy pauses mid sip. 'You've lost me. Does this mean we can do it or not?'

River smiles. 'We can. If Bridget places the tracker on Alexandra's stalker and—'

Alex sighs in frustration. 'But we don't know who that is.'

'True, and that's going to be a challenge, but we have to work with what we've got. So, I'll target Bridget's stalker Charlotte, Lucy will put a tracker on Vanessa, and Alex will go after Marcus.'

'How will I put a tracker on Vanessa?' Lucy asks. 'You don't know where she is.'

River runs a hand over his stubble. 'I'll have to give that some thought too but I'm thinking we could lure her to—'

Alex holds out a hand as her phone starts ringing. 'Excuse me guys, just one sec—'

She shifts the laptop onto the sofa and gets up.

'Hello?'

There's a pause, then – 'Is this Alexandra Raynor?'

'Speaking.' She walks from one side of her small living

47

room to the other. There's something about the voice on the other end of the phone that she doesn't like; an officious tone she's heard before.

'Hello Alexandra, I'm sorry I'm ringing so late. I'm DC Ian McGowan, Met Police.'

Alex stops walking. Her eyes have become a pinhole camera, her vision constricted, a shaft of light surrounded by darkness, a low hum ringing in her ears.

'As the surviving next of kin of Arthur and Alice Raynor, we wanted you to know that Colin Sutherland was released from HMP Belmarsh three weeks ago. I can only apologise that you weren't told sooner but it's taken us a while to track down a phone number for you . . . Alexandra . . . Alexandra can you hear me? Alexandra? Are you still there?'

She drops, rather than snaps back, into herself. 'Yes, I'm here. I heard you. He got out three weeks ago. Thank you for telling me. Goodb—'

But DC Ian McGowan isn't done yet. 'He's currently housed in a hostel run by a charity, and he's due to move in with a family member soon.'

Family. The word floats through her, the ghost of a life she once knew.

'The reason I'm calling,' he continues, 'is because Sutherland is keen to attend a restorative justice meeting with you. It would be an accompanied meeting, you wouldn't be alone with him, and you'd have the opportunity to tell him how his crime affected you and to ask him any questions you might have. It's perfectly normal to feel anxious at this prospect,' he adds quickly, 'and there is a restraining order in place, but—'

'They don't work.'

'Sorry?'

'My parents had a . . .' She fights to find the right words as memories swoop like crows, '. . . he was served a Community Protection Notice, to protect them, and it didn't make any . . .' her throat dries and she has to fight to get air past her windpipe and into her lungs.

Her grip tightens on the phone and she's only vaguely aware of Samuel calling out from the bedroom, 'Babe? Is everything okay?'

'It didn't make any difference.' She focuses on a spot on the wall. 'Colin Sutherland still murdered my parents. You can take your restorative meeting and your restraining order, and you can shove them up your arse.'

Chapter 10

Lucy

Seven days until someone dies . . .

There is a part of Lucy – the horrified, empathetic part – that is urging her to log out of Zoom and shut down her computer. The other part, fascinated and voyeuristic, is unable to move: her fingers clasp her wine glass; her gaze fixes on the embossed metal of one of the running medals, hanging on the wall to the right of her desk.

'Alex?' River's voice breaks the silence. 'Alex are you still there? Can you hear us?'

Bridget is looking down; presumably at her phone, from the focused expression on her face.

'Did you all just hear that?' River's voice, barely more than a whisper, drifts out from Lucy's laptop.

She makes a soft 'Hmm' noise in the back of her throat and reaches for her phone. There's already a message from

River in the FYST chat: *Alex, is everything okay? We're worried about you.*

'River,' she says, 'I think we should remove Alex from the Zoom. She probably needs a bit of time alone.'

'I was only listening to check that she's okay,' he says, as his throat flushes pink. 'She's gone very quiet.'

'River, please, could you just remove her?' Lucy says again, 'This is feeling a bit intrusive now. I don't feel comfortable, us listening in. She's at home, she's safe. She'll get in touch if she needs us.'

For a couple of seconds River does nothing, indecisiveness wrinkling his forehead, then Alexandra's living room blinks and disappears. Lucy's shoulders sag with relief.

'I've just found an article online.' Bridget looks up from her phone, her eyes bright and questioning behind the sheen of her glasses. 'Looks like a journalist did some digging about ten years ago when Alex got the part on *Southern Lights*. They found out her real surname and discovered that her parents were murdered when she was ten. Colin Sutherland was their next-door neighbour. There was some kind of ongoing dispute about land boundaries and then Sutherland snapped. He . . . well it all came to a head one day when he—'

'Don't.' Lucy turns her head sharply as though the murder is on her laptop screen instead of playing out inside her head. 'I don't want to hear any more.'

'It's tragic.' River's voice is flat. 'Poor Alex. I had no idea.'

'Who looked after her? Afterwards?' An image of the tiny Year Sevens waiting at the gates for their parents flashes into Lucy's mind. To have your parents taken away from you when you're so young in such a horrific, violent way . . . it's the most awful thing she's ever heard.

'Her extended family, it says here.' Bridget removes her glasses and rubs at her eyes. 'There's a quote from "a friend" saying Alex has always felt responsible for what happened. It doesn't say why.'

'God.' River runs a hand over his face too. 'How do we . . . what do we say?'

'Nothing,' Lucy says. 'She'd have told us if she wanted us to know.'

River sighs deeply. 'I guess we're going to have to rethink the tracker plan.'

Bridget, whose eyes look smaller and deep-set without her large tortoiseshell glasses, leans closer to the screen. 'Why's that?'

'Because we can't let you put a tracker on a murderer!'

'Hang on a second,' Lucy raises a hand as though interrupting a staff meeting. 'River, you're assuming that Sutherland is Alex's stalker. Don't you think that's unlikely, given the fact he was in prison until three weeks ago?'

'They do have mobile phones in prison you know,' he says, 'Smuggled in, obviously.'

His patronising tone makes her prickle with irritation. Does he really think she's that naive? 'Yes, I know, but she's been stalked for six months. Why would Sutherland start sending her abusive messages when he only had a few months left to serve of a twenty-five-year sentence? Why risk screwing up his parole hearing?'

'Your guess is as good as ours.' River's dismissive shrug makes her want to punch the screen.

'Lucy has a point,' Bridget says. 'The dates don't really add up and how can he take photos of her from prison? Not to mention—'

'We can't assume anything.' River cuts her off. 'This is a murderer we're talking about. God knows who he's working with. Maybe we should just ditch the whole thing.'

'Don't be ridiculous!' Bridget leans closer to the camera, her eyes and nose filling the frame. 'If you don't hand out those trackers, River Scott-Tyler, then I'll go and buy some myself. Did any of us think Jamie would murder Natalie when he got out of jail? No, we didn't. Do I think Charlotte would murder me given half a chance? It's certainly a possibility. Could you forgive yourself if your ex did anything to Meg? If Marcus does anything to Lucy? We have seven days, just *seven days* until the date on the wreath. We have to do what we can to protect ourselves.'

'I think,' River says cautiously, 'that we should just leave this to the police. Alex will want them involved now.'

'Are you sure about that?' Lucy says. 'Because I'm pretty sure she just told them to stick their restraining order up their arse.'

'One second,' River looks distracted. 'Alex is requesting access.'

The screen flickers and Alex's face appears beside Bridget's.

Lucy had expected her to look distraught, but her nose isn't red and swollen and her face isn't blotchy from tears. She looks exactly as she did when she first logged on.

'Sorry about that.' Alex props her chin on her hand, defiance in her eyes as she stares into the camera. 'When are we getting the trackers then, River? Because this shit needs to stop.'

Chapter 11

Alexandra

SATURDAY 14TH OCTOBER

Six days until someone dies . . .

Alex approaches Highgate Wood, a floral design incised into the green metal gates, and pulls her leopard-print coat tighter around her body. The sky is still dark, but the birds are awake, their chirpy calls adding shrill notes to the low drone of traffic on the roads nearby. It's also freezing cold.

Samuel, who hasn't stopped talking since they left the house, makes a big act of patting his face and then hers. 'Are you real? Am I? It must be a dream because why else would we be out in the freezing cold this bloody early in the morning?'

Alex removes his hand from her cheek. It's 6.30 a.m. and she's so tired she feels like her skin is melting.

'Look,' she says for the third time since they dragged themselves out of bed. 'I really appreciate you coming with me, but could you please stop dicking about?'

'Wait what?' He raises his eyebrows, his tired eyes glinting with mischief. 'This is serious? Proper MI5 spy shit? Quick, take cover! Enemy sighted at twelve o'clock!'

Alex knows laughter will only encourage him, but she can't help herself. He is a comedian after all. She knows why he's doing this, playing the fool and trying to make her laugh. He couldn't stop her tears last night but he's doing his best to stop her thinking about Colin Sutherland now.

He kisses her on the top of the head. 'Come on then, let's go and find your weirdos.'

'Sam, they're not—' she clocks the grin on his face and catches herself. 'No more than I am, anyway.'

The others are a couple of hundred metres down the path, huddled around a bench, surrounded by trees. River is wearing a backpack and is jogging on the spot, Bridget is whirring a set of keys around her forefinger, while Lucy, bundled up in a red coat, blue beanie and multicoloured scarf, is checking her watch. Alex raises a hand in hello then nudges Samuel, 'No comments, no jokes, no dicking about. Okay?'

'Yes boss. I'll just stay here, boss, and keep watch, boss.' She hears the smile in his voice as he comes to a halt.

'Sorry, sorry,' she says as she draws closer, then she sneezes – five times in rapid succession. From behind her she hears Samuel laugh. He finds it amusing that she can't sneeze once like everyone else.

Lucy slides up to her, her eyebrows pinched in sympathy 'Is everything okay?'

She'd obviously overheard every word of her conversation with the detective last night. They all did; she could see it in their faces the moment she rejoined the Zoom. No one had brought it up and Alex had moved the conversation on.

'I'm good, thanks,' she tells Lucy. 'Sorry we're late. We had to wait longer than we thought for a tube.'

River shrugs off his rucksack, drops it onto the bench and unzips it. He takes out four small square boxes and hands them around.

Alex turns the box over in her hands, examining it. She can feel the excitement and fear radiating off the other two women as they do the same.

'There's a QR code on the back,' River says, keeping his voice low. 'If you scan it with your phone it'll take you to the app. Enter the code at the bottom of the box and it's up and running. Obviously, we'll need to swap codes with each other later, so we can track our own stalkers. I was going to keep a list of them all but, given that I'm sometimes called a control freak,' his gaze slides towards Alex, 'I thought I'd leave it to you guys. The hardest bit will be planting it so it can't be found. It's magnetised so you should be able to slip it under a tyre arch or similar or, if the target has a rucksack, look for a small pocket, like this one.' He taps a zip on the side of his bag. 'Same for coats; look for unused pockets or maybe a tear in the material where you can slip the tracker in. For a handbag, um . . . you could perhaps create a secret pocket with a sharp knife if you have time, or—'

Bridget gives him a scathing look. 'What kind of woman wouldn't notice damage to her handbag?'

'I wouldn't,' Lucy says. 'There's so much crap in my bag you could probably graffiti the lining and I wouldn't notice.'

'What about women who alternate handbags?' Bridget says. 'Or people who wear different coats?'

'Oh,' Lucy says. 'Good point. Although,' she glances down at her own red coat, 'I pretty much live in this, and I only get my good handbag out if I'm going to a wedding.'

'There we go then,' River says. 'It's a risk, but a small risk. In my experience, when it gets cold, most people stick to one favourite warm coat. Remember, Bridget, you're not allowed to place a tracker on—' he glances warily at Alex.

'Sutherland,' she fills in the name for him. 'It's fine. I know you all know about him.'

'Hang on one second, River,' Bridget says indignantly. 'You're not *allowing* me—'

'Wrong word,' he waves a dismissive hand through the air. 'But the fact remains, he's a dangerous man.'

Lucy groans. 'Didn't we already have this conversation last night? The dates don't add up. No one apart from you thinks he's a threat.'

'If that man comes anywhere near Alex,' Samuel's voice rings out from behind her, making her jump, 'then we ring the fucking police. I don't care how much you distrust them, babe. We're ringing them.'

'Sure,' she lies. 'Of course.'

'Are we done?' Lucy asks, 'The sun's coming up and I really need to get to—'

'One more thing, just quickly,' River says, to a collective groan. 'We still need to talk about the—'

He breaks off, listening intently as branches snap and crunch and leaves rustle in the thick coppice to their left. Someone's in there, walking around. Alex listens, staring into the darkness, the hairs raised on her arms. Beside her, Bridget and Lucy are doing the same.

The only person who doesn't looked scared is Samuel.

He's moving towards the source of the sound, his hands clenched into fists.

'Who's there?' he shouts.

The crunching and rustling stops instantly.

'Who's there?' Samuel shouts again.

There's no reply. He holds out a hand to the group, warning them to stay where they are then, stepping lightly, moves into the bushes.

'Sam, no!' Alex shouts, but he's already disappeared into the darkness. She moves to go after him, but Lucy grabs her arm.

'Don't! It's not safe.'

'Which is exactly why I should—' She isn't sure what she hears first: the rustling in the bushes, River's shout of alarm, or the rock whistling past her ear.

It bounces off Bridget's arm, making her shriek, then it drops to the ground, nestled in mud and leaves.

'What the—' River reaches to pick it up as Alex turns back towards the bushes, fear spiking in her belly. Where is he? Where's Sam? Stupid twat, charging off like Rambo. She'll never forgive herself if anything's happened to him.

'Sam!' She yanks her arm from Lucy's hand and heads after him. 'Sam!' She turns on the torch function on her phone and sweeps the light over the branches and leaves. 'Sam, where are you?'

From behind her she hears River's shout of surprise, then a horrified chorus from the two women.

'Sam!' She sets off towards the entrance of the park, just as a tall, dark figure bursts out from the bushes to her left.

'Jesus!' She presses a hand to her chest as Sam makes his way towards her. 'You scared me.'

Her boyfriend turns in a slow circle, scanning the park with the kind of laser focus Alex has only ever seen in Jason Bourne films. She doesn't know this version of Samuel: narrow-eyed, alpha, vibrating with adrenaline.

'Fuck.' He presses his lips together, disappointment replacing the determination in his eyes. 'Stupid fucking tree roots.' He pulls at his trouser leg and examines the scrape on his shin, then looks back at her. 'Sorry, babe. Lost them.'

'Them? How many were there?'

'Just one. I'd guess male but I couldn't be sure. Big coat, hood up, moved fast. He . . . they . . . headed towards the entrance. They're probably long gone.' He runs his hands over his face, huffing and puffing as though he just ran a marathon, and when he looks at her again he's back, the Sam she knows – silly, kind, never takes the stairs if there's an escalator nearby.

She puts her arms around his neck and presses herself into him, feeling the softness of his belly against hers, and the firmness of his back beneath her palms. 'Don't do that again.'

'Sorry to interrupt, but you guys need to see this.' River has appeared at her shoulder, anxiety rolling off him like a damp mist.

Alex's gaze travels from his eyes, large and haunted behind the sheen of his glasses, to the rock in his outstretched hand. For a moment she's not sure what she's looking at but then she sees it, the hard jagged lines scratched into the surface, as though a knife was repeatedly scraped over the stone.

'It's a six,' she says.

Lucy steps into her eyeline, shivering in the cold morning light. 'It's a reminder about the date on the wreath. Six days. That's all we've got until one of us dies.'

'No one's dying,' Bridget says. Her tone is confident, but her eyes betray her; she's barely blinking, her gaze fixed on the bushes and the trees.

'No?' Lucy says. 'Well, someone followed us here.'

'They had to be staking one of us out,' Alex adds. 'Literally, watching all through the night.' Her stomach lurches as she looks back at the bushes. Could it be the same person that scrawled on her dressing room mirror? Could it be Sutherland? Do the police know something she doesn't? Is that why the detective decided to inform her about his release, three weeks after he left prison? No. She pushes the thought away. It can't be Sutherland, he was still in prison when the stalking started. Besides, there's a three in four chance that the wreath wasn't even meant for her.

'Did you see their face?' Bridget asks Sam. 'Were they male or female?'

Lucy and River stare at him intently, waiting for his answer.

'I didn't see.' He shakes his head ruefully. 'I'm sorry.'

'Whoever it was,' River says in a low voice, 'it's even more important now that we place the trackers.'

'What if they overheard us?' Alex asks. 'And know what we're planning?'

For the first time all morning River's bravado slips. Doubt clouds his eyes for a split second then his confidence returns. 'All the more reason to be careful, and put in place a Plan B.'

'What's that then?' Samuel slings an arm around Alex's shoulders and pulls her closer.

'We hide,' River says. 'On the twentieth of October. Somewhere no one can find us.'

'And then what?' Bridget asks, before Alex has a chance to object.

River presses his glasses into his face with his middle finger then reaches into his pocket for a tissue and noisily blows his nose. 'We set a trap.'

Chapter 12

Bridget

Six days until someone dies . . .

It's been twelve hours since the conversation in Highgate Wood and Bridget is still irritated with River. What kind of fool does he take her for? Not allowed indeed! She's more than twice his age. If anyone needs supervision, it's him – what a ridiculous idea to meet in a public park. Any sensible person would have suggested meeting in a private home where a stalker couldn't turn up and throw rocks at them. And she's still waiting for him to share more about his mysterious 'trap' idea. When pressed to tell them more he had made an excuse about 'ironing out the creases' and said he'd be in touch. She didn't have the energy to tell him to just spit it out.

Six days. Her mind skips from the crude carving on the rock to the sight of Natalie's mother, pale-faced and broken

62

as she followed her daughter's coffin out of the church, and she shivers. No one else will die, not if she's got anything to do with it.

She turns off the TV, reaches for her handbag, takes out the tracker and turns it over in her hands. The technology is really quite astonishing. Her home address showed up in the app within seconds of her entering the tracker's details.

She shoves it back into her bag as the front door clicks open. Gary's home, and he's late. She hears his boots being dropped onto the shoe rack and his soft whistle as he walks down the hall. She shoves her feet into her slippers and hurries out of the room.

'How was work?' She hovers beside the kitchen door.

Gary, partially hidden behind the open fridge door, doesn't reply.

'That's if you've actually been at work this whole time.'

His sigh fuels her irritation. She's sick of the way he blocks her out; like she's the one at fault, not him.

'Why have you started taking your phone into the bathroom with you?' she asks. 'Is there something I should know?'

The fridge door slams shut, and Gary emerges, a pack of ham in his hand. 'Can I not take a shit and read the news any more?'

'That's not what I'm talking about, and you know it.'

'Just leave it. I'm tired.' He shoves a wad of ham into his mouth, puts the packet back in the fridge then brushes past her and heads into the hallway.

'Gary, we need to talk about this.'

When he turns and looks at her, *really* looks at her, her heart leaps. If he could just be honest with her, they might

63

be able to save their relationship; *might* being the operative word.

'I love you; you know that don't you?' He kisses her lightly on the cheek and as he pulls away she smells the scent of cigarettes, beer and ham on his breath. 'But please,' he squeezes the top of her arm, 'stop meddling. Stay in your lane.'

'I love you too!' Bridget calls after him as he heads down the hallway. 'But you have to earn my trust!'

Gary pauses outside the spare bedroom, then walks inside and closes the door. Sighing, Bridget heads back into the kitchen and takes the bottle of white wine she opened yesterday out of the fridge. She sits at the small table where she and Gary used to have dinner together, pours herself a glass of wine, necks it, then rests her head in her hands. Gary's never going to talk to her; not properly. They're going to continue to live separate lives until she tells him that enough is enough, and she wants him out. But he's all she's got; he's her whole world.

She sits up sharply, remembering something, and rushes from the room. The tracker! She's a genius. Now she'll know where he is, every minute of every single day.

Bridget perches on the edge of the sofa, the tracker in her hand.

Where to leave it isn't an issue. Gary only owns two coats – a faded denim jacket that he wears in the summer, and a dark green Parka he wears when it's cold. It'll be easier to hide the tracker in the Parka: all that material, the hem hanging below his knees. Scissors! She jumps to her feet, rummages in the drawer in the TV unit where she keeps her cross-stitch stuff and finds a pair of nail scissors. Perfect, nice and sharp.

As she closes the drawer, the bathroom door opens then closes. Gary's going to have a shower, as he does every day when he gets home. He's not one to luxuriate under the spray – he belts out a single song, then turns off the water and gets out. She's got about three minutes to get the job done.

Heart racing, she pokes her head around the living room door; then, as the strangled sound of Gary singing 'True' by Spandau Ballet escapes from beneath the bathroom door, she speeds towards the coat rack. She runs her hands over the Parka's lining. Probably best to make the cut vertically, just beneath the zip. Or will he feel the tracker banging against his inner thigh as he walks? Would it be better at the back instead? Or somewhere near the hood? Beads of sweat bud at her temples as panic sets in. What to do? What to do?

As the last verse of 'True' drifts down the hallway she cuts a small hole just beneath the zip, then as Gary reaches the last 'Oooo' of the song she pushes the tracker through the hole. She darts into her bedroom just as the bathroom door opens, and a cloud of steam is released into the hall.

Fifteen minutes have passed since Bridget placed the tracker in Gary's coat but she still feels jittery as she pulls on her coat, hat and gloves.

She keeps her tone light as she sticks her head around the living room door. 'I'm going out, having dinner with some friends.'

Gary, slumped against the sofa, continues to scroll through his phone.

'Seriously?' she says. 'Is this where we are now?'

He doesn't so much as glance up at her. 'Haven't you got somewhere to be?'

Bridget bristles. She wouldn't let him get away with talking to her like that normally, but she doesn't want to be late for Alex. When she and Gary row it can go on for hours.

Bridget settles herself at her table, reaches for the wine menu, opens it and peers over the top, a self-conscious smile pricking at her lips. It's all so ridiculously spy-like, dining alone, incognito in a cosy Italian restaurant in Soho as rain batters the windows and soaking wet pedestrians hurry past outside. She watches everyone that passes, making sure they're not Charlotte. When she left home she double-checked that she wasn't being tailed, but Charlotte is cleverer than she looks. If she discovered where she works she could definitely have followed her here.

Alexandra and Samuel are a couple of tables away, in the centre of the room, bathed in candlelight, looking to all the world like a couple on a date. Which is exactly what's happening. The meal was planned weeks ago but now she's along for the ride in the hope that she'll identify a stalker where Alex has failed.

She waited for the couple to leave Alex's flat at eight p.m. as planned, trailed them to the tube station and sat in the same carriage but suitably far away. She subtly observed everyone who got on and off and, while she didn't spot the man who murdered Alex's parents, she did surreptitiously snap anyone she deemed suspicious. She'll send the pictures to Alexandra later, along with the notes that she took.

*

Bridget is twirling strands of pasta around her fork when she notices Alexandra twisting around in her seat, staring around at the other diners with the intensity of a witness surveying a police line-up. Several heads turned when Alex walked in, and several diners surreptitiously whispered to each other – presumably because of her fame – but if she noticed, she didn't let on. She looks stressed now, though. Bridget puts down her fork and taps out a message on her phone.

What's the matter?

Alexandra doesn't reply. Instead, she continues to stare around the room, her brow furrowed. Samuel reaches across the table and says something that Bridget can't hear. Alex whips her hand from under Sam's and stands up, clutching her phone. She looks the picture of elegance in her form-fitting black dress, her wild curls pinned into a low bun. Her spine is rigid, the muscles in her jaw clenched.

'Who took this?' Her voice rises above the chatter of the other diners as she holds her phone aloft. 'Who took this photo of me?'

As heads turn, conversations dry up and cutlery is lowered, Bridget grabs the sides of her chair, itching to rush over and ask her what's wrong. She pushes down her curiosity and picks up her phone instead to subtly record the scene, angling the camera from left to right to capture every diner she can see.

'No one?' Alex says, and it's almost as though she's centre stage, a ceiling light illuminating her face. Samuel joins her in the spotlight, another character in the play, quietly asking her to sit down.

'You're just going to sit there and eat your dinner, are

you?' Alex continues, 'pretending you didn't just send me the most disgusting message I've ever received.'

'Madam,' the Maître D says, a tall angular man in a well-fitting suit, 'If I could please ask you to . . .' he lowers his voice as he puts a hand to Alexandra's elbow, but she won't be reasoned with and she twists away, still glaring at the other diners as she demands her coat. Samuel digs around in his wallet then presses several notes into the Maître D's hand.

Where are you going? Bridget texts as she watches them leave, her carbonara congealing on the plate. *What just happened?*

'Waiter!' She raises her hand. 'Waiter, the bill! As quick as you can.'

She watches, desperate to leave as Alexandra and Samuel appear beyond the window. They're having a heated argument in the rain. Is it mission aborted? Are they going home? Should she?

'Waiter! Please!' She waves her arm from side to side, but he's got his back to her, taking another table's order, and now Samuel's trying to flag a taxi outside. She shoves her phone into her bag and thumbs through her purse. She's only got a twenty-pound note. That's nowhere near enough to cover her meal and a tip.

'Waiter!' She beckons him as he turns away from the table, but he's spotted some empty dishes in front of a couple and of course he's going to pick them up. Beyond the window a taxi's pulled up outside, its yellow light a flare in the gloom.

'Oh, for god's sake.' Bridget tosses the twenty-pound note onto the table and gets up so quickly that her chair tips over and clatters to the ground.

She hears the waiter calling after her as she hurries out of the restaurant, down the short hallway and out onto the street.

'Alex!' She waves wildly as the rain flattens her hair to her head and her dress to her skin. 'Alex, wait!' but the taxi's already halfway down the road.

Chapter 13

WhatsApp group: FYST

21.22
Alexandra: Bridget, I'm so sorry I abandoned you in the restaurant earlier. I know I've already apologised and explained but I feel awful just leaving you there.

Bridget: I understand. I'm sure I would have done the same.

Lucy: What happened?

Alexandra: My fucking stalker was in the restaurant. Bridget sent me a video she took of the other diners, but I didn't recognise anyone. Anyway, whoever it was took a photo of Sam and me having dinner. From the angle of the photo they sent me, they must have been in the corridor. They sent me another photo, of two skeletons lying together in a grave. It was what they wrote that made me feel sick.

River: What did they write?

Lucy: Oh my god, Alex. Did they just walk in off the street then? Or could it be a waiter? Has the restaurant got CCTV?

21.28

Alexandra: They wrote 'You'll be with your mum and dad soon.'

Lucy: Oh, Alex. That's awful. It's so cruel.

River: I know I'm stating the obvious but that's the second death threat you've received.

Alex: Sam thinks that the wreath was meant for me. He's insisting I go to the police.

River: So you should.

Lucy: Bridget, did you see anything?

Bridget: Nothing. I was sitting in the wrong place to see anyone in the doorway. I could kick myself for not choosing a different table. I won't make that mistake again.

River: There's not going to be an again.

Alexandra: You don't get to make that decision, River. Bridget does. And before you jump down my throat I'm going to the police on Monday.

River: Why not ring them now? Or go tomorrow?

Alexandra: Because it's half past fucking nine at night. Because I'm upset. Because I need to plant the tracker on Marcus at the gym tomorrow morning. Is that okay, River? Do I have your permission to make my own fucking decisions?

River: I know you're upset but you're taking it out on the wrong person. It was just a question.

Alexandra: And that was my answer. Lucy, are you still okay to plant the tracker on Vanessa for River?

Lucy: Absolutely. I'll be there tomorrow afternoon.

River: I think we should stop. It's too dangerous.

Alexandra: Seriously? This morning you were all gung-ho and 'we need to hide and set a trap'. Do I have to remind you that we just buried Natalie Beare days ago? That there are four stalkers here, not just mine? And that we only have six days left until the date on the RIP card? If we place three of the trackers we'll know where Marcus, Charlotte and Vanessa are on the 20th. If the three of you hide, you'll all be safe.

Lucy: Aren't you going to hide?

Alexandra: Sam can walk me to the theatre and back. I'll be fine.

River: But what about when you're on stage? How can you ensure your safety in what's essentially a room full of strangers?

Alexandra: It's a THEATRE, River. This isn't America and I'm not Abraham Lincoln.

River: No, but your stalker's already been in your DRESSING ROOM! I don't want to scare you but if they can scrawl on your mirror, they can get to you on the opening night of the play.

Lucy: River! Stop it.

Bridget: I'll find her stalker before then. They're bound to slip up and show themselves, then all I need to do is place the tracker and we'll all be safe on the 20th.

Bridget: We can work that out. You said you had a plan to trap them. Still waiting to hear more about that . . .

Lucy: We have to at least try this plan, River. It's the only way we can take back any kind of control.

River: Okay, okay fine. But if anything goes wrong tomorrow, we're done.

Chapter 14

Lucy

Five days until someone dies . . .

Lucy sits up in bed, pyjama top clinging to her back, her blonde plait unravelling after four hours of broken sleep. A noise, like a fist against glass, startled her out of a dream. She holds herself still, blinking in the darkness, listening to the low rumble of the central heating and the water flushing in the flat upstairs. Was that what woke her? Her neighbour, going to the loo?

It's 3.07 a.m. The neon display on the alarm clock taunts her. She can't remember the last time she slept for eight hours. She slips off the bed, conscious of her own full bladder, and she's halfway across the bedroom when she hears it again: a dull knocking from the living room. She shakes uncontrollably, frozen, her gaze fixed on a beam of light in the hallway. Did she forget to turn the bathroom light off when she went to bed? Her phone is on the bedside table but even if she could move to pick it up who would she ring? She could scream, try and alert the neighbours, but if Marcus has found her, and he succeeds in breaking into her flat, she could be dead before the police show up.

I'm going nowhere.

That's what he said in the note. She'd ripped it into tiny pieces when she fled back into the school, but his words are tattooed on her brain. Was she distracted when she drove home from school on Friday? Did she forget to keep an eye on the rear-view mirror, to vary her route? Did he follow her? Has he been watching her ever since? Her pulse quickens as she remembers the dark figure she glimpsed in the bushes in Highgate Wood, and the rock that whistled by her head. Had he followed her there too? Does he know about the trackers? Is she the one who's going to die?

If she puts the lights on, he'll know that she's heard him. He'll know she's scared and on edge. She wants to make sure the front door is locked; check the windows in every room; but she's too scared that she'll see him, that his face will loom out of the gloom. She thinks of Natalie, standing at her front door, almost inside, almost safe. Did she hear Jamie behind her? Did she turn and look into his eyes, then see the knife?

Tap-tap-tap. Tap-tap-tap. The sounds continue and Lucy's bladder loosens; urine floods her pyjama bottoms, streaming down her thighs. She drops to her knees, then her stomach and inches her way beneath her bed. She presses her hands over her mouth to smother her loud, laboured breathing and smells dust and sweat and fear.

She waits and she listens, and the alarm clock ticks from

75

3.12 a.m. to 4.30 a.m. to 5.45 a.m. and her urine-soaked pyjamas feel cold and wet against her skin. She continues to listen, barely breathing, until daylight creeps from between the gap in the curtains then she edges her way out from the bed. She pulls a dressing gown around her stiff, damp body, grabs her phone and edges towards the living room. She stands beside the window, too terrified to pull back the curtain and check the glass in case Marcus is still out there. Sobbing, she runs back to her bedroom.

Outside, a cigarette burns on the steps to her flat.

Chapter 15

Alexandra

SUNDAY 15TH OCTOBER

Five days until someone dies . . .

Alex wipes an arm across her forehead as she reaches Marcus's gym. It's a little after eleven a.m. and she's so nervous she's broken out in a sweat.

Samuel had still been snoozing beside her when she got up a little after nine. He hadn't returned from his gig until two a.m. so she'd tiptoed around the bedroom as she got ready, taking care not to wake him.

She'd barely slept. For all her bravado in the group chat, she's scared to go back to the theatre. River was right, her stalker has already found a way to get into her dressing room – what's to stop them from stabbing her to death in full view of the audience? She could miss the opening night and hide with the others, but then what? Never set foot in the theatre again? Allow the stalker to control her career?

She could open up to Liz – tell her about her stalker and ask whether the company could provide additional security during the play's run. Liz might well agree, but it would be the last role she'd ever be offered. Word would get out that hiring her was too risky, too expensive. In a room full of auditioning actresses, her name would be moved to the bottom of the list.

Angry tears had filled her eyes as she pulled on her gym gear and tucked her phone into the pocket in her leggings without bothering to turn it on. She couldn't check for messages from friends without worrying that her stalker had found a new way to message her. She couldn't leave the house without peering through the window, walk somewhere without looking over her shoulder, have a meal without a camera zooming in on her face. She couldn't even relax in her own home knowing that her stalker might be outside watching, waiting, planning their next move.

There was a moment, as she reached for the front door handle, when the urge to run back up the stairs, throw off her clothes and get back into bed with Sam had been unbearably strong, but she'd managed to make it outside into the cold North London air.

Bridget was waiting for her in her van. She was up early to visit the flower market on Columbia Road – to see if anyone had any jobs – and had offered her a lift to Marcus's gym. Bridget had the heating on full blast, so Alex slipped out of her coat and tried not to think about what she was about to do. Instead, she'd chatted to Bridget about theatre, plays, and her time in *Southern Lights*. Bridget hadn't seen it, but everyone had questions if they knew you'd been on TV.

There was a tense moment, ten minutes into the journey, when Bridget glanced at her rear-view mirror and swore under her breath.

'I thought it was Charlotte. But it's just someone who looks like her. Don't worry, it's fine.'

Bridget had insisted on dropping her outside the gym, then had spent several minutes making sure that she wanted to do this, reminding her that it wasn't too late to change her mind. She'd been so jittery Alex jumped out of the cab as soon as Bridget drew breath. If she hadn't been nervous before, she certainly was now.

'Text me when you're done,' Bridget had shouted after her. 'I'll come and get you, drive you home!'

Now, she slips into the building, flashes a smile at the receptionist as she touches her day pass on the turnstile and follows the sign to the ladies' changing room. She leaves her bag in a locker, steels herself, then strolls into the gym as casually as she can, her water bottle in her hand.

Her plan rests on two things: one, getting Marcus chatting and two, slipping the tracker into his pocket or bag without him noticing.

All the treadmills are in use, as are two of the bikes, most of the elliptical machines and one of the step machines. She scans the room, looking for a tall man with long fair hair who matches the photo Lucy sent her, and spots Marcus on the treadmill, running at an easy pace. Slow enough that he'd be able to hold a conversation with her, but both treadmills either side of him are in use. She's going to have to use a rowing machine instead and bide her time.

She slots her feet into place, lifts the bar and gets into a slow, steady rhythm: no point building up too much of a sweat. As she pushes and pulls, she casts sneaky glances in Marcus's direction. She knew he was young, but he looks even younger in person, despite the fact he's at least six foot two. His long fair hair is pulled back into a ponytail and there's a hint of acne below his cheekbones and above his sparse stubble. Whilst his face looks young his body is strong and muscular with wide shoulders, a broad chest and thick arms. His chiselled thighs suggest he cycles a lot.

Her phone bleeps on the floor beside her and she instinctively glances at it. Sam's messaged her.

Where are you? Woke up and you were gone.

After what happened at Highgate Woods she didn't tell him that today was the day she'd be placing a tracker on Marcus. He'd only try and talk her out of it.

She yanks at the bar and pushes harder with her legs, upping the pace of her strokes. Sam hasn't been back to his own place for several days and she's starting to feel like she can't breathe. If she's not at rehearsals he's following her from room to room, asking her if the stalker has been in touch and nagging her about going to the police. She's overheard him on the phone a couple of times, talking about her to someone. He hangs up if she so much as clears her throat.

He's trying to protect her, but she feels like she's suffocating. She always gets like this a couple of months into a relationship. It doesn't matter who the man is, the moment she catches herself falling in love a switch inside is flicked and emotionally she shuts down.

Her focus switches back to Marcus. He's finished with the treadmill and is heading over to the free weights area. She selects a couple of five-kilogram dumbbells, props one leg up on a bench and starts doing deliberately bad tricep extensions, her elbow flapping around instead of tucked into her waist.

Marcus doesn't so much as glance in her direction but a woman doing stretches on a mat in the corner of the room gives her a funny look. Alex repeats the move on the other side, watching as Marcus grunts through a set of bent-over rows.

'That looks tough,' she says, openly watching him now. His gaze flicks towards her, then just as quickly away. He continues to grunt and row, grunt and row. Engaging him in conversation is proving trickier than she anticipated. Maybe he hates small talk while he's working out, or he's so obsessed with Lucy that other women are completely invisible to him? She waits for him to finish his reps, then, as he adds some weight to the barbell, she slides over.

'I don't suppose you could spot me?'

He gives her a long slow look and something inside her contracts and twists. It's there in his eyes, the unnerving intensity that Lucy warned her about; that makes her feel uncomfortable in her own skin.

'Do I know you?' he asks. 'You look familiar.'

It's a question she's heard hundreds of times. During the soap's peak popularity, when her character was part of a major abduction storyline, she couldn't get the tube or walk into a restaurant without being approached by a fan. 'It's possible.'

'Were you a teacher at St Paul's?'

She shakes her head. 'You must be thinking of someone else.'

'I'll help you.' The 'staring from the mat' woman has

81

appeared beside them. She's a chirpy ponytailed blonde in a neon pink crop top and pink and black camouflage leggings.

'Do you know how many kilograms you normally press?' the woman asks.

Before Alexandra can object, the woman takes her by the elbow and angles her towards the weights stand. As she waffles on about form and reps and sets, Marcus makes his way towards the elliptical trainers.

Shit.

He's suspicious of her; why else would he have abandoned the weights part-way through his set? She can't follow him or she'll look even dodgier.

'Thanks so much for your help,' she says to the woman who's added twenty kilograms to the barbell. Alexandra bends at the knees, lifts the barbell without too much trouble and carefully lowers it onto the hook above the bench. Then, as the woman hovers over her, wittering words of encouragement, she lies back on the bench and grips the metal bar. She lifts and lowers, lifts and lowers, all the while trying to work out how the hell she's going to place a tracker on a man who doesn't want to be anywhere near her. Her phone continually vibrates as she completes her third set.

'Excuse me for a second. I need to get this.' She heads across the room towards the women's changing room. Feeling the weight of someone's gaze, she turns slowly. Marcus, pumping the handles of the elliptical trainer, stares straight back at her. Suppressing a shudder, she yanks open the door to the changing rooms, her phone still vibrating in her hand with a call.

It's Sam again.

She hovers her thumb over the answer icon, then changes

her mind and taps 'decline'. He's obviously worried, but now isn't the time. It's Lucy she needs to talk to. She finds her number and holds the phone to her ear as the call connects.

'It's me. I need your help. Marcus seems suspicious of me. I've made a couple of attempts to chat to him and he's not into it at all. There's no point me trying the male changing rooms because his stuff will be locked away. I don't know what else to try.'

There's a pause on the other line, then Lucy sighs softly. 'It's okay, I appreciate you trying but it was always going to be . . . wait, I've just thought of something. He might have brought his motorbike. I should have mentioned it before. It's a Yamaha, black with yellow wheel rims. It looks like something Batman might ride. The best place to put the tracker would be under the seat. But don't feel you have to do this. If he's freaking you out just leave.'

Alex glances at the door to the gym, imagining Marcus on the other side, still pumping away at the elliptical with that strange, steady stare of his, and pushes down the flicker of fear that she feels.

'Black and yellow Yamaha.' She tucks the phone between her shoulder and her jaw, opens her locker and pulls out her stuff. 'Got it. I'll talk to you later, okay?'

She pulls on her hoodie, slings her bag across her body then heads for the corridor. She hurries past the reception area and leaves the building. There aren't a huge number of spaces in the car park outside and she spots the motorbike straight away – black with yellow rims as Lucy described. It's the only motorbike amongst half a dozen parked cars. It's also in full view of reception, thanks to the glass wall and door that make up the front of the building. The receptionist is deep in conversation with a colleague and there's no one else in the foyer; she's got to make her move now, while she can.

She speeds across the car park and stands next to the black BMW that's parked beside the motorbike. She opens her bag and slips her hand into the front pocket. Her fingers spider around the small space, feeling for the smooth circular shape of the tracker. She shivers in her thin hoodie, cursing herself for leaving her coat in Bridget's van.

Where the fuck is it? She moves her hand into the body of the bag and shifts her purse, her hairbrush, make-up removers, a small make-up bag, tissues, pens, a notepad and other bits and bobs out of the way. Where is it? She can't have lost it. Surely. Did it fall out of her bag somehow? Is it lying on the floor of the changing room? Is it in her locker?

She hears a noise and glances up. Marcus, in a long dark coat with a rucksack over one shoulder and a motorbike helmet in his hand, is walking through reception. Fuck. *Fuck*!

She sweeps her hand around in the bottom of her bag but the tracker's not there. She must have lost it and now it's too late. Marcus has opened the door to the gym and he's heading straight for her. She turns her back on him so she's facing the black BMW. She's going to have to pretend that it's hers, that she can't find her key. With any luck he'll just drive off. She was so close to placing the tracker on his bike. She won't get a second chance. He's seen her face now.

She frantically pats the pockets of her hoodie. No tracker. She can hear trainers crunching over the gravel. He's getting closer. He's only a few metres behind her. She slides her hands over her thighs and her palm curves over something solid. It's the fucking tracker. She'd transferred it from her bag to her leggings when she was in Bridget's van.

'Alexandra?' Marcus says her name and fear explodes through her body. She turns slowly, pulling short sharp breaths deep into her lungs. How does he know her name? He's so close she can smell the sharp tang of his sweat mixed with the pungent musk of his deodorant.

She looks up at him, the tracker buried in her damp palm. 'How do you—'

'Your water bottle.' He holds it towards her, her name printed in black on the shiny silver metal.

'Right. Thanks.' She closes the distance between them, her thigh nudging the motorbike's seat. All she needs to do is tuck the tracker beneath it. River said the trackers were magnetic, so it should cling to the metal. Or did he? Fear clouds her brain as Marcus waits for her to take the bottle. If the tracker isn't magnetised it'll drop to the floor. It'll be game over the moment he spots it. He's still looking at her expectantly, his arm outstretched. Should she place the tracker under the seat or not? She won't get another chance. She made the wrong decision twenty-five years ago and paid the ultimate price.

'Thank you.' She leans towards him, blocking his view of the seat with her body as she reaches out her right hand for the bottle. At the same time the fingers of her left hand slide over the leather of the seat, then move down and under.

She lets the tracker go. And it sticks.

'You should be careful,' Marcus says as she straightens up, and adrenaline spikes through her body, 'with the things that are precious to you. If you don't look after them, they could disappear forever.'

85

'It's just . . .' She shakes the water bottle lightly, so the water sloshes around inside. 'It's just a bottle.'

He smiles broadly, revealing the gap in his front teeth. 'I think you're cleverer than that, Alexandra.'

She takes a step away from him. 'I don't know what you're talking about.'

His smile widens, then disappears as he pulls his helmet down over his head. 'I don't know if you're a private investigator or a honey trap, but please, send Lucy my love.'

Chapter 16

Lucy

Five days until someone dies . . .

Lucy hasn't slept. She hasn't eaten. But she's showered, put on clean clothes and she's made it out of her flat and into an Uber. She hovered by her front door for a full five minutes before she left the house, paralysed by indecision: frightened to leave in case Marcus was out on the street, and scared to stay in the flat in case she couldn't escape. Claustrophobia – and River's barrage of texts asking if she was still coming to the pub – won out, and she eventually sped out of the flat, locked the door, sprinted up the steps and jumped into the taxi before she could change her mind.

The further she gets from home the more convinced she becomes that Marcus wasn't anywhere near her flat last night. The tapping sound she heard could have been anything – a water leak upstairs, a pigeon on her patio,

87

the boiler or mice. She's been obsessive about taking a different route home from work every day, constantly on watch for Marcus's motorbike, or any vehicle that follows her for too long. There's no way he could have found out where she lives. But Natalie's death has made her more fearful; made her wonder if maybe all basement flats are cursed.

A message notification flashes up on her phone as the taxi creeps closer to the mock Tudor pub where River and Meg are having Sunday lunch. It's from Alex but she's too scared to look at it. If Marcus has done anything to her, she'll never forgive herself.

She opens the message, bracing herself.

IT'S DONE! Tracker in place. Here's the code for your app.

She slumps back in her seat, releasing all the tension in her body in a long, slow sigh.

'That'll be eighteen quid please, love,' the taxi driver says.

She touches her bank card to the payment machine then tucks it back into her purse and plucks at the door handle, steeling herself for what's to come. She's not like Alex. She's not confident, determined or strong. She has no idea how Vanessa will react and it's the unpredictability of the situation that's scaring her. She doesn't do spontaneous or improvised. She's suffered from anxiety since she was thirteen and right now it's almost as bad as it gets.

The exterior of The Badger and Butcher is exactly as she anticipated it. She Googled the pub last night, and again this morning, and looked at as many images as she could. She also studied the photographs of Vanessa that River sent her and researched her online. But Vanessa is more than an

88

image and a LinkedIn CV; she's real and unpredictable and what happens next is something Lucy cannot control.

'All right, miss?' the taxi driver twists round in his seat. 'The handle's just there, can you see it, just below the—'

'Got it, thank you.' She yanks at the handle and steps out of the taxi before she changes her mind.

As the cab pulls away, she mentally steadies herself. All she has to do is get close enough to Vanessa to slip a tracker into her coat pocket or her handbag. When that's done, she can go home and hide.

The pub is packed. There isn't a single empty table and the sound of chatter, laughter and cutlery on crockery is so loud that Lucy can only vaguely hear the gentle jazz soundtrack that's being piped into the room. She's perched on a stool at the end of the bar, the smell of roast beef, Yorkshire pudding and gravy hanging heavy in the air, a Diet Coke in her hand. She spotted River and Meg as soon as she walked in. They were sitting at a table at the window as planned, perfectly placed for her to keep an eye on them from the bar. River caught her eye and shook his head sharply. No sign of Vanessa. Maybe she hadn't seen River's Twitter post about his excitement at going out for a roast, Lucy thought hopefully. Maybe she wouldn't turn up at all.

Now, as a waitress swerves between tables, a tray in each hand, Lucy spots movement at the door. It's Vanessa. She recognises her immediately, even with an oversized grey beanie partly obscuring her long, dark hair. A grey scarf is wound around her throat and she's wearing a loose-fitting purple coat – with pockets. A black handbag dangling from the crook of her elbow. Pockets and a handbag. Lucy takes a sip of her drink, feeling like she's about to throw up.

Vanessa pauses in the doorway and surveys the restaurant, her gaze resting on River and Meg. Neither of them has spotted her, they're too busy tucking into their food. As she heads for the bar Lucy surreptitiously slides her handbag off the stool beside her. Here comes the 'friend' she's been saving it for.

She turns back towards the bar, feigning interest in the barman who's darting back and forth, preparing drinks.

'Excuse me?' A female voice says to her left. 'Is this seat taken?'

'No, no. It's fine.' Lucy shoots Vanessa a smile.

Up close she can smell the floral fruity scent of her perfume, can see the red lipstick on her lips and the winged eyeliner that creates sharp, neat ticks on either side of her eyes. She looks like a perfectly normal woman in her mid-twenties, made up for a nice Sunday lunch, dressed for a cool October day. As Vanessa climbs onto the stool beside her Lucy pretends to look at her phone, but secretly she watches every move the other woman makes. Her hat's off; so is the scarf, bundled into her lap; but the coat's still on, and the bag.

'Excuse me,' Vanessa says, but when Lucy turns her head she realises it's the barman's attention she's trying to get, not hers.

He's alone at the bar, focusing on the waitresses who are dropping off drinks orders, and ignoring everyone else.

'I hope you're not thirsty,' Lucy gestures at her half-empty Diet Coke. 'It took me fifteen minutes just to get this.'

'I'm not in a hurry.' Vanessa keeps her elbow propped up

on the bar, a ten-pound note between her fingers and twists around in her seat zoning in on River and Meg.

Her bag is on her right hip, within easy reach. It's the type of bag with a flap, closed with a postman's lock. In order to open it Lucy would need to twist the metal clasp horizontally and then lift the flap. Vanessa would have to be distracted for at least thirty seconds if she's going to get the tracker inside.

'Makes me sick,' Vanessa says under her breath.

'Sorry?' Lucy looks at her in surprise.

'The way he's touching her. She was trying to eat her food and he grabbed her hand. Look at him, gripping her fingers like he's being romantic when she's probably just said something he doesn't agree with, and he wants her to stop.'

'Who are you talking about?'

'Those two.' She gives a nod across the room. 'The guy with the messy hair and glasses and the girl with the mullet in a pink cardigan.'

Lucy takes a sip of her Diet Coke. She's so nervous her throat has dried. 'Oh, okay. Do you know them?'

Vanessa gives a sharp laugh. 'He's my ex.'

'Awkward.'

Vanessa's gaze slides towards her. 'Only for him. When his girlfriend goes to the toilet I'm going with her.'

Shit. Lucy subtly slides her hand across the bar, searching for her phone. She needs to warn River.

'She's got no idea what she's let herself in for,' Vanessa's cheeks have pinkened, whether from excitement or the warmth of the packed pub, Lucy can't tell. 'She's no idea the hell he'll put her through. Have you ever been out with someone controlling?'

Lucy's hand retreats from her phone as she meets Vanessa's eyes, trying to read the emotion behind the strong, steady gaze. Is this part of her game? Did she clock her own vulnerability the moment she sat down?

'Yes,' she says. 'I have.'

'How long were you together?' Vanessa asks but before Lucy can answer, the barman slides over and says hi. Vanessa shoots him a smile. 'Gin and tonic, please, and my friend will have . . .' she raises her eyebrows questioningly at Lucy.

'I'm fine. Thank you.'

'You sure?' Vanessa eyes her near-empty glass.

Lucy wavers. Will it look suspicious if she stays at the bar without a drink? At some point Vanessa will probably ask if she's waiting for someone. 'I'll have a Diet Coke, please,' she says. 'That's very kind.'

After the barman nods and moves away she adds, 'We were together for a year.'

'Hard to get away, isn't it? Once they've reeled you in? I was with River for nearly two years. Biggest regret of my life. Was he charming, your ex? Did he love-bomb you after you first met? Make you feel like you were the most incredible woman in the world?'

Lucy twists her hands in her lap. She feels uncomfortable, talking about Marcus with River's stalker, but there's a part of her that wants to open up. She's kept quiet for so long. 'You could say that.'

'Was it exciting? At the start? Magical?'

Lucy nods, although she's not sure 'magical' is the word she'd choose. Her relationship with Marcus didn't start with a spark or eyes meeting across the room. Back then she'd have described it as a slow burn, a meeting of minds, a growing attraction, a drunken encounter that caught them both by surprise and led to a desperate, passionate love affair. Now she'd describe their relationship as toxic, controlling and coercive, a trap set by Marcus that she stumbled into and couldn't escape. She tried to leave him multiple times, and each time he talked her into taking him back.

'It's how they get you, isn't it?' Vanessa shifts her bag onto her lap, unbuckles it and takes out her phone. She checks it then tucks it back inside. Lucy's gaze flicks to Vanessa's coat pocket. It's wide open, exposed.

'They lure you in,' Vanessa's practically quivering with anger now, 'and then they chip away at you, bit by bit, until there's only shards of you left. I won't let him do that to anyone else. He should be locked up for what he does.'

River's sipping his drink, listening as Meg talks. Or at least, he's pretending to listen. One of his legs is jiggling so violently it's obvious that he knows he's being watched. He's hating every moment but he's going through with it because he's so desperate for Vanessa to be tracked. She has to be lying. Maybe she was the coercive one and everything she's just shared is her deluded justification for trying to ruin his life. But what if River is the one who isn't telling the truth?

'You know I'm basically homeless now?' Vanessa reaches for the gin glass the barman places on the bar in front of her. 'I had to move out of my flat because he wouldn't leave me alone. I'm sofa-surfing, going from one friend's house to the next so he can't track me down.'

'He's stalking you?' Lucy asks.

'No, but only because he doesn't know where I live. Before I moved though, he'd come over regularly to *warn* me off.'

She makes quotation marks around the word with her index fingers. 'I'm the enemy now because I escaped, and he'll do anything to make sure he doesn't lose Meg. She keeps blocking me on social media, so I've got no idea if any of my messages are getting through. That's why I need to talk to her in person. She needs to hear what I've got to say, without him getting in the way.'

Lucy subtly slips her hand into her pocket and rubs her thumb over the tracker's smooth surface. Vanessa's version of the truth is the complete opposite to River's. He said she's on the run so the police can't arrest her, and that she sent his nudes and texts to Meg. He claims she's let down his tyres, that she sends him abusive messages via the contact form on his website, and emails his clients to try and ruin his reputation.

Across the room Meg has turned her face to window. She's dabbing at her eyes with her napkin, openly crying while River observes her with his arms crossed and a stony expression on his face.

Could he be the liar? They only have his word for it that Vanessa's been stalking him. He claimed Meg knew about the tracker he put on her but what if she didn't? What if he is as possessive and controlling as Vanessa claims? What if he dreamed up the whole tracker scheme to stop her from getting to Meg?

He seems caring, harmless and geeky, but appearances can be so deceptive; God knows Marcus taught her that much. And River's mask has slipped a couple of times. She saw his paranoid side when he got worked up about Natalie not adding him to her fake Facebook account and he had his ear to his laptop when Alex took a phone call during their Zoom. There's a patronising side to him too, that slips out from time to time.

Does she really know enough about him to help him track Vanessa? She's been manipulated by a man before. Has she inadvertently let it happen again? She rubs her thumb over the tracker again. Vanessa's on her phone, her body angled away leaving the pocket of her purple coat wide open and exposed. Lucy's pulse races as she closes her grip on the tracker and slowly slides her hand out of her pocket. She won't be in this position again. What's the right thing to do?

As she reaches for her glass, she feels the weight of River's gaze and raises her chin to look at him. His hands are on his thighs, a frantic expression on his face.

He raises his eyebrows at her, and a silent question wings its way across the pub – is it done?

She takes a sip of her drink, observes him over the top of the glass and minutely nods her head. It's the first lie she's told him but, if Vanessa is right, then he's told a lot more.

Chapter 17

Alexandra

SUNDAY 15TH OCTOBER

Five days until someone dies . . .

Freaked out by her conversation with Marcus, Alex had sent Lucy a quick message (missing out the part about Marcus guessing they knew each other, so she didn't panic her) then jogged all the way from the gym to Walthamstow underground station, glancing behind her the whole way. How the hell had he worked out what she was up to? Had he read it in her body language? Were her intentions really that obvious when she walked into the gym?

She collapsed into a seat on the tube, still shaking with adrenaline. Marcus might be young but there was something about his energy that was as intimidating as hell.

Now, as she leaves Covent Garden underground, she stands back, letting the crowd flow away from the station, and checks her phone to see how the others are doing. There are no updates from River or Lucy, but several messages from Bridget:

11.30 Have you left the gym yet? I can come and get you at any time.

11.39 Can you update the group that you're okay. I know I won't be the only one worried about you.

11.41 I'm done at the flower market, just waiting for your call.

11.52 I'm outside the gym. Are you still in there?

12.00 Alex?

12.05 I've tried calling but it's not going through. Please ring me asap. I'm so scared that something's happened to you.

Alex looks at her watch. Shit. It's nearly twenty past twelve. Bridget must be going out of her mind.

I'm fine! she types and hits send.

I'm so sorry, Bridget, she begins another message, *but I've already left Walthamstow. Your texts must have gone through when I was on the tube. I'm sorry if I scared you but it's done. I put the tracker on Marcus's motorbike. I've let Lucy know.*

By the time she hits send Bridget has replied to her first text,

Oh, thank goodness. I don't know what I thought Marcus might have done to you in a gym full of people, but I'm so glad you're okay.

Sighing, Alex looks back at her messages. Sam hasn't been

in touch since he called her at the gym. She hadn't planned on travelling home via Covent Garden, but he told her last night that he was popping into the Freemasons Arms, where they run a comedy club, to meet a mate for lunch, so that's where she's heading. After her encounter with Marcus, she just wants to be with someone who makes her feel safe. The fact that that person is Sam, who she's been pushing away for days, isn't lost on her. But she's too jittery to give her contrariness any more thought.

Her phone vibrates with a new message, from an unknown number.

I can see you.

Instinctively she looks up, searching the crowds for the sender. It's not the number she blocked after she was sent photos in the restaurant, but it has to be the same person, she's sure of that. But who is it? It could be any of the people milling around her: the tourists, the shoppers, the selfie takers; it has to be someone still, someone watching, a voyeur to her fright.

But you can't see me can you? Another message pops up on her phone.

It's a three-minute walk along Long Acre to the Freemasons Arms. Should she go and find Samuel, or should she get back on the tube?

All alone, Alex? No one to talk to? Now you know how it feels.

She looks across the street to the shops opposite. Is her stalker hiding behind one of the reflective glass panes? Are they in Tiffany's, Regal House, or the Nag's Head? Is her stalker behind her? She turns sharply, scans the inside of the station, the ticket barriers, the machines, the commuters, the staff. She's breathing more quickly now, but her senses are heightened; she sees movement out of the corner of her eye – a dachshund, pulling on its lead – smells the spicy, citrussy scent of Dior Sauvage, hears a toddler shouting at his mother to look. Her stalker could be any of the people around her or they could be at home, at work, in the cinema, having lunch, sending her messages, revelling in her fear.

She takes off, heads down Long Acre, walking quickly past shops, cafés and pubs, her phone still vibrating in her hand. She tries telling herself that her stalker's not in Covent Garden, that she's not in any danger; then she remembers the photograph in the restaurant – they took it less than five metres from where she was sitting and she had no clue they were there. They could have approached her and stabbed her, or thrown acid in her face. She needs to get to the pub. When she finds Sam, she'll be safe.

She flinches as someone overtakes her, their arm brushing hers, but it's just a woman running towards a taxi, her arm in the air. Alex glances over her shoulder, looking for a face she recognises from her tube carriage, from the station, from the crowd in the street, but everyone looks like strangers, one face melding into another, their clothing muted shades of black, brown and grey.

She speeds up, lengthening her stride but still walking. The Freemasons Arms is in sight now, less than a hundred metres away, a black canopy over white pillars, the bases gilded and shiny like the windowsills and the embossed name of the pub. She hurries towards it, a refuge from fear, and pushes open the doors.

Sam!

She searches the faces of the punters at the bar, the groups at the tables, the bent heads of diners shovelling fish and chips into their mouths. She can't see him. She moves around the pub and searches more carefully, curious eyes swivelling in her direction as she drifts from one table to the next. She looks from one face to another, none of them Sam's.

'Excuse me,' she grips the polished wood of the bar and leans towards the barman. 'Have you seen Samuel Myers? Comedian. He said he'd be in with Paul?'

He shakes his head. 'Sorry love, I haven't seen Sam all week. Can I get you a drink?'

Alex turns away, tears welling in her eyes. She's not going to cry here, in front of him and all these strangers. She heads for the ladies' loos, slams open the door and locks herself in the nearest cubicle. She deletes the stalker's messages unread, blocks the number then texts Sam.

I'm at the Freemasons Arms. Where are you?

It takes four minutes for him to reply:

You're not there are you? Sorry babe, we decided to go to the Coach and Horses instead. I'd invite you to join us, but it's work talk. Everything okay?

She stares at the words, fighting the urge to reply, *Actually everything's not okay. One hour ago I put a tracker on a psychopath, then my stalker caught up with me and for some fucked-up reason I thought of you, and how seeing you would make me feel safe. But you're not here, and now I'm pissed off with myself.*

Instead, she types,

Enjoy your work talk. I'm getting an Uber home. I'm busy tomorrow. I'll be in touch the next time I'm free.

100

As texts go it's as passive aggressive as hell, and Sam doesn't deserve it. With any luck he'll dump her, so she doesn't have to make that decision herself.

Chapter 18

River

SUNDAY 15TH OCTOBER

Five days until someone dies . . .

River had been on tenterhooks for the last hour, dreading Vanessa walking into the pub, whilst also desperate for her to show up, and then waiting for Lucy to give him a sign. There had been a moment earlier when he was worried that Lucy wouldn't be able to go through with it. She'd looked terrified as she'd climbed onto the bar stool, her face white, but somehow she'd engaged Vanessa in conversation and he'd watched, simultaneously fascinated and horrified, as the two women chatted away like old friends.

He'd felt terrible about inviting Meg to the pub under false pretences (a lovely Sunday lunch together), knowing how she felt about his ex, but it was the only way he could ensure that Vanessa would show up. Vanessa had become fixated with Meg, repeatedly contacting her, rather than him.

It was part-way through Lucy and Vanessa's conversation when Meg spotted her, and her reaction had almost ruined the whole thing. Instead of responding with terrified silence as he'd anticipated, she'd grabbed her phone from the table and threatened to call the police. He'd had to snatch it away to get her to stop. Then, as he had explained what was happening and why, she'd burst into furious tears. He was starting to think he'd have to take her out to the car when Lucy nodded at him, confirming that the tracker had been placed.

Now he arches his spine and stretches out his arms. He feels like he's spent all day in the gym, not an hour pushing food around a plate in a pub.

'Meg,' he says, straightening up again, but the chair across from him is empty. His girlfriend is winding her way through the tables, heading for the bar where Vanessa is waiting and smirking.

'Meg, wait!' He jumps to his feet. 'Stop!'

Heads turn and chairs shift as he pushes past the other tables to reach her. Lucy's on her feet now too, her gaze darting from Meg to Vanessa to River, lips parted, unsure what to do.

'Meg!' River reaches out an arm and fastens his fingers around his girlfriend's wrist. 'Meg, stop!'

She snaps around, her cheeks flushed, her eyes shining with anger. 'Get off me!' She tries to shake him off, but he holds firm. 'River, get off me.'

'Please,' he begs. 'Don't do this. It won't end well. This is what she wants.'

'I don't care what she wants. Someone needs to tell her to get out of our fucking lives.'

103

He's never seen her like this before. She'll stand her ground in an argument, but she never loses her temper, and she rarely swears. She shakes her arm again, then pulls, straining to get away from him.

'Meg, please.' He drops his voice. 'People are watching.'

There's a noticeable drop in volume in the pub. Several of the diners have stopped eating, their cutlery abandoned, the food cooling on their plates. Startled glances are being swapped, eyebrows are being raised and low whispers are being exchanged. A toddler's shout punctuates the silence as he excitedly slams his hands against his highchair's plastic tray.

'Look at her.' Meg continues to squirm and pull, her eyes still fixed on Vanessa. 'She's smirking. She's fucking smirking. Let's see how much she laughs when I—'

'This is what she *wants*,' River hisses again. 'She's enjoying seeing you upset. Don't stoop to her level. You're better than this. *Please*. Please can we just go?'

He isn't sure whether it's the comment about Vanessa enjoying seeing her upset, or if she's just run out of steam, but Meg visibly sags, and her arm relaxes beneath his grip.

'Let go of me. I'm not walking out of here with you holding onto me like I'm a misbehaving child.'

Vanessa has uncrossed her arms and she's winding a grey scarf around her neck. Lucy is quietly remonstrating with her, pointing at the barman, presumably trying to get her to stay for a drink.

'You promise you're not going to confront her?' River asks Meg.

She glares up at him, her eyes shining with tears. 'Ask me that one more time and let's see how long this relationship lasts.'

Shock relaxes his grip on her wrist, and he watches, horrified, as she storms out of the pub.

'Tosser,' says a bloke at the table beside him. 'She deserves better.'

River turns sharply to see an acne-pitted twenty-something staring up at him. 'Fuck off, mate. You have no idea.'

River indicates left and turns the car into their road. Meg, in the passenger seat, hasn't said a word since they left the pub. She hasn't looked at him either. She's spent the whole journey determinedly staring out of the window.

'If you want to have a go at me,' he begins hesitantly, 'then I completely understand.'

Meg says nothing, but as she touches a hand to her face and swipes at her eyes something inside him twists painfully. He can't stand it, seeing her so upset.

'I should have told you what the plan was,' he says.

'Yes, you fucking should.' Still, she doesn't look at him. 'Why would you do that to me, River? Why would you let me think that we were going out for a nice Sunday lunch and then—'

'It was all part of the—'

'Can you let me finish?' She whips around to look at him, her eyes puffy, the tip of her nose swollen and red. 'For once in our relationship could you let me finish a bloody sentence?'

He nods, says nothing, keeps his eyes on the road. She's got every right to be angry.

'Can you imagine how horrible it was,' Meg continues, 'to think we were having a nice meal together only to look up and see her staring at us from the bar? Have you got any idea how shocked I was? How scared?'

That was why I didn't tell you, River thinks but doesn't say. I wanted your reaction to be genuine otherwise Vanessa might have suspected that something was up.

'I'm sorry,' he says.

'What I don't understand,' Meg says. 'Is why you didn't just ring the police and tell them the plan to lure her to the pub? If you'd done that, she'd be in a cell now. She'd be out of our lives.'

Would she? River thinks. Or would she have fled as the police car pulled up outside? He saw the number of times she glanced at the windows. She had to suspect there was a reason why he'd posted his plans so publicly on Twitter. What the police want – what he *needs* – is Vanessa's address. Once the tracker reveals that he can pass the info on to the police. They'll turn up and arrest her. It will all be over, until she gets out of prison at least.

'Well?' Meg says, her tone shrill and impatient. 'Did you? Did you even think about that?'

'I did.' River pauses, waiting to see if she has more to add. 'But I didn't think the police would go along with it.'

'You assumed, you mean?'

'Yes,' he's treading warily now, not wanting to further upset her. 'I assumed.'

'And you didn't think to run this *plan* by me?'

'I'm sorry, Meg. I made a mistake.'

'Nice of you to admit that for once.' Her words are sharp but her tone's softened, and as River pulls into an empty spot outside their flat, the fear he's been feeling for the last half an hour loosens its grip on his chest.

*

106

He joins Meg on the pavement outside their building and sorts through the keys in his hand to find the right one.

'Do you still want to go to the cinema later,' he asks, 'or would you rather stay in and— Ow!' He presses a hand to the back of his head as something hard clunks against his skull. He turns sharply at the exact moment a teenage boy on a bike, ten metres away, hurls another rock at him.

'What the—' River grabs at Meg's hand and ducks. The rock sails over their heads and lands on the pavement with a clunk.

'Fucking paedo!' The boy gives him the finger then twists the front wheel of his bike and pedals away.

'Oh my god, River.' Meg touches a hand to the back of his head, then looks at her fingers, slick with blood. 'You're bleeding. Let's get you inside.'

'No.' He moves to get back into the car. 'The police will want a photo. You can't throw rocks at strangers in the street and get away with it.'

'Come inside,' Meg pulls at his arm. 'Please. What if he's got friends at the end of the street? Let's get inside where it's safe.'

'But I need—'

'One of the neighbours will have CCTV.'

River stares down the street, willing the boy to return, as Meg takes the key from his hand and slots it into the front door. Out of the corner of his eye he sees one of their neighbours peer out at him from between the blinds of their living room window. The moment he turns his head the blinds flip back down.

'Oh god.' Meg groans softly. 'River look.' She presses a piece of paper into his hand.

Keep your daughters safe, the flyer announces in large red letters. Then *Petition your local MP. Registered sex offender River Scott-Tyler lives on your street at number 29.*

'They're everywhere.' Meg is on the verge of tears. 'In every letterbox.'

River turns slowly, as though in a dream. He looks from left to right, along his side of the street and on the opposite side of the road. Flyers, dozens of them, hanging out of letterboxes and tucked under the windscreen wipers of cars, red lettering against a white background, fluttering in the breeze.

Chapter 19

Lucy

Five days until someone dies . . .

There's a van unloading outside Lucy's flat so the taxi driver drops her off on the corner. There's only one thought in her mind as she makes her way down the street – *open wine, get drunk*. It's Sunday afternoon, just after five p.m. and there's a pile of marking and lesson prep waiting for her, but what she wants, more than anything in the world, is to lock all the doors, close all the curtains and get so drunk that she passes out.

Every last drop of adrenaline that got her through the last hour has evaporated and she's having to drag one foot in front of the other to make her way home. She was convinced there was going to be a fight, right there in the pub in front of her. River's girlfriend stormed over, fists clenched, eyes narrowed, lips pressed into a tight line, and if he hadn't grabbed her by the wrist god knows what would have happened.

Vanessa spotted her before Lucy did and, in an instant, her energy changed. She sprang off her seat and waited, arms crossed, stance wide, waiting for the confrontation. Lucy remonstrated with her, telling her not to do something stupid, but Vanessa looked straight through her. Only after River and Meg had left the pub did she allow Lucy to talk her into sitting down and having another drink.

Now, Lucy pauses outside the corner shop at the end of her street and takes out her phone. No messages from River, and no new posts in the FYST WhatsApp group. Unusual. The last message she received was from Alex. With a jolt she remembers the app. With everything that just happened she completely forgot to enter the code.

She stiffens, sensing danger, as though the air around her has compacted, displaced by another body nearby. Cars drone in the distance, children's laughter carries on a cool light breeze, and then she hears it; the low, rhythmic whisper of his breathing.

'Where've you been?'

Marcus is in front of her, his hands in the pockets of his long grey coat, the collar turned up, his wavy fair hair falling over his shoulders. A motorbike helmet is nestled between the crook of his elbow and his waist.

She tries to speak but adrenaline has spiked from her stomach to her throat and stolen her voice. He knows where she lives. He said he'd find out and he has.

'I watched you getting dressed earlier.' His dark eyes sweep from the top of her head to the toes of her boots, and she shudders, stripped naked by his gaze. 'You made an effort. Who was it for?'

'I . . . I . . .' She fumbles with her phone. 'I'm going to call the police.'

'No, you're not. Who is this for?'

'No one.' She takes a step backwards. Out of the corner of her eye she sees an elderly woman leave the corner shop, a bag of shopping in one hand, a stick in the other.

'Don't lie.'

'I went to the pub, for lunch, with friends.'

'The brunette, in the purple coat.'

She stares at him in horror. He was watching the whole time.

'Shall we go in?' He takes one of his hands from his pockets and, with a theatrical sweep of his arm, points in the direction of her blue front door.

'No.' She shakes her head rapidly; takes another step back. 'No.'

'We've got a lot to talk about, don't you think?'

'I want you to leave.'

'You still love me, Lucy.'

'No, no I don't.'

'I think you do.' His hand moves towards her face and, for one terrifying second, she thinks he's about to hit her. Instead, he cups the back of her head and presses his lips to hers. She tries to pull away, to slide her lips from his, but he's holding her head so tightly she can't escape as he slides his wet tongue into her mouth. He's held her by the back of the head before. It was the last time they had sex. She was between his legs, and he kept her down there as she pressed her hands to the sheets and fought to escape. He laughed when he eventually released her, kicked off the duvet, reached down to ruffle her hair. 'Did you like that, miss?'

She swore then that she'd never let him touch her again.

'Get the fuck off me!' She raises her knee and thrusts it up and between his legs, then she shoves him as hard as she can in the chest. He tumbles backwards, twisting as he falls, his hands pressed to his groin, his mouth open, an anguished groan filling the air. He lands heavily, his elbow hitting the pavement, then his hip.

'I hate you.' She quivers with rage, standing above him as he continues to groan and moan, curled up on his side. 'I cannot express how much I fucking hate you. You are the biggest mistake of my life. I don't blame your mother for leaving you. She must have known what an evil bastard you are.'

At the mention of his mother something dark sparks in Marcus's eyes and he shifts on the ground, gets into a sitting position and presses a hand to the pavement, trying to get up. Terrified, Lucy kicks out at him but he's ready for her this time and he grabs her foot before it can connect. She hops desperately, trying to keep her balance, then yanks her foot out of her shoe and runs as fast as she can towards the corner shop.

'I'll fucking destroy you,' he shouts after her. 'When I'm finished with you, you'll wish you were dead.'

Lucy bursts into the shop and slaps her hands on the counter, making the young bloke behind it jolt in surprise. 'You have to help me. Is there somewhere I can hide?'

His startled eyes flick wildly from her face to her hair to her body as he tries to make sense of what's happening.

'Can we lock it? Please?' She gestures towards the door. 'My ex is out there. He's violent. He—' She can't get the words out she's breathing so hard. 'Please. Please.' Outside Marcus is picking himself up from the pavement, checking his motorbike helmet for any sign of damage. He senses Lucy watching and looks across at her. The emptiness in his eyes makes her stomach roil and lurch.

'Oh god please.' Her desperate squeal shocks the shopkeeper out of his stupor, and he hurries to her side and peers out of the window.

'That man?' he asks as Marcus stands up and heads towards them, a slow smile plucking at his lips. She's trapped and he knows it.

'Yes.' In less than a minute he'll be inside the shop. 'Please just lock the door. Lock the door!'

'Miss . . .' There's indecision written all over the shopkeeper's face. He glances towards the back of the shop where there's an archway that leads to a storeroom. 'I can't lock it. I don't have the keys. I'm covering for my uncle. He'll be back in ten minutes and then—'

'No. Please. There's no time.' She looks back towards the storeroom. There must be a back exit. She risks another glance out of the window and her heart leaps into her throat. Marcus is less than five feet from the door. 'Hold the handle,' she tells the shopkeeper. 'Please don't let him in.'

And that's when she sees it, the metal deadbolt at the top of the door, painted in the same deep green paint. She reaches for it but the shopkeeper's in the way and she's at the wrong angle to lift the thumb latch and move the bolt across.

'Please,' she begs him as she plucks desperately at the metal. Marcus is two paces away and he's staring straight at her. 'Please lock the door.'

Marcus is there, on the other side of the window, and the shopkeeper still isn't helping so she turns and runs towards the back of the shop, praying that there's an exit.

She's halfway down the aisle when a voice calls after her, 'It's okay miss, the door is now locked. Shall I call the police?'

She turns sharply. 'No! No don't. Don't call the police.' Sensing she's being watched, her gaze flicks towards the door. Marcus is still on the other side and he's staring straight at her. His eyes rest on her for the longest time, moving from her lips, to her chest, where they linger before they return to her face.

He smirks as a shiver runs through her.

'See you soon,' he mouths; then he turns and strolls back to his bike.

Chapter 20

Bridget

Five days until someone dies . . .

Bridget had been creeping around the spare room when Lucy's name flashed up on her phone. Gary had gone out to a greyhound track in North London (a fact that the app confirmed), which gave her at least four hours to log into his laptop and to search through his things. As the phone vibrated on the dressing table Bridget had tucked the pair of women's knickers that she'd found back under the mattress (size ten, black and lacy) then shoved the shirt covered in lipstick marks to the bottom of the laundry bin and roughly wiped the tears from her cheeks.

Lucy had never called her before and she'd felt a frisson of delight as she answered the call. Lucy was frantic. Marcus had turned up on her street and confronted her and she'd had to take refuge in the back room of a newsagent's. Her stalker was waiting for her outside and she didn't know where to go if she snuck out of the back entrance. She couldn't go home because he knew where she lived.

'Please,' Lucy had begged. 'Please. Is there any way you can collect me? I don't care where we go. Just promise me that you won't call the police.'

Bridget hadn't thought twice about going to her aid.

As she'd pulled up outside the newsagent's, she'd felt giddy with excitement, and fearful too. Keeping an eye out for Alexandra's invisible stalker was one thing; confronting a grown man with malicious intentions was another. But there had been no sign of a long-haired man in a grey coat, holding a motorcycle helmet. No sign of a motorbike either.

Lucy had been a quivering wreck and she'd had to help her out of the shop and across the small patch of pavement to the passenger side of the van. She'd reminded Bridget of an animal being released into the wild, the way her eyes darted from left to right, watching for predators, flinching at every loud sound. As they'd headed back to her flat, she'd asked the younger woman several times if she was sure she didn't want to go to a police station or a friend's house, but Lucy had repeatedly shaken her head.

'Your tea's just next to you,' she says now as she lowers herself onto the sofa beside Lucy. 'And here are some tissues.' She nudges a box of Kleenex against Lucy's thigh and is shocked when Lucy grips her hand.

'Thank you.' Her voice is barely a whisper beneath her mop of blonde hair. 'I don't know what I'd have done if you hadn't answered the phone.'

She squeezes Bridget's hand tightly then releases it to

pluck a tissue from the box. It disappears under her curtain of hair, and she blows her nose noisily.

Bridget reaches for her tea. 'Really not a problem. You'd have done the same for me.' She pauses, unsure whether to bring up the thought that's been niggling at her since Lucy's phone call, then decides what the hell. If she doesn't ask, she'll never find out. 'Why did you ring me, rather than River or Alexandra?'

Lucy tucks a lock of hair behind her ear and sits up. Her eyes are pink and swollen and her cheekbones are black with smeared mascara. 'I figured . . . I figured . . .' Bridget waits expectantly. Is it because she's the kindest? The most understanding? Because she has access to a car? 'That Alex and River have been through enough this weekend.'

Bridget puts down her tea, her ego deflated. That was the only reason why?

'That's very true,' she says, 'about Alexandra. Those skeletons and that message. Just horrible. What happened to River? I've not been kept in the loop.'

She listens attentively as Lucy describes, between sniffles and nose blows, how Vanessa joined her at the bar, Meg's attempt to confront her, and the argument with River in the middle of the pub with all the other diners listening in.

'Good god,' Bridget says as Lucy draws the story to a close. 'But you planted the tracker? That all went ahead?'

'Yeah.' Lucy raises the tissue to her nose and blows it again.

'How are you feeling now? Any better?'

Lucy laughs dryly. 'I feel safer. Thank you.' She squeezes Bridget's hand again and Bridget has to use all her willpower not to run off to the bathroom to wash it immediately, given all that snot.

'Would you like to stay here tonight? I'm afraid we don't have a spare room but you're very welcome to the sofa. I've got blankets and you could have one of my pillows.'

Lucy gives her a watery smile. 'You're so kind, Bridget. I'd really appreciate that. Gary doesn't mind, does he?'

'No, no. Not at all. He's gone to the greyhound track. He won't be home for hours.'

'If you don't mind. I just . . . I just don't know what to do.' Lucy dissolves into tears again and Bridget waits patiently for her to stop. 'I can't go into school tomorrow,' Lucy says between sobs. 'All my working and lesson prep is at home.'

'I could come with you to collect it?' Bridget suggests, but Lucy shakes her head.

'He might be waiting. He knows where I live.'

'We could . . .' Bridget treads carefully, knowing Lucy's views on the matter, '. . . we could go to the police?'

'No.' There's steel in the word. 'No police.'

'Could I ask why? You were sexually assaulted in the street. You've been plagued with notes and unwanted visits at school, and now he knows where you live.'

Lucy twists the piece of tissue paper in her hands and stares down at her feet, then she raises her chin and looks around the room, taking in, Bridget imagines, the tired decor, the floral eighties pelmet around the window, the china dogs either side of the fireplace and the dried flowers, crumbling in a vase. She looks around the room for what feels like forever, then she shifts on the sofa, so her body is turned towards Bridget.

118

'Can I trust you?' she asks softly. 'With something I haven't told anyone else in the world?'

A jolt of excitement passes through Bridget's body. She can't remember the last time someone told her a secret.

'You'll judge me. You'll see me differently.'

'I'm sure I won't . . .' Bridget says carefully. She can't imagine what Lucy might be able to tell her that would change her perception of the nervy young schoolteacher.

'My stalker. My stalker is . . .' Lucy looks down at her hands, '. . . one of my ex-pupils.'

Bridget's eyebrows shoot up towards her hairline and her mouth forms a neat, horrified circle.

'You're shocked, aren't you? I don't blame you. I'd be shocked too. It's awful. It's the most awful thing in the world.'

As she dissolves into tears again, Bridget shifts in her seat. 'I think we need something stronger than tea. I'll go and open some wine.'

She can hear the younger woman continue to sob as she heads down the hallway and into the kitchen. A schoolboy, she thinks as she slides a bottle of rioja out of the rack. Her stalker with a motorcycle helmet is a child? Her mind races as she pours two large measures of red wine into her best glasses. Why would a schoolboy stalk his teacher? More importantly, why can't Lucy go to the police? For the second time in as many minutes Bridget's eyebrows rise. She was having an affair with the boy when he was still at school! Dear god. No wonder she can't go to the police.

No judgement, she tells herself as she carries the glasses back to the living room. Do not judge her, or appear to judge her, or she'll instantly clam up.

119

'Here you go,' she hands a glass to Lucy and perches beside her, her own glass resting on her thigh. 'It may help.'

She waits what feels like an interminable amount of time as Lucy sips at the wine, places it on the coaster, sighs, reaches for the glass, takes another sip and then places it back down.

'When you're ready,' Bridget nudges. 'I'm here to listen. You're in a safe place now.'

Lucy makes a sound that's either a dry laugh or a snort of denial, and picks up her glass for the umpteenth time.

'It was the sixth form leavers' party at Churchill Trinity,' she says softly. 'I was Marcus's A Level English teacher.'

'He joined to do his A Levels?' Bridget suggests, and Lucy nods.

'He was very bright. I noticed that immediately. He was well spoken – posh, as the other kids called him – and eloquent. He was the sort of student the others would listen to when he spoke. He was more mature than the other boys his age. One of the other members of staff told me that his father was a respected barrister, but his mother wasn't in the picture. She'd walked out on the family when Marcus was fourteen, to be with another man.'

'Oh dear,' Bridget says. 'So he was troubled then?'

'Not that I noticed. Not straight away anyway. There was something . . . fascinating . . . about him. I can't really explain it. He had this cool don't-give-a-shit attitude, that drew people to him. I'm pretty sure all the girls, and some of the boys, in the class were under his spell.'

'Were you?' Bridget asks. 'Under his spell?'

'No. Yes.' Lucy shakes her head. 'I was twenty-one when I started at that school, fresh out of university. It was my first job, and I was keen to impress. It felt strange, teaching students who were so close to me in age. At the leavers' party several of the students had already turned eighteen.'

'Had Marcus?'

'No.' Lucy twirls the wine around her glass. 'He was a couple of months away from his eighteenth birthday. I was nearly twenty-three.'

'I'm assuming something happened at the party?'

'Yeah.' Lucy leans back on the sofa, cranes her neck to the ceiling and sighs. 'I shouldn't even have been there. My grandfather had died the day before and I was still reeling. The Head said I could take some time off, but I felt I owed it to the students to go to the Leavers' Ball. I had a few glasses of punch over the course of the evening, non-alcoholic – or at least it was supposed to be. I don't know if one of the students had spiked it to liven up the party – it didn't taste alcoholic,' she glances at Bridget, who shrugs, 'but I felt drunk. I went outside to clear my head and suddenly Marcus was there, beside me, asking if I was okay. I hadn't seen him for a few months because he'd been off sick – I wasn't told why. Anyway, he thanked me for being such a good teacher and he told me that I'd made a big difference to his life. He said my boyfriend was lucky to have me, that I was a good person. I started to cry – it was a combination of the drink, my grandfather's death and the fact I'd recently been dumped. When Marcus hugged me, I didn't push him away. It didn't feel wrong. It felt like one lost person comforting another and then, somehow, he ended up kissing me and . . .' she closes her eyes, lost in thought or in horror, '. . . I kissed him back.'

'Well . . .' Bridget fights for the right thing to say and settles on, 'a kiss isn't that bad. Is it?'

'We had sex.' Lucy squeezes her eyes shut, as though trying to block the memory out. 'Not there and then. I got on the back of his motorbike, and we went back to my flat.'

'Oh.' Bridget reaches for her wine, takes a sip, struggling not to show the revulsion she feels on her face. Whatever was Lucy thinking? Seventeen! The boy was still a teenager, a grubby, smelly one at that. She can still remember the pong of her brother's football boots, stinking out her parents' hall.

'He never stopped reminding me of that after we started a relationship.' Lucy opens her eyes to look at her. 'Jokingly at first: "You had sex with me when I was officially still at school. You could go to prison for that", then it became a threat.' She reaches for her wine glass, then her hand falls away as she realises that it's empty. 'That's why I can't go to the police, Bridget. Because if I report him, he'll report me. I could go to prison for two years. I could be on the sex offenders list for the rest of my life.'

'Oh dear. That is worrying.' Bridget reaches for Lucy's empty wine glass. 'More wine?'

Chapter 21

WhatsApp group: FYST

19.58
River: Two trackers placed, two to go! Lucy, thank you for what you did today. I can't tell you how it feels knowing that Vanessa's nowhere near us. She's been on the move all day, last location was Heathrow airport. With any luck she's decided to move abroad! (Wishful thinking, I know).

20.06
Alexandra: Let's hope so, River! Lucy's asleep in my spare room by the way.

River: She's at your house? Is she okay? What's happened?

Alexandra: Marcus approached her in the street near her flat and she had to hide in a newsagent's to escape. She rang Bridget to collect her and went back to hers for a bit before she caught a taxi to mine.

River: Marcus has worked out where she lives? Didn't she spot him on the app?

Alexandra: She said she forgot to input the code because she was too focused on putting the tracker on Vanessa.

River: Shit, I feel responsible for that. Has she got the app working now? Can you tell where he is?

Alex: She thinks he's at home in Walthamstow.

River: Thank god for that. Are you okay, Alex? How's your day been?

Alexandra: Shit. But the tracker's on Marcus and that's all that matters.

River: Sorry to hear that. Crap day here too. Meg said I tricked her into going to the pub. Cue argument. Then, when we got home, we found flyers in all my neighbours' letterboxes (presumably posted by Vanessa before she went to the pub), calling me a sex offender. I'm going to ring the police tomorrow, once the app updates and tells me what country she's in. With any luck they'll arrest her at the airport when she comes back. Bridget, I'm going to need all the info you've got on Charlotte, please, so I can do my part.

20.26
River: Bridget, are you there? Are you okay?

20.32
Alexandra: Bridget? Can you please let us know you're okay.

20.46

Bridget: Charlotte knows where I live. She pushed a note under my front door, after Lucy left. I was in the kitchen and didn't hear a thing. I just spotted it when I was heading to the living room. I can't stop shaking. I can't believe she's found out where I live.

Alexandra: Oh god, Bridge. Is Gary home? Are all the doors and windows locked? Have you rung the police?

Bridget: Gary's at the pub. Everything's locked. I've rung the police and they said to enter the note into my harassment diary. Still no mention of arresting or cautioning her. I don't think they took it seriously because the note's only threatening to me. It sounds harmless to anyone else. Which is exactly why she worded it that way.

River: What did it say?

Bridget: How are the birthday preparations going?

River: That's it?

Bridget: Yep. See what I mean? She's reminding me of what she said when my old boss Frank mentioned my birthday party – 'if it happens'. Like I was going to die before the 20th October. I know she was jealous of the fact Frank and I got on so well, but I don't understand what I've done to make her hate me so much. She hounded me out of that job, and now this one, but that's not enough for her. She sent the wreath, I know she did.

River: The sooner we get a tracker on her the better. Have you got any idea where I could find her?

125

Bridget: I thought of something earlier – it's a long shot but she used to go to salsa classes in Soho. I looked it up and it's on tomorrow night. Are you okay to go along, River? I can send you a description of her.

River: Absolutely, just tell me where and when.

WhatsApp private messages: River and Bridget

River: I hope this isn't insensitive given what just happened to you but we really need to talk about formulating a plan for the 20th. We need to set a trap to lure whoever sent the wreath somewhere where the four of us will be waiting – with cameras, CCTV, anything we could use in evidence. I've got a YouTube gaming channel, nearly 3,000 subscribers. We threaten to publicly shame them if they don't stop, say we'll make the video go viral, like paedophile hunters do. I need you to back me up on this so we can convince Alex and Lucy to go along with it.

Bridget: Charlotte's planning on killing me and you think you can shame her into putting the knife down? Are you mad?

River: Yes, maybe, but what's the alternative? Kidnap her? Kill her? It's the only solution I can think of that doesn't involve the police.

Bridget: We need another in-person meeting. ASAP. Tomorrow ideally. We'll all brainstorm what to do.

River: Or we convince Lucy to go to the police. Alex has already agreed to speak to them tomorrow. If Lucy is on board, we can tell the police everything. They have to take us seriously – the note on the wreath was essentially a threat to kill. I went back to the church by the way, to see if I could find it, but it was gone.

Bridget: Have you still got the rock?

River: No.

Bridget: What?

River: It was passed around the group and I didn't get it back.

Bridget: You're kidding?

River: I wish I was.

Bridget: Well, it's one of five people – us four or Sam. We need to find it. Without the florist's card, the rock is the only evidence we've got.

River: We'll find it. So, we meet at your place and convince Lucy to go to the police?

Bridget: How about your place instead? Let's tell the other two about the plan to meet up. Don't mention the police or Lucy will feel bamboozled. We'll talk her round tomorrow.

WhatsApp group: FYST

20.54
River: Hi guys. I think we should all meet tomorrow to discuss what we're going to do on the 20th to stay safe. We can do it at my place. It won't be until around 10.30 p.m. though as I need to try and track down Charlotte. Alex, are you okay

with that? Can you check that's okay with Lucy when she wakes up?

20.55
River: Have any of you got the rock that was thrown at us?

21.14
River: Alex, are you ignoring me again?

128

Chapter 22

Alexandra

MONDAY 16TH OCTOBER

Four days until someone dies . . .

Alexandra slowly climbs the steps of Wood Green police station, her hands pushed deep into her pockets, a black beanie pulled low over her ears. This is it: the beginning of the end. No more texts, Tweets, emails or photos. No more messages in her dressing room or flowers on her doorstep. No more paranoia, fear or tears. For her stalker to be arrested and sentenced she just needs to open the door and tell the police what's been happening.

Just. There's never been a weightier word.

She pauses on the top step and turns back towards the street, looking for Bridget. It takes her a while to spot her, with so much traffic speeding past, but she's exactly where she promised she'd be, outside the café near the park, on the other side of the street. As Bridget raises a hand and waves, Alex groans. She's supposed to be watching discreetly, not advertising the fact that she's there.

Last night she had rung her director and told her she wouldn't be in. Liz had been so sympathetic about Alex's pretend stomach upset she'd wondered if she should just tell her the truth instead. It had been a fleeting thought, one she'd immediately dismissed. She didn't want to be viewed as a victim; she'd lived with that tag long enough. It was the cast and crew's respect she wanted, not their pity.

Now, as she opens the door to the police station, it's not work she's thinking about, it's Sam. He hadn't replied to her passive-aggressive text, and it was strange, waking up in bed alone, his side of the bed unwrinkled and cold. She'd briefly considered texting him to tell him where she was going, then swiftly changed her mind. He'd want to come with her and, while there's a part of her that aches to have him beside her again, she doesn't want him to hold her hand, not for this. She's been getting too comfortable, too dependent on him for support and affection, and that's dangerous. It's better for them both if they take a step back.

It's smaller than she imagined inside the police station, more run down too, with peeling posters on the notice boards and grimy glass separating the small waiting room from the reception desk. There's no one sitting behind it. She's completely alone.

'Hello?' The word sounds small and meek as she steps towards the reception desk. She ignores her phone vibrating in her handbag. She needs to do this before she completely loses her nerve. 'Hello? Is there anybody there?'

She spots a fluorescent yellow vest, slung over a filing

cabinet beyond the dirty glass, and images flash up in her mind like scenes in a film: police officers turning up at her door, yellow vests, crackling radios on their shoulders, wide-brimmed hats with black-and-white bands above furrowed brows. She can see her father's hands, large and expressive, gesturing in the direction of the house next door; hear his deep, resonant voice. 'Next-door neighbour's been causing trouble again.' She sees the two officers exchange looks. They don't believe that Colin Sutherland has been making their lives a nightmare, that he turned up at the garden centre where her dad works and stared and stared and stared. They think her dad's making a big fuss about nothing. They like Colin Sutherland. He's one of them.

The scene changes and now she's watching from an upstairs window as they chat to him outside his house, laughing and slapping him on the arm and calling him 'Guv'. Her dad says that Colin Sutherland is a retired police inspector, that they're never going to take his complaints seriously because they're all 'buddy buddy' and 'look after your own'.

Now her mum's at the kitchen table, with her head in her hands saying there's not much more that she can take. She can hear Ben blaring out music from the tinny stereo in his bedroom.

Another scene now: her dad's in the garden, Ben's upstairs and Mum's in the kitchen with the radio on. There's a knock at the door. She peers out of the upstairs window, where there's a wooden bowl of pot pourri on a narrow wooden table. She can smell the musky floral scent, see the top of a man's hooded head, see the pizza box in his hands. Now

131

she's flying down the stairs because they don't get pizza very often, only for birthdays and special treats and maybe it's because she got Star of the Day at school and her parents got her a pizza to say well done. She pauses at the front door, indecision gnawing at her. Maybe she should get one of her parents; they've always told her not to answer the door, but this is a surprise. They've arranged it because they're proud of her. She yanks at the door handle, pulling hard because it always sticks. She looks up expectantly, a smile on her face.

'Oi!' A face appears in front of her: large and round, broken veins on the cheeks, grey-threaded eyebrows above dark sunken eyes. 'Enough with the shouting.' The face looms at her, swimming in and out of focus. 'What's the problem?' The man's lips are moving but she can't understand a word that's being said. The glass panel has become a box that's encasing her, trapping her in the past.

'Miss, you were shouting for help. What exactly is the problem?'

Details jump out at her as though a dimmer switch has been twisted, illuminating the man that's staring at her with a look of concern on his face. He's wearing a white shirt, black tie, black jacket, lapels on the shoulders, a chequered blue-and-white stripe across the chest, the word 'Police', white on blue above the heart.

The memory shatters as she realises where she is and the glass box becomes a panel again, separating her from a man who's staring at her like she's mad. How can she trust him with her life when his colleagues couldn't – wouldn't – save her parents? When the person who murdered them was a cop?

132

'Miss?' the desk sergeant says, but it's not his voice she hears as she runs out of the police station and sprints across the road and into the park. It's her mother's scream.

'Are you okay?' Bridget appears beside her, pink-cheeked and panting with strands of hair stuck to her cheeks. 'I thought you were never going to stop running. You know the last time I moved faster than a brisk walk was . . .' She tails off and parks herself beside her, on the bench. 'What happened? You look . . . awful.'

'I feel it.' Alex rests her elbows on her knees and cradles her head in her hands. She should have trusted her gut – going to the police was a bad idea, but she'd convinced herself that she could stroll in, sit down at a table with a cop and tell them everything. Not trusting her gut was a bad idea. It always was.

'So did you tell them?' Bridget asks.

'I couldn't.'

'Oh.'

There's something in the singular syllable – a note of caution or worry – that makes Alex properly look at Bridget in her grey coat and grey scarf, perched on the edge of the bench with her grey gloved hands pressed between her knees. The only touch of colour in her whole outfit is a slash of pink lipstick on her thin, wide lips.

'Oh what?' she asks.

A muscle twitches in Bridget's jaw and she twists her hands together, her gaze fixed on a lone pigeon on the path, pecking at invisible crumbs.

'Bridget,' Alex asks again, 'what was that oh?'

Bridget swallows nervously. What is it that she won't say?

133

'Just tell me.'

'I saw him.'

'When?' Alex doesn't have to ask who.

'When you got out of the taxi. He was trailing you, in a black car. He pulled up around the corner, outside a shop, on double yellow lines. I tried to warn you. I rang but you didn't answer your phone.'

Alex squints into the distance, looking for the face that swam in and out of her vision in the police station, the face that glared down at her – his eyes dark and empty – before he pushed his way into her home.

She's only vaguely aware of Bridget calling her name, of the gloved hand that clutches her. 'Breathe Alex, breathe. It's okay. He's gone.'

Chapter 23

Lucy

Four days until someone dies . . .

Lucy is nervy and unfocused, jumping each time a door bangs, turning sharply whenever someone walks past the glass panel in the door. Her students have noticed that she's jittery. They're playing up more than normal: swinging on their chairs, chatting and sneaking looks at their phones. She hasn't got the energy to lay down the law. When the bell rings for the end of the lesson she presses her palms to her desk, limp with relief. She can hear her phone vibrating in her bag, but she doesn't bother to get it. It'll be Alex or River or Bridget, checking up on her, making sure she's okay to meet up later. She doesn't want a meeting, not least because she'll have to look River in the eye.

It's been bothering her for days, the decision she made in the pub, with Vanessa sitting beside her and River pushing food around his plate, trying desperately not to stare. Had Vanessa convinced her that River was controlling and coercive, or had sleep deprivation and her relationship with Marcus made her doubt her friend? Since that day River has done nothing but try and protect them all. He was planning a trap, trying to convince them all to hide. She has to tell him the truth, face-to-face. If anything happened to him, she'd never forgive herself.

She leaves the classroom, her mind still whirring as she spots Jada, hurrying down the corridor alone, head down, shoulders hunched, making herself as small as she can.

'Jada!' she calls. 'You weren't in tutor time this morning. Is everything okay?'

Her student doesn't reply, and instead quickens her pace.

'Jada?' Lucy says again. She considers going after her but she's obviously not in the mood to talk. She'll catch her later, check up on her then.

She closes the door to the classroom and heads to the staffroom. As she walks inside several colleagues turn their heads in her direction and nod or smile hello.

Last night Bridget had insisted that she stay over, that the sofa was comfier than it looked. Although she'd initially jumped at the offer, the second time Bridget brought it up, she had politely declined. She was grateful to Bridget for rescuing her from the newsagent's, but she didn't want to spend a moment longer in her flat than she had to. It wasn't because the flat was so cluttered and messy that she felt overwhelmed by the detritus of Bridget and Gary's lives (although that didn't help). What had made her desperate to leave was the fact she felt more wretched in Bridget's presence than she had crouched on the shopkeeper's floor.

She'd told her the truth about her relationship with Marcus, hoping to find acceptance and understanding. Instead, she'd watched as Bridget's expression switched from sympathy to revulsion. She'd heard the judgement in her voice.

She couldn't go home because Marcus might be there, she couldn't afford a hotel and she didn't have any friends she could call. All of the friends she'd made during her degree were dotted around the country and she couldn't ask any of the teachers she'd befriended because she'd have to lie to ask for their help.

So it was Alex that she'd texted from Bridget's bathroom, asking if she could stay at hers for the night. Alex had replied within seconds, telling her to jump in a cab, and Lucy told Bridget the new plan. She'd thought she'd seen a flash of pain in the older woman's eyes, but Bridget quickly rallied, saying of course Lucy should go wherever she felt safe, and to take Alex's coat with her – she'd found it in her van after dropping her off at the gym.

When Lucy's eyes had flickered open on Monday morning, hungover but comfy in Alex's spare room, she'd felt relaxed for the first time in months. Then fear had walked its way back up her spine. She'd evaded Marcus for over twelve hours, but the moment she walked through the iron gates of Thames View Academy she'd be back where he wanted her; in a predictable routine. She lay in bed, listening to Alex bustling around in the bathroom, and tried to work out what to do. She could call in sick, but she'd essentially be keeping herself prisoner in Alex's flat. And what about Jada? There'd be no one to give her breakfast after tutor time and she might not have the money to buy lunch. To hide away would tell Marcus that he'd won, that he'd successfully controlled her behaviour again. She'd pushed the warm duvet away, sat up, and swung her legs over the bed. Alex had got up too and, when Lucy had left, pulling her thin cardigan around her, she'd insisted she take her leopard-print coat.

Now, Helen Corry pops her head around the staffroom door, her greying hair held back with a hairband, a sombre expression on her face. 'Lucy, could I have a quick word?'

A quick word with the Deputy Head? Worry buries itself deep in her gut, but she nods her head sharply and follows Helen out of the room.

'Everything okay?' Lucy asks as they walk down the corridor towards Helen's office, the sound of student chatter and laughter creeping through the walls and windows from the playground outside.

'I'm sure it will be,' Helen replies, but there's a curtness to her tone.

After they enter Helen's office (door closed, never a good sign), Lucy takes a seat, her hands pressed between her knees, her spine rigid, each breath shallower than the last. Has she been called for a chat because she's been giving food to Jada? Is it Marcus? Has someone spotted him hanging around the gates? Or have the students been complaining about working in a room with the blinds pulled down? Helen clears her throat and rests her forearms on her desk and there's that look again, the one that makes Lucy's guts churn.

'Right,' she clasps her hands together. 'This isn't the easiest of conversations I'm afraid, but there are a couple of matters that, in the Head's absence, I need to clear up.'

'Okay.' Lucy sits up taller.

'Firstly,' Helen consults a piece of paper on her desk. 'Jada Arnold.' She pauses, waiting for a response.

138

'Yes, she's in my tutor group. Difficult home life. I . . . I give her a piece of fruit and a breakfast bar sometimes because she doesn't always eat at home.'

'I see, right, and have you ever had contact with Jada outside of school?'

'No, never. Why?'

'You've never contacted her on social media?'

'No!' Her heart misses a beat as she frantically tries to work out what's going on. 'I'd never contact a student out of school.'

'So you didn't send her a SnapChat message telling her you'd developed feelings for her?'

For several seconds Lucy can't speak. She stares at Helen, blinking uncomprehendingly, mouth agape. Did one of the other students see her giving Jada food and decide to stir up trouble? Did they do it for a laugh? Or could it be . . . her legs tremble as she remembers Marcus's parting shot. *I'll fucking destroy you. When I'm finished with you, you'll wish you were dead.*

'That wasn't me.' She stares into Helen's eyes, silently begging her to believe her. 'I swear to god. I don't even have a SnapChat account and I would never, *never* contact a student or . . . or . . .' as the phrase *develop inappropriate feelings for a student* swirls through her mind she begins to stutter. 'My relationship with Jada is strictly professional – teacher and student – nothing more. Call her in here, ask her if I've ever done or said anything inappropriate. She'll tell you the truth.'

'I've already spoken to her. And that's as much as I can say about that.'

Lucy's shock turns to horror as she reads the expression

139

on the other woman's face. Was Jada the one who filed the complaint? Surely she wouldn't believe that a random SnapChat in Lucy's name was genuine. The students wind each other up all the time by imitating each other and spreading rumours and lies.

'The other issue, although they are both connected,' Helen continues, looking back at her, 'is your OnlyFans account.'

Lucy goes limp, tears welling in her eyes. What has Marcus done?

'This is you, isn't it?' Helen slides a printout across the desk. Lucy glances at the image, then buries her face in her hands. She'd watched as he'd deleted the photos they'd taken of each other after a drunken night in. He'd promised there were no copies. He *swore* they weren't on the cloud. She'd let it go because she loved him, and she didn't want to make him angry by questioning his word.

'This photograph, along with a link to OnlyFans, was sent to Jada when she expressed disbelief that you'd contacted her on SnapChat.'

'I didn't . . . do . . . either . . . of . . . those things.' Lucy's chest convulses between words as sobs steal her breath.

'Can you tell me who did?'

'My ex.'

'Can you tell me the name of this person? Because if what you're saying is true, we'll have to involve the police.'

'No. No.' Her face is hot and sticky, still nestled in her hands, each breath shallow and jagged as though she's slowly suffocating herself.

'Lucy.' She hears Helen get up from her chair then feels the weight of her hand on her back. 'If what you're saying is true then it's very serious indeed. Revenge porn is a crime.

140

Whoever did this to you will be arrested, and they could end up in jail.'

Lucy says nothing. If she has Marcus arrested, he'll get his revenge and she'll potentially end up in jail. She'll be all over the news, another sick and twisted teacher who couldn't keep their hands to themselves. It would destroy her grandmother, already weak from the effects of chemotherapy for bowel cancer, and it would break her parents' hearts. There wouldn't be a person in the UK who wouldn't think she was a vile, disgusting human being. Even if, by some miracle, she didn't end up in prison, her life would be ruined. Every potential date, every potential job, they'd only have to Google her to discover what she'd done.

'Would you like me to call the police now?' Helen asks. Her hand feels like a weight on Lucy's back, keeping her in place, pinning her down.

'No,' she croaks and shifts in her seat until Helen removes her hand.

'I can't force you, but I do think it's something you should seriously consider if what you're saying is true. Obviously, there will need to be an internal investigation,' Lucy hears the creak of her chair as she sits back down, 'and you'll need to remain at home until a decision is reached.'

There's a pause, during which Lucy tries to work out how the hell she's going to get her bag from the staffroom without anyone asking what's wrong. She uncurls herself, plucks a hair from her cheek, stuck there with tears, and takes a tissue from the box that Helen has slid across the desk. Her mind is whirring, running through scenarios and outcomes, none of them good. She just wants to escape, to get as far away from the school and London as she can.

'I know you'll do the investigation anyway,' she forces herself to look Helen in the eye, 'but I'll make things easier for you. I quit. I'm handing in my notice with immediate effect.'

Chapter 24

Bridget

Four days until someone dies . . .

Bridget stares in wonder at Alex's mug cupboard. She's always believed that mugs can say so much about a person. Her mother was fond of 1980s Worcestershire china, Evesham pattern featuring fruit, leaves and hops. She has an eclectic mix of mugs herself – some were gifts, some charity shop finds and the odd one or two from craft fayres.

Alex seems to favour tasteful and classy, or at least wants to appear that way: four blue-and-white hand-fired china mugs proudly line the front of the cupboard. Hidden behind them are several 'comedy' mugs that make Bridget cringe. She takes a blue-and-white mug for herself and reaches into the back for a mug for Alex: 'Queen of the Fucking World'. She dearly hopes it was a gift.

143

As the kettle boils her phone bleeps with a message from River:

As mentioned, I've booked a place at Charlotte's salsa class for tonight. I've been watching YouTube tutorials for the last hour and have been trying to replicate the moves. If any of the neighbours have spotted me through the window, they'll think I'm insane, as well as a sex offender!

Bridget smiles to herself, imagining Rigid River trying to wiggle his hips. More Tony Adams on *Strictly* than John Whaite, she's sure.

Thank you so much for doing this, she types back. *I'm terrible at dancing too. The nearest I've got to tripping the light fantastic was watching the Strictly tour for my birthday. I just hope Charlotte still goes to salsa class. I'm pretty sure part of the reason she signed up was to try and snag a man.*

River sends a gif in response of Forrest Gump speeding away in response, then, *Still planning on getting to Lucy's for half ten tonight. How did it go with Alex earlier?*

Bridget grimaces. *She had a panic attack in the police station. She wasn't able to talk to anyone. And worse . . . I spotted Colin Sutherland nearby. Now we know he's her stalker I need to place a tracker on him.*

As River composes his reply, she hears Alex moving around in the living room. It had taken some persuading to get her to agree to Bridget taking her home after her failed attempt to report her stalker to the police. She'd been insisting on flagging a cab alone but Bridget had talked her round, telling her the van was quicker and safer, that it would be dangerous to stay there any longer in case Colin Sutherland returned.

Her phone vibrates on the kitchen counter. River has replied:

No! Absolutely not. Far too dangerous. The man's a murderer, he's been in prison.

Bridget swishes the teabags around in the mugs, mentally composing a response, then opens the fridge for the milk. Like mug cupboards, the contents of a fridge can say a lot about a person too; and this one says its owner is too busy to go shopping, exists on takeaways and likes a drink. Bridget reaches inside, twists a bottle around to get a better look at the label then yanks out her hand at the sound of Alex's voice. But Alex hasn't come into the kitchen to check up on her. She's talking to someone in the living room.

Bridget edges her way out of the kitchen and into the hallway and hovers beside the coat stand.

'What fucking right have you got to do that?' The shrill notes of Alex's anger escape from the living room. Is it the detective again? Did Alex ring him to report a sighting of Colin Sutherland in Wood Green?

'If I'd wanted him tracked down, I would have done it myself.' The floorboards in the living room creak as she paces back and forth and Bridget holds herself very still, barely breathing. She feels like an intruder, not just in Alex's flat, but in her life. Who is she talking about? Might it be an ex-agent? Ex-friend? An actress? Director?

'I've looked after myself for the last fifteen years, Sam. I don't need his help now.'

Bridget frowns. It can't be her father, he's dead. Grandfather? Uncle?

'And *this* is exactly why I don't open up, Sam. Because

145

it's always used against me. Which bit of 'Ben blames me for their death' didn't you understand?'

Bridget shivers. Ben? Is that who they're talking about? He was mentioned in the online article she read about the murder. He's Alex's older brother. She didn't realise that they were estranged.

'No! I don't want to know what he said. Seriously Sam, I don't know how much more of this I can take. If it's not you smothering me, it's Conrad making snidey remarks or it's Colin Sutherland—No! Nothing's happened. My life's imploding and we're days away from the opening night of *Gabler*, the biggest night of my career. I'm sorry.' There's a pause, a sniff. 'I know you're only trying to help . . .' Alex's voice is thicker now, raspier, as though she's fighting back tears, '. . . but I can't deal with this right now. No, Sam! Didn't you listen to a word I just said? Please, just leave me alone!'

There's a strangled grunt of frustration then the flump of something – presumably her phone – landing somewhere soft. Bridget, still pressed up against the hall wall, lets out a soft sigh of relief as the flat falls silent. She's always found other people's rows to be simultaneously fascinating and embarrassing. They're almost as intimate as sex, not that she's ever deliberately eavesdropped on someone doing that!

She steps softly into the living room to find Alex by the faux fireplace, gripping the wooden mantlepiece and breathing heavily. 'Are you okay? I couldn't help but over—'

'Oh, for fuck's sake!' Alex whips around, wide-eyed and startled, as though Bridget nudged her with a cattle prod instead of asking how she was.

'I was just—'

146

'It's creepy, Bridget. The way you keep following me around. For god's sake.'

'You're under a lot of stress.' Bridget takes a tentative step towards her. 'With very good reason, given the fact Sutherland followed you to the police station. I know you'll be feeling very—'

'Why does everyone keep telling me how I feel?'

Bridget stares at her in wonder; she's never seen anyone shake the way Alexandra is shaking now, as though her entire body is vibrating with rage.

'Let me help you,' she says. 'I could still try and track him down, get a tracker on him and—'

'No!' Alex throws her hands up in the air and strides towards her so determinedly that she takes a step back, fearing she might be struck. But Alex doesn't hit her; she swerves around her, stalks towards the front door and throws it open. 'Out!'

'You're angry. Let me get your cup of tea and then we can sit down and talk all this—'

'Please, Bridget.' Alex's eyes shine with tears. 'I appreciate everything you've done for me. But please, please just fuck off home.'

Bridget stands on the street outside Alex's flat, her arms crossed over her chest, her favourite long scarf wrapped around her neck, the ends lifted and whipped by a cold October wind. Two floors up, the light is still on in the living room but there's no sign of Alex – she's probably raiding the fridge for wine. Bridget sighs softly to herself and tucks her flyaway scarf into the collar of her coat. If Samuel hadn't called and upset her, they might be drinking the wine together

147

now, sitting on either side of the crushed velvet sofa, laughing at the thought of River stumbling around trying to get his salsa footwork right.

But that's not going to happen. Alex is inside and she's out in the cold. As the wind whistles around her trying, and failing, to claim her scarf, Bridget thinks about her own home: full to the rafters with memories, gifts, trinkets and toys; cosy and closeting, so very different to Alex's minimalist, arty and carefully arranged home. It might explain why Lucy was in such a rush to leave the other night.

Bridget's been rejected twice now – first by Lucy and now by Alexandra – and it stings. They're supposed to stick together, to look after each other, to be friends. She thinks fleetingly of River and reaches into her pocket for her phone. She should probably respond to his text.

She taps out a reply, tucks her phone back into her handbag then gives herself a little shake and heads down the street to her van. Back home to an empty flat, and a meal for one.

Chapter 25

Lucy

Four days until someone dies . . .

There is a rhythm to Lucy's frenzied packing: throw something into the suitcase, check the tracking app, search through bathroom cabinets, check app, unplug chargers, check app. According to the app, Marcus is at home but she's not taking any chances. The moment that tiny red dot so much as twitches she's throwing everything into the car and she's off.

She rang her mother in tears from the school car park, explaining through sobs that her mental health was wrecked, she'd handed in her notice, and she just wanted to come home. Her mother didn't immediately respond. They didn't have the kind of relationship where they told each other everything. They were more of a 'put up and shut up' type of family: keep the dark stuff private and put on a happy

149

mask to show the world. Her parents had no idea about the stalking, or even about Marcus. It was a burden Lucy felt she had to shoulder alone.

'Oh, Luce,' her mother said eventually. 'I had no idea. I'm so sorry. Daddy and I decided to go to Cumbria tomorrow to do a spot of hiking before we celebrate our anniversary on the 20th. Where better than on the top of a mountain? I've cancelled the meal. Did I not tell you? Sorry, sweetheart, my mind's been all over the place recently. We haven't talked properly in ages, have we? I assumed you've been as busy as me! If you think you'll feel better here, then you must come home. Let me talk to Dad about changing our plans.'

It wasn't quite the outpouring of sympathy and love that Lucy had hoped for, but it was home, and it was safe. She'd never taken Marcus to meet her parents, and he doesn't know where they live.

Now, she speeds from room to room in the small South London flat, throwing open drawers and cupboards, abandoning anything that isn't essential, or so precious that she can't leave it behind. A thought flashes through her mind as she tosses underwear, jumpers and socks into one of the suitcases: she needs to text the others to let them know that she can't make the meeting any more. She also needs to tell River the truth about Vanessa and the tracker.

Both thoughts vanish as she touches a framed photograph of her grandfather, feeling like her heart might break. She doesn't need to take him with her: he'll still be there when she gets back.

Two suitcases packed and zipped up, she wheels them to the front door then returns to the living room to collect the laundry basket of houseplants she can't bear to leave behind to die. She's got no idea how long she's going to be gone for but, when she does return, it'll be to move her stuff out.

She carries the laundry basket through the narrow hallway and places it next to the suitcases then checks the tracker app again. She lets herself breathe. Marcus still hasn't moved.

She wishes she was brave enough to drive over to his flat and scream in his face; to tell him how much she despises him, to tell him how angry she is, to pick at his scabs and his insecurities until he feels as small as she does. The expression on Helen's face as she slid the photograph across the desk still makes her feel sick.

She didn't tell Marcus about Jada; she wasn't working at Thames View when they were together. So how did he know about her, that she'd taken her under her wing? She's only talked to her mum about Jada, and Alice, an old friend who lives in Bath.

She scrolls through her sent messages and finds the email she sent to Alice two weeks ago. Yes, there it is – the bit where she mentions Jada by her full name, asking Alice for advice. What the hell was she thinking, putting Jada's full name in an email? Had she been drinking that night? It's the only explanation she can come up with for talking about a vulnerable student in a non-work email. Did Marcus hack her email? Is that how he found out? She scrolls through her inbox looking for anything unusual and pauses at a LinkedIn email about Ben Bryan, a colleague she doesn't particularly like. She never bothers opening LinkedIn messages and she certainly wouldn't open one about Ben, but this one's been read. And not by her.

She scrolls further down then, finding nothing, looks through her sent messages. There aren't many: one to a dressmaking course she wanted to join, another to a massage therapist cancelling an appointment, and one to her GP's surgery when she moved house, letting them know her new address. She presses a hand to her mouth. That's how Marcus found out where she lives. Was he watching when she logged onto her laptop when they lived together? Had he written down her password, or memorised it? Set up keystroke spyware? Has he been monitoring everything she does online since she left? She feels sick. Why the hell didn't she change her passwords when she left him? Why didn't she renew her anti-virus software instead of telling herself she'd renew it when she was a bit less skint? Because she never thought he'd do this. When she left him, she thought it was over: she never dreamed that he'd stalk her, and try to destroy her life.

Fear licking at her heart like a flame, she checks the app again, certain that this time she'll see the tiny red dot by her own front door. But Marcus still hasn't moved. Whatever he's doing, whatever he's planning next, he's doing it from home.

Fingers fumbling over the keyboard, she changes the password to her email account then takes one final look around her flat. At some point, after she's given her landlord notice, she'll have to return and clear everything out, but not now. She's got everything that she needs.

She hauls the suitcases up the steps of her basement flat one by one and grunts as she lifts them into the boot of the car. She returns to the top of the steps to get the basket of houseplants and slides it onto the back seat. She shivers as she straightens up, rubbing at her arms as a cold breeze whistles down the street and cuts through the thin cotton of her jumper. She's forgotten her coat. She glances up and down the street, instinct nagging at her to just get in the car and go, but it's a long drive to York and her car's heating is lukewarm at best.

I've got time, she tells herself as she locks up the car and rushes back down the steps to the flat. Her coat isn't where she left it and she hasn't got time to search so she grabs Alex's coat from the hook behind the living room door and throws it over her arm. She'll post it back to her once she gets to York. She heads for the door then spots a hefty Yucca plant that she missed and picks that up too. Once outside the flat she struggles to lock the front door, shuffling the coat and plant in her arms, as she tries to find the right key.

'Let me help you with that.'

There's a split second where she's flooded with gratitude, someone wants to help her, then her brain registers the familiar tenor and the ground beneath her feet seems to sag. He shouldn't be here. She checked the app less than a minute ago and she was still safe. How can someone cross London in the blink of an eye? It can't be happening. She's imagining his voice. Fear is playing with her mind.

She turns slowly, her heart pounding against her ribcage, trying to make its escape.

'Going somewhere, Lucy?'

His voice is expressionless, matching the set of his face, but there's a darkness behind his eyes that she's seen before.

She's trapped. She can't run back into the flat or he'll follow her, and she can't get around his six foot three and fourteen stone frame. He's been working out since she left him, and there's a hard swell to his shoulders and biceps beneath the soft, grey wool of his coat.

'I'm going on holiday,' she says flatly.

'With two suitcases and all your houseplants?' There's the spark again, in his eyes. She'd always see it when he caught her out in a lie.

'No one said I was going abroad,' She forces herself to maintain eye contact. She doesn't want him to know how afraid she feels, 'and I don't want to leave my plants to die.'

The word hangs in the air between them, like a shard of glass, waiting to fall.

Die.

Marcus once told her that he'd kill himself if she ever left him. He said a lot of things to get her to stay. He told her about the abuse he'd suffered as a child at prep school. He told her that his controlling behaviour was down to depression, that he'd see a therapist and go to a doctor for SSRIs. He promised to attend anger management classes, and said he'd talk to his father about his abandonment issues. Every time she tried to leave him, he made himself so vulnerable, so soft and so needy that she'd feel sorry for him and give their relationship another chance. She'd tell herself that he'd suffered and lost so much and if she left him too, he'd have nothing left. If he killed himself, it would haunt her for the rest of her life.

None of his promises ever came true. He never visited the GP or a therapist, called his father or booked a place on an anger management course. He was a master manipulator. There wasn't anything he wouldn't say to get her to stay.

She gave him everything and, in return, he took her self-confidence, her self-belief and her self-worth. He broke her down into smaller and smaller pieces until she didn't know who she was any more. Shame was her bedfellow and crying

154

herself to sleep became normal; silent tears dampening the soft cotton pillowcase beneath her head.

'I could do with a holiday,' Marcus says now.

Lucy says nothing. She's too terrified to speak. This can't be happening. She was so close to leaving. As she packed up the car, she could almost smell the warm, comforting scent of her mother's perfume, feel the gentle pressure of her father's arms around her as he pulled her into a hug.

'Come on then,' Marcus takes her by the elbow and angles her towards the steps that lead to the street. 'Where are we off to? Anywhere nice?'

She twists away so sharply his hand falls away. The plant pot slips out of her grip and smashes on the patio as she speeds towards the stairs. She gets a hand to the handrail, a foot on the first step, then her feet slip out from beneath her as she's yanked backwards, a handful of her jumper in Marcus's clenched fist.

'Help!' The word comes out as a strangled squeak in the back of her throat. 'Help!' Her arms whirlwind and flay, connecting with nothing as she tries to escape.

There's a split second, when the pressure of the jumper across her chest eases, when she thinks that he's released her, that's she's free, that she can still make it to the safety of her mum and dad's house. But Marcus hasn't let her go. He's throwing her across the patio. 'Think you can fucking track me, do you?' is the last thing she hears before her head connects with a brick wall and everything goes black.

Chapter 26

River

Four days until someone dies . . .

River Scott-Tyler has never felt as awkward, uncoordinated and humiliated as he does right now, and he's fairly certain that the reason his partner keeps pausing to wipe her hands on her skirt isn't because she put on too much hand cream earlier, as she's claiming; it's because she can't stand the sensation of his sweaty palms in hers.

'One, two, three, five, six, seven. One, two, three, five, six, seven.' The teacher, a short dark-haired man named Florian, shouts from across the room as River desperately tries to get his legs and body to move in time with the beat.

Thirty minutes ago, he walked through an unfamiliar pub in Soho into a room in the basement that was lined with mirrors and almost entirely full of women. The shout of 'Fresh meat!' as he looked wildly around, trying to locate

156

the salsa teacher, was almost enough to make him walk straight back out. There was no sign of Charlotte, not that he was entirely sure who he was looking for. Bridget didn't have a photo and, when he Googled the full name she'd given him, he couldn't find anything on her at all. All he had to go on was Bridget's description: small, blonde bob, blue eyes and a posh voice.

Women outnumbered men four to one and he wasn't alone for long.

The first two women he danced with were brunette (Imelda and Janice), then he danced with a woman with long blonde hair called Flo, a woman with braids called Ira and now he's dancing with Jo (also brunette). His head's pounding from the music, his feet are sore and he's pretty sure he'll hear the instructor shouting out numbers in his sleep, and there's still no sign of Charlotte. It's hugely frustrating. He could have spent the evening with Meg, attempting to mend their relationship, instead of torturing himself by learning a dance he knows he'll never do again.

As he tries, for the umpteenth time, to master a turn without crushing his partner's feet, the door swings open and a diminutive blonde bursts in. For someone so small she makes quite the entrance, hopping around on one foot as she tries to do up her shoe, a fake fur coat thrown over one arm and an expensive-looking handbag hanging from the crook of one elbow.

'Sorry I'm late, darlings!' She raises a hand in apology, loses her balance, smacks into the wall with her shoulder, rights herself, swears then drops onto her bottom to do up her shoe.

'Charlotte's drunk again,' Jo hisses as River twirls her

around. 'I swear she's sleeping with Florian. It's the only explanation I can come up with for why he hasn't kicked her out. Oh shit, watch out—'

'Ooh, who do we have here?' Charlotte has appeared beside them, her skin flushed, eyes shining, beads of sweat above her top lip. Without so much as an 'excuse me' she dips under River and Jo's clasped hands so she's standing between them like the filling in a sandwich, looks up at River and says, 'May I cut in?'

'Looks like you already have.' Jo releases River's hands, rolling her eyes as she moves away.

River forces a smile as Charlotte assumes the holds. 'I'm River. I'm new.'

'You certainly are.' Even with her slurring there's no mistaking the lascivious look in her eyes. Up close he can see the creases either side of her eyes and the slight sagging to her jaw that contrasts with her wrinkle-free brow and full red lips. Bridget told him that Charlotte was mid-forties and he's not sure if the work she's had done makes her look older or younger than her actual age. She's certainly flirting as if their twenty-year age difference doesn't exist.

For the next couple of minutes he does his best to keep his balance, and protect his toes, as Charlotte repeatedly steps on him, presses against him, or moves in completely the wrong direction, despite his best efforts to lead. As he steps backwards and forwards, he can feel the tracker in his pocket, pressing against his leg. He's spent most of the day worrying how to plant it on a woman without being accused of inappropriate touching or trying to steal her purse, but Charlotte's so drunk he could probably put a frozen chicken in her handbag, and she wouldn't even realise until the next day.

'All right, everyone!' Florian calls from the corner of the room as he turns down the track. 'That's it for today. I'll be posting a new block of dates on my website tomorrow so make sure you sign up. First come first served.'

As the other dancers collect their belongings and file out of the room Charlotte loops her arm through River's, anchoring him in place.

'Keep me company.' There's that lascivious look again. 'Join me for a drink. There are some proper creeps in the bar.'

He glances at his watch. 9.30 p.m. He needs to get home for the group meeting in an hour.

'Just a quick one,' he says, but Charlotte's already swaying across the room in search of her coat and bag. He hovers, unsure whether to help her or wait until she's done. He thinks of Meg, at home alone, eating a meal for one and watching the TV. She knows what he's doing and why, but he can't shake the feeling that he's being unfaithful, indulging Charlotte's flirtatiousness and agreeing to join her for a drink.

'Come on then, darling!' she calls from the doorway, and he pushes the feeling away. He's doing this for Bridget, for her safety, so she'll feel as secure as he does, knowing where Vanessa is every minute of every day.

'Hey, Bryan!' Charlotte calls again, completely forgetting his name. 'Are you coming or what? Mine's a G and T.'

Puppy-like, River follows Charlotte into a corner of the dark bar where she's found two available seats on a banquette around a table. The seats on the other side of the table are occupied by a couple who don't even glance up as River sets down a gin and tonic and an alcohol-free Indian Pale Ale. They're obviously in that early stage of a relationship where they can't keep their eyes, and their hands, off each other. All the cheek-stroking, and the sound of their baby talk makes him simultaneously nauseous and horribly nostalgic. The beginning of his relationship with Meg, eight months ago, was so magical, so right, so ripe with possibility that he craved her like a drug. Being around her made him feel optimistic and excited for the future. He hadn't felt like that for so long, he wanted to drink in every last second. And then Vanessa waded in and ruined it all.

Talking of his ex . . . He sneakily checks the tracker app on his phone as Charlotte digs through her bag beside him, muttering something about her 'fucking lipstick'. River frowns, confused as Vanessa's location updates. Bangalore? What the hell? Is she backpacking around India? She's never been the type. They always used to argue about where to go on holiday. He's a city break kind of guy whereas Vanessa was more of a one week in Rhodes or Kos beach holiday type of girl.

He can't make sense of what he's seeing. Lucy gave him the nod when he asked if she'd tagged Vanessa. Has something gone wrong or has his ex-girlfriend had a personality transplant over the last few days?

'Cheers, darling!' Charlotte nudges him in the ribs, lipstick reapplied, and waves her G and T in the air.

He hastily shoves his phone into his pocket and reaches for his beer. 'Cheers!'

As their glasses clink together, he feels her calf press against his. He can't move his leg away because he's already on the edge of the bench. If he moves over any further he'll fall off. Instead, he brings his knees closer together and presses his feet into the floor. It's going to be trickier than he thought, placing a tracker on her, because her bag and coat are on the other side of her. Either he waits for her to go to the toilet, ideally leaving the coat behind, or he'll have to come up with a way to get her to move the bag within reach. Given how closely she's pressed up against him now he couldn't squeeze a lolly stick between their warm, slightly sweaty bodies, never mind her bag. He shouldn't have checked his phone while she was rooting through her bag. He should have distracted her as she searched for her lipstick and dropped the tracker inside.

Charlotte taps him on the knee, making him tense. 'Thank you, for this.'

'Oh, it's nothing. What's a five-pound gin and tonic when I crippled your feet?' He laughs at his own joke whilst desperately trying to avoid looking at the couple opposite who are sucking face with a fervour he hasn't seen since Matt Aldridge and Sara Jennings snogged for so long at the Year Nine disco that Sara's lips and chin looked sandpapered for days.

'No, I mean it.' Charlotte's hand remains on his knee. 'I've had a terrible time recently and I need a friend. Not that you're a friend, you're a stranger really but I think we could be friends. Very good friends.'

'Right, yes.' River nods but he's not really listening. All his focus is on the hand on his knee and how desperately he wants her to remove it. This might be the only chance he gets to put a tracker on her and help Bridget out. Is this how women feel, he wonders, when their bosses casually throw an arm around their shoulders, or brush past them

161

when there's plenty of space to walk around? He wants to say something: thanks, but no thanks. I've got a girlfriend. Keep your hands to yourself.

But he does none of those things. Instead, he says, 'Shall we swap numbers? I'm not sure I'll be coming back to class again, but it would be nice to stay in touch.'

Light sparks in Charlotte's hazy eyes and she yanks her handbag back onto her lap, abandoning his knee. 'Yes! Yes! Let's!'

As she digs around inside her bag, searching for her phone, River slips his hand into his pocket and palms the tracker. He glances at the couple opposite but they're still chewing each other's faces off, oblivious to anything but each other's wet tongues. The inside of Charlotte's bag appears to be a dark jumble of receipts, hairbrushes, leaflets, lipsticks and perfume. She even removes a grubby dog collar and a roll of Sellotape, placing them on the table alongside her purse as she searches for her mobile.

'I need to get a brighter phone case,' she mumbles to herself as she places a handful of used tissues on the table. 'Why do I insist on buying everything in black?'

River jiggles on the bench, the tracker in his palm. Any second now he's going to reach across Charlotte, point at the window and say, 'Isn't that Florian kissing someone outside?' Then, when she turns to look, he'll slip the tracker in her handbag, make his excuses and leave.

'Oh!' Charlotte says excitedly. 'Found it.'

River lunges towards her, desperate not to miss his chance. His lips part, but before he can speak, Charlotte presses her mouth to his. In his shock he almost lets go of the tracker, then something in his brain shouts 'Do it, now! Do it now!'

and he feels for Charlotte's handbag and drops the tracker inside. As he pulls away, he sees something flash out of the corner of his eye.

He whips around, searching for the source of the light, but even before he spots the phone pointed in his direction, he knows who just took his photo.

Vanessa's not in India. She's standing three feet away.

Chapter 27

Alexandra

Four days until someone dies . . .

'Is there a bigger arsehole in the world than me?' Alex stares at herself in the living room mirror. Her reflection stares back, anger and accusation burning in her mirrored self's eyes.

'No.' She shakes her head, and her reflection does the same. 'No. You, Alexandra Jane Raynor, win the fucking Oscar for being an ungrateful bitch.'

It all happened so quickly, the way her past subsumed her present and memories smothered her. Colin Sutherland. Colin Sutherland. Colin Sutherland. His name was still ringing in her head like a bell when Sam called her and casually announced that he'd tracked down her brother on Facebook.

'You shout out Ben's name in your sleep,' Sam's voice

buzzed in her ear, making her brain rattle in her skull, 'did you know that? I know you said you didn't want to see him . . .' oh how she regretted getting drunk on her fourth date with Sam and telling him about her brother. She'd told him everything: about the drunken accusation Ben had thrown at her on the night of her twentieth birthday. How he'd left a grovelling voicemail apology the next day when she wouldn't pick up the phone. How he'd sent flowers and banged on her front door, begging to be let in. Her heart had broken when he'd blamed her for their parents' death, then iced over with every clumsy attempt he'd made to put things right. How could she ever look him in the eye again, knowing what he truly believed? The only way she could deal with that was to convince herself that he'd died too.

'. . . but that's your guilt speaking,' Sam continued, 'and, after everything that's happened recently I think the time is right to talk to him, to forgive him, you could use his support.'

She blew up at him then and threw her phone across the room. Before she'd had time to pull herself back together Bridget had tiptoed in, all whispery and sympathetic, talking about Colin Sutherland and how she imagined Alex must feel.

He'd been lodged in her brain since Bridget saw him outside the police station; malignant, deadly, like a tumour or a clot, wrapped with questions. How had he managed to stalk her from prison? Did he have a mobile phone? Did he convince someone to find her, to follow her, to leave 'gifts' on her doorstep? A corrupt cop, an ex-con, his son? He knows where she lives. He saw Sam enter her apartment. He's been biding his time, waiting to stalk her, to torture her, to kill her for putting him in jail.

165

Colin Sutherland, Colin Sutherland, Colin Sutherland.

She screamed at Bridget to get out, not because she'd done anything wrong, but to get her to stop talking. So the bell would stop ringing, so she could throw off the blanket of the past, so she could drink; scream; breathe.

Now, she slumps onto the sofa, lies still for a couple of seconds, staring at the white washed ceiling, then gets back to her feet. She walks into the kitchen, opens the fridge, stares into the icy emptiness, then closes the door and drifts into the bedroom. She spots one of Samuel's socks on the floor at the end of the bed and crouches to pick it up, remembering the first time they had sex, four months ago, at the end of their first date.

She'd called him a deviant for keeping his socks on and he'd laughed and valiantly battled to remove them, still above her in a press-up position, the toes of one foot scratching at the ankle of his other foot, digging at the sock like a dog with an itch. She can't remember what he said, or what she said, but she remembers his arms giving out and the howl of their shared laughter as he collapsed on top of her.

They'd met at a friend's party, three days earlier, and she'd disliked him on sight. He was loud, brash and confident; the sort of man who told a story to a room, not an individual, who basked in the limelight of a dozen laughing eyes. She'd sloped off to the kitchen, empty wine glass in her hand, still pissed off about a comment Conrad had made during the readthrough earlier in the day. Sam had followed her and hovered beside the sink as she grabbed the nearest bottle of wine and emptied it into her glass.

'If I get you to laugh in the next three minutes, will you go out on a date with me?'

166

'Nope.' She'd turned to look at him. Up close his brown hooded eyes were warm and friendly, and his full cheeks dimpled when he smiled. He was tall, dark and, while he wasn't conventionally good looking, she couldn't deny the fact that she found him ridiculously attractive. Irritating, given the fact that he was a professional show-off and she had more than enough drama in her life.

'Really?' he'd said. 'You sure?'

'I'm sure.'

'Fair enough.' He'd turned to walk out of the kitchen, then paused as he reached the open door and looked back. 'Has anyone told you how beautiful you are today?'

She'd rolled her eyes. 'No.'

He'd leaned against the doorframe, angling his body into an idiotic, comedic shape. 'Oh well. Better luck tomorrow.'

She'd laughed despite herself, then quickly said, 'That doesn't mean I'm going on a date with you.'

He'd glanced at his watch. 'I've got one minute, forty-seven seconds left to change your mind. Knock, knock . . .'

She sinks onto the bed, the sock pressed to her chest. What kind of bitch pushes away a man who makes her cry with laughter? Who listens when she freaks out, who wants to protect her, who reaches for her in the night when a nightmare jolts her awake? What kind of fuck-up screams at someone who tracks down her brother because the man who killed their parents has been released from jail?

No wonder Ben hasn't spoken to her for fifteen years. She's thought about contacting him a hundred times, but his silence tells her all she needs to know. Anyone in their right mind would stay as far away from her as they could. She's never thought of herself as toxic before, but she has to be, doesn't she? She pulls people close, then she shoves them away. She formed the WhatsApp group to get support and how does she thank the others? She screams at Bridget, who was there for her at her lowest, who ferried her home because she was worried about her, and she repeatedly tells River that he's a twat. The only person she hasn't been horrible to is Lucy, but that's probably only a matter of time.

She glances at the alarm clock beside the bed – 9.30 p.m. – then checks her phone to see if she's had a reply from Lucy, or any of the others. There was a group message from her at 6.05 p.m. saying, *I don't want to be part of this group any more. My mental health can't take it. Going to stay with my parents. I hope you all stay safe.* Alex rang her immediately but there was no answer, and she hasn't replied to any of the texts she's sent since.

What happened to Lucy between her leaving the flat that morning and sending that text at 6.05 p.m.? The more Alex thinks about it, the more out of character the message feels. The group is Lucy's lifeline, it's all their lifelines. Would she really just walk away knowing one of them could be dead in four days' time?

Dread worms its way into her chest as she checks the last time Lucy logged onto WhatsApp.

6.15 p.m. is almost exactly the same time Natalie stopped responding to texts. One minute she was reading every message, the next she was gone.

The dialling tone sounds as she calls Lucy's number. It rings and it rings, then WhatsApp gives up. She sends her a message instead: *Where are you? Call me asap.* One tick appears but not two.

Fuck. Fuck.

She calls Lucy from her phone, rather than the app and it connects to voicemail.

'Lucy, it's Alex. Where are you? I understand if you want to leave the group but please, just call me back.'

She types a message into the FYST group:

Bridget, River – have either of you heard from Lucy since she sent that text about wanting to leave the group? She hasn't checked WhatsApp since 6.15 and I'm getting worried. Bridget, you know where she lives. Can you check if she's still there? Or tell me the address and I'll go (I'm so sorry I was such a fucking bitch earlier. It wasn't your fault).

A single tick appears next to her message. It's been sent but it hasn't been delivered. What's happening? Where is everyone? It's as though they've all just disappeared.

Chapter 28

River

Four days until someone dies . . .

Later, when the fight-or-flight part of River Scott-Tyler's brain has stopped firing, he will wonder why he didn't just call the police when he saw Vanessa standing in the middle of the pub with her phone in her hand. But he's not thinking logically now. He's on his feet, screaming in his ex-girlfriend's face.

'Give me your phone!' He lunges for the white iPhone in her hand, but she sidesteps him and whips it away.

'Get your hands off me!' Her eyes dart from left to right, checking she's got an audience, then she lowers her voice so only River can hear. 'If you so much as touch me I'll get you beaten to a pulp.'

Her threat is like a shove to the chest, and he takes a half-step backwards. She's not bluffing – she'd call him a

170

sex offender in front of all these people. They'd believe her too, this diminutive, sweet-looking woman with her breathy, Marilyn Monroe tone. Her voice was the first thing he noticed about her, and it lured him in like a siren's call. It took him nearly a year to discover that what he found so alluring and endearing was a weapon, used to disarm and deceive. She'd only have to convince one pissed man with a hero complex that she was in trouble, and he'd find himself knocked to the floor.

'Delete the photo.' He's breathing shallowly through his nose, hands twitching at his sides, body quivering as he fights to keep the anger out of his voice. She wants a reaction, for him to be angry, to lose control.

'What photo?' She smiles – all sparkly eyes and prettily pouting lips – and River feels his resolve slip. He's never hated anyone more in his life than he hates her right now.

'Everything okay, darling? Who's this then?' Charlotte appears beside them, so unsteady on her feet that she has to clutch hold of his arm to stay upright.

Vanessa's gaze slides towards the interloper. Her smile is still in place, but her lips have thinned. 'Going for the older woman now are you, River? What does Meg think of that?'

'Who's Meg, Bryan?' Charlotte gazes up at him, her lipstick smudged all over her chin from their kiss. He wipes a hand over his mouth; the back of his hand is smeared with red lipstick too.

'Why don't you get us both another drink?' He takes a twenty-pound note out of his wallet, angles Charlotte towards the bar and presses her lightly in the small of her back to send her on her way. She totters away like a wind-up robot, her question forgotten.

'That wasn't what it looked like,' River turns his attention back to his ex. 'And you know it.'

'Who am I to judge?' She rocks back on her heels. 'It isn't me you have to answer to any more, is it? I'm sure Meg will understand.'

River flinches, as though struck. 'You sent the photo to her?'

'Speedy, aren't I?' She laughs. 'Useful, you cheating on her. I won't have to kill her if she dumps you. Let's see how you like losing someone you love.'

'You fucking bitch!' He lunges for her, his arm outstretched, reaching for her throat. His mind is white noise – logic and control damped down with blind rage. He wants to hurt her, smother her, to wipe the smirk from her face. He just wants her dead. A gasp – a squawk of terror from somewhere behind him – punctures the white noise in his brain and he snatches his hand from Vanessa's neck, her skin striped red where his fingers had been.

The pub fills with noise, female voices raised in concern, the screech of chair legs on the wooden floor and a single shout: 'Someone call the police.'

Vanessa presses a hand to her neck, jubilation in her eyes. 'I suggest you run.'

River slams open the front door of the flat, then stumbles, his legs giving way beneath him, and steadies himself against a wall. He sucks in air like a drowning man, one hand pressed to his chest, willing his heart to slow down. He can't remember the last time he ran anywhere, never mind six miles, and he's so light-headed he feels he might faint. A police car followed him as he sprinted down Oxford Street, siren whooping, as he weaved his way through late-night drinkers, dawdlers and tourists. He stopped running and held his hands in the air, only for the car to zoom straight past him. He burst into tears, right there on the street, sobbing as people swerved around him, glancing but not stopping; another weirdo on London's streets. He just wanted to get home, to Meg, to put everything right. It would have been faster to catch the tube but there was no way he could sit down or stand in one place: he had to keep moving. Fight or flight. Even if Vanessa hadn't told him to, he would still have run.

Now, as the blood stops pounding in his ears, he listens for the sound of his girlfriend bustling around their home: for the chatter of the television, the clank of pots and pans in the kitchen, the whirr of her sewing machine in the bedroom, the sound of the shower. The flat is silent. He sniffs the air, catches the faintest aroma of a meat-based dish. Chilli con carne? Spaghetti bolognese? His broken legs carry him into the kitchen, and he turns on the light. There's a single portion of spaghetti meatballs on the little table by the window, a knife and fork either side of the place mat. The washing up has been done, a frying pan, saucepan, chopping board and various utensils drip-drying beside the sink.

The door to the living room is open and, even though the light is off, he turns it on and looks inside. The blanket they normally snuggle under in the evenings is still spread over the back of the sofa, untouched and unused.

'Meg?' He walks past the dark bathroom without looking inside, opens the bedroom door and turns on the light. A cold chill settles in his heart as he looks around the small

173

room: the wardrobe doors are open and there's a suitcase missing. He bargains with his fear, telling himself that maybe Meg's gone on a training course she forgot to tell him about, or she's travelled back to Bournemouth to see her mum. His phone vibrates in his pocket, and he grabs for it desperately. It'll be her, telling him where she's gone.

But it's not a message from Meg that causes his phone to alert him; it's a comment from Alexandra in the WhatsApp chat. He doesn't bother to read it. His eyes have already skipped down to a message from Meg, unread. She must have sent it when he was running, and he was too focused on getting home to notice his phone vibrating against his leg.

He reads the message over and over again, but Meg's words don't change:

River, I don't know who that woman was that you were kissing, or what you're up to, and I don't want to know. Vanessa wins. I can't do this any more. I'm going to stay with a friend. Don't try to find or contact me. I'll be in touch at some point. Right now I just need some space.

Chapter 29

Lucy

Four days until someone dies . . .

Lucy groans as she slowly regains consciousness and touches a hand to her neck. Why is it sore? Sleep pulls at her, unwilling to let her go, and her thoughts drift between confusion and concern. Did she pull a muscle in her sleep? Her whole body aches. Why—

'Ow!' She lets out a yelp as the left side of her skull knocks against something hard and pain radiates through her head like a dozen shards of glass. Another jolt, another knock and she opens her eyes, blinking into the darkness. She's in a car, and it's moving quickly. Did she fall asleep? As she grips the glovebox, braced to crash, there's a snort of amusement to her right.

Memories flash through her mind: packing up her flat, loading the car, going back for a coat; and then Marcus blocking her way, staring down at her, gripping her, throwing her against a wall.

'Relax.' He touches a hand to her thigh and gives it a squeeze; a casual, familiar caress. Two lovers off on holiday, not a kidnapping after a brutal assault. 'Are you warm enough? I can turn up the heating if you want.'

She fumbles for the catch on the door, instinct kicking in – *get out, jump* – but they're speeding down a motorway, surrounded by other cars. If she escaped now, she wouldn't survive. Her hand falls away and she gathers the coat from her lap and pulls it over her shoulders; not because she's cold, but to shield her body from Marcus's gaze.

'Take me back. Now.'

He snorts again, with derision this time. 'We're going on holiday, remember?'

'You don't have to do this. We can . . .' She searches for something, anything that will convince him to turn the car around. 'We can go back to mine and . . . have a cup of tea or a drink. We'll talk about this, about where it all went wrong.'

'I'd say it went wrong when you left me.' Anger creeps into his voice and she tenses.

'I know, and you're right. But if we just—'

'We'll talk at the cottage.'

She looks out of the window, searching for road signs that will give her a clue where they're heading, but she's pretty sure she already knows. She's been to his grandmother's cottage before. Less of a cottage and more of a five-bedroom mansion in Newton Abbot, in six acres of woodland with views across Dartmoor. When she died, Marcus's dad inherited it, and the family uses it for holidays. If Marcus

176

takes her there, she'll be completely isolated. If she screams no one would hear.

'You won't find it,' Marcus says as she reaches into the footwell, feeling for her bag. 'I've got your phone.'

'Please . . . just . . . just let me ring my mum. I was supposed to be going home. She'll be wondering where I am.'

There's a beat; a loaded pause. She can feel the anger radiating off him, see it in the clench of his jaw.

'So, no holiday then? Another lie, Lucy. You just don't know when to stop.'

Her eyes flit over his body, looking for a phone-shaped lump in a pocket. 'She'll worry about me. She'll call the police.'

'No, she won't. You sent her a text, telling her you'd changed your mind, that some girlfriends had offered to take you on holiday to cheer you up.'

'She won't believe that. I was in tears when I rang her. She'll want to talk to me, to check I'm okay.'

A smile plays on his lips. 'You sure about that? She sounded relieved to me. She said a holiday was a great idea, that a bit of time away with your girlfriends was just what you needed, and to give her a ring when you get back.'

'I don't believe you.'

'She also said that phone reception can be a bit patchy in Cumbria and not to worry if you call and you can't get through.' He indicates left, exiting the motorway via a junction. 'By the way, that's quite the WhatsApp group you're part of. Proper little spies, aren't you? Following innocent people around and intruding into their lives. I've sent them a little message too.'

177

Lucy stiffens, fear running through her veins like ice.

'I met Alex briefly, at my gym. Terrible actress. I knew you'd sent her. Strange that she thinks I'm the creepy one when she's the one placing trackers on people's motorbikes. How long have you all got now until one of you dies? Three days, is it? Four?' He gives her a sideways look. 'I wonder who sent that wreath?'

Chapter 30

Bridget

Four days until someone dies . . .

Bridget lets herself into the flat and turns on the light. 'Gary? Are you home?'

She knows, even as she calls out into the silence, that he's not. He's never home these days. She takes off her coat and hat and hangs them on a hook in the hallway then makes her way into the kitchen. She turns on the kettle, takes a mug (cheap but tasteful), from the cupboard and sits down at the table as her phone bleeps in her bag. She hopes it's not Alex again. She read her last text after she parked up the van – a hurried apology, utterly insincere. That's twice Alex has apologised for her behaviour: first for abandoning her at the restaurant and now for telling her to fuck off and kicking her out of her flat.

Creepy; the word whirs around her brain, echoing Alex's

179

tone. It's so creepy the way you keep following me around. She didn't kick Lucy out of her flat and call her names. She let her stay there all night. Bridget reaches for a piece of kitchen roll and dabs at her eyes. How is it creepy when she's just trying to help? Lucy couldn't get away from her fast enough, Gary barely speaks to her, and Charlotte nearly stabbed her with her own secateurs. What's wrong with her that makes people dislike her so much?

She blows her nose noisily. Still no message from River. It's almost ten p.m. and the salsa class should have finished at half past nine. She's going to have to leave soon to get to Lucy's for 10.30 p.m. but there's no point if River can't make it. They both need to be there to convince her to go to the police.

Maybe he didn't make it to the class? Or maybe Charlotte wasn't there? She taps on the app and waits for the tracker location to load. It was River's idea to give her the code before the tracker was placed. Jack Solomons Club, Great Windmill Street. He's at the salsa class then, but is the tracker on him, or on her?

Everything okay, River? she taps out a private message and waits. Two ticks appear but River doesn't respond. It's killing her, not knowing what happened. He *has* to get that tracker on Charlotte. She needs to know where she is every minute of every day.

Irritated, she navigates back to the group chat and clicks on Lucy's name. She hasn't logged onto WhatsApp since 6.15 p.m. That's the same time Alex mentioned in her message. Bridget chews on her fingernails as the kettle bubbles to a boil and clicks itself off. There could be multiple reasons why Lucy hasn't checked WhatsApp in the last three

180

and a half hours – she lost her phone, it's out of battery, she's gone somewhere where the signal is poor – but none of them ease the tight feeling in Bridget's chest. She needs to check on her; make sure she's okay.

It's quiet and peaceful on Lucy's road. The lights are off in most homes and the newsagent's on the corner has shuttered its windows. A streetlamp buzzes, casting a wan orange light onto the pavement as Bridget steps out of her van. She sighs softly as she glances up and down the street.

She walks a couple of metres along the pavement and pauses at the gate to the steps that lead down to Lucy's flat. Natalie lived in a basement flat too. It's a thought that makes Bridget shiver, so she pushes it away.

The gate's open, but that's not overly concerning. The only person she's ever known who was obsessed with closing gates was her mother; she'd bark at visitors to close the gate before they came in and fly into a fury if postmen and work-men strolled out of the front garden leaving it wide open. Marjorie Bauer was a strange fish in many ways and Bridget's childhood wasn't particularly happy, but the memory sends a pang of nostalgia through her, then a swell of grief that she hasn't felt in years.

She turns on the torch app on her phone and makes her way down the steps then crosses the small patch of paved patio, hesitating as she reaches the front door. It's been left ajar.

'Lucy?' She pushes at the door then glances behind her. She can't shake it: the creeping feeling that someone's out there, watching every move that she makes.

'Lucy?' She steps into the flat and closes the door behind

her, then opens it again. She's not sure which is worse: being trapped in the flat with someone awful, or someone awful following her in.

She turns on the light in the living room and glances around. She's only been in Lucy's flat once before, when she picked her and River up to go to Highgate Woods. She wasn't in Lucy's hallway for more than a couple of seconds before she was ready to go, but she peeked into her living room as she waited. Everything still looks in its place. No, that's not strictly true. The last time she looked there were several plants on the mantelpiece and windowsill. Now, there are gaps, and small sprinklings of soil where the plants used to be. She continues down the narrow hallway until she reaches a bathroom and pulls on the light; no toothbrush or toothpaste, not in any of the cupboards or on the shelves. No shampoo or shower gel either. Maybe her theory about Lucy going somewhere with no mobile reception was right? She moves on to the bedroom and raises her eyebrows at all the open drawers and the pile of clothes on the bed. If Lucy has gone somewhere, she left in a rush.

She takes a cursory look around the kitchen – nothing unusual there – then hurries back down the hallway to the front door. She doesn't want to spend a minute longer in Lucy's flat than she has to; she'll text Alex and River from the safety of her van. She steps back out onto the patio and slams the front door shut (wherever Lucy is she won't want to be burgled). She sweeps her torch over the patio, taking one last look before she heads back up the steps: bins lined up along one wall, a plant lying on its side, soil spread across the tiles and brick walls with—

She moves closer to the dark stain on the wall, touches her fingers to the brick and shines the light onto her fingertips. It's dry, and it's crumbly, but it's definitely blood.

Chapter 31

WhatsApp group: FYST

23.22
Bridget: I'm in the van outside Lucy's flat. The door was open when I got here, and it looked like she packed in a hurry. A plant had been dropped on the patio and, I don't want to overreact, but there was blood on one of the walls, at roughly head height.

Alexandra: What the fuck? Is her car still there?

Bridget: Not that I can see.

Alexandra: Shit. Do you think Marcus found her? Is his motorbike there?

Bridget: What does it look like?

Alexandra: It's a black and yellow Yamaha. Black tyres with yellow rims.

Bridget: I didn't spot a motorbike, but I'll take a look further down the street.

23.38
Bridget: I found the motorbike.

Alexandra: Can you feel around under the seat and see if the tracker is still there?

23.43
Bridget: I can't find anything.

Alexandra: Did you use the torch on your phone?

Bridget: I'll have another look.

23.46
Bridget: Nothing. I felt around and looked everywhere. Definitely no tracker.

Alexandra: Shit. Either it fell off or he found it. I really hope it fell off.

River: It won't have fallen off, the magnets are strong.

Alexandra: He's taken her. I know he's taken her. FUCK. If he was the one who sent the wreath he'll kill her.

Bridget: We need to find her!

Alexandra: How? What do we do?

River: Tell the police. As soon as possible.

Alexandra: Wait. Before you call. Are you sure about that? She was adamant about not getting them involved.

Bridget: Do I need to remind you that I found blood on the patio wall?

River: I'll call them. We'll find her. We'll get her back.

Chapter 32

Lucy

Four days until someone dies . . .

It's nearly eleven o'clock as Marcus drives the car up the isolated track to his grandmother's cottage. As he parks up outside the house the headlights flood the tarmac with an eerie orange glow. The whitewashed house, with its triangular, jutting roof and the smaller spiky roofs of the porch, summer room and extension, looks bigger than Lucy remembers. She sits up taller in her seat, nervy, desperate, adrenaline coursing through her. He's brought her to the cottage to kill her. The wreath was meant for her; the rock too. He's been biding his time, toying with her, terrifying her, waiting for his chance to strike. She thinks of Natalie, just trying to get home when Jamie crept up behind her and stabbed her to death, and her throat tightens. She can't let Marcus take her into the house. Once the door's locked behind her the countdown

187

will begin. Four days until he kills her: god only knows what he'll do.

Her only hope of escape is to get to the nearest town – Chagford, which is four miles away. She visited it with Marcus about a year ago and thought it was charming, full of character and cute little art shops. Now it's her refuge, if she makes it there. She's got no idea what she'll do when she does; maybe look for a pub and ask to borrow a phone. And if she can't do that, she'll knock on someone's door. Who she'll ring or what she'll do afterwards she doesn't know. She just wants to live.

There's a can of de-icer under the sole of her right shoe. She became aware of it, rolling around in the footwell, about an hour ago, and pinioned it with her foot, hiding it from Marcus. Now, as he turns off the engine, pockets the car keys, and unbuckles his seatbelt, she readies herself. He's always opened and closed car doors for her. The first time he did it – in a taxi on a night out – she was confused when he told her not to open the door because he'd do it. 'Are you Mr Darcy?' she'd asked, laughing, as he'd offered her a hand as she stepped out of the car and onto the pavement. 'It's good manners.' The base of his throat had flushed red. 'My dad taught me that much.'

Now, as he steps outside and closes the driver's side door, the interior of the car darkens. She undoes her seatbelt and reaches into the footwell for the de-icer but she's shaking so much it slips from her fingers. She grabs for it again, tightening her grip around the can as Marcus rounds the car, his boots crunching against the gravel driveway. As the door opens, she angles her body towards him, her right hand – and the can – hidden behind her back.

188

'Madam.' He mock bows and holds out a hand.

She lowers her gaze, certain he'll see the terror in her eyes, and places her left hand on his. She swings her legs out of the car and onto the gravel, then, as Marcus tightens his grip on her hand, she swings her right arm from behind her back and presses the nozzle on the can. A cloud of vapour fills the air and Marcus jumps back, coughing and covering his face with his arm. In an instant Lucy is running, out of the gate and back down the track. Darkness wraps itself around her as she continues to run, the cold air dragging at her lungs, her head pounding, her ankles tensing and turning as her feet catch on indents and cracks in the old, neglected road. She can vaguely make out the sign ahead of her – *Chagford 4 miles* – and her heart gives a little leap of hope. Four miles from freedom. She's got no idea if there's a police station in Chagford but, even if she has to spend the evening in the porch of a church, at least she won't be with him. Her shadow appears – stretching before her like a dark stain on the road, surrounded by light – then she hears the low rumble of the car behind her. She risks a glance over her shoulder, hoping, praying; but she already knows that it's him.

'Lucyyyy!' He calls her name from the open driver's side window. 'Bit late for a run, isn't it?'

His taunting tone makes her pick up her pace. She knows, as she sprints down the road, the car idling behind her, that she's got no hope of out-running him, but she can't – won't – stop. As long as she's running, she's free.

'Come on, Lucy, let's not be silly now.'

She veers off the road and clambers over a wobbly metal gate, heart pounding, her breath jagged and shallow. She

189

lands lightly in a field of damson trees, the branches bowing under the weight of the soft, ripe fruit, and takes off, leaping over roots and rocks, weaving between the trees. She glances over her shoulder as the car slows to a stop, headlights on full beam. He's coming after her! She continues to run as the car door opens and closes; the gate clangs as he leaps over it. She can hear his footsteps slapping against the damp earth as he closes the distance between them. He's thirty or forty metres behind her. She keeps running, arms pumping, feet skimming the damp earth, the cold night air filling her lungs. There's a dense wood on the other side of the field, beyond a straggly hedge which has a gap in the branches at the base, probably made by an animal. She should be able to crawl through it, but he'll struggle. She can still lose him; it's so dark in the wood he'll never find her if she hides.

He's gaining on her; he's so close that she can hear him breathe, but she's reached the edge of the field. She drops to her knees and crawls headfirst into the hedge, oblivious to the branches and brambles that catch in her hair and scratch at her skin. The hole is made for something far smaller than her, but she ploughs through it, eyes half-closed, sweat rolling down her temples.

The hedge shakes violently and, before she knows what's happening, Marcus's fingers close around her foot. She kicks out at him then pulls her leg back sharply, yanking her foot out of her shoe.

'Fuck's sake!' His shout fills her ears as she scrabbles forward, the scent of damp earth in her nose, her breath rasping in her throat. She's made it through though; she's out the other side.

She scrabbles to her feet, takes a step and falls, her foot catching in the dense undergrowth. It's even darker in the wood than she thought, the heavy canopy above her head blocking out the light of the moon. She can't see the ground beneath her feet but she ploughs through the trees, searching the gloom for somewhere to hide.

A yelp of surprise catches in her throat as her foot snags on a tree root and she falls heavily, her wrists breaking her fall. She tries to stand, but her ankle can't take her weight and she overbalances, grabbing a tree for support. She holds herself still, listening, trying to locate Marcus, but all she can hear is the rapid rhythm of her own breath.

She slides to the ground and, on hands and knees, crawls towards a felled tree. She slides over it, her ankle pulsing with pain, and flattens herself against the cool earth, her face pressed into the crevice between the tree's trunk and the mossy ground.

'Lucy!' Marcus's shout rings out like a gunshot, making her flinch. He can't be more than a few metres away. 'There's no point hiding. You know I'll find you.'

She's shaking now, every part of her body tremoring and trembling. Tears spill onto her cheeks, winding their way through the grime on her skin. She doesn't want to die. She wants to travel, to get married, to have children. She wants to be normal again. She wants to go out with her friends and get drunk, go for a walk without looking over her shoulder, open a window at home when it's hot. She wants to try Tinder, go on dates, swap stories and moan about the weirdos she's met. Normal weirdos – men who talk over her, or ghost her, or have hobbies that bore her to tears. She wants to turn back time, turn down a glass of punch, leave the party early, accept a different job; to take the path that meant she and Marcus would never have met.

She lies there, pressed up against the tree, for what feels like hours, but can't be more than a few minutes. She wants to open her eyes, to peel her cheek from the tree's rough bark, to shift away from the rock or the root that's pressing into her left thigh, but she daren't move. She isn't the only one listening and waiting. Somewhere, out there, Marcus is doing the same.

Where is he? He was so close when he shouted; she felt sure he'd discover her hiding place. She holds herself rigid, barely breathing, listening for the snap of a twig or the crunch of a leaf – something, anything that will give him away – but there's nothing, not a sound. It is as though the wood is holding its breath too, watching, waiting for him to find her. Even the breeze that plucked and pulled at the baby hairs at the nape of her neck as she pressed herself up against the fallen tree has grown still.

She breathes through her nose, inhaling the dampness of the bark, frowning as a new scent mingles with the woody, earthiness of the tree. It's strong, bitter and acrid and it catches in the back of her nose. She's smelled it before, so many times, but her brain's struggling to identify it. Cigarette smoke!

She turns sharply, adrenaline flooding her body as she prepares to jump to her feet and run, but Marcus has already grabbed the back of her cardigan and he's dragging her away from the tree. She twists around, the cardigan cutting into her neck as she hits out at his face and chest with her fists, her palms and her nails. She kicks out at him with her one good foot and she screams until her mouth is smothered by his hand. She continues to fight, to wriggle, to bite at his hand until he throws her away from him and punches her square in the face. As she falls, the stars paint white stripes in the midnight sky, then completely disappear.

Lucy comes to as Marcus cable-ties her wrists together and attaches them to the rickety metal bed frame in his grandmother's room. Fear brings her leaden limbs to life. He's going to rape her. She twists and turns and screams, shaking the bed as she jolts and jerks and tries to get free.

He glances down at her as he tests the stretch of the cable ties, pulling on her wrists, making her skin sing out in pain. He sees the fear in her eyes and his top lip curls in disgust.

'Don't flatter yourself. You'll be begging me to fuck you soon enough. Besides,' he jabs a finger into the soft mound of her belly, 'you've let yourself go. But we'll soon sort that out. I told you; you need me. We're good together.'

He looms over her, staring into her face, waiting for a reaction. She returns his gaze, focusing on the black pits of his pupils – the darkness she's looked into so many times before – and feels . . . nothing. Not anger, sadness, regret or guilt. Nothing.

Learned helplessness, that's what a psychologist would call it. She didn't always switch off when faced with Marcus's aggression. In the first six months of their relationship, she gave as good as she got, arguing as furiously as he did. How dare he try and shame her, questioning the way she lived her life before she met him. How dare he criticise her choices, her past and her friends. She stood up to him, determined to defend herself, to make him see how wrong he was; but the harder she fought the more defensive,

193

indignant and aggressive he would become. He wouldn't back down, and he wouldn't apologise; his ego demanded that he win.

She'd lie in bed afterwards, her back turned to him, silently fuming, waiting for a 'sorry' that never came. If they continued to ignore each other she'd always crack first. She didn't know how he could bear the coldness and awkwardness, the tiptoeing around. She found it so unbearable she'd always breach the silence first.

'Can we at least talk about this?' she'd say, and Marcus's blank expression would be replaced by a smile.

His eyes would light up the more she talked, and she'd feel warm and happy, as though the sun had come out, pushing a dark cloud away.

For the longest time she subdued any suspicion that she was in a coercive and controlling relationship with a narcissist. She argued with him, didn't she? She didn't let him walk all over her. She fought back. She wasn't subservient, weak and quiet. But she had been his teacher. She'd overstepped the mark. She'd done something reprehensible. If anyone was in the wrong it was her.

He wore her down. She learned that switching off was less exhausting than arguing. She thought she deserved the way he treated her. No one could hate her as much as she hated herself.

'All right then. Time for bed.' Marcus straightens up and moves his head towards one shoulder, then the next, stretching out his neck.

'I *was* going to surprise you with some new pyjamas,' he says as he rounds the bottom of the bed and pulls his t-shirt over his head, 'but the little stunt you pulled earlier put paid to that. If you behave yourself tomorrow, I'll give them to you. Tonight, you can sleep in your clothes.'

His naked torso is more muscular than it was the last time she saw it: his chest is wider, his pecs are fuller, and his biceps and triceps are so large that his arms jut out from his shoulders at a forty-five degree angle rather than hang by his sides. He was on the verge of manhood when they met – long and lanky, strong but lean, hair that curled over his ears and fell over his eyes and a bassy voice that seemed too deep, too confident for someone his age. Now he's a man and, while once she would have found his muscles appealing, now she finds them terrifying. Something drove him to work out that hard, to lift heavier and heavier weights, day after day after day; she's pretty sure it was hate.

Chapter 33

Alexandra

TUESDAY 17TH OCTOBER

Three days until someone dies . . .

Alex has gone blank. Conrad is staring at her, waiting for her to say her line, but her head is empty. She should know it; they've rehearsed the scene dozens of times, she knows the character inside out. The pause stretches and a bead of sweat rolls down her lower back. The play is opening in three days' time and she's forgotten her bloody line. Conrad's left eyebrow twitches upwards: the soap actress has forgotten her lines – quelle surprise. He prompts her with an ad-lib, but she still can't remember the line. Her mind is empty, whitewashed, the script of the play gone. Her bare feet are planted on the wooden boards – her body is on the stage, but the rest of her disappeared with Lucy last night.

She was going to call in sick again, but River had convinced her not to. There was nothing any of them could do to help Lucy until he'd reported her disappearance to the police. Alex had paced her flat, striding from the kitchen to the living room and back, her phone in her hand, her thoughts becoming darker and darker until she was convinced that Lucy was dead and Colin Sutherland was waiting for her in the street, with an axe in his hand. The more she'd paced, the smaller the flat had become, and the thicker the air. She'd shoved her feet into her trainers, called an Uber, strapped her bag across her body and forced herself down the stairs to the front door. If she hadn't left the flat today, she'd never have left it again.

'All right guys,' Liz calls from the stalls. 'Let's take a little break. We're all tired and, I don't know about you, Alex, but I could do with a coffee. Let's take ten minutes, everyone.'

Relieved, Alex heads for the wings, but a stagehand steps in front of her, blocking her escape.

'The gun.'

She looks at him blankly.

'You can't leave it on the stage. I need to lock it away.'

'Fuck, sorry.' She returns to the stage, picks up the gun and hands it to him, just as she has a dozen times before. The gun is only a prop – it doesn't even fire blanks – but it's a deactivated weapon and the theatre is strict about it being locked up when not in use.

She heads back to her dressing room, picks up her script and flicks through the pages until she reaches the scene where she blanked.

For once in my life I want to feel that I control a human destiny.

Just fifteen words, but so important to the story, to Hedda's fate; a moment when she realises she can't control her own destiny so she chooses to control someone else's. Alex says the words aloud, then she says them again, louder this time; but they still sound hollow and forced. She didn't sleep more than two or three hours last night. Faces loomed behind her closed eyelids like spirits – Lucy, Ben, Sam, her parents – and when she did finally sleep, Colin Sutherland haunted her dreams, taunting her, telling her he had Lucy hidden in his basement, that he was going to kill her and it was all her fault. She woke up screaming, the sheet drenched in sweat and the duvet wrapped around her like a shroud.

Now, a tap on the door makes her jump.

'Could we have a quick word?' Liz walks into the room, closing the door behind her.

'Sure, sure.' Alex gestures for the director to take the only seat in the room, then perches on an upturned crate.

Liz smiles across at her, but her lips are pressed too tightly together, and her body language is too rigid for Alex to feel reassured. She's going to get a bollocking, she can sense it.

'So,' Liz rests her forearms on her thighs and leans towards her. There are dark circles beneath her eyes and patches of dry skin on her jaw. She looks as tired as Alex feels. 'I just wanted to check in, see how you are.'

Alex runs a hand over her face, a self-soothing motion that does little to quell her panic. 'I fucked up the scene. I don't know why.'

A frown settles between Liz's eyebrows. 'Is everything okay? At home? In your personal life?'

If she tells Liz the truth – that she's being stalked by the man who murdered her parents, that she split up with her boyfriend, that he contacted her estranged brother, that one

198

of her friends has vanished into thin air – she'll start crying and never stop. Her mental health is a rope that connects her to reality, and there's only the thinnest of cotton threads left. If she tells Liz the truth it will snap.

'No. Yeah. Everything's fine,' she lies.

'Okay.' Liz says slowly. She's watching her intently, her eyes never leaving her face. 'Because you've seemed a little unfocused over the last week or so. Like your mind's on something else. Conrad's noticed it too.'

Any softening, any bend to tell the truth that Alex may have been feeling, instantly hardens. They've been talking about her, criticising her, gossiping behind her back. She's ten years old again, walking into the playground to a rumble of whispers, eyes following her, mouths behind hands.

'I gave your agent a ring,' Liz continues, 'and she said she hasn't heard from you for ages – that you haven't returned any of her calls. She's concerned too.'

Alex breathes faster, taking in short, shallow gulps as a wave of panic passes through her. The air in the room has become heavier, thicker, and harder to breathe. They're all talking about her, worrying about her, smothering and suffocating her, trying to decide what to do for the best.

Now she's sitting in a beige-walled, windowless room, surrounded by police officers, social workers and relatives. Their voices clash above her head as they try to decide where she and Ben will stay the night, whilst she tries to interrupt. Ben glowers at her and tells her to shut up, as she attempts to make herself heard, to tell these adults that they can stop arguing because it's obvious isn't it, they should go home, once they've been to the hospital to see Mum and Dad. She's been taught to be polite to adults, to speak when she's spoken

199

to, not to interrupt, but she's frustrated, so frustrated and she can't sit on the cold, hard chair a minute longer. She stands up and tugs at her Auntie Genevieve's sleeve. She is her dad's sister; she gives her ten pounds in a card for her birthday and she bought her a make-up set for Christmas when her mum said no.

'Auntie, can we please—'

Her auntie presses a reassuring hand to her shoulder but the adults continue to talk, everyone on their feet now, gathering in a huddle in the centre of the room.

'Auntie G, can't we just—'

Her aunt reaches into her pocket for a tissue then dabs at her eyes.

'Excuse me, Auntie, but—'

'Stop it!' She feels her brother's arms around her, rough, tight and pitching as she's hauled away from the adults. 'Alexandra, stop! We can't go home. We can never go there again and it's all your fault. You opened the door to him. After you were told not to! And now Mum and Dad are dead.'

'Alex?' Liz touches a hand to her arm, but she sees rather than feels the embrace; she's still locked in the memory, trying to fight her way out. 'Are you okay? You're shivering. Have you got a cardigan anywhere?'

Alex stands up in her tomato-stained slip and pulls on her coat. She slides her feet into her shoes and picks up her bag. For the last six months she's been speaking someone else's words and for the last fifteen years she's been living other people's lives. There was a time when she could lose herself in make-believe, but not any more. The protective armour that acting gave her has gone.

200

'Alex? Where are you going?' Liz calls as she opens the door to the dressing room. 'Alex! I haven't finished talking to you. Alex, come back!'

Chapter 34

River

Three days until someone dies . . .

River shifts on the police station's hard plastic chair and stretches out his shoulders. He's been waiting to speak to someone for over forty minutes and he's not sure how many more times he can check for messages from Meg or re-read the guidance for reporting a missing person. Last night, after Bridget broke the news about Lucy's disappearance, his first instinct was to ring the police. As he'd tapped the first two of three nines, worry had made him put down his phone. You couldn't report a person as missing without answering a LOT of questions: he'd watched enough police dramas to know that.

He'd found a website – missingpeople.org.uk – and a list of questions the police might ask him. He was stumped by the first few bullet points: name, age, date of birth and address of the missing person. He knew Lucy's first and last name but had no idea of her date of birth (neither did Alexandra or Bridget). He could provide a physical description of her but not what she was wearing at the time of her disappearance, and he had no idea if she had any tattoos, scars or birthmarks. Nor could he provide the number plate of her car, her last-known movements or what she'd taken with her. He couldn't ring friends and family because Lucy's social media accounts were hidden or locked, but he knew the name of the school where she worked. Maybe they could help with her last-known movements and what she'd been wearing. But it was midnight, he'd have to wait at least eight hours until someone at the school answered the phone.

He'd paced his flat, trying to decide what to do. Ring the police with next to no information or wait eight hours and contact the school? A lot could happen in eight hours, and none of them knew what Marcus was capable of. River had gone online again, done some more googling and found a list on a police website that said you should search the home of the person who was missing and ring round the hospitals before you called it in. You should check the loft and garden and look for clues. Bridget had already checked every room in Lucy's flat and identified clues: signs of hurried packing, an open front door, a dropped plant pot and blood on the wall of the patio. She'd also shut the front door, locking it, so there wasn't anything else River could do there. He rang the hospitals instead, working his way through a list he found on an NHS website, and by the time he rang the last one it was two in the morning. Lucy hadn't been admitted to hospital. Six hours to go until Thames View Academy opened. He'd tried to report Lucy missing using the online form but there were too many questions that he couldn't answer. He'd had no choice but to wait.

He'd slept fitfully – Meg, Lucy and Vanessa swimming in and out of his dreams, laughing, running away, telling him that he wasn't wanted, and to leave them alone – and woke with a start at four a.m., five a.m., six a.m. then seven. He'd checked his phone and found messages from Bridget and Alex asking for an update, but Lucy still hadn't logged onto WhatsApp since 6.15 p.m. the night before. Tired and worried, he'd swerved his normal sparkling kombucha and gone on the hunt for coffee. He'd found half a pack of granules in the back of the cupboard and drunk two cups, one after another, then paced the flat and watched the minutes on his phone slowly tick away as it got closer to eight.

It had taken a couple of minutes before he got through to the school office – answerphone, answerphone, then the call finally connected and the woman he'd spoken to sounded harassed and tired. Miss Newton wouldn't be in today, he'd been told, and no, she couldn't remember seeing her the day before. He'd asked to speak to the head teacher and was told she was otherwise engaged. He'd left a message with his name and number saying it was very important that she call him back.

'Rover?' A tall, rangy man in his mid-thirties with grey at his temples pops his head around the door. 'Misper?'

'Sorry?' River stands up. 'What was that?'

'Missing person, right? You're . . .' he squints at his notebook. 'Mr Rover.'

'River. Scott-Tyler.'

'DC Thompson.' The detective beckons him through the door, 'Come through.'

*

204

'Right then.' the detective says. Unlike River, whose backside hasn't yet touched the thinly sprung sofa, the detective is already sitting down, his notepad propped open on his knee, his pen in hand. He has the air of a man who has a thousand things to do and no time in which to do them but there's something reassuring about his brisk, efficient manner that makes River feel slightly less panicked than he did ten minutes ago.

'So, you're reporting Lucy Newton as missing then?' Thompson glances down at his notes. 'You told the desk sergeant she stopped checking her messages sometime after six p.m. last night, left her front door open, signs she packed a case, a dropped plant, blood on the patio wall.'

'Yes.' River presses his hands between his knees. 'Yes, that's right.'

'And your relationship to Lucy is . . .'

'Friends.'

'Okay. And you're worried about her because—'

'She's being stalked. By her ex. Marcus. I'm sorry, I don't know his last name.'

'Okay.' He scribbles in his notebook again then glances up. There's something about the way his eyes narrow that makes River feel as though the detective is looking straight into his soul. 'Is this recent then? The stalking? I checked our database, and I couldn't find any kind of stalking or harassment report regarding a Lucy Newton.'

'She didn't report him.' River glances away, as though he's the guilty one. 'I'm not . . . er . . . I'm not entirely sure why, but she was very insistent about not going to the police.'

'Okay.' The word is longer this time, as though Thompson is mulling something over as he speaks. 'And I'm right in

205

thinking that you don't know Lucy's date of birth or have contact details for other friends or family?'

'Yes. No. No, I don't know those things. I don't . . . I don't know Lucy all that well really. I did ring the school where she works though – Thames View Academy – they said she hasn't been in today. No, that she's not coming in. Yes, yes that's it.' Sweat beads in his hairline and he wipes his sleeve over his forehead. He has no reason whatsoever to feel guilty – he's not the one who abducted Lucy – but DC Thompson keeps glancing at him as though he's hiding something. It's like he knows about the trackers, even though he hasn't mentioned them once.

'Unusual,' Thompson says. 'That you're the one to report Lucy as missing if you don't know her very well. We haven't received Misper reports from her family.'

'I . . . um . . . ' River shrugs awkwardly. 'Maybe they haven't noticed yet. We, um . . . we noticed she was missing because we're a . . . we're part of a . . . I suppose you'd call it a stalking survival club.'

The detective raises an eyebrow, prompting him to continue.

'There's four of us. Me and the three girls . . . women. They're definitely women. Lucy Newton, Bridget Hopkins and Alexandra Raynor. We're all being stalked and we, we support each other. You'll have my record, my report of my stalking case on file. Vanessa Griffiths. My ex. I've been waiting for someone to arrest her for . . . a while.' He feels heat rise from the base of his neck to his unshaven jaw and wonders if he's blushing. He's not ashamed of being stalked; he's angry that it's still ongoing, when he's done everything that he can to get her to stop. 'A couple of days ago I reported a new threat she's made. She basically threatened to kill my girlfriend.'

'Right.' Thompson's narrowed eyes sweep over him. 'I'd have to check who's dealing with that.'

'But this isn't about that,' River says. 'It's about Lucy. A week ago we attended the funeral of one of our friends. Natalie Beare. She was stalked and murdered by her ex-boyfriend.'

The detective raises his eyebrows in acknowledgement. 'I know the case.'

'A wreath was delivered after the service, to the four of us. A florist's card was attached to it, with RIP written at the top and a date for ten days' time.'

'I'm not sure I'm following.'

'It was a threat. That one of us would die, like Natalie did. Then we all met, in Highgate Woods, early one morning a few days later, and someone threw a rock at us. It—'

'Why were you in the woods?'

'To talk about the threat, on the wreath.'

'In a park, early in the morning?'

'Yes. We didn't want to be overheard, or risk one of our stalkers following us.' River blunders on, terrified the detective will somehow trick him into confessing about the trackers. 'But one of them did – one of our stalkers, I mean. They hid in the bushes and threw a rock at us. It had a six carved into it. They were trying to scare us, to warn us that there were only six days left until one of us was killed.'

The corner of the detective's mouth twitches and he runs a thumb over it, smoothing away the half-smile.

'I know it sounds ridiculous,' River says, 'but—'

'Have you got this . . . rock? Or the wreath?'

207

'No. They . . . we don't know where they are.' The detective's looking at him like he's completely lost the plot and it's taking all his willpower to stay in his seat and not bolt from the room. 'Anyway, that's why I'm so worried about Lucy. I think Marcus has kidnapped her and he's going to kill her in three days' time.'

The detective says nothing for the longest time – he just stares at River, his brow furrowed, as though he's trying to work him out – then he sighs noisily, interweaves his figures and stretches out his arms.

'Well, you did the right thing, telling us about Lucy. We'll look into it. I'll give you the reference number.'

'I'll put it in my phone.' River slips his phone out of his jacket pocket. A message has arrived since he last checked it. It's from Florian, the salsa class instructor, asking if he can pass his number on to Charlotte. *Absolutely-bloody-not*, River thinks, but doesn't say. Instead, he taps the reference number that DC Thompson tells him into his phone then carefully repeats it back.

'If anything else comes to light,' the detective gets up from his seat, 'ring 101 and quote that number. Or if Lucy comes back. We'll need to double-check that she's okay.'

'Do you think she is?' River asks as the other man holds the door open for him. 'Okay, I mean.'

DC Thompson presses his lips together. 'Let's hope so, eh?'

Chapter 35

Lucy

Three days until someone dies . . .

Lucy rubs at the red indents that circle her wrists like bracelets, her gaze flicking from Marcus – frying onions on the ancient Aga and humming to himself – to the knife on the chopping board beside him.

'I'm using *lean* mince for the chilli.' He glances across at her as he tips a plastic tray of pinky-red meat into the pan. 'Less *fat*.'

Last night, as he'd lain beside her in the gloom staring into her face (he'd kept a lamp on all night), she'd flipped onto her side, her arms twisted like a pretzel above her head, and tried to plan her escape. Marcus had caught her heading to Chagford so if she vanished again that'll be the first place that he'll look. She'd either have to escape in the night when he was asleep and hope that gave her an hour or two to get

209

to Chagford and hide, *or* she'd have to find a way to stop Marcus coming after her. She'd wriggled her wrists against the plastic of the cable ties and remembered a random TikTok clip she'd seen about a woman snapping cable ties by bringing her hands down over her knees. That wouldn't work, not with her hands bound above her head and tied to the bed frame. She'd craned her chin towards her hands and shuffled up the bed, trying to get her teeth closer to her wrists. If she couldn't twist her hands out of the ties, maybe she could chew through them instead? The motion had made the bed rock and Marcus had shifted closer to her and thrown a heavy arm over her waist.

'*Why* can't you just go to sleep?' He'd grunted irritably, got out of bed and turned on the ceiling light. 'Flip onto your back.'

Lucy had stared at him in horror.

'I'm not going to fuck you, you stupid bitch. Lie on your back.'

She couldn't have rolled over if she'd wanted to; she was frozen with regret. Why hadn't she waited longer to try and chew through the ties? She should have listened to his breathing, waited until it was deep and slow.

'For fuck's sake. Why do you have to make everything so bloody difficult?' He'd grabbed her by the ankles and pulled them towards him. As he'd done so her arms had straightened. She'd whimpered, not in fear but frustration, as he'd snapped cable ties around each ankle and anchored her feet to the ornate metal frame at the base of the bed.

'Marcus,' she'd whispered as he'd switched off the light and the bed sagged under his weight. 'Marcus, I wouldn't have done anything. I just . . . I just wanted to put an arm around you.' She'd hated herself, even as the words left her mouth.

He'd laughed, a hard-edged snort of disbelief. 'Don't make yourself look more stupid than you already do.'

'It doesn't have to be like this, please. I can't go to sleep. It already hurts. You say you love me, but this isn't how you treat someone you love. You can't—'

'Shut the fuck up.' He'd twisted onto his side, propped himself up on his elbow and glared down at her. 'Or am I going to have to gag you too? I've played this game by your rules for fucking months and now I get to make the decisions. Shut up and go to sleep. Do you understand?'

She'd nodded mutely. There would be no escaping while he slept. The only way she could guarantee her freedom would be if he was dead.

She'd slept fitfully, shifting and sweating, unable to get comfortable, shifting her weight to try and relieve the tightness in her triceps and calves; but it was one or the other, something always hurt. At six a.m. the urge to use the toilet had become so unbearable she'd had to waken him. She'd said his name repeatedly, louder and louder until his eyes finally flicked open and he'd stared at her, a look of confusion, then delight, on his face. He'd cut through the ties around her ankles with scissors but kept her wrists tightly bound. He'd stood, smirking, by the open bathroom door as she'd struggled to undo the buttons on her jeans.

'Close the door!' She'd glared at him, her thumbs hooked around the waistband of her jeans.

'Not going to happen.'

'I can't escape with my wrists bound, can I?'

'I'd like to see you try.'

211

'For fuck's sake, Marcus. How is humiliating me going to make me fall in love with you?'

His eyes had darkened. 'Who said this had anything to do with love?'

She'd yanked her jeans down to her thighs, taking her knickers with them, and sat on the toilet. She'd stared back at him, defiance bubbling within her as she released the urine she'd been holding for hours. He'd always been so prissy about bodily functions, so judgemental of women who were vulgar or rude, but he hadn't so much as blinked as her piss hit the ceramic toilet bowl, the rushing and tinkling the only sound in the room. He'd continued to watch her – his eyes narrowed, his arms crossed over his chest – as she'd struggled to tear toilet paper from the roll, clumsily wiped herself and then stood to pull up her knickers and jeans.

Neither of them spoke as she'd washed and dried her hands, but rage had been drumming against her chest bone, growing larger, more powerful, desperate for escape. She'd crossed the bathroom, chin up, shoulders back, hands clasped in front of her, and looked him in the eye. He'd filled the shape of the door frame, arms still crossed, feet wide, watching her. She'd moved closer, closer. He hadn't moved a muscle. He wasn't going to step back into the hallway to allow her to leave.

'Fuck you!' She'd raised her clasped hands and swung them like a hammer. Her fists had glanced off his chest, like a coin thrown at marble. 'I fucking hate you.' She'd hit him again and again, as images swirled through the whirlpool of her mind – the playground note, the closing blinds, Jada's revulsion, Helen Corry's face, the near-naked photos, the messages, the emails, the flowers, the house moves, the

212

motorbike, his coat, his face, his face, his face . . . She'd wanted to tear her nails through his skin; to rip the hair from his head; to strip him, shred him and reduce him to nothing; to tear up all she had lost. She'd driven her knee up between his legs, but he'd been too fast for her: he'd twisted away, one hand clasped around her bound wrists, the other twisted in her hair. He'd shoved her roughly into the bathroom then pushed her over the sink, so her nose was pressed against the mirror. He was breathing heavily, raggedly and quivering with rage. His fingers had tightened in her hair, and he'd yanked her head back sharply, forcing her to look at her reflection.

'Tell me why I shouldn't just smash your face into the mirror right now.'

Lucy had tensed, her thumbs sliding over the underside of the sink, her mind racing, her breaths coming in short, sharp gasps. There was nothing she could do to stop him. She couldn't overpower him, she couldn't argue with him, she couldn't plead with him. If he wanted to smash her face into the mirror, he would. If he wanted to kill her, he could. She'd rather be dead than scarred for the rest of her life, to wake each day and see his hatred etched into her skin.

'Just do it.' She'd closed her eyes, readying herself for the pain. Afterwards she'd find a way to kill herself; disappear somewhere he'd never be able to find her. If her only reason to live was to find a way to die, then so be it. She'd felt him tense behind her, his thighs pressed against her bottom, his breath quickened in her ear. She'd waited and she'd waited, certain that the moment she relaxed he'd throw her against the glass. What was he waiting for? For her to beg? To fight? To pretend she loved him?

Eventually she'd heard him sigh.

He'd pulled her away from the sink and pushed her towards the door, making her stumble. 'Unlike you, Lucy, I have some self-control. Anyway, let's get some breakfast now. I'll cook. You can entertain me with your sparkling conversation. French toast still your favourite? I thought we could snuggle up on the sofa afterwards; watch some Netflix or a film.'

He'd followed her down the stairs to the kitchen, only pausing his continuous stream of consciousness to say, 'That's where you respond, Lucy,' or 'Did you hear what I said?'

As they'd moved through the house Lucy had scanned her surroundings: all the windows were closed, presumably locked; the outer doors, the same. There were several ornaments dotted around on shelves and surfaces, all of them ceramic and twee, none of them capable of doing any damage unless she were able to smash them and use a jagged shard on Marcus's throat. A quick glance into the living room had revealed that he had removed the fire set – including the poker – from the fire surround. As she'd taken a seat at the long wooden table that ran the length of the kitchen, she'd noticed that he'd removed the knife block too. He'd prepped the cottage for this exact scenario; her abduction had been planned.

She'd watched as he'd taken a keyring from the pocket of his jeans, selected a key, then unlocked a metal box to the right of the Aga. He'd removed a bread knife, then locked the box and pocketed the key. He'd taken a floury loaf from the bread bin, sawn two identical slices, then washed and dried the knife, unlocked the box and returned the knife to it, locking it again before he returned the key to his jeans.

214

It was a meticulous process, accompanied by the smallest of smiles on his face.

'The secret to the very best French toast,' he had reached into a cupboard for a carton of eggs, 'is the freshest ingredients, and the hottest oil.'

That was six hours ago; the longest six hours of her life. Since then, she's endured two films (his favourite, *Dawn of the Planet of the Apes*, and hers, *La La Land*), five games of backgammon, several albums that he'd decided she 'had to hear' and several hours of a podcast about a missing teen in Texas. Earlier in the day Marcus was jumpy and hypervigilant, particularly as he cooked the French toast, but as the day has progressed, he seems to have settled into the fantasy land he's created, of them as infatuated lovers, having a lovely time at Granny's house. Earlier, when they were watching *La La Land* on the sofa, he'd pulled her closer, so she'd had to lean against him, and put an arm around her shoulders. He'd reached for her hand, tutted when the cable ties meant he couldn't weave her fingers through his, then reached into his pocket for some nail clippers and released the bonds on her wrists. She'd said nothing as the plastic fell away, and tried not to tense as he eased his fingers between hers. If he wanted to play at boyfriend and girlfriend, then she'd do the same. She'd play the role for as long as it took for his defences to drop; for him to trust her again, to completely lose himself in the fantasy.

Then she'd kill him.

They've only had two meals together and he's already become sloppy about locking the knife back in the box. It's been on the chopping board beside him for the last five minutes and he hasn't so much as glanced at it. She could risk it. She could cross the tiles in three or four steps, grab the knife and plunge it into his guts as the low-fat mince pops and sizzles in the pan. But if he grabs it first then every wretched, torturous minute of this everlasting day will have been wasted. She rubs at her wrists, still free of their restraints, then slides her fingers under her thighs. If she sits on them, she can't snatch the knife. She'll kill him eventually. Not now, but she will.

'That smells *lovely*.' She injects as much enthusiasm as she can into her voice. 'Are you using a pre-made sauce or are you making it from scratch?'

Marcus snorts loudly. 'Really?' He gestures at the individually potted herbs, lined up along the windowsill. 'You think I bought fresh oregano to use sauce from a jar?'

'Oh yeah.' She forces a laugh. 'I didn't see them there.'

Her gaze slides back toward the knife. She saw that though. She definitely noticed the knife.

216

Chapter 36

Alexandra

Two days until someone dies . . .

Alex taps her debit card against the electronic gates at Temple underground station then glances behind her to check she's not being followed. She's been running on adrenaline ever since she left the flat an hour ago. She jumped at car horns as she made her way to the station, then, as the train slowed at Monument, she saw a man on the platform who looked so like Colin Sutherland that her legs gave way beneath her. If she hadn't been gripping a pole she would have fallen where she stood. She used to think having a faceless stalker was torture; now she sees Sutherland's face everywhere she goes.

She turns off her phone as she exits the station. She's had three missed calls from Liz since she left the house, one from her agent and several texts from Sam, asking if they could talk. Only his texts make her heart ache. She nearly caved and rang him last night. She'd been sitting at her laptop for hours, knocking back red wine when a wave of loneliness crashed over her, so intense that she burst into tears. She'd walked out on the role of a lifetime and there was no one she could talk to about it. Not her parents, not her brother, not the FYST group and not Sam. Yes, there were acting friends she could call, and one or two friends from school, but they'd all tell her she was mad. They'd chastise her, tell her not to be so stupid, to get her arse back on stage. She wasn't sure she could explain why she'd done it, even if they did ask her why.

She hadn't called Sam. Instead, she'd splashed her face with cold water, made a pot of coffee, and sat down at her desk. Lucy hadn't told her much about Marcus but there was one detail that might help her find him: he'd asked in the gym if she was a teacher at St Paul's. A quick Google search revealed that it was a private boys' school in London. Another search, on Facebook, brought up the St Paul's alumni page. There was no way of searching the followers and a search for 'Marcus' on the main page revealed no results. Irritated, she'd returned to Google and typed 'Marcus St Paul's School London' and hit return. Result! Two Marcuses – Marcus Seymour and Marcus Wordsworth – had listed St Paul's as their school on LinkedIn. There was also a link to the Old Pauline News: an online magazine for alumni of the school. She'd clicked on the LinkedIn links first, neither of which had photos, but Marcus Seymour was forty-one years old. Marcus Wordsworth, on the other hand, was only twenty-one. He had to be the Marcus that she'd met at the gym. She'd tried social media next, searching Facebook,

Twitter, Instagram, TikTok and Snapchat. Nothing. He wasn't on any social media apps apart from Instagram and, even then, his profile was private.

She'd stared at the screen, knocked back a coffee, then rubbed her hands over her face. His LinkedIn profile hadn't been updated for years. The only job listed was a week's work experience somewhere called Hawthorne Law. A quick glance at their website revealed them to be a commercial law firm in London. She'd clicked on the 'Team members' link and her heart leapt as she scrolled through the page. Anthony Wordsworth, Partner. She'd only met Marcus once, but he *had* to be his father – she could see the similarity in the shape of the jaw and the wide-set eyes.

I've found Marcus's dad, she'd typed into the new WhatsApp group that was just her, Bridget and River. They all felt weird talking about Lucy in the other group, when she wasn't there. *I'm going to go and see him tomorrow. Find out where the fuck his son is. I think I'll get more out of him than a cop.*

A split second later Bridget had responded. *I'll come with you. Unless that's going to creep you out.*

Alex had groaned at the pointed comment. She really *didn't* want Bridget to go with her but agreeing was the only way to salvage their relationship. She'd hurt her, and she really didn't deserve it.

Alex isn't entirely sure why Bridget has come dressed like the Queen in a tweed jacket, frilly collared blouse, A-line skirt and pearls around her throat, but she's decided not to ask.

'Do we have an appointment?' Bridget asks as they walk

through Victoria Embankment Gardens and pass a memorial to someone called Lady Henry Somerset.

'Nope. But he's not in court. I rang to ask before I left.'

'Okay, well that's good. Do we just turn up and ask to speak to him? I've never visited a barrister before.'

'Me neither.'

'I imagine he's posh.'

'He probably is. I looked up the fees to go to St Paul's. Nearly ten grand a term. That sounds pretty posh to me.'

Bridget gives a low slow whistle and touches the pearls at her throat. 'Who can afford money like that?'

'Not anyone I know, that's for sure. It's a different world. Talking of which, how the hell did Lucy even meet him?'

Bridget presses against her as they swerve around a man throwing breadcrumbs into a crowd of frenzied pigeons. 'They met at her first teaching placement, Churchill Trinity.'

Alex glances at her, confused. 'I didn't know he was a teacher too'

'That's, um . . .' Bridget clears her throat lightly. 'That's the impression she gave me anyway.'

Alex side-eyes her. Why is she suddenly so uncomfortable? What is it that she knows? When Lucy arrived in a taxi from Bridget's she couldn't get a word out of her about Marcus. She made it pretty clear that he was the last person she wanted to talk about.

'He's younger than her,' she tells Bridget. 'Did you know that? I'd assumed he was older.'

'Did you? Can't say I've given it much thought.'

Something has shifted in the older woman's expression. She's hiding something, but Alex hasn't got the first clue what.

They continue to chat, making small talk about the weather, London, what they've watched on TV, until they reach Middle Temple Lane and draw to a halt.

'That's it there.' Alex gestures towards a large black door with a gold knocker in the shape of a lion's head. To the right is a gold plaque that reads *Hawthorne Law*.

Bridget rubs her palms on her tweed skirt. 'What do we do now? Go in together? Is there a receptionist we need to get past do you think?'

She isn't the only one who's nervous. Alex feels faintly ridiculous, standing outside a law firm in a trouser suit and heels.

'Okay.' She touches a hand to Bridget's shoulder. 'I've been thinking how best to do this all night and we need a two-pronged approach, just in case it fucks up. You should go in first – say you're a friend of Marcus's and you need to speak to Anthony because he's disappeared. Then—'

'A friend?' Bridget's eyebrows twitch upwards. 'Why would a twenty-whatever man be friends with a fifty-something woman?'

'Why not? Maybe you know him from work.'

'But we don't know what he does for a job.'

'Doesn't matter. I very much doubt the receptionist is going to give you the third degree.'

'But what if his father does? What if Marcus doesn't work? Or he does some kind of job that a woman my age would never do?'

Alex rolls back her shoulders and blows out her frustration with a short, sharp breath. Why is Bridget so anxious? She's normally more composed. Is it the posh setting that's freaking her out, or the pressure to find Lucy? Either way, she's making her feel more stressed than she did five minutes ago.

'Bridget, you're overthinking it. If he asks how you know Marcus say "work" and then move the subject on. We want to know where he could be. We don't—'

'But he's a barrister. They cross-examine people for a living.'

Alex presses a hand to her forehead. 'Right, we're scrapping Plan A and going straight to Plan B. You wait here. I'll go in.'

'Are you sure?' Bridget looks up and down the street as though expecting an army of barristers in black capes and white wigs to jump out at her.

'Or in the park. Wherever you want, wherever you feel most comfortable.'

'I'll wait at the end of the street. Then it won't look suspicious if he glances out of his window.'

Alex fights very hard not to roll her eyes. What's she expecting to happen? For Anthony Wordsworth to chase her down the street with a baseball bat? For the police to arrive?

'That'll be fine,' she says, squeezing Bridget's hand. 'I'm going in now. Okay?'

The reception area of Hawthorne Law is exactly as Alex imagined it: dark, understated, elegant and absolutely stinking of class and wealth. The receptionist, a pretty, young blonde with her hair tied back in a ponytail, in a white shirt and black suit, looks up from her laptop and smiles.

'Good morning. How can I help you?'

Alex approaches the desk. In her mind she's a powerful female CEO of a human rights charity and she's come to see Anthony Wordsworth about suing the arse off . . . oh god, what was her cover story? Oh yeah. Suing a bank for mis-selling her company a one-million-pound loan (she found a similar story in the *Evening Standard* last night).

She returns the receptionist's smile.

'Hi, I'm Imogen Goldmann-Harding, to see Anthony Wordsworth.'

A frown creases the receptionist's otherwise line-free brow. 'Oh. I wasn't aware that Anthony had any meetings pencilled in for this morning. One moment please.'

Alex waits, hands gathered loosely in front of her, as the receptionist taps away at her keyboard, frown deepening. 'I'm afraid I don't have anything in the diary.'

'No, no, sorry, crossed wires.' Alex laughs lightly, the sort of tinkling non-threatening laughter she hopes will put the other woman at ease. 'I don't have an appointment. I rang earlier to check he was in and thought I'd pop in on the off-chance he could see me. Imogen Goldmann-Harding from Liberty, the human rights organisation. It's about a mis-sold loan.'

'Oh. Okay. Sure.' Indecision is written all over the receptionist's face, but she picks up the phone anyway. 'Hi Anthony. I've got an Imogen Goldmann-Harding from Liberty here, about a mis-sold loan. Are you available to talk to her?'

Alex holds herself very still, a half-smile fixed to her face. He *must* agree to see her. There is no plan C.

'Umm . . . yes, yes I know.' The receptionist's gaze flits in Alex's direction. 'Oh. Really? Ten minutes. Oh, okay then. I'll send her up. Thanks Anthony, bye.'

Inside Alex does somersaults. He's agreed to see her. Fucking YES. Outwardly she widens her smile.

'He can give you ten minutes,' the receptionist says. 'If you take the door to the left there, it's up the first set of stairs and his office is on the left.'

'Wonderful. Thank you so much.'

Alex takes the stairs one at a time. Winning over the receptionist was the easy bit. There's a reason Marcus is such an arsehole, and she wouldn't be the slightest bit surprised if the apple hadn't fallen far from the tree.

She steels herself as she taps on Anthony Wordsworth's door then takes a short sharp breath as he shouts, 'Come!' and walks inside.

Anthony Wordsworth looks just like his photo on the law firm website, other than a few additional grey hairs at his temples and about thirty pounds. He's dressed in an expensive navy-blue suit with a white shirt, white handkerchief in his breast pocket, and a tastefully swirled navy and purple tie. He's in his late forties or early fifties with a handsome but lived-in face, a wry expression and a slow, sardonic smile.

'Imogen.' He rises and holds out a thick hand.

'Anthony, thank you for seeing me.'

'No problem. Sit. Please.' He gestures at a plump leather chair. 'What can I do you for? A loan, was it? Mis-sold? By whom?'

He pulls a notebook closer and reaches for a pen. The nib hovers over the page as he leans his weight into the desk.

Alex shifts in her seat. This is the part she's been dreading; the bit she rehearsed over and over again last night.

'I'm afraid I'm here under false pretences.' She shoots him what she hopes is a winning smile. 'I assumed it would be the only way you'd agree to see me.'

Anthony Wordsworth pushes his chair away from the desk. 'Oh yes?'

'It's about your son, Marcus.'

'Oh for fuck's sake. What's he done now?'

'Do you know where he is?'

He laughs hollowly. 'God knows. He's a law unto himself.'

'He doesn't live with you then?'

She can see the faces of the four people in the silver-framed photograph on Anthony's desk. It's him, a very attractive blonde woman, and two young children, both with white-blonde, curly hair.

'Is that Marcus?'

'No.' He reaches for the photograph and turns it face down. 'What's this all about?'

'Marcus. We think he's kidnapped his ex-girlfriend, Lucy Newton.'

A guffaw explodes from Wordsworth's mouth. 'Kidnapped? Fuck off. The boy's an idiot but that . . .' he shakes his head. 'No. Absolutely not.' As his laughter fades away the mood shifts, and he looks at Alex through narrowed eyes. 'Who are you anyway?'

'Alexandra Raynor. I'm a friend of Lucy's. Have you met her?'

'Lucy who?' He laughs. 'I haven't met any of his girlfriends. Although he was caught snorting cocaine off some brunette's tits at St Paul's. Whether she was a girlfriend or not – who cares. To be honest with you, Miss Raynor, my son and I live very separate lives. He's been living on his own in a studio flat in Walthamstow since he was sixteen. Quite the fall from grace.' He watches her carefully, looking for disapproval or judgement. 'I thought he'd grow up if I sent

225

him to a comp and made him stand on his own two feet. That was a mistake. I had to withdraw him and send him to rehab. He didn't even sit his A Levels, bloody twat. He insisted on going back for the leaver's party though. "Oh, hey guys. I've been to rehab. Aren't I cool?"'

'Do you know where he might be?' Alex asks.

'Not a clue. He'll be in touch when he needs money, I assume.'

Alex takes her phone out of her pocket. 'Could you give me the address? Of his flat?'

'Nope.' He looks at his watch.

Alex's breathing quickens. Anthony Wordsworth is their only connection to Marcus. If he won't tell her where he is they'll never find Lucy. 'Please, it's important. We think he'll harm Lucy if we don't find them soon. You have to tell me where he is.'

'No, I don't.' He stands, opens the door and looks at her expectantly. 'I'd like you to leave now, before I call the police.'

'Please.' Alex hates herself for begging, even as she says the word. 'Don't tell him that I've been here.' She leans over the desk and scribbles on his notepad with his pen. 'My number. If you change your mind about speaking to me, then—'

'Don't make me ask again.'

'Okay. Okay.' She smooths down her skirt and runs a hand over her hair. She could beg him all day and he still wouldn't tell her what she needs to know. It's been one massive waste of time.

Chapter 37

WhatsApp group: Find Lucy

11.46
River: Alex and Bridget, how did you get on with Marcus's dad?

Alexandra: Not great, he told me fuck all then kicked me out. All I got out of him was that Marcus was expelled from private school for snorting cocaine, then he was kicked out from home too. Lived on his own and was sent to a comp. Bridget told me Lucy met him at Churchill Trinity. I'd assumed he was a teacher but now I'm wondering if he was a pupil. Given the fact he's younger than her the timing sounds about right.

River: SHIT. No. You think he was her student?

Alexandra: I'm pretty sure I'm right.

River: I really hope you're wrong, but the name of the school might help us track them down. By the way, have you or Sam got the rock?

Alexandra: The one from Highgate Wood? No, I thought you had it.

River: Are you sure Sam hasn't got it?

Alexandra: I don't think so, but I'll text him and ask.

River: Thanks, we need it as evidence. Have you heard from Bridget?

Alexandra: Not since we said goodbye earlier. Have you heard back from the police?

River: Nothing. And at 6 p.m. tonight it'll be 48 hours since Lucy disappeared. I've got a lead though. I did a deep-dive search on Marcus, found a forum for musicians and a post from him looking for a replacement drummer for his band. They're called The Disciples of London, he's the bassist, and they're playing tonight!

Alexandra: We've got to go.

River: Won't he recognise you from the gym?

Alexandra: Have you ever been on stage? You can't see anything beyond the edge of the stage, never mind individual faces in the audience. But I get it ~ if we follow him home, or whatever, we can't be spotted. I've got a wig that should help. Don't worry, River. I'm not going to fuck this up if it's going to help us find Lucy.

River: Okay, fair enough. They're playing at a pub in Camden. I'll send you the address. Doors open at 7pm.

Alexandra: I'll see you there.

Chapter 38

Lucy

Two days until someone dies . . .

Lucy sits up abruptly. Marcus does the same. They'd both been curled under blankets on the sofa – Lucy at one end, Marcus at the other – when a sound neither of them has heard since they arrived cuts through the sound of the TV.

Lucy hadn't been paying attention to the film anyway; her mind had drifted ages ago. She was thinking about what she'd do after she killed Marcus: take the car – the fob was in the pocket of his jeans along with the other keys he hefted around – then drive back to her flat and grab her passport. Everything else she needed was in a suitcase in the boot of the car.

A phone is ringing somewhere in the house. She looks around the room, trying to locate the source of the sound.

Has someone realised that she's missing? Have they

managed to track her down? Forty-two hours have passed since Marcus ambushed and kidnapped her and, while she wouldn't expect the school, her parents or her friends to have noticed her disappearance yet, she's pretty sure the WhatsApp group will have. But would they have reported her missing? She's told them time and time again that she doesn't want the police involved, but they know Marcus has tracked her down. They'll be worried, she knows that for sure.

Marcus gets up from the sofa and retrieves a landline from under a sideboard on the other side of the room.

'Hello?' He holds the phone to his ear.

His expression changes from suspicious to pissed-off as the person on the other end of the line responds.

'That's fucking bullshit.' He spits the words into the phone. 'Whoever this Alexandra person is, she's a lying bitch.'

Lucy goes cold. Alexandra? Her Alexandra? What has she done?

'Of course I haven't kidnapped someone,' Marcus continues. 'I don't even know a Lucy. Dad, I think you've been played. You—'

His top lip retracts as he's interrupted, and his free hand curls into a fist.

'My phone's out of battery, okay? And I haven't got my charger. I came up to Granny's cottage because I'm going through some shit right now – not that you'd know because you never fucking call me. No. I won't keep my voice down. This is fucking typical of you. You always assume the worst about me, always—'

'Come up here and check then! Or kick me out. Send me

back to what is essentially a minute, basic prison cell while you and your new family live in the house that used to be—'

'Fuck you! I'm not having this conversation any more.' He jabs at the handset then hurls it away. It arcs through the air, hits the fireplace and smashes onto the rug in pieces. Lucy stares at them for a second then jumps up and gathers the shards of plastic into a pile.

'Leave it!' Marcus grabs her by the wrist and pulls her to her feet.

She stumbles after him as he drags her towards the bedroom. 'Marcus, let's talk about this. I could help. I could ring your dad and tell him that I've got no idea what all this is about, that—'

She cries out in shock as he shoves her onto the bed. She lands on her stomach, arms splayed.

'He's got no idea who you are. No one does.' He heads for the dresser, opens a drawer and pulls out a handful of cable ties. 'I could kill you now and no one would know.'

'Marcus, please.' Lucy flips onto her back and scrambles off the bed. Her heart's beating so quickly she feels unsteady on her feet. 'You don't have to do this. We could still make things work. If we think . . . if we go back to when we were happy . . . we can . . . we can put all this behind us.' She reaches out and touches his cheek. For a split second he softens, then his eyes darken, and he pushes her – hard – so she tumbles back onto the bed.

'Stop fucking talking.'

She doesn't struggle as he cable-ties her wrists and ankles and attaches them to the bed. Instead, she keeps her gaze lowered and counts her breaths to slow her pulse. She's still counting as the bedroom door slams shut and pounding rock music fills the house.

She was so close. If Marcus had let her touch him for more than a second, she would have pulled the pointed shard of plastic from the waistband of her jeans and stabbed him in the neck.

Chapter 39

River

Two days until someone dies . . .

River stares at his laptop screen then takes off his glasses and rubs his eyes. He's been trying to respect Meg's wish to give her some space but he can't stop himself from worrying. He's barely slept since Vanessa made a threat to kill her, and he rushed home from the salsa class to find her gone. He'd texted her, telling her about the threat, then, when she didn't reply, he'd begged her to just let him know that she was still alive. Five words appeared on his screen in response:

I'm alive, River. Stop worrying.

The whole of Tuesday, he'd monitored Meg's WhatsApp. She'd logged on at 6.05 a.m. That was good; Vanessa didn't know where she was, and she'd survived the night. But would she be safe at work? He held off on texting her until 9.22 p.m., by which time her shift would definitely have ended.

Please tell me that you're at your friend's house and you're safe.

She made him sweat for a whole ten minutes then replied briefly:

I'm fine, River. I'm safe. I'm with Emily, but I need to come round to collect my stuff soon. Don't reply, PLEASE. I'll send you another message, telling you when.

The compulsion to respond was more than he could bear. Instead, he selected the broken-hearted icon as a response to the message, then swiftly changed it to a thumbs up instead. He could still save their relationship but that was something he'd have to do in person, not by text.

He's suffered nearly forty-eight hours of torture and the detective in charge of his case still hasn't rung him back. He's due to go and see the Disciples of London with Alex in a few hours' time but, instead of getting on with his work, he's googling Bridget Hopkins. It's stopping him from repeatedly texting Meg, at least.

Something Bridget said has been bothering him for a while. At Natalie's funeral, when the wreath was delivered, three of them had freaked out because the date was significant. Alex's play was debuting, Lucy was due to attend her parents' wedding anniversary dinner, and it was Bridget's birthday; at least that's what she'd said. She'd also claimed, in a WhatsApp conversation with him about Charlotte's salsa class, that she went to see *Strictly Come Dancing* for her birthday. He's read the exchange several times and it's there in black and white:

I'm terrible at dancing too. The nearest I've got to tripping the light fantastic was watching the Strictly tour for my birthday.

235

He's looked it up online and the *Strictly Come Dancing* tour runs from late January until mid-February. It doesn't, and has never, taken place in October. Either Bridget lied about her birthday being the twentieth of October or she lied about going to watch the *Strictly* tour. She also lied about leaving her job after Charlotte tracked her down. He rang the florist where she works half an hour ago and the guy who answered said she's taken a few days off; she definitely hasn't left.

He's done a deep-dive search for her online and found . . . NOTHING. Absolutely nothing. There are Bridget Hopkins scattered all over the globe, but he hasn't found a single one who could be her – not on Facebook; not on LinkedIn; nowhere. Either she's lied about her last name, she's never used social media, or she's managed to completely hide her internet footprint to stay one step ahead of Charlotte, but she doesn't seem tech savvy enough for that.

He picks up his phone, running his teeth over his bottom lip as he re-reads the text that Florian sent asking if he could pass his number on to Charlotte. Two days ago, he replied with a definitive no, but there are questions he needs answered and he's got a feeling that Charlotte might be able to help. He doesn't want to give her his number though. He's got one stalker already; he really doesn't need two. At Natalie's funeral Bridget mentioned that Charlotte was a colleague at the last florist shop she worked at.

His thumbs fly over the screen as he taps out a reply to Florian: *I don't suppose you know the name of the florists that Charlotte works for? I said I'd use them to send my mum some flowers.*

It's a lie of course. Charlotte didn't tell him anything about

236

her job – she was too busy trying to hold his hands and stick her tongue down his throat – but if Florian does know where she works then he'll be able to pop in and speak to her about Bridget. There are two advantages to this approach. One: she will be at work, so she'll have to act professionally. Two: she'll be sober.

River squeezes his way into the packed pub and makes his way to the bar, craning his neck for any sign of Alex. He looks automatically for wild curly hair and it takes him a while before he spots the slim bespectacled woman with a sleek brown bob standing over by the window, with her back to the wall. As their eyes meet, he makes a 'want a drink?' gesture and she nods. Ten minutes later he makes his way through the crowd towards Alex, a bottle of beer in each hand.

Her cheeks are flushed, her eyes glazed, and when she smiles her grin is wide and lopsided.

'You okay?' he asks.

'Yeah, yeah, fine.' She takes one of the bottles and pulls him into a clumsy one-armed hug.

He hugs her back then looks into her face. 'Have a couple at home before you came out, did you?'

She raises her gaze to the ceiling and blinks rapidly, as though she's trying to stop herself from crying, and when she looks back at him there's a vulnerability behind her eyes that he hasn't seen before.

'What is it?' he asks. 'What's happened?'

'You mean other than the fact we've got forty-eight hours until one of us dies?' She takes a slug of beer.

He watches her, frowning. He's never seen Alex like this – drunk, emotional, unstable – and he doesn't like it. He finds comfort in predictability, solidity and routine; it's part of the reason he loves Meg so much, because she doesn't swing wildly from one emotional state to another. She's sensible and grounded and her behaviour never wavers from its set path. If he surprises her with flowers she'll smile, hug him and put them in water. If they have an argument she'll storm off to the next room, calm down, then return to talk it through with him. She gets drunk, of course she does, but even that's predictable – she'll get louder and louder, probably burst into song, and hug everyone in the vicinity and tell them she loves them.

Drunken Alex, on the other hand, is an unknown quantity. When so much rests on finding where Marcus is keeping Lucy, he's already regretting telling Alex about the band.

'Are you sure you want to do this?' he asks. 'We could get you a cab?'

'Are you fucking kidding me? Absolutely not. Let's go and find the band.'

He follows her through the crowd towards the thumping bassline at the back of the pub, desperately wishing he had Samuel's number so he could ring him to come and pick her up.

'Hey! Annalise! What the fuck are you doing here?'

Alex jerks to a stop, forcing River to do the same. A short, stocky bloke in his twenties, with a blue fringe and a septum piercing, is pulling on her arm.

'I don't know what you're talking about.' Her tone is bored and weary.

'Mate, mate!' Still keeping hold of her arm, Blue-Fringe slaps one of his friends on the back. 'Look who's here to see The Disciples of London. Mate, mate look!'

'Excuse me.' River reaches across Alex and plucks at the man's hand. 'We have somewhere to be.'

'Fuck! You're right. I almost didn't recognise her with the glasses and the hair.' Now a tall, angular man, barely out of his teens, is gawping at Alex. 'Oh my god. My mum loves that show. Can we get a selfie?'

'No,' River says at the same time as Alex says, 'Fine.'

He lets go of her arm as she turns to have her photo taken. The angular teen thrusts his phone at a girl with heavy black eye make-up, then he and his friend stand either side of Alex. A muscle twitches in River's cheeks as they lean into her. She isn't the only one who's drunk.

'Hey!' she says as Angular slings his arm around her shoulders. She shifts her weight to try and shake him off, but he tightens his grip.

'Chill out, Annalise,' Blue-Fringe slips an arm around her waist. 'It's only a photo. Someone buy this woman a drink.'

'That's not my name,' Alex says from between gritted teeth as she pulls at his fingers. River moves closer, ready to step in. He knows she's perfectly capable of looking after herself, but not when she's drunk, and these guys are taking the piss.

'Smile!' says the girl with the phone. She snaps a photo then looks at the screen and wrinkles her nose. 'She's got her eyes closed.'

'Take it again,' says Blue-Fringe, 'and move back a bit. You're too close.'

The girl takes a step backwards and knocks into a guy with long dark hair and ripped jeans. He whips round, irritated, then spots Alex.

'Fuck me, it's you! Hey guys . . .' he turns back to his

mates and gestures over his shoulder with his thumb. 'You'll never guess—'

'That's it. We're done.' As Alex tries to pull away from Blue-Fringe and Angular, River catches a note of panic in her voice.

'No, wait!'

'The photo's shit, you were all moving.'

'No, no, no, Annalise. Don't go!'

There's a chorus of disapproval as Alex tries to get away, then a yelp of surprise as she elbows Angular in the side. As his arm slips from her shoulders, she signals to River with her eyes: *Let's get out of here, now!* He doesn't hesitate. He grabs her by the hand and shoulders his way through the crowd, as shouts of 'Bitch!' 'Stuck up' and 'Celebrity twat' follow them out of the bar and into the room at the back. He finds a tiny pocket of space – the corner of a wall that hasn't been claimed – near the female toilets and turns to check on Alex, still holding tightly onto his hand.

'Are you okay?' he shouts over the boom of the music. 'Should I call you an Uber?'

She stares back at him, incredulous. 'You think those twats scared me off?' She gives him a shove. 'Come on, the band are on stage.'

The music is exactly the kind of guitar-heavy, shoegazing, overly stylised crap that River can't stand but the crowd seem to love it. Everywhere he looks people his age and younger are bouncing, singing, dancing and pounding the air with their fists. For an unsigned band still playing back rooms in pubs they seem to have a dedicated following. On stage the singer, a slim-hipped guy in skinny jeans, is gripping the microphone and staring dolefully into the crowd as he sings about the end of a relationship feeling like surgery without the good drugs. Begrudgingly, River can relate.

He leans over to Alex, who's drunkenly swaying and repeatedly closing her eyes. 'Where's Marcus?'

She shakes her head then shouts in his ear. 'Not here! Some other bloke's playing bass.'

River swears under his breath. This is worse than he thought. The fact Marcus isn't on stage suggests he's either been kicked out of the band since his online post or he's disappeared with Lucy. If it's the latter they need to find him, and quickly.

'I think we should wait until the end of the gig and try to talk to the band.'

'What?' Alex pulls a face. 'Wait until what?'

He cups his hands over his mouth and leans closer. 'Wait until the end then talk to the band. They might know where he is.'

She nods enthusiastically then mimes going to get another drink.

'Are you sure about that?' River says. 'We might run into—'

But Alex is already squeezing past him, heading towards the door.

He's got no choice but to follow her.

'Four?' he says after she shouts her order to the barman. 'We don't need two each. I wasn't even going to have one.'

'Then I'll drink them!' She side-eyes him, grins, then grabs the closest bottle, raises it to her mouth and drains it in three or four gulps. 'One.' She sets it down and picks up the second.

River reaches for the bottle as she raises it to her lips. 'I really think you've—'

'Don't.' She shoots him a warning look then takes a swig.

'Oh, look who it is! The Z-list celeb.'

River hears them coming before he sees them. Blue-Fringe, Angular, the girl, and two other guys who'd make millennium-era Pete Doherty look well-groomed and healthy, are heading towards the bar.

'Fuck off.' Alex turns her back to them and raises the bottle to her mouth.

'Think you're too special to talk to us, do you?' Angular bumps her back with his elbow – a hard, deliberate prod – and the bottle clinks against Alex's teeth.

'Hey!' River lunges towards him and gives him a shove. 'Leave her alone.'

Angular is taller and heavier than River, but he's also drunk, and he has to grab hold of the edge of the bar to stop himself from falling backwards. His friends shout a collective 'Wooooah!'

'Who the fuck are you?' Angular asks as he straightens himself back up again. 'Her sugar baby? Or her really shit minder?'

Alex spins around and shoves him hard in the chest. 'Who are you calling a cougar, you twat?'

Angular stumbles backwards, into the girl and Blue-Fringe.

'Take a selfie of that!' Alex shouts, then before River knows what's going on, she grabs him by the hand and heads for the door.

*

Hand in hand they stumble for fifty, maybe sixty metres, then Alex yanks River into a side alley and pulls him to the ground behind a large metal skip. She presses a hand over her mouth, shaking and squeaking as she tries, and fails to stop herself from laughing as River hovers beside her and peels a piece of newspaper (coated in god-knows-what) from the sole of his shoe. He peers around the side of the skip scanning the passersby for anyone with a blue fringe, scruffy clothes, an angular frame or a pissed-off expression. Given they're in the heart of Camden, he spots four people who fit the bill in as many seconds, but none of them are the blue-haired, scraggy-looking gig-goers they just escaped from, and he rocks back on his heels and sighs with relief.

'We can't just sit here!' Alex thumps the skip with her fist, making River jump. 'We need to go back there, talk to the band. They'll know where Marcus lives.'

'I don't think—' River breaks off as his phone vibrates 'Hang on, I need to check this.'

Please be Meg, he silently wishes as he slips his mobile out of his pocket. He's been giving her the space that she asked for. He hasn't chased or cajoled her, but it's been two days since she left, and he's desperate to hear her voice. But it's not a voice note from his girlfriend, it's a missed call notification from Bridget, and a reply from Florian. He clicks on the message, his stomach tight.

Charlotte – a florist? Florian has written. *I don't know where you got that idea. She's a comedian, does stand up, adverts, that sort of thing.*

'What is it?' Alex cranes her neck to look at the screen then sneezes, loudly, five times in a row. River angles his

243

phone away. Earlier, at the bar, he'd nearly shared his concerns about Bridget with her, but now is not the right time. He needs to know exactly what he's dealing with before he stirs that pot.

Give Charlotte my number, he types back to Florian. *I need to talk to her asap.*

As he hits send, a shadow falls across his face.

Bridget looms over them. 'What on earth's going on here?'

Chapter 40

Bridget

Two days until someone dies . . .

It was never part of Bridget's plan to make an impromptu trip to Camden and squeeze her way through a crowded underground station in search of a hot and smelly dive bar. After the morning's trip to Temple, she'd shepherded Alex into a black cab in case Colin Sutherland was lying in wait in the park, checked her app to ensure Charlotte wasn't near, then taken herself off to WH Smiths and bought a notepad and pen. She'd found a café, ordered a cappuccino and a Danish pastry and opened her new notebook. There was something about the anonymity of the situation that made her breathing deepen and her heart rate slow. Eight days had passed since Natalie's funeral, but so much had happened it had felt like eight weeks. There was so much noise in Bridget's brain, so many thoughts clamouring for attention, so much worry, so much fear. The moment she'd quietened her own internal dialogue, River or Alex would message her and their voices would fill her brain, making her absorb all their fears and worries too. It was too much. There were some days when she felt like her head might explode.

She'd put the pen to the notebook and underlined two headings: 'Lucy' and 'Marcus', then wrote down everything she knew about them. She'd always written lists: everything from holiday packing lists to shopping lists to Christmas present lists to 'to do' lists. She'd even written them as a child, compiling an inventory of her books complete with location and date (if borrowed by a friend) so she knew exactly where each one was. Lists made an out-of-control world feel less terrifying.

Only as she'd put pen to paper did she realise quite how little she knew about Lucy, and even less about Marcus. Why hadn't she asked Lucy more about herself when the young woman had sought refuge in her home? Why had she escaped to the kitchen for wine and reprieve after Lucy had made her confession? If she'd been calmer, reacted non-judgementally, she might know where she was now.

After an hour in the coffee shop Bridget had returned home downhearted, made a late lunch and flicked between TV shows, unable to concentrate on any of them. It had made her want to cry, not knowing where Lucy was or what was happening to her. River and Alex seemed to think that they had forty-eight hours to rescue her, but there was every chance she might already be dead. Bridget had drowned the thought from her mind by going into the kitchen and turning on the radio, ear-piercingly loud. She couldn't just sit around doing nothing, so she did what she always did when she was stressed – she baked.

When Gary returned from work, they'd had dinner (together, unusually) in the living room with trays on their laps. She knew not to push him to talk, or he'd only escape to the spare room again, and took comfort in the fact that she knew where he was and what he was doing. After dinner she'd served him a huge slice of frosted carrot cake, beamed when he commented on how good it was then watched, dejected, as he returned to his room.

She'd remained on the sofa, the foam-filled seat beside her slowly reinflating, filling the indent Gary's backside had left behind, and checked her phone. There'd been no update to the WhatsApp group since the morning when River and Alex had arranged to see Marcus's band. It was frustrating, not knowing exactly what was going on. She'd opened the tracking app: one triangle showed Gary in their flat, another showed Charlotte in a bar in Soho and the third triangle – her brow wrinkled in confusion – that wasn't at all where she'd expected it to be.

She'd purchased the extra tracker four days ago, a couple of hours after the meeting in Highgate Wood.

Not wanting to arouse suspicion, she hadn't asked River where he'd bought the trackers, and she'd googled instead. There were several shops in London that sold spyware, drones and trackers, but the only one that sold the same make and model was in Walthamstow.

It was an unassuming little place, wedged between a vape shop and an off-licence. You couldn't peer through the window because a black curtain framed the display of drones, doorbell cameras and voice recorders. But once she'd stepped inside, her eyes were opened to a whole new world. Lining the shelves, lit up with spotlights to cut through the gloom, were mains sockets, extension leads, and computer mice that were actually listening devices; USB pens and tiny black gadgets the size of paperclips that were audio voice recorders; clothes hooks and smoke alarms with hidden cameras and motion detectors; even a voice-activated pen. There were also, for the more paranoid shopper, bugs and hidden camera detectors that fitted into the palm of the hand. Bridget had wandered from shelf to shelf open-mouthed. She'd never seen anything quite like it in her life. It was Disney World for stalkers, a spyware utopia for a cheating partner's spouse. Looking around, she couldn't believe that River hadn't bought more. If, somehow, he'd managed to get a listening device into Vanessa's house or her car he might have known what she was planning as well as where she was; forewarned as well as forearmed.

She'd paused beside a listening device, deliberating. If she bought one, would it actually be useful? If she put it in a pocket how much would it actually pick up – street noise, the rumble of trains, footsteps, someone clearing their throat? She'd have to listen to an awful lot of nothing much to catch anything interesting. A camera would be better; but did she really need to see everything?

No – she'd shaken her head decisively – a tracker was all that she needed. For now, at least; she could always come back.

She'd paid at the counter, tucked the plain black plastic bag into her handbag, and left.

*

248

Fields? Tracks? Where the hell had London gone? She'd pinched at the screen, pulling the view further out until a place name appeared. Chagford? Where the hell was that? Dartmoor National Park. Dartmoor? That was in Devon. What the hell was going on?

She'd flicked out of the app and returned to WhatsApp. There it was, in the 'Find Lucy' chat, the conversation between River and Alex, discussing going to see a band in Camden. So why was the app showing Devon? Either Alex had lied about going to see the band or something unusual had happened since.

Where are you? she'd tapped out, then waited for the ticks to appear. One tick appeared but not two. It hadn't been read. Or had it? Maybe River had read it, but not Alex. Or vice-versa.

Bridget had called River, first on WhatsApp, then when there was no answer, she'd tried a normal call. It had gone straight to voicemail.

'River?' She'd scrabbled to find the right words. 'Just wondering, are you and Alex still watching the band?'

She'd perched on the edge of the sofa, bewildered and scared. What should she do? Go and check up on them? Sit it out and wait? She'd re-opened the app and looked at the small red triangle in the middle of Dartmoor. Either the app had malfunctioned, or Alex had upped and gone to Devon for no reason that she could discern.

She'd stood up, suddenly decisive. There was only one way to find out.

Now, as Bridget stands beside the skip, looking down at River and Alex, she tries not to show her confusion. Five minutes ago, as she'd trawled through the music venue trying to find them, she'd become convinced that the WhatsApp conversation about the band had been faked to throw her off the scent. What the scent was, she wasn't entirely sure, but she didn't like being lied to, or left out.

She wasn't bullied at school, but she was always a tagger-on, rather than the heart of any friendship group. If her classmates were asked by the teacher to form groups of three or four, no one shifted their chairs closer to hers or desperately clutched at her arm. No one called out her name – 'Bridget! Bridget! Over here!' She was sidelined and ignored, forced to form a reject group with the other dregs and outcasts while the girls she thought of as friends gathered together, giggling, oblivious to her miserable face.

As she'd wandered through the pub, wincing at the pounding bassline and the discordant guitars as she wound her way through the packed crowd, she'd texted the group. I'm in the venue. Where are you guys? Still no reply. There was no sign of them anywhere. River would have been hard to pick out: Bridget was surrounded by rangy bespectacled men; but Alex should have been easy to find with her loud leopard-print coat, though she had no idea what her wig looked like. They'd either been and left, or they hadn't turned up at all. Despairing and disappointed, she'd wandered back onto the street, scanning the faces of the pedestrians in both directions before she headed back towards the tube. Five loud, echoing sneezes had made her pause as she passed an alleyway. Slowly, tentatively, she'd headed towards the skip. There was every chance that danger lay behind the large metal bin – a wired drug addict, a desperate alcoholic or two, or someone doing something that would make her feel sick – but she'd heard Alex sneeze before, five times in succession in the cold morning air of Highgate Wood. Devon or no Devon, she wouldn't sleep that night if she didn't check it was her.

And lo and behold, there they are – Alex and River – crouched behind the skip like two grown-up children playing hide and seek. Hiding from someone else, or from her?

'Fuck, Bridget! We thought you were them.' Alex scrambles to her feet, wobbles and presses a hand to the wall to steady herself.

'Thought I was who?' Bridget's gaze slides towards River. While Alex is obviously drunk, River looks altogether more sober.

'Just some idiots who had a go at Alex in the bar.' River stands up too and dusts himself off. 'Marcus wasn't playing.'

'I know,' Bridget says. 'I went in.'

'Why are you here?' River asks bluntly.

'I was—' Bridget begins, then breaks off as she looks Alex up and down, from her wild curly hair to the wig in her hand, to her grey bomber jacket, skinny jeans, high-heeled maroon boots, then back to the jacket. She's not wearing the leopard-print coat. She wasn't wearing it that morning either, when they went to see Anthony Wordsworth, but she'd assumed it was because she was wearing a smart suit and the leopard print would have looked gauche. She'd assumed the coat was her favourite – she'd worn it to Highgate Wood, to the restaurant with Sam, then left it in her van en route to Marcus's gym. Bridget had returned it to her, via Lucy, the evening that Marcus turned up on her street.

'Where's your coat, Alex?' she asks, her stomach tightening. 'The um . . . the lovely leopard-print one?'

Alex, who's been staring past her to the street, her eyes dulled with alcohol, turns her head sharply. 'What are you on about?'

'Guys,' River says. 'I think maybe you two should head home and I'll go back to the venue to see if I can talk to the band.'

Bridget ignores him. 'Your leopardskin coat, Alex. Where is it?'

'Probably in Lucy's flat. I lent it to her after she stayed at mine.'

'Was she wearing it?' Bridget asks, her urgent tone attracting a curious glance from River. 'On the day she disappeared?'

'I don't know.'

'Why does it matter?' River asks.

Bridget hesitates, unsure what to say next. The truth is, after she'd dropped Alex off near Marcus's gym, she'd driven straight home with Alex's coat then spent an hour in the bathroom carefully pulling apart the fraying seams of the coat's lining so she could slip a tracker inside. She'd planned on giving the coat back to Alex the next day, but when Lucy said she was heading over there, she'd given it to her instead.

There's only one reason the tracker is showing a Devon location – that's where the coat is. And if the coat's in Dartmoor, maybe Lucy is too.

'Bridget?' River says. 'Is everything okay?'

A hard, tight knot forms in Bridget's stomach. This is where she tells them she knows where Lucy is, when she rallies the troops so they can rescue her. But telling them would mean revealing her secret. The moment she confesses that she's been tracking Alex: all the trust, all the friendship,

252

all the camaraderie she's worked so hard to cultivate over the last few months would vanish in an instant. Alex would never talk to her again.

Save Lucy or save herself? There must be a way to do both, but it's going to need some thought.

'Bridget!' River says again, louder this time. 'What's going on?'

'Nothing.' She forces a smile. 'It was a nice coat. That's all.'

Chapter 41

Alexandra

Two days until someone dies . . .

There's someone in her flat. Alex presses a hand to the wall of the shared hallway, steadying herself, and listens at the door. She'd been thinking about River and Bridget until she heard noises from inside.

The mood in the alleyway had switched suddenly after Bridget had arrived. She'd stared down at them – like a small, cuddly batman in her long dark coat and her beanie with two pom-poms sewn to the top like spherical ears – while River had eyed her nervously. When he'd asked her why she'd changed her mind about an early night she'd mumbled something about the group sticking together, then flushed red from the base of her neck to her cheeks.

'What was that all about?' Alex had asked River as he bundled her into a black cab. 'Bridget just turning up like that?'

He gave a little shrug. 'Maybe she's lonely.' But he didn't meet her eyes.

Now she touches her hand to the door handle, then hesitates. It's exactly the kind of brainless move someone in a horror film would make – creep inside, get clubbed to death by a stalker and left in a pool of her own blood. But what's the alternative? Call the police? Call River? She's drunk, but not so drunk she can't run if she needs to. There have been no sightings of Sutherland since the police station: not by Bridget, nor by her. Has he been biding his time? Waiting for her to leave the flat so he could sneak inside? He's not planning on killing her until the twentieth so what's he doing? Trashing the place? Scrawling a message on her mirror? Telling her what a worthless, untalented piece of crap she is? What a slut, what a liar, what a fake?

It was your fault.

Rage sparks in her belly at the memory, and booze makes her bold. How fucking dare he scare her, stalk her, harass and abuse her. She slips her iPhone out of her coat pocket and holds her thumb over the side button and one of the volume buttons. If she holds them down for long enough, the phone will call the emergency services automatically. She won't even have to dial 999.

She pushes at the door so it opens a crack, and listens for the sound of movement. He's in the kitchen. She can hear him opening and closing cupboards, and the sound of footsteps on the tiles. She opens the door a little wider and slips through the gap into the hallway. Through the open door to the living room, she spots a pool of blood on the pale beige rug.

Her heart beats faster as she tiptoes towards the kitchen,

255

then turns sharply as her booze-soaked brain registers how much danger she's in. Her hip knocks against a small side table and a large ceramic ornament of a woman dancing totters on the edge of the table then crashes to the floor.

She runs back towards the front door gripping the iPhone, and a spark of fear explodes in her belly as a male voice shouts her name.

'Alex?' he says it again.

She stops running and turns to see her boyfriend standing outside her kitchen, his hands raised in shock, a yellow tea towel dangling from one hand.

'Sam?' Her brain cycles through multiple emotional responses: shock, horror, incredulity, joy and relief. 'What the actual fuck?' She presses a hand to her heart. 'What are you doing here? I thought you were—'

'Your spare key.' He digs around in his back pocket and holds it out to her. You gave it to me, remember? So I could let myself in, after the gig. I know it's late, but I wanted to make you dinner. I've got some making up to do.'

She wrinkles her nose and sniffs. Either he's lying or he's invented aroma-less food.

'I haven't started yet,' he says, giving the tea towel a shake. 'I opened a bottle of wine so you could have a drink when you got back – assuming you came back – obviously I had no idea where you'd gone and you won't answer my calls. Anyway, I knocked one of the glasses over. I was just looking for some salt to put on the rug.'

That's what she saw on the living room carpet: red wine, not blood.

'I was looking for salt. White wine and salt, that's what you put on red wine, isn't it?'

He has such a beseeching tone and a little-boy-lost expression that her irritation at him just casually letting himself into her flat softens.

'Why are you doing this, Sam? I wanted you to give me some space.'

'Because . . .' he shakes the tea towel again. 'Sorry, can I just sort out the rug? I don't want it to stain.' Before she can respond he pops back into the kitchen then returns with a salt cellar and half a bottle of wine. She follows him into the living room and stands in the doorway, watching as he drops to his knees and performs emergency surgery on the wine-splattered rug.

'We could get takeout?' Sam says, looking up at her as he glugs white wine onto the salt. 'Save me cooking. Probably be nicer too.'

An objection forms in her brain but she hasn't got the energy to voice it, so she drops onto the sofa instead. 'Yeah, fine, whatever you want.'

'Been anywhere nice?' He scrubs at the rug with the tea towel. It looks worse than it did five minutes ago, but she hasn't got the heart to tell him. It's only a rug. 'Tonight, I mean? God, I sound like a hairdresser. Going anywhere nice on your holidays this year?' He laughs to himself. She doesn't join in.

'Where were you really? Sunday lunchtime?'

'What? On Sunday? I told you, I was in Soho, with Paul.'

'When did you change the plan?'

'What?' he says again, and she feels her blood pressure climb.

'When did you decide to go to Soho instead of Covent Garden?'

257

'Before I left the house. Paul texted. I don't know why he . . .' he frowns as his eyes search her face. 'What is this? I'm not seeing someone else, you know.'

'Can I trust you, Sam?'

'Yeah, of – oh fuck. This is about Ben, isn't it? You think I'm up to something else, don't you? You think I lied about going to the Freemasons Arms.' A light goes on behind his eyes. 'Did you . . . did you go there to check up on me?'

'No. I . . .' she hasn't got the energy to explain about the texts or how scared she was. 'Sam, Lucy's been kidnapped.'

He rises up on his knees, the tea towel abandoned. 'What the fuck?'

'She vanished two days ago. The front door to her flat was left open, and some of her stuff was gone.'

'Was she burgled? Maybe she's just gone away to hide from . . .' he pauses, trying to remember Marcus's name.

'She was kidnapped. Bridget found blood on the patio wall and a dropped houseplant on the ground. It looks like she was interrupted when she was trying to leave.'

'Shit.' Sam glances down at the rug. 'I've really fucked this up, I'm sorry. I'll buy you a new one.'

'Fuck the rug.'

He notes the warning tone in her voice and gets up from the floor, abandoning the wine-scented crime scene, to join her on the sofa.

'I'm sorry.' He swallows, suddenly nervous, his easy, self-assured vibe gone. 'About Lucy. About everything. About getting in touch with your brother. Seriously. I thought I was doing the right thing, but I fucked up. It wasn't my place.'

'No.' Alex shakes her head. 'It wasn't.'

She stares at her hands, runs a nail over the cuticle of

one of her thumbs. She desperately wants to ask him about Ben – what he's up to, whether he's happy or not, how he's spent the last fifteen years – but she keeps her questions to herself. To voice them would mean opening up a part of herself that she's kept locked away for so long. Resurrecting her feelings towards her brother would break her, and she's barely clinging on to her sanity as it is.

Sam breaks the silence. 'I miss you, Alex.'

When she doesn't respond he inches closer, puts his hand over hers. The sensation, of his fingers rubbing circles into her skin, makes something flair within her, something urgent and desperate.

Wordlessly she reaches for him, cups a hand to his face and leans closer, presses her lips to his. He kisses her back then pulls away.

'Alex, you're drunk.'

'Not drunk enough to regret this.' She kisses him again, runs her hands over the muscles of his shoulders, then slides them down the hard planes of his back; feels the strength of him, the solidity. Her world is crumbling but now, in this moment, Samuel feels real.

Chapter 42

Lucy

One day until someone dies . . .

There are guns in the cottage, two of them – an air pistol and an air rifle – in a locked glass-fronted cabinet in one of the other bedrooms. The last time Lucy visited (voluntarily, back when she'd hoped that a change of scene might get Marcus to relax and turn him back into the man she'd fallen in love with), he'd taught her how to shoot. They'd taken the guns into the woodland at the end of the garden where he'd set up empty Coke cans as targets. She'd felt like a sniper, crouched behind a log with the rifle pressed against her shoulder and her eye at the sight. Her first few shots had whizzed over the cans and vanished between the trees. The next few were closer, but still missed. She'd gritted her teeth, determined to hit something. Ping! A pellet had hit the can on the top of the stack, sending it tumbling to the ground. She'd whooped in delight, taken aim again and fired. Another can fell, then another.

'See!' Marcus had crouched beside her. 'I told you it wasn't hard. Now try the air pistol. If you hold it with two hands you'll feel like a cop from *The Wire*!'

'Could you kill someone with one of these?' she'd asked as she swapped guns and felt the weight of the pistol in her hands.

'Only if you were at close range or got a lucky shot through the eye.'

Back then she'd shuddered at the thought. Now, as she watches Marcus move around the kitchen, she can't think of anything more satisfying than a pellet piercing his cornea, rocketing through the pupil, popping out through the retina and lodging itself deep into his brain. But the air guns are going to be as hard to get hold of as the knives. Any progress she may have made in getting him to relax and trust her was lost the minute his father phoned. Now, if he has to leave the room, he'll shackle her to the nearest available piece of furniture – and if she needs the toilet he'll stand in the open doorway and watch. She no longer has the shard of sharp plastic from the destroyed landline phone. When she woke up this morning it had worked its way out of her waistband and down towards her thigh. When Marcus untied her legs, but not her arms, so she could go to the toilet she felt it slip down the leg of her jeans. She couldn't risk it falling out en route to the bathroom with Marcus behind her, so she did a subtle little dance to dislodge it as she got out of bed. When it reached her ankle and dropped onto the carpet, she nudged it under the bed with her toe.

'Scrambled eggs or fried?' Marcus asks now.

She imagines picking up a hot pan, bubbling with fat, and smashing it into his face. 'Fried please,' she says.

'Okayyy. I'm using spray fat; saves on calories. We *will* have a trim little Lucy again.' He says the sentence in a strange chirpy voice that makes her want to rip off her own ears.

'Can I have—'

She's interrupted by an insistent rapping on the front door. Marcus pales and puts the eggs back in their box.

'Stay here.' He takes a couple of cable ties out of his back pocket and ties her wrist to a cupboard. He leaves the kitchen then, but as the shout of 'Police! Open the door,' drifts in from outside, he doubles back, shoves a washing-up sponge into her mouth and slaps a piece of thick black tape over her lips. She gags as the sponge catches the back of her tongue and a foul, soapy liquid rolls down her throat.

'Coming!' Marcus calls. He takes one last look around the kitchen then leaves the room.

Lucy stands up and moves across the kitchen, towards the closed door. The cupboard door she's tied to opens and the cable ties bite into her wrist as her arm reaches its maximum extension. She can't scream but she could create an almighty noise if she wanted to. With her free hand she could slam the cupboard door open and closed. She could kick at the cabinets. She could throw the kettle across the room or take a glass off a shelf and throw it to the floor.

There are a dozen different ways that she could signal to the police that she needs their help, that she's being held prisoner and wants to escape. She could do any of these things, but she doesn't. She stands as near to the kitchen door as she can get, barely breathing, and listens. She can hear the low rumble of a man's voice – presumably a police officer – then Marcus's clearer, higher tones saying, 'Yes of course, I'll just fetch her for you. She's in the kitchen. One sec.'

She darts back to where he left her and waits.

'The police want to talk to you.' He returns to the kitchen and closes the door behind him. 'A "welfare check" apparently.' He makes quotation marks with his index fingers then tugs the tape from her lips. She uses her tongue to try and push the sponge out, but Marcus slaps a hand over her mouth, keeping it in place.

'Now, listen and listen carefully. If you so much as breathe a *word* about what's going on here, I will finish you. If they arrest me, I'll tell them that you groomed me – that you fed my insecurities about Mum leaving to build a friendship with me, then initiated a sexual affair. I'll tell them that it made me feel dirty and used but you were my teacher, so I had no choice. Oh, and I'll cry.' He blinks rapidly, bringing tears to his eyes. Lucy watches, disgusted, as a tear rolls down his cheek. 'Your arrest and trial will be covered by the national press. Your parents will read about it; your little granny; Jada; all your colleagues from school. Everyone who's ever met you, and everyone who hasn't, will read about what a dirty little predator you are. You'll go to jail, and when you get out, I'll be waiting for you. There's nowhere you can run where I won't find you. You made this happen, Lucy, not me.'

He moves his face so close to hers that she can smell the toothpaste on his breath. 'Do you understand?'

She nods desperately. Her mouth has filled with saliva and she's struggling to swallow with the sponge lodged so close to her throat.

'All right then.' Marcus yanks the sponge out of her mouth, making her gag, then cuts through the cable tie around her wrist. 'Keep your cardigan over your hands.' He pulls her sleeve until it hangs over her fingers then angles her towards the door. 'Now, let's see your smiley face.'

She forces a grimace.

'Happy.' Marcus says through clenched teeth. 'You look like you're going to a funeral.'

I wish I was going to yours, she thinks as she attempts a cheery smile.

'Better.' Marcus pushes her towards the door. 'Remember, I'll be listening to every word that you say.'

'You must be Lucy.' A friendly looking woman in her early thirties, with dark brown hair tied back into a neat bun, smiles at her from the doorstep. 'I'm DC Elizabeth Martin, Devon and Cornwall police, and this is my colleague, PC Aasim Khan.' The uniformed man beside her gives a little nod of hello.

Lucy resists the urge to wipe her palms on her jeans and returns a smile instead. 'Lucy Newton. How can I help?'

'Nothing to worry about. We just wanted to have a quick word.' DC Martin's gaze flickers towards Marcus, who is standing so close Lucy can feel each rise and fall of his chest against her back. 'Alone, if that's okay?'

'Sure. We could talk in the living room.' She turns to gesture across the hallway and digs Marcus in the stomach with her elbow. He groans softly and clutches his abdomen.

'Careful, Luce.' He laughs to cover the threat then bends to kiss her on the cheek. 'I know when I'm not wanted. I'll go back to the kitchen, where I belong.'

His forced laughter accompanies him across the hall.

'Shall we chat out here? Go for a little walk?' The detective's gaze drops to Lucy's bare feet. 'Have you got a jacket and shoes?'

'Yeah, of course.' She grabs Alex's leopardskin coat from the hook and pulls it on, then, with only one of her shoes on the mat, slips her feet into Marcus's size 11 trainers instead. Her ankle's still sore after her fall and, as she makes her way outside, it takes all her concentration to mask her slight limp.

'This is a lovely place,' DC Martin says as they round the side of the house, and the enormous tree-lined garden opens up before them. 'Airbnb, is it?'

'No.' Lucy says. 'It belonged to Marcus's granny. His dad owns it now.'

PC Khan gives a low whistle from behind them. 'Very nice.'

'He rents it out,' Lucy adds. 'When family isn't using it.'

'Right, right.' DC Martin casts an eye over the back of the house. 'Five bedrooms, is it? Six?'

'Five.' Despite the cold October breeze, Lucy feels a trickle of sweat roll down her lower back. She'd be terrible in a police interview room. She feels so intimidated by the cool, collected detective and her breezy questions that she wouldn't last five minutes. She'd probably confess to crimes that she hadn't even done.

'And you like it here?' the detective asks.

'It's nice to get away from the hustle and bustle of London, and the countryside's beautiful.'

'It certainly is.'

'Did you leave London in a hurry, Lucy?' DC Martin

turns to look at her. 'My colleagues in the Met tell me that you left the door to your flat open, and blood was found on the patio wall.'

Lucy glances back towards the house, jolting as she spots Marcus in one of the upstairs bedroom windows. He's watching every move she makes.

The detective follows her gaze. 'Are you scared of him? Has he made threats to hurt you if you tell us the truth?'

'No.' She shoves her hands deep into the pockets of Alex's coat.

'Are you sure about that? Your friends are very worried about you. They think you've been coerced into leaving, or were taken by force.'

This is it: the fulcrum on which the remainder of her life rests. She could tell the detective the truth and have her freedom taken from her, or she could lie and take her fate into her own hands. The weight of the decision makes her feel light-headed, but she's made her choice. She knows what she needs to do.

She turns and looks DC Martin in the eye. 'Marcus has never hurt me. I got this,' she touches a hand to the rough red patch on her forehead, 'because I went out and got drunk after I resigned from my job. I tripped on an uneven paving slab when I got home. Marcus must have left the door open when he came to pick me up to come here. I was so desperate to get away that I shouted at him from the car to hurry up with my bags. If there's anyone you should be worried about it's him, with me being so high-maintenance and all.'

The police officers exchange a look. She's gone too far. They're more concerned than they were before.

'Okay, okay, that's fine,' the detective says good-naturedly.

'You understand that we need to check these things out though, don't you? Maybe give your friends a ring, let them know that you're okay.'

'Yeah, sure. I'll do that now.' Lucy turns to walk back to the house just as Marcus leans out of the window.

'Everything okay down there?' he shouts.

'All good.' Lucy flashes her first genuine smile of the day. That's it now; she's made her decision. She refuses to be like Natalie and spend the rest of her life looking over her shoulder, wondering if today is the day that she'll die. Sending Marcus to prison won't set her free, but killing him and then disappearing abroad will.

Chapter 43

WhatsApp group: Find Lucy

13.13

River: Just wanted to let you both know that the police have done a welfare check on Lucy. She's okay – she's alive! She's in a house that belongs to Marcus's family.

Alexandra: Oh, thank God. That she's alive, obviously. Not that she's still with that fucker.

Bridget: Agreed!

River: The officer I spoke to said his colleagues in Devon reported that Lucy appeared to be well and happy, that she'd gone away for a few days with Marcus after she left her job.

Alexandra: She's left teaching?! I don't believe that for one second. She loves that job. He must have made her lie to the police.

Bridget: WHAT? What about the blood and the plant and the open door?

River: I didn't ask about those things specifically but the guy I spoke to sounded like it was a closed case. Lucy's fine, nothing to worry about.

Bridget: Absolute rubbish.

Alexandra: I don't believe it either. Marcus must have pressured her into saying she was fine. Tomorrow's the date on the wreath. We need to rescue Lucy and hide.

River: How? We've got no idea where she is, other than 'Dartmoor'. It's a big place. I asked the sergeant for the address, but he wouldn't tell me.

Bridget: Dartmoor, you say?

River: Yeah why?

Bridget: Marcus's surname is Wordsworth, right? I know someone who's lived there her whole life and she knows EVERYONE (bit of a busybody if you ask me). If his family has property there she'll know about it.

Alexandra: Ring her now!

Bridget: I will!

WhatsApp private messages: River and Alexandra

15.16
River: Alex, if Bridget gets hold of an address, someone needs to go there.

Alexandra: Abso-fucking-lutely.

River: Are you up for it?

Alexandra: Of course. Are you going to tell Bridget, or should I?

River: Let's just keep it between us for now.

Alexandra: Why? What's going on?

River: Nothing. I'm just trying to work out how this can happen. We need to be careful about who we trust.

Chapter 44

Alexandra

One day until someone dies . . .

Alex stands at the window of her flat, looking out onto the rainy street below. Still no sign of Sutherland. The fact she hasn't spotted him yet is scaring her more than Bridget's sighting did. She logged onto Twitter that morning to see if he was still sending her messages, and found twenty-seven tweets from six different accounts, calling her a bitch, a whore, a liar and the reason her parents were dead. So he's still out there, but he's biding his time. Either that or he's too well hidden for her to see. She's not sure which option scares her the most.

The wind's blowing furiously outside, stripping the orange-brown leaves from the trees and hurling them at the road. Bridget still hasn't found Marcus's address in Dartmoor and Alex feels impotent, useless; a bystander on a beach watching someone else drown.

271

It's been nine days since Natalie's funeral and they're still no closer to discovering who sent the wreath. Initially she had assumed that it was Marcus; that he'd snatched Lucy to hide her away as the days ticked down. But what if she's wrong? What if River's supposed to die, or Bridget, or her? Their plan to hide or lay a trap was abandoned the moment Lucy disappeared.

Assuming they all survive Friday, what then? Their stalkers will continue to haunt them. There will be new threats, new messages, new photos: more cruelty, more fear. She'll never be able to walk down the street without looking over her shoulder, never go for a meal without listening for the beep of her phone.

She lifts the empty wine glasses from the coffee table and carries them into the kitchen. The flat feels empty without Sam, and she feels his loss as keenly as if her clothes had been stripped from her skin. They'd had sex on the sofa, in the shower, then in bed, and she'd fallen asleep in his arms drunk on wine and his smell. The next morning, as she'd peered at him from beneath weighted, hungover lids, his eyes had flickered open, and his lips had curled into a lazy, self-satisfied smile.

'This is nice,' he'd murmured; then his expression had changed. 'You can remember, can't you? What happened last night?'

'No,' she'd said, then, unable to bear his pained expression a moment longer, 'Yes, Sam. Of course I remember. You spilled red wine all over my rug.'

'And the rest?'

She'd laughed. 'Are you looking for a compliment or what?'

'It would make a nice change.' His eyes had crinkled as he looked at her.

'Okay, fine.' She'd touched a hand to his cheek, scratched at his stubble with the side of her thumb. 'You were hot as all hell.'

They'd had sex again, less frenzied than the night before; gentler, slower; and when she'd looked into his eyes after she'd climaxed, the tenderness of his gaze had made something inside her break. She'd been pretending to herself, and to him, that what they were doing was casual, no strings attached sex: no expectations, no feelings, no love. She'd seen more in his eyes though. He wanted her. He cared.

She'd searched inside herself for the right thing to say, but instead of softness and warmth, she was flooded with fear. She couldn't let herself fall for him. If anything happened to him, it would rip her apart.

'Shower!' she'd said decisively, pecking him on the lips before she swung her legs out of bed. 'Alone!' she'd ordered as he moved to join her. She'd cried as the hot water ran over her face, her hair and her body. She'd let it run cold for a minute before she got out, shivering under the icy blast, shocking herself back into her skin.

Now, as she fills the wine glasses with hot, soapy water, her mobile rings in her pocket.

'River?' She taps the speaker button and continues to wash up the glasses, 'what's up?'

'Good news and bad.'

'Okay. Give me the good news first.'

'Bridget's got an address for Marcus, in Dartmoor.'

Alex stares at her phone, the wine glasses forgotten. 'You're kidding?'

'Nope. I've looked it up on Google Streetview and it's pretty remote. If I was going to kidnap someone it's where I'd take them.'

'Fuck.'

'Sorry, I didn't mean to be morbid. I just—'

'No, not you. I can't believe we've found her; potentially found her.'

She snatches up her phone, heads into the hallway and pulls on her boots.

'Alex, off topic, but have there been any more sightings of Sutherland? Lucy's not the only one in danger here and I really think you need to go back to the police station and—'

'Please, don't start this again. I'm fine. He hasn't been anywhere near me.' The bells, which she's managed to mostly quieten over the last few days by focusing on Lucy's disappearance, begin to chime, and she wonders if she was too hasty, washing the wine glass when she could have refilled it instead.

'Anyway,' she says, 'back to Lucy. Are you ready to go?'

When River doesn't reply she looks at her phone to check they haven't been cut off.

'River? Are you still there?'

'Yeah . . . yeah sorry. This is um . . . this is the bad news bit.'

Alex stops lacing her boots. 'Go on . . .'

'I can't come.'

'What?'

'I can't help you rescue Lucy.'

'Why not?'

'Because . . . because . . .' his voice is thick and raspy, like he's fighting back tears. 'Because I'm terrified that it's Meg

274

who's going to die tomorrow. Vanessa's obsessed with her. She knows where she works and where she gets her hair done. She threatened to kill her, when I went to Charlotte's salsa class.'

'What?' Alex stares at the phone in horror. 'I didn't know that.'

'I couldn't say anything. Lucy had disappeared and I . . . I didn't want to make it all about me.'

'Oh my god, River.' She feels as though her heart might break. 'You should have told me.'

'Well, now you know.'

'Can't Meg . . .' she tries desperately to think of a solution. 'Can't she come with us?'

'She'd never agree. She won't call in sick, not even to protect herself. She wouldn't do that to the other nurses when they're so overstretched. I messaged her to tell her not to go in tomorrow, to lock all the doors and hide, but she refuses to do it. She says she won't let Vanessa control her like that.'

'Oh River—'

'She's coming round to the flat tonight, to get her stuff, and I need to be there. Maybe she'll listen to me in person. I have to at least try.'

Alex sits back on her heels and runs her hands over her face. It hadn't even occurred to her that Meg, Sam or Gary could be in danger too. Sam hasn't been sent any threatening messages as far as she knows and, other than the text the other night, calling her a dirty whore because he was staying over, he's rarely been referred to.

Fuck their stalkers: fuck them for destroying their lives, for trying to control them, for making them live in fear.

Fuck them, fuck them, fuck them. She'd kill them all if she could. She'd serve twenty-five years in jail if it meant her friends were safe.

She stands up and shakes out her hands, trying to ground herself, to dislodge the despair.

She'll text Sam before she leaves, tell him to cancel his gig, but she won't tell him where she's going. He'd only try and go with her. 'It's okay,' Alex says. 'I'll go to Devon. You stay here with Meg.'

'No.' There's fear in River's voice. 'Not on your own. Promise me.'

'We can't leave Lucy with Marcus.'

'He knows who you are, Alex. It wouldn't be safe.'

'I'm not leaving her with him.'

'Fuck!' River's shout rings out from her phone. 'Maybe I should go with you. Maybe . . . maybe if I leave Meg a note, then—'

'You know that won't work; not if a text couldn't convince her.' Dark clouds are gathering beyond the living room window. Even the weather isn't on their side. 'I'll go with Bridget. We can take her van.'

River takes his time responding. 'I don't know if that's a good idea.'

'Why not?'

'She's said a few things that aren't adding up.'

'Like what?'

He sighs heavily. 'Firstly, she claimed that she used to work with Charlotte, and that she had to switch jobs after the stalking started.'

'Yeah. And?'

'Bridget's a florist, right?'

276

'Yes.'

'Charlotte's a comedian. She does voiceover and gigs at comedy clubs.'

'What? How do you know that?'

'Her salsa teacher told me.'

'And you trust him?'

'Why would he lie?' He pauses. 'What I can't work out is, why would a florist be stalked by a comedian?'

'She sent her shit flowers once?'

Neither of them laughs.

'There's something else,' River says. 'When we were at Natalie's funeral and the wreath was delivered, Bridget said that her birthday was on the twentieth of October. Do you remember her saying that?'

Alex nods. Across the street a woman is fighting a losing battle with her umbrella. The wind keeps whipping it inside out, and she's getting wetter and wetter by the second.

'Yeah, of course.'

'She was lying,' River says. 'She told me that she went to the *Strictly Come Dancing* tour for her birthday earlier this year. I looked up the dates. The tour takes place in late January to mid Feb.'

Alex frowns, trying to make sense of what he's telling her. 'Why would Bridget lie about something like that?'

'I don't know. Do you think she might be mentally unstable? I just . . . I can't shake the feeling that something about her stalking story doesn't add up.'

'You think she's doing it for attention?'

'Maybe. There are people out there who'll do anything to get people to feel sorry for them. How many stories have you read about people pretending to have cancer?'

'Lots. Although most of them do it for money don't they – setting up fundraisers and then going on holiday or buying a new car or whatever.'

'Exactly. Bridget hasn't asked any of us for money, so I don't think it's that.'

'So what? It's like Munchausen's by stalking?'

River laughs, then his voice becomes serious again. 'I don't know. Just . . . if you go to Dartmoor with her, take everything she says with a pinch of salt. Okay? I don't think she's dangerous. I'm just . . . I'm not sure how much we can trust her.'

'Okay, all right.' Alex runs a hand over the back of her neck and squeezes it. There isn't a muscle in her body that doesn't feel tense. 'I'll be fine, River. Don't worry. I've met some liars and bullshitters in my life; I can handle Bridget. I hope it goes okay with Meg later. Look after yourself too.'

'And you.' She hears a softening to his voice. He's relieved that she's essentially given her permission not to go.

She stares out of the window as the call ends, her heart pounding as though she has just run a mile. Why would Bridget lie about her birthday? Did she do it so she'd feel like part of the gang, to pretend that she felt threatened too? That was fucked up if so. The job thing though . . . she hadn't *actually* lied about that; just said that that she worked with Charlotte. Might a florist have worked somewhere with a comedian? Decorated a venue or something? It was a bit of a stretch. Maybe Charlotte had lied to the salsa instructor about her job – she wouldn't be the first stalker to lie. She texts Sam:

Do you know any comedians called Charlotte on the circuit? One that goes salsa dancing. Maybe has stalkery tendencies? Bit of a long shot, but let me know if that rings any bells. Also, Sam, this is really important, but I need you not to go out tomorrow. It's the 20th October, the date on the wreath.

The phone rings almost immediately, as she knew it would.

'Are you at home? I'm coming over?' She can hear the worry in his voice.

'I'm not at home,' she lies. 'I'm staying with a friend in Birmingham.'

'You got there quickly!'

'I'm not as slow as I look.' The lightness in her tone doesn't match the seriousness of the text she sent, and Sam picks up on it immediately.

'What's going on, Alex?'

'Nothing. I'm just . . . I'm hiding.'

'In Birmingham?'

'Yes. And I need you to hide too. Is there somewhere you could stay?'

'Yes, with you. Alex, if you're worried about the threat then I need . . . I *want* . . . to be with you.'

'No! You . . . you need to stay at home, your own home . . .' Her heart twists in her chest. It's killing her, lying to him, but she can't let him know what she's really doing because he'd try and talk her out of it. He'd tell her to leave it to the police. Or worse, he'd insist on coming with her and she doesn't trust him not to put himself in danger, not after she saw the way he charged into the bushes in Highgate Wood. 'I'm fine here, I'm safe. I promise. Harriet's looking after me.'

'You've never mentioned a Harriet before.'

'I've got loads of friends I've never mentioned. Would you

like me to start with primary school? I was best friends with Adrienne Walters then when she went off with Amy—'

'Can I talk to her? To Harriet?'

Alex's chest tightens. Her flat's too quiet. He knows she's not in Birmingham and he's calling out the lie. Maybe she is a terrible actress after all.

'She's just gone to the shop, for wine.'

There's a pause, loaded with suspicion, then Sam says, 'She's not exactly keeping you safe if she's left you all alone.'

'Sam, stop it. I'm fine. Just promise me you won't go out tomorrow. No gigs? No drinks with mates, no trips to the corner shop. Please, please just stay at home.'

His sigh is so loud she knows it's accompanied by an eye roll. 'Fine. I'll stay at home. But I want you to stay in touch, and I want us to talk about this when you get back from Birmingham. You can't live like this. You need to get back in touch with the police.'

'I know. Take care, okay. Speak soon.' She *almost* adds 'love you' before she ends the call, but she catches herself just in time.

A couple of seconds later, it's Bridget's number she calls.

Bridget's van smells. Not of cut flowers and all things floral, but of the warm dust that's trapped in the heating vents, and the artificial fragrance of the half-dozen air fresheners hanging from the rear-view mirror. The audiobook that was playing when Alex got into the van ends on a happily-ever-after wrap-up and Bridget reaches across and turns it off.

Alex taps the air fresheners with her index finger. 'Have you got a dead body in the back or something?'

280

Sam isn't the only one that makes jokes when he's nervous. It's not that she thinks Bridget's dangerous, but River caught her lying and, until Alex finds out why, she's treading carefully. In her experience, if you've unearthed a couple of lies, keep digging because, invariably, there are more.

Bridget turns sharply and looks at her with wide, uncomprehending eyes. 'What did you say?'

'Trying to mask the smell of something rotting in the back?' Alex taps the air fresheners again. 'Gary piss you off, did he?'

Bridget's laughter is half shocked gasp, half maniacal cackle. 'Oh, I've been tempted,' she says, her eyes creasing with amusement. 'How are things between you and Sam?'

'Well, I haven't killed him, if that's what you mean.'

'Are things better, between the two of you? I didn't mean to listen to your phone conversation when I was at your flat, but it was very—'

'Loud?'

'It is a small flat. Was it very bad news?'

Before River's revelation, Alex might have opened up to her. She might have shared how conflicted she's feeling, how she hasn't stopped thinking about her brother since Sam mentioned his name. But she's not about to make herself vulnerable to someone she can't trust. 'No, no it's fine. All sorted now. How about you? Are you feeling more in control now you know where Charlotte is?'

Bridget doesn't immediately respond. She's frowning into the distance, a faraway look in her eyes.

'Bridget?'

'Yes, yes.' She gives a little shake and blinks rapidly. 'It's a huge help. I don't have to look over my shoulder wherever I go. I'm sorry I haven't been able to help you, though.'

'No one expected you to put a tracker on Sutherland, least of all me.'

'Yes, yes indeed.' She indicates left and pulls off at the junction. According to the Google Maps app on her phone – propped up in a tissue box between the seats – there's only half an hour until they reach their destination. It's a quarter past six and the last streaks of sunset have disappeared from the sky. In fifteen minutes it will be completely dark.

'So where was it,' Alex asks, 'that you and Charlotte first met?'

'At work.'

'And where was that?'

The frown reappears between Bridget's brows. 'One second, I can't navigate roundabouts and talk at the same time.'

Alex waits as Bridget manoeuvres the van into the correct lane and takes the second exit.

'I hope Lucy's all right,' Bridget says at the exact moment Alex says, 'A florists, was it?'

There's a pause then Bridget says, 'No. I met her at a comedy club.'

'Oh!' Alex's voice squeaks in surprise. She'd expected a lie.

'I've always done a bit of this and that,' Bridget says, 'not stand-up comedy. I'm more of a behind-the-scenes sort of person. I've done all kinds of jobs. I've been a postwoman, florist, obviously – but I learnt that from my mother, helping out in her shop from time to time. I'm not officially trained.'

282

'What did you do in the comedy club? You know Sam's a comedian?'

'No.' The word comes out sharply. 'No, I didn't know that. I was a stagehand. Like I said, I've turned my hand to most things, over the years.'

'Sounds that way.'

'So it's always been acting for you?'

'Yeah. I did a degree in drama, and it was pretty much acting jobs or waiting tables from then on until *Southern Lights*. It changed my life.'

'Shouldn't you be at work now? The play, I mean . . .' Bridget leaves the rest of the sentence hanging.

Alex plucks at the neckline of her jumper. 'Do you mind if I open a window, or—'

'I'll turn the heating down.' Bridget jabs at a button on the dashboard and slightly cooler air billows from the dusty heating vents.

Alex has no idea how to answer her question. Yes, she should be at work, preparing for the preview that evening. The cast and crew will invite their friends and family to watch the play before it opens to paying theatregoers tomorrow. She hasn't invited any friends and family because she won't be there. She won't be onstage on the opening night either, even though her face and name are on the poster, pamphlets and programme. Taking the title role in a West End show has been her lifelong dream but, right now, she can't ever imagine acting again.

Before Sam had left her flat, he'd begged her to ring her agent.

'Please, Alex.' He'd grasped her hands and shook them lightly as though the motion would travel through her body and wake up her brain. 'Just be honest with her. Tell her about Colin Sutherland. Tell her that it's triggered you, given you PTSD. It's okay to be open about mental health issues these days. No one's going to judge you. You're not going to kill your career.'

Alex shook her head. She couldn't imagine anything worse than being that vulnerable with Felicity – one of the most fearsome agents in the business. In her early sixties, Felicity was still a force of nature, one of the 'pull yourself together for god's sake' brigade.

'Email her then,' Sam had said. 'I'll do it for you if you want.'

She'd nodded mutely, too exhausted to put up a fight. If an email would stop Felicity from ringing her multiple times, day and night, then so be it. Felicity would talk to the producers, and they'd put out a statement saying she was stressed and exhausted. She just hoped the papers didn't chase the story: she could do without a Colin Sutherland feeding frenzy, or the paparazzi camped outside her door. She'd watched over Sam's shoulder as he'd logged into her email account and tapped out an email on her behalf. He'd looked at her every couple of words to gauge her reaction and she'd shrugged or nodded until she couldn't bear to read any more. The moment he'd hit *send* she'd deleted the email app from her phone. She didn't want to know what Felicity's reaction was – she had a good enough idea.

'Alex?' Bridget says now. 'If you don't want to talk about it just say? I'm just so confused. I thought this was your dream job.'

'So did I,' Alex says, 'until everything changed.'

284

They both lapse into silence until the awkwardness becomes unbearable and Bridget presses play on another audiobook.

Bridget kills the headlights as she steers the car up the small track that leads to the house where Marcus may or may not be keeping Lucy prisoner. She parks up by a bend fifty or sixty metres away, near a cluster of trees that block the car from view.

'Are you sure they're here?' Alex whispers. There's something about the darkness – they haven't passed a streetlamp for at least ten miles – that makes the small cab space feel like a hot, airless metal coffin. She needs to get out, to breathe fresh air.

'Yes,' Bridget murmurs. 'Margaret was certain that the Wordsworths own this house.'

'All right then.' Alex unclicks her seat belt. 'I guess we just . . . we need to make sure she's in there. That she's . . .'

Still alive. That's what she wanted to say, but the words caught in her throat.

She touches a hand to the catch on the passenger side door, but her fingers are trembling so much she can't hook them around the black, plastic handle. She's back there, in her childhood house, crawling out from the cupboard beneath the stairs.

There are bloody fingerprints on the wall outside the living room. The TV is blaring, no other sounds. She can't hear the low rumble of her dad clearing his throat, or her mum moaning that he hasn't put the bins out yet.

Her chest aches and she's breathing shallowly. Bridget is talking to her, but she can't hear her for the ringing in her ears.

'Mum? Dad?'

She feels like she's choking, like thick fingers are fastened around her neck.

Blood. Everywhere she looks there is blood. On the walls, on the TV, on the sofa, on the floor. Two bodies, human but not human: empty, lifeless, one sprawled on the carpet, the other on the sofa, one arm outstretched.

'Mum? Dad?'

'Alex! Alex! Look at me! Alex, look at me! Take a deep breath. Slower. Alex, breathe slower. Look at me!' Bridget swims in and out of her vision. 'That's it. *In* two three. *Out* two three. You're safe, Alex. No one's going to harm you. Keep breathing, *in* two three. *Out* two three. Name five things that you can see. Alex, focus. Name five things you can see . . .'

Chapter 45

River

One day until someone dies . . .

River stares into the mirror and moves his hands over his hair, crunching his curls so they hide in his palms. He releases them, sighing as they spring back to life. He sniffs his armpits; still fresh. Should he change his shirt? He's wearing the green one. Meg used to say that it matched his eyes. But she also liked the blue denim shirt. She said it was soft. Will she hug him when she arrives to pick up her stuff? Or will she be reserved and distant? Changing his shirt isn't going to save his relationship. Or Meg's life. He's going to have to beg her to hide.

He reaches for antiperspirant, rubs it over his pits once again then checks his watch. 6.25 p.m. Three minutes since he last checked. She's late.

He tears his eyes from his reflection, unwilling to examine

287

his flaws a moment longer, and paces the flat. The bins are all empty and the bed is freshly made. He's put on a pot of coffee in case Meg isn't drinking, and chilled a bottle of Sauvignon Blanc in the fridge in case she is. He popped to Waitrose earlier and spent an entire day's salary on nice little nibbly bits in case she's hungry, then doubled back on his way home and bought breakfast things – fresh croissants, a new jar of jam and a pat of salty butter – in case she stayed overnight. He felt sick as the cashier scanned the items. Meg *had* to stay overnight with him – if not in the flat then somewhere that Vanessa didn't know. They should stay together for the whole of the next day too. He had to believe that he could keep her safe, or he'd cry.

All her things are exactly where she left them – books on the bookshelves, muddled in with his favourites, vinyl in the record boxes, clothes in the wardrobe and her favourite utensils in the kitchen drawers. Although it's in his nature to be helpful, he hasn't been able to bring himself to touch anything she owns. If she insists on packing it all up into boxes it will buy him more time to talk to her, to prove to her that the threat is real, to beg her not to leave.

He moves to the window and, cupping his hands to the glass, stares out into the darkness, looking for the familiar shape of Vanessa's blue Fiat Uno. A violent rage sparks within him at the thought of her outside watching, grinning jubilantly as Meg carries her belongings out of his flat in beige cardboard boxes while his life falls apart.

He can't understand how she found the tracker so quickly. The app was working when he got back to the pub and showed the tracker moving around London, then it sped off to Heathrow and reappeared in India. Had Vanessa got a

288

taxi home, looked through her bag and found it? Had she left it in the taxi? No, she had to have put it *on* someone for it to make it onto a flight. Meg was right: he should have rung the police the moment she turned up at the pub. By pursuing his own harebrained scheme he's put both of their lives at risk.

He picks up a plant and hurls it across the room. It hits the far wall with a thump, then bounces back and lands on the carpet, showering it with soil. Horrified by the mess, he rushes into the kitchen, grabs a dustpan and brush from the cupboard beneath the sink and runs to the living room. If Meg sees what he's done she'll think he's completely lost the plot. He sweeps the soil into the pan, then bursts into tears just as the front door buzzes.

Meg has arrived.

His girlfriend's face creases with concern as she stares up at him. She's got a tree's worth of flattened cardboard wedged under each arm, but she looks beautiful in her floral tea dress and pink cardigan, make-up free and pale. Her eyes dart over his face.

'Have you been crying?' she asks.

'No.' He swipes at his cheeks and takes a step backwards to allow her into the hallway. 'Yes. Doesn't matter. Come in.'

Shit, he thinks as he leads her into the flat, *their* flat; that wasn't how it was supposed to go. He was supposed to be calm when he answered the door, not tear-stained with soil under his nails and his hair askew. He steps into the living room, expecting Meg to follow him, but she continues towards the bedroom without another word.

'Can we talk?' he calls after her, hating the plaintive whine in his voice. 'Please? I've made coffee, or we could have wine.'

The flat falls silent. Meg has stopped walking. She's thinking, considering what he said.

Please, River prays. *Please.*

'Okay.' Her reply is short, sharp, and when she walks into the living room her arms are free of cardboard boxes, but her eyes are downcast.

'Coffee or wine?' he asks, as she perches on the edge of an armchair instead of joining him on the sofa.

'Neither. I don't want to be here long.'

The insinuation stings but he tries not to show the pain he feels on his face.

'I think . . .' he shifts forward on the sofa, mimicking her posture, and rubs his sticky palms together, '. . . that I need to listen to how you're feeling.'

Meg sighs heavily.

'No?' River says. 'Should I go first?'

'River,' the word is pure exasperation. 'Could you give me a moment to think without immediately taking control? Please?'

'Of course, of course.' He dips his head.

'Who was she?' She stares at him defiantly, daring him to lie.

She's talking about the kiss.

'The . . . um . . . the photo. It wasn't what it looked like. I swear to you. It was . . . the woman's called Charlotte – she's Bridget's stalker. I was trying to put a tracker in her bag, and she lunged at me. She was drunk and got the wrong idea. I didn't kiss her back. I swear on my life.'

290

Meg runs her hands over her face then looks at him through her fingers. 'I actually believe you,' she laughs dryly, 'because that's exactly the kind of screwed-up shit I thought would happen. You were lucky she didn't stab you.'

'Meg, please, I'm sorry. I love you.'

'I love . . .' her voice catches on the word, '. . . I love you too, but I can't do this, not when work's so stressful. I've tried to support you, to get through it together, but I feel like . . . I feel like you've become as obsessive as she is, if not more.'

'I was doing my best to protect us, to protect you. Tomorrow is the date on the wreath and we need to hide, just in case my ex was the one who—'

'See!' Meg jumps to her feet, hands clenched into fists. 'This is exactly what I mean. I sit down thinking you want to talk about us when all you really want to do is pull me deeper and deeper into this . . . into this mess.'

All the hope, all the nervous energy that had sent River whizzing round the flat in a tidying frenzy leaves his body in a soul-sucking whoosh.

'Could you at least agree to hide somewhere tomorrow?' he says. 'If not with me, then at your parents' place, or with a friend? Somewhere V doesn't know about. I just want you to be safe, Meg. I'd never forgive myself if anything happened to you.'

'And then what?' Meg asks. 'If she wants me dead what makes you think she won't try and do it on the twenty-first, or the twenty-second, or in two months' time? Do I just hide for the rest of my life? I don't want to lose you, but I can't live like this.'

'Shall we have some wine?' he says desperately. She's not

291

softening, and he needs a couple of minutes to regroup, to think.

'Okay,' she sighs, resigned. 'I'll have a glass.'

He throws open the fridge and takes out the Sauvignon Blanc. Baby steps, baby steps, he tells himself, as he takes the corkscrew out of the drawer. He turns the metal spiral into the cork and, as the cork is extracted with a loud pop, he hears the faintest of dings from the living room. He's just been sent a text, but he's in no hurry to read it. He takes two glasses from the cupboard, pours the wine, relishing the soft glug of the pale amber liquid as it leaves the bottle, then he searches through the fridge for some snacks. Olives, hummus, sun-dried tomatoes, kettle chips, sourdough and artichokes – he arranges them carefully on a plate then adds another few slices of bread. Meg's bound to be hungry. She's always starving when she finishes a shift; nurses in A&E barely get a chance to go to the toilet, never mind eat.

Should he take the wine in first then return for the nibbles, or do it the other way round? It's not a decision he would have given a second thought to before, back when it was just him and Meg chilling out on an ordinary evening, sinking into the sofa, their legs pretzeled as they devoured a gripping new Netflix show. But everything he does feels more weighted now, more important: he doesn't want to put a single foot wrong. Wine, that's what they need – it'll relax them both. He reaches for the glasses and carries them into the living room. Meg's seat is empty. She must have popped to the loo. He places the glasses on the coffee table then returns to the kitchen for the food and delivers it back to the empty living room.

He sighs contentedly, pleased that everything looks perfect, then looks for his phone. It's not on the sofa where he left it. Strange: it's on the arm of the chair where Meg had perched. He picks it up, sees the snatch of a message on the locked screen. It's from Charlotte – *I need to see you asap, darling. Are you free tomorrow for brunch? I know a nice little place by Primrose Hill. I'll reveal everything then. ;) xx C*

'Shit!' He straightens up and heads to the bathroom. 'Meg!' He raps on the door, but it swings open before he can knock a second time. There's no one inside.

'Meg?' He heads for the bedroom. There's a pile of cardboard on the bed but no sign of his girlfriend.

'Shit! Shit!' He speeds out the flat, down the stairs and onto the street. He looks left and right, scanning for any sign of the diminutive woman he loves more than anyone else in the world. 'Meg!' he shouts. 'Meg, it's not what it looks like!'

But Meg has gone.

Chapter 46

Bridget

THURSDAY 19TH OCTOBER

One day until someone dies . . .

Bridget blows on her hands then shoves them under her armpits. With the engine off she's getting colder and colder and bitterly regretting not grabbing a pair of gloves before she left the house. According to the app Gary had headed straight for the pub, and she'd scribbled out a note telling him that she'd gone to visit a friend and she wouldn't be home until Friday. She'd left it in the kitchen, next to a plate of spaghetti bolognese. It's been nearly five hours since she left the house and she's itching to check the app, but she can't risk Alex seeing the screen.

Alexandra appears to have calmed down over the last five minutes anyway; she's breathing normally again, and the strange, haunted look has faded from her eyes. That's the second time she's had to talk her out of a panic attack, and it doesn't take a genius to work out what it's connected to. Alex is terrified that they'll discover Lucy's body. So is Bridget, particularly as she's known Lucy's location for days, which is something she's struggled with. Her gaze flicks back towards the large house at the top of the drive. All the downstairs lights are on but none of the curtains are closed.

'Are you up for taking a look?' she asks Alex. 'Or do you want to stay here, and I'll go on my own?'

'I'm coming with you.' Alex pulls at the door handle and climbs out of the car.

Abandoning the car at the bottom of the drive, Bridget and Alex creep closer to the house, hugging the side of the track, pressing themselves close to the bushes, bent double, moving in single file. The Devon countryside is quiet, save for the occasional rush of a car from the main road or the hoot of an owl, and every breath, every footstep Bridget takes sounds altogether too loud. A thought occurs to her, and she stops walking so abruptly that Alex clips the back of her shoe.

'What is it?' Alex whispers. 'What's wrong?'

'The wrench.'

'What wrench?'

'There's one in the back of the van. I need to get it.'

'Why?'

'Self-defence.' It's occurred to Bridget that, other than 'Let's check if Lucy's in there', they haven't got a plan at all. What if they do see something terrible through one of the windows? They won't be able to save Lucy without some kind of weapon, not if Marcus is armed.

'I thought we were just going to see what the situation is,' Alex whispers back.

'And then what?'

'We come up with a plan to get her out.' She gestures for Bridget to retreat a few paces, so they're closer to the van. 'What I'm thinking – assuming she's okay – is that one of us lures him out, you probably, because he's seen my face. Then, while you distract him, I break in and get her out.'

'Won't he hear that?'

Alex looks almost ghostly in the light of the moon. 'Not if there's an open door or window. Or if you manage to get him out of earshot.'

'I need to get him out of earshot. Okay,' Bridget says, sounding braver than she feels.

'I hope I won't need the wrench,' she adds as they continue to creep towards the house.

Bridget and Alex have reached an impasse. The hedge has ended and, if they want to get any closer to the house, they'll have to run across a huge expanse of driveway.

'No security lights,' Bridget whispers, gesturing at the house. 'No cameras.'

Alex squints. 'How can you see so well in the dark?'

'Carrot addiction.' She gives a small laugh. 'Not really. You just need to know where to look.'

'Fair enough.' Alex picks up a stone. 'Let's make sure you're right.'

Bridget grips her wrist, yanking her hand down. 'Careful. Throw it low so it doesn't make too much noise when it lands.'

Alex gently tosses the stone halfway between their hiding space and the front door. The stone gently clacks against the gravel. No lights come on and Marcus doesn't come rushing out of the house.

'Okay then,' Bridget says. 'Let's run to that car. We'll get a better view from there. Ready?'

The moment Alex nods she takes off, keeping low and moving as quickly, and as lightly, as she can. The car, a Ford Fiesta, is parked lengthways, to the left of the front door. From the tyre tracks in the gravel Marcus must have been in a hell of a hurry to get Lucy into the house. Bridget twists around and gestures at Alex, still crouching by the hedge, to make the run too.

'Can you see her?' Alex breathlessly joins her. 'Is she inside?'

'I haven't looked yet.'

Almost as one they rise from their knees to a squat and peer through the windows of the car.

'She's in the living room.' There's relief in Alex's voice. None of them have voiced it publicly but, ever since Lucy disappeared, Bridget knows they've all feared the worst. 'She's sitting on the sofa. She looks okay.'

Bridget nods. She's spotted her too, and now she's trying to work out how the hell to get her out. There's a row of long-dead plants on the outer living room windowsill; the kitchen windowsill too. The paint's peeling on the window surrounds and the glass looks original; no double glazing here. None of the windows are open; hardly surprising given the time of year.

She plops back down again and takes a few slow, deep breaths to still her racing heart.

'I'm going closer,' Alex says. Her pupils are huge, dark holes, but there's a focused intensity to her gaze. She's either terrified or excited; maybe a mixture of the two. 'See if I can hear anything.'

Bridget touches her arm. 'I'll keep watch from here. Be careful, okay?'

Alex nods and takes off, edging her way around the bonnet of the car, then, keeping so low she's practically on her hands and knees, she scuttles over the gravel towards the house. A dark shape appears at the window, making Bridget press a hand to her mouth. Marcus is crossing the living room, carrying two mugs in his hands. Alex doesn't spot him: she's still head down, crawling towards the side of the house. Panic sparks in Bridget's chest. She isn't going to try and peer through the window, is she? Not when Marcus is inside. She gestures frantically to try and catch Alex's attention, to warn her to move away, but Alex can't see her. She's crouched on her haunches beside the window, tilting her head, trying to listen to what's being said inside.

'Alex!' Bridget hisses.

She watches, horror stricken, as Alex slowly rises, gripping the windowsill for support. In a matter of seconds her head will be above the parapet. If Marcus glances out of the window, he'll see her straight away. If she runs to warn her, she won't make it in time. She grabs a handful of gravel instead and hurls it across the driveway, keeping her aim low, so as to avoid the windows. Alex flinches as the small stones hit her leg. As she snatches her hand from the sill, she dislodges two plant pots and, almost in slow motion, they totter, wobble then fall. There's a sharp crack-crack as they hit the gravel, like gunshots through the air.

Bridget catches a glimpse of Alex's stricken face as Marcus strides out of the living room. He heard the noise! Bridget flattens herself to the gravel and presses her hand to her

298

mouth. She stiffens as a shaft of light appears on the ground. He's standing at the open front door.

'Who's there?' His deep, bassy tone makes her shiver. 'This is private property.'

From beneath the car, she sees his black boots move towards the window, hears the crunch of the soles on the gravel.

'What the fuck?' Marcus crouches down, examines the pieces of broken pot, then stands back up. She can almost feel him, listening for the sound of her uneven breathing, scanning the darkness for her shape. She holds her breath, praying that Alex is out of sight; that she found a way to blend herself into the gloom.

She swears she can smell him – musky aftershave, cigarette smoke and the tang of unwashed clothes.

For the longest time there is silence – Marcus looking, Bridget hiding – before he finally, *finally* trudges back to the house muttering something about bloody foxes always making a mess.

It's fifteen minutes since Marcus went back into the house, and Bridget and Alex have reconvened at the van.

'What do we do now?' Bridget whispers, pulling the bobble hat she found in the glove compartment low over her ears.

Alex glances back towards the house, then smothers a yawn. She doesn't just look ghostly now; she looks drawn and exhausted. 'We need a Plan B. Marcus is going to be edgy; he'll be suspicious if you knock on the door.'

'Agreed. Have you got a Plan B?'

'We set fire to the house.'

'What?' The word comes out too loudly and Alex raises her eyebrows.

'Fine. Too dangerous, but how else are we going to get him out of the house? We set fire to something else – the hedge?'

'Too wet. It's been raining on and off for days.'

'So we go round the back, see if there's a wooden shed or a summerhouse or something.'

Bridget pulls a face. 'Isn't a spontaneously combusting shed going to look suspicious?'

'Well yeah, but he'll put it out, won't he? Before he does anything else. And that'll give us enough time to rescue Lucy.'

'Arson.' Bridget says the word idly, as though mulling over whether it's a crime she's prepared to commit. 'It could work. I've got a lighter in the van, and some pieces of paper.'

'Lighter fluid?' Alex asks and Bridget shakes her head.

'We can still make it work.' She glances back towards the house and bounces lightly on her toes, like a sprinter before a race. She's desperate to get Lucy out. 'So, we're decided?' You set fire to the shed, I rescue Lucy and we meet back here?'

Bridget gnaws on her thumbnail, remembering Marcus's deep, bassy voice and the way the air changed as he prowled around in front of the house, like a predator searching for its prey. Alex might be a fast runner, but *she's* definitely not. What if he catches her setting light to the shed? Or grabs her before she makes her escape? As afraid as she is, she's not going to back out. They have to get Lucy to safety. She might be alive now, but for how long?

'Sure,' she says. 'Good plan. Do we do it now?'

Alex shakes her head. 'No, he'll be too nervy. I think we sit it out—'

'In the van?'

'No, near the house. We don't know what's going on in there when we're all the way down here. Find some bushes or something, near the shed, assuming there is one – a shed I mean – and stay in text contact with me. When it looks like they're going to bed, when all the lights go out in the house, I'll message you. When you start the fire I'll make some kind of noise to alert him, then you go back to the van while I get Lucy. Okay?'

'Can we take blankets?' Bridget asks. 'There's some in the back of the van. It's going to get cold.'

'Oh for—' Alex seems to catch herself and her expression softens. 'Fine, let's get the blankets, and the lighter and paper. Be careful, Bridget, okay? We've already fucked up once. This cannot go wrong.'

Chapter 47

Alexandra

One day until someone dies . . .

Alex follows Bridget around the side of the house, keeping one eye on where she's stepping and another on an upstairs window with the curtains pulled back. With the lights still on inside it's unlikely Marcus could even see them, but she stays close to the wall anyway. Being spotted is a risk she's not prepared to take. As she reaches the back of the house she stares out into the darkness trying to make out the shapes and shadows in the garden. It's so quiet she can hear the soft nasal sigh of Bridget breathing beside her, and the tinkle of a water feature. Something small and jagged swoops low over the garden before it disappears into the black silhouette of a tree.

'Bat,' Bridget breathes, as Alex swears under her breath.

Unlike London with its buildings and its people, its lights

and its sounds, there's something unnerving about the countryside at night. It's like a great dark vacuum, stretching into forever. With nothing to observe, she feels like the one that's being watched.

'There.' Bridget nudges her, keeping her voice low. 'Shed, back left corner. I think it's wood.'

Alex follows her eyeline, trying to push the thought out of her head that, somewhere out there, Colin Sutherland is staring out into the same dark night, wishing that she were dead. 'I see it. Got the lighter and the paper?'

Bridget juggles the blanket in her arms to reveal what's in her hands. 'Yep.'

'Okay. Hide out near the shed, keep your phone on silent, and listen out for my text.'

Bridget nods again, then, keeping her gaze fixed on the house, edges towards the hedge that circles the garden. Alex waits until she's disappeared into the darkness then continues to inch her way around the back of the house, looking for open windows or insecure doors. She tries the door to a glass conservatory – locked and sturdy. The kitchen door is the same. She can only hope that whichever door Marcus throws open when he sees that the shed is on fire, he doesn't lock it behind him.

Reconnaissance complete – or as near as it can be, given the fact she's avoiding a psychopath – she returns to the front of the house, throws the blanket over her head and body and crawls into a suitably sparse section of the hedge. The ground is cold and damp beneath her palms, and thorns catch on the blanket as she crawls through the branches. When she's sure she's far back enough to ensure that she's hidden, but can still see out, she turns back to face the house, like a dog curling in its bed. Bridget's blanket suggestion was genius. She'd be scratched and bleeding without it, not to mention even colder than she is now.

She fishes her phone out of her pocket and, shielding the light with the blanket, looks at the screen. She's got five per cent battery. Shit. Why didn't she charge it before she left the house?

Dozens of messages have appeared since she last checked it: texts from Samuel, Felicity, Liz, River and half a dozen actor friends (who've no doubt heard the news about her 'mental health' break). She messages Bridget: *Have you found somewhere to hide?*

A reply appears almost immediately: *Yes, near the shed.*

No sooner has she read it than another one appears: *Are you sure Marcus didn't see us? I'm terrified he's going to come out of the back of the house and pull me out of this bush by the hair.*

Alex blows into her hands, wishing she'd had the foresight to bring some gloves. It's got to be less than five degrees and only growing colder.

He didn't see us. I just watched him walk to the kitchen. You can do this, Bridget. We're going to get Lucy. In a couple of hours all this will be over, and we'll be driving back to London. Stay strong.

Her text is more confident than she feels. For a start she hasn't got the first clue what time Marcus will head up the stairs to bed. It could be half nine, it could be two o'clock in the morning for all she knows, and it's only going to grow colder with every hour that passes. Maybe Bridget was right, maybe they should have waited it out in the van. But Marcus isn't the only one who's moving around in the house: Lucy is too. She's still alive and she's going to stay that way.

She checks Sam's messages next, keeping one eye on the house.

Hey babe, how's Birmingham? I still wish you'd let me come with you. There are a few Charlottes working the circuit that I know of. You're going to have to be more specific than 'she likes salsa'!! What's this about?

She opens River's messages next:

Let me know what happens. Don't do anything dangerous. If in doubt call the police. This isn't just about you any more.

Another message, a couple of minutes later:

Any weirdness from you know who? (She presumes he means Bridget).

Then:

Meg's coming over to pack up her things. Any news on Lucy? Have you found her yet?

And:

Meg's just left. I don't know where she's gone. I don't know what to do.

Followed by:

I'm going to go and try to intercept Meg when she goes to work tomorrow. I'll spend all day in the hospital if I have to – make sure she's okay. Charlotte wants to meet for brunch in Primrose Hill to talk about Bridget, but I don't think I can do that now. Any update on Lucy?

His last message says:

Alex, please text me back. I don't want to ring you in case it's dangerous but I'm getting really worried here.

He sounds terrified so she texts him back:

305

We're here and we've seen Lucy through the window. She's still alive. Plan is in place to rescue her. With any luck we'll be back in London in the early hours.

He answers immediately: *Oh thank god. I was so scared you were dead.*

Another text appears from Sam: *You've finally read my message! Can we FaceTime? I need to see your face.*

We can't because—

She stops typing to glance at the battery in the corner of the screen. There's only three per cent left. She can't reply to Sam or River. She needs that three per cent to tell Bridget when to set the fire; without it they're screwed. She turns off the phone, pulls the blanket tighter around her, smothers a yawn with her hand, and stares at the house.

Go to bed, Marcus. She tries to send him a psychic message as he walks back into the living room. *For god's sake, go to bed.*

Chapter 48

Lucy

The day someone dies . . .

It's been less than twenty-four hours since Lucy told the visiting police officers that she hadn't been abducted by Marcus. Any hope that her lie would convince him to trust her had vanished the moment she stepped back into the house. He'd ordered her to sit at the bottom of the stairs where he could see her, then stood at the hallway window, waiting for their uninvited visitors to leave. He had become more and more agitated with every second that passed.

'They're still just sitting in the car, talking.' He'd turned to look at her. 'What exactly did you tell them?'

'That we've come away for a minibreak after I left my job.'

'Did they ask why you resigned?'

'No.'

'So they just accepted what you said, blithely? Didn't give you the third degree?'

Panic rose in her chest. If she told him they'd accepted her explanation he wouldn't believe her, but if she told him they'd mentioned the open door and the blood on the wall then he'd panic. If he moved her from the house, she wouldn't be able to go through with her plan to kill him.

'They mentioned a plant,' she'd said after a pause. 'One of my house plants. They said it had been found on the patio, overturned.'

'And?' His eyes had darkened.

'I said I'd dropped it when we were loading the car, that I'd just left it there because I didn't want a load of soil in the boot.'

'And they believed you?'

'Yes, of course! Who hasn't dropped something in a rush and left it behind?'

Marcus had looked back at the window as an engine started up outside. Rather than relaxing, Lucy tensed. The moment the police left it would just be her and Marcus again – and the countdown to the date on the wreath.

Marcus had been nervy for hours after the police departed. He'd re-bound Lucy's wrists and told her to lie on the sofa while he stood at the living room windows, watching, waiting for them to return. He didn't even take his normal early evening shower. As darkness fell, he'd finally begun to relax. He allowed Lucy to sit back up, and turned on the TV. It couldn't have been on for more than thirty or forty minutes before there was a crash from outside. Marcus had jumped to his feet, ordered her not to move, and hurried out the front door. She'd remained on the sofa, dry mouthed, knowing he'd punish her later if she dared to stand up. She heard him shout that it was public property, then nothing until he walked back into the room. She didn't ask him what the noise was, and he didn't offer an explanation. Instead, he turned off the TV and sat beside her, listening, his body rigid, for what felt like hours.

In the silence, she'd readied herself. If someone had found them – if they knew what he was up to – then he only had two options: move her or kill her. There was no way he'd release her. Her only chance of killing him first was if he took a shower.

That time is now. It's eight o'clock in the morning on the day she's due to die and she's got five minutes, maybe seven, until Marcus comes out of the shower. Last night, around three a.m. he got out of bed and disappeared for an hour. As the minutes ticked by and he still hadn't returned she'd begun to panic. Had she left it too late to kill him? Had the police spooked him and he'd left her tied to the bed to die? She waited, and she waited, and when he finally returned she kept her eyes tightly shut as the bed sagged under his weight, and let out the softest of sighs.

Now, she grunts in frustration. She's still attached to the metal bed frame and, ever since Marcus left the room – two minutes ago according to the bedside clock – she's been sawing at the cable tie around her wrist with the shard of broken phone that she retrieved from under the bed with her toes.

She's worn away the sharp ridges but there are still several millimetres of plastic to get through before she's free. She places her feet against the metal bedstead, bends her knees, then yanks at her arm. The cable tie bites painfully into her wrist, but she doesn't make a sound. Instead, she sets to work with her teeth, gnawing at the plastic.

Four minutes have passed.

She must get it off. If she doesn't Marcus will see the damage she's done when he removes it, later. He'll know that she tried to get free. She grinds her front teeth back and forth, then bites into the plastic with her incisors.

The clock's digital display taunts her: five minutes since Marcus left the room.

She bites, yanks, bites, yanks. Her restraint is thinner now, ridged with bite marks, but it still won't yield. She hears a click from the landing. Has Marcus opened the bathroom door?

She presses her bare feet against the bedframe and pulls on her arm. She can hear footsteps now, slapping against the cold wooden floorboards. Marcus swears and the footsteps recede. He's left something in the bathroom. It's bought her seconds at most.

She clenches her teeth against the pain as she continues to pull at her arm. There has to be a way to escape – there has to. The half-remembered TikTok video of a woman bringing her cable-tied hands down over her knees flies into her mind again.

With just seconds until Marcus re-enters the bedroom, Lucy shifts around on the bed so she's sitting on her bum with her knees together. She clasps her hands together and, with every ounce of energy she's got left, brings them down and over her knees. The cable tie snaps and pings across the bed. In an instant Lucy's on her feet. She grabs the brass lamp from the bedside table and yanks the plug out of the wall, then she tucks herself behind the open bedroom door.

The scent of shower gel and shampoo fills her nostrils. He's coming back, he's nearly at the door. She's breathing quickly now, her chest rising and falling, the heavy lamp raised above her head, clasped with both hands.

Step into the room. Step into the room.

He won't be able to tell that she's moved from the bed until he's cleared the arc of the door.

Step into the room.

She can hear him breathing in the doorway, less than a foot away from her. Why has he stopped walking? Has he realised something's wrong? She glances back at the bed at the exact moment that Marcus walks into the room. He crouches down and plucks a piece of black plastic from the carpet. It's the cable tie; she didn't have time to retrieve it when it pinged across the room.

It all happens in an instant. As Marcus steps into the bedroom Lucy leaps out from behind the door and swings the heavy base of the lamp at his head. It smashes against his temple, knocking him off balance. She hits him again around the back of his head before he can recover, and he slumps to his knees. He's too dazed and disorientated to snatch the lamp from her but he raises an arm to block the next blow. She smashes the metal against his forearm then takes another swing at his head. It connects and he collapses to the ground, blood pouring from a wound on the back of his head, turning the pale carpet a bright red.

He's on his stomach, naked, the towel in a heap on the floor. His head's turned away from her and he's groaning, his fingers twitching against the carpet, his arms spread wide.

She steps over him and, still gripping the lamp, moves closer to the chair where he's neatly stacked his clothes. Still watching him, she runs a hand over the clothes until she finds his jeans. Tucking the lamp under one arm, she feels around in the pockets until she finds her car fob, a bunch of keys and her mobile phone. She could make her escape now and hope that he bleeds to death alone, or she could hit him with the lamp until she's sure that he's dead. There's one more option open; something that will ensure his death, something she's been fantasising about for days. She stares down at Marcus, still on his stomach, groaning, and heads for the spare room and the guns.

Lucy jabs the key into the gun cabinet lock but her hands are shaking so much that she drops it. She dips down, picks up the weighty keyring, and tries again. The key jabs at the lock and the wooden surround, everywhere but into the hole.

She shakes out her arms and tries to steady her breathing, but she's vibrating with adrenaline. No amount of swearing or shaking is going to make her calm down. She listens for the sound of Marcus's groaning in the bedroom across the hallway. It's stopped. He's either dead or she's made the worst mistake of her life.

Shielding her eyes with her arm she swings at the panes of the cupboard with the base of the lamp. The glass explodes. Sweat drips down her face as she pulls her cardigan over her hand and reaches for the air rifle inside the cabinet. The magazine's empty. Shit. She grabs for the air pistol instead and looks inside the chamber. One pellet. Just one pellet out of nine, that's all that's inside.

She yanks open the drawers, searching for more, but the

only carton she finds is empty. One shot, that's all she's got. She can't miss.

Abandoning the lamp she runs back to the bedroom, the pistol in her hand. She pauses in the doorway, her chest rising and falling. A close range shot or straight through the eye, the only way to kill someone, that's what he said.

She tightens her grip on the air pistol and steps into the room. She just wants to be free.

Marcus isn't where she left him. Somehow, he's managed to pull himself into a sitting position with his back resting against the bottom of the bed and his legs outstretched. A slow, mocking smile spreads across his bruised, blood-splattered face as his eyes meet hers.

'An air pistol? Right . . .'

She fingers the trigger, her arm straight and locked, her stance wide.

'You're not that kind of person, Lucy.'

She closes one eye and shifts her arm half a centimetre to the right, so his eye is neatly framed in the gun's sight. It's perfectly positioned for no more than a millisecond before it judders towards his temple, then swings back the other way, to the space between his eyes. Her heart's thudding so violently it's sending tremors from her chest to her shoulder, shaking her arm and her hand.

'We love each other,' Marcus runs a hand over his forehead, pushing his sweat-soaked hair away from his face. 'That's never going to change.'

Lucy grips her right wrist with her left hand to try and stabilise her arm. The sooner she pulls the trigger the better. The more he talks, the more chance she's got of missing.

313

'You could never live with yourself,' Marcus says from the floor. 'It would haunt you. I know you, Lucy, this isn't who you are.' He shifts his position, putting one hand to the carpet as he bends his knees. He's readying himself to get up.

She has to shoot him. Now!

Teeth gritted she crooks her index finger, increasing the pressure on the trigger. Pull it! screams a voice in her brain. Pull it! This is what you want.

'You're not a murderer, Lucy.' Not taking his eyes off her, Marcus rests his weight into his palm and the ball of his right foot. He leans forward. There's tension in every muscle in his body, like a tightly wound spring.

'Don't move!' she screams. 'Don't move or I'll shoot.'

Pull the trigger! The voice in her head is desperate now. Kill him before he kills you. But her finger won't move. She can't do it.

Do it! Do—

Before she knows what's happening, Marcus springs to his feet and knocks the gun from her hands.

Chapter 49

Alexandra

The day someone dies . . .

Alex wakes with a start, ripped from her dream by the frantic cawing of a crow somewhere nearby. A wave of panic surges through her as her brain struggles to make sense of the dirt beneath her fingertips, the blanket wrapped around her like a shroud, and the branches and leaves that claw at her face. For one terrible, paralysing second, she thinks she's been attacked and dragged into foliage to die, then her mind pedals through her memories and her breath catches in her throat. She fell asleep! It's daylight. It's the twentieth of October. She was supposed to rescue Lucy and she fucking fell asleep. She throws off the blanket, twists onto her hands and knees, starts crawling, heading for the gap where the hedge meets gravel, then stops and pats her pocket for her phone. Bridget! She never gave her the signal to start the fire. A dozen notifications flash up on the screen, from River, from Samuel, but none of them from Bridget.

Bridget, she taps out a frantic text. *Where are you? I fell asleep!*

One tick appears but not two.

I've got 1% battery left. Her heart's pounding so violently she feels sick. *Please reply if you see this. I'm coming to find you. If you're still in the bushes, stay where you are.*

As her phone dies, she continues her crawl. She pauses as she reaches daylight and looks up at the house. There's a light on in the bathroom window, but nowhere else. *Please let Lucy still be alive. Please let Lucy still be alive.* Her brain chants a frantic prayer as she sprints across the gravel, rounds the house and the hedge, keeping low, and heads for the shed.

'Bridget! Bridget!' She hisses. She ducks down and peers into the nearest bush. 'Bridget, are you there?'

She tries another bush, and another, then runs the length of the hedge, continually glancing up at the house as sweat soaks her scalp and the roots of her hair. She increases the volume of her whisper – 'Bridget! Bridget! It's me.' In the silence of the morning, it sounds like a scream.

Either Bridget's comatose, or she's gone. Was she right last night, about Marcus spotting her? Has he taken her too? Did he pull her out by the hair?

The van. The van. She sprints back along the side of the house and down the driveway. If it's still there then Marcus has got her. And if he hasn't, then—

She stops running and stares.

The van's gone. Vanished. As though it were never there.

316

'What the fuck?' She grips her stomach as she stares at the empty space. Why would Bridget just up and leave without her? Without trying to find her? Without even sending a text? She's alone, in Dartmoor, with no phone, no car and no plan. Even if, by some miracle, she manages to rescue Lucy alone, how the hell will they escape?

Although . . . she turns back to look at the house. A car is still outside. They could use that.

She heads towards it, walking slowly up the driveway, keeping close to the bushes to avoid being seen, her brain scrabbling for a plan. Could she throw a brick through a window? Break in and rescue Lucy when Marcus leaves the house? There wouldn't be much time though. Maybe—

She stares up at the house. There are two figures in the bedroom window, lurching violently from left to right. He's doing it; he's killing Lucy.

Her stomach lurches and she takes off at a sprint, heading for the front door. She turns the handle. Locked. She tries it again, this time shouldering her weight into the door, but it doesn't so much as creak. As she darts round to the back of the house, images from her childhood flash up in her mind. Hide, screams a little voice in the back of her brain, hide, just hide; but she keeps on running.

She tries the kitchen and conservatory doors – still locked – then runs her hands over the kitchen windows. They're old and wooden, the paint peeling from the frame, made up of three panes of glass per window, a black metal latch on the inside, halfway down. She scans the ground, looking for a large rock or a brick, anything she can use to smash the glass, then spots a small concrete angel next to a planter. It's heavier than it looks, and she heaves it into her arms then hurls it at the window. The glass shatters, covering the sink, the floor and the work surfaces.

She pauses, catching her breath, listening for the sound of footsteps, speeding down the stairs towards the kitchen, but all she can hear is the frantic pounding of her pulse in her ears. She reaches a hand through the shattered pane and unlatches the window then hauls a planter closer, rests a foot on it and pulls herself in, pushing glass out of the way with her coat-covered hand. As she slides off the sink onto the tiled floor, she hears a loud thump from upstairs, like someone falling to the floor.

Frantically she stares around the kitchen looking for something, anything, she could use as a weapon, but there aren't any knives. She takes off empty-handed, speeding through the hallway and up the carpeted stairs, the sound of a struggle getting louder and louder the closer she gets. She can hear Marcus grunting and swearing, and Lucy groaning and shrieking in pain. She pauses to glance into an empty bedroom, spots a smashed cabinet on one side of the room, a rifle on one shelf, covered in glass and a weighty-looking lamp, slick with blood, on the floor.

She deliberates for what feels like an age but can't be more than a split second – she's never used a rifle in her life, and she hasn't got time to learn – then grabs at the lamp. Please be his blood, she offers up in silent prayer as she runs on the balls of her feet, in the direction of the noise. It's only after a couple of steps that she realises that the house has fallen quiet: the silence is more terrifying than the crashing violence of a fight.

She stops running metres from the room she saw from

the driveway and takes a shuddering breath. Memories paralyse her again: the cupboard under the stairs, the scent of old shoes, discarded paint tins and moth-eaten blankets and the warmth of her palms against her ears.

She slips into the room, the lamp raised, her breath quickening as she spots a gun on the floor, a pool of blood at the base of the bed, and Lucy up against a wall, Marcus's hands around her throat.

Alex leaps over the gun and brings the lamp down on the top of his head. A sharp crack fills the air and he stumbles backwards, releasing Lucy. She slips down the wall, one hand to her throat, eyes wide, deathly pale. Alex hits Marcus again. His arms flail as he tries to grab at her, but she wrenches her arm away, and tries to hit him again. Her mind is empty and, as she wields the brass lamp, it's as though someone else is attacking him – someone taller, stronger, angrier, more powerful.

'Alex! Alex!' A voice calls her name and she turns, expecting to see Ben cowering beside her, pulling frantically at her coat, but it's not her brother with red-blue bruises blooming on his neck and collarbone, it's Lucy, trying to haul herself off the carpet and up, onto her feet.

Keeping one eye on Marcus, groaning and writhing on the carpet at the base of the bed, Alex grabs the gun from the floor and tucks it into her handbag, then she reaches a hand down to Lucy and helps her to her feet.

'Give me the key,' Alex says as she slides into the passenger seat of the Ford Fiesta. 'I'm driving.'

It's an argument that's been raging ever since Lucy

produced a bunch of keys and a car fob from the pocket of her jeans, unlocked the front door and limped across the driveway to her car, with Alex at her side.

As Lucy silently starts the engine Alex slumps against her seat. There's no point arguing with her, she's completely shut down.

'If you take a left at the bottom of the driveway, then the first right,' Alex says as the car gathers speed, 'then we'll hit a town called – fuck, Lucy! Slow down.'

The car swings out of the driveway, the passenger side clipping the hedge as Lucy yanks the wheel to the left.

'Jesus!' Alex grips the handle above the door with one hand and the seatbelt with the other. She glances across at Lucy. 'Pull over! You haven't got your seatbelt on.'

'I couldn't do it,' Lucy says as the speedometer ticks from fifty miles an hour, to sixty, to sixty-five, and the verges either side of them flash past in a blur. 'He told me that if you shoot someone in the eye with an air pistol they'll die.' Her gaze is fixed and glassy as though she can't see the road at all. 'But I couldn't pull the trigger.'

The speedometer ticks from seventy to seventy-two to seventy-five and the back tyres slide and skid on the wet tarmac as the car swings round a bend.

'I was going to go abroad,' Lucy continues, as though in a dream, 'somewhere no one would ever find me.'

'You can still do that, just please, slow down! You don't know these roads.'

Seventy-six, seventy-seven, seventy-eight.

'You're going to kill us. Lucy, stop! Slow down!'

Seventy-nine, eighty, eighty-one. The speedometer continues to climb. If a truck meets them around a bend it'll be over.

320

They'll die on impact. Alex twists to look at Lucy – seatbelt off, zombie-like, her foot pressed to the floor. She could grab the wheel, but then what? They'd just plough into a hedge.

'Wherever I go he'll find me,' Lucy says flatly. 'But he can't do that if I'm dead.'

'Stop the car!' Alex screams, scrabbling around in her bag for something sharp as they hit eighty-two, eighty-three, eighty-four miles an hour. Her fingers close over a pen. The car's juddering and shaking; it's going to spin out of control. 'I'm really sorry,' she says as she leans across Lucy and jams the pen into her right thigh. Lucy gasps and reflexively lifts her leg, releasing the accelerator. Her eyes widen as the pain kicks in.

'What . . . what . . .' She looks from her thigh – a deep indent in the denim of her jeans but no blood – to Alex, to the speedometer, and she touches a foot to the brake. The car slows – seventy-five miles an hour, seventy, sixty – and her hands, arms and shoulders begin to shake – subtly at first, then so violently it's as though she's trying to yank the steering wheel clear off its shaft.

'Pull over,' Alex says, and this time Lucy does as she says. She slows the car to a crawl and pulls into a layby by the gate to a field.

For several seconds neither of them speaks, then Alex rests her elbows on the dashboard and howls into the gap between her arms.

'I'm sorry,' Lucy whispers. 'I'm so sorry.'

Alex says nothing. Maybe Lucy's right, maybe death is the only escape. What else can they do? Sending their stalkers to prison only delays the inevitable; and now River's tracker plan has failed, they're in as much danger as they ever were,

321

if not more. She's willing to take a chance with her own life but she won't let Lucy die.

She's got ten grand saved up. Lucy can have it; she can have it all.

'I can help you,' she says, sitting back in her seat. 'I've got money, and friends in Greece, Portugal and France. They're good people, they'd put you up until you're back on your feet. You've got fight left in you; I know you have. Just promise me you won't do anything stupid until we've at least tried to get you on a plane?'

Lucy shakes her head miserably. 'He'll find me or he'll tell the police what I did, and let them track me down.'

That's what she's so scared of – Marcus telling the police how they met? Alex stares out into the darkness, picking through the conversation she had with Anthony Wordsworth. Maybe that visit wasn't such a massive waste of time after all. 'Lucy,' she turns to look at her, 'when did you and Marcus get together?'

'Don't.'

'I know it was when you were teaching.'

She sees Lucy flinch. She's right, she's hit a raw nerve, that's the secret Lucy doesn't want shared. Is that why she stayed with Marcus for so long – as punishment for what she had done?

'Please,' Alex says, 'it's important. When exactly did you get together?'

'At the leavers' party.'

'At the end of term, after A Levels?'

Lucy nods minutely and closes her eyes, blocking her out.

'Have you got any texts that prove that? An email? Anything he sent you that would have the date on it?'

'I don't know. No, I deleted everything he sent me when I left him.'

'Are you sure? Are you absolutely sure?'

'Why?'

'Please, Lucy. Think. Was there anything you kept?'

Lucy shakes her head again then inhales, sharply. 'There was one email that I kept. He sent me the most beautiful poem the day after we slept together, and said the loveliest things about me, and how he felt now we'd got together. It made me cry. I'd made the worst mistake of my life, but I also felt like I'd met my soulmate. I couldn't reconcile the two.'

'Oh thank god you kept that.' Alex sighs noisily. 'There's no way he could lie about when you got together because the email will be dated. Lucy, Marcus wasn't a student then. His dad withdrew him from school to send him to rehab. I went to see him – Anthony Wordsworth – two days ago.'

'It was a temporary withdrawal, because of illness.'

'Originally maybe, but it became a permanent withdrawal. That's what his dad told me, and he had no reason to lie. Marcus only attended the leavers' party to show off about rehab to the other kids. Lucy . . . you didn't do anything wrong. He just made you think you did.'

A single tear winds its way down Lucy's cheek, but she doesn't say a word.

As the silence continues, Alex starts to doubt herself. Maybe she was wrong; maybe Marcus's hold over Lucy is stronger than guilt. Maybe there isn't any fight left in her. She waited too long to try and rescue her and now Lucy thinks killing herself is her only escape.

'He definitely said that?' Lucy says softly. 'That it was a permanent withdrawal?'

'Yes!' Alex squeezes her hand. 'Lucy, Marcus has been lying to you this whole time. He wasn't your student when you got together. He'd already left school.'

'I can't . . . I can't let myself believe that. It feels like another cruel trick.'

'It's not a trick, I promise you. Lucy, Marcus has been keeping you prisoner by holding this over you but it's not real. It's never been real. You've got nothing left to fear any more. You can—'

'I've got everything to fear.'

'Of course you do. Of course.'

Lucy's hand, lying limply in hers, suddenly twitches and shifts, and now it's Alex's hand being squeezed.

'If I leave. If I move abroad,' Lucy turns her tear-stained face towards her, eyes clouded with worry, 'who'll look after you?'

'I'll be okay.'

'Sam loves you, you know. I only met him once, but I saw it in his eyes.'

She saw it too; it's why she jumped out of bed and made an excuse about needing a shower. 'I can look after myself.'

'You've been doing that for a very long time,' Lucy says quietly. 'Would it be so bad to let someone else take a turn?'

'It would if they died.'

'Oh, Alex . . .' There's empathy in Lucy's soft sigh. 'Keeping a wall up won't protect anyone.'

'It might protect me.'

There's a pause, then:

'How's that working out for you?'

She laughs – a sad, dry bark of acknowledgement. She's lost count of the times she's drunk herself to sleep, woken

324

from a nightmare screaming, or stayed out late to delay a return to her empty flat, and her thoughts.

'What happened to you was awful,' Lucy continues, her cheeks pinkening, the colour returning to her skin. 'It was tragic, the worst thing in the world. But you have to stop punishing yourself. It wasn't your fault. You were a ten-year-old girl, just a child.'

'They'd still be alive if I hadn't opened the door.'

'Would they? Are you sure about that? Because it sounds to me like Sutherland could have snapped at any time: when you were at school, on a trip, or spending the night with a friend. You were a *child*, Alex. You can't hold yourself responsible for something a psychopath did. You can't live the rest of your life in fear.'

'I'm not afraid of him.'

'That's not what I mean.'

Alex looks at Lucy in her blood-stained jeans and ripped sweatshirt, her blonde hair greasy and straggly, framing a plump, line-free face; how can someone so young be so bloody insightful?

'We need to text River,' Alex says, changing the subject as she reaches for the charger lead that's hanging from the USB port and plugs it into her phone. 'Let him know we're okay and that Bridget went AWOL. He's probably having kittens right now. I should probably text Sam too. Anyway, let's get back to London, grab what you need from your flat and book you a flight. And by the way . . .' She gives Lucy a loaded look, then smiles. 'I'm driving now.'

Chapter 50

River

The day someone dies . . .

It had been the longest night of River's life. He hadn't bothered going to bed; instead he'd sat at his laptop and searched for Vanessa. It's something he'd done dozens, maybe even hundreds of times, since she began her stalking campaign, but now the clock was ticking. If he was right, and she was the one who'd sent the wreath, then he only had a matter of hours to track her down and send the police to arrest her. It made him want to cry, thinking about the opportunity he'd let slip through his fingers. He should have told the police that he was going to lure Vanessa to the pub, or had a friend park up outside to follow her home. He was so convinced that his tracker plan would work that he hadn't allowed for it to fail.

There had been nothing on the internet, just like every

326

other time he'd looked: Vanessa had wiped every last footprint from social media. She'd vanished, just like in real life. As dawn broke, he'd checked his phone for the umpteenth time that night, hoping for an update from Alex. He hadn't heard from her for hours and he felt sick with fear . . . There was no way he could keep everyone safe; he'd been forced to choose. It was as though their stalkers had conspired to split them up.

At six o'clock he'd stretched, stood up and made himself a coffee. Then he'd showered and changed into clean clothes. Meg hadn't revealed where she was staying – despite several texts begging her to tell him. He'd have to wait for her at the hospital.

As he'd packed a bag to take with him his phone bleeped with a message. It was from Meg!

I'm at my parents' house in Enfield. You've scared me into calling in sick for the first time in my nursing career. I can't believe this is what my life has become. I'm so angry, River, I don't know what to think. Please don't call me. I've been talking to my parents, trying to decide what to do. Mum thinks you should tweet that we've split up, so your ex leaves me alone. But how does that help you? You need to get onto the police again. They're not doing enough to find her. Stay safe.

He'd punched the air, then read the text again and again. Meg was safe, that was all that mattered; her parents would look after her – he could finally breathe. The tweet was a good idea, whether or not it was true.

He'd returned to his laptop, posted a meme to Twitter about letting the person you love go, then he'd checked his phone again. Charlotte was awake too, wanting to

327

know if he wanted to meet for brunch at 11 a.m. in Emily's Eats, a little café in Primrose Hill. He'd ummed and ahhed over the invitation, drummed his fingers on the coffee table, then sat back in his seat. With Meg out of reach would Vanessa come after him instead? He'd stood up, sat down again, tried to think logically. His head was telling him to stay in his flat, but his gut was telling him to go. He could ring Charlotte instead of meeting her, but he wouldn't be able to read her body language, or the micro expressions on her face. Either Charlotte, or Bridget, was lying about the way they'd met, and he was pretty sure that Bridget was.

'Fuck it.' He'd tapped out a reply to Charlotte, saying that he'd love to have brunch. Vanessa was smaller than him, and lighter. If he saw her coming, there was no way he would die.

He'd continued to stare at his phone, mulling over his decision. What would be *very* telling would be Bridget's reaction to the meeting he'd just planned. He tapped out a message to the 'Find Lucy' WhatsApp group, telling the other two where he was going to meet Charlotte, and then, utterly spent, stumbled to the sofa and stretched out. He'd meant to rest for just a minute or two, but his eyes had grown heavy and his breathing grew slow and steady.

Three hours later his eyes flew open as his phone vibrated on the coffee table. He snatched it up, horrified, hating himself for falling asleep. Two messages: one from Lucy, using Alex's phone, letting him know that she and Alex were okay and heading back to London, but that Bridget had disappeared in the middle of the night.

He was ecstatic that Alex had managed to rescue Lucy (and they both sounded unharmed) but why the hell had Bridget vanished?

He was pretty sure that Charlotte might know.

River's stomach rumbles as he takes a sip of his coffee; no sign of Bridget, and no answers from Charlotte either. At eleven-thirty, when the waiter finally came over to their table Charlotte had ordered eggs benedict on potato rosti while he shook his head and he claimed he'd already eaten. He hadn't expected to stay in the café for more than an hour and, somehow, it's already twelve fifteen and he still hasn't been able to ask Charlotte about Bridget because she hasn't stopped talking since they sat down.

She's launched into another monologue now – this time it's about an English professor at uni whose nose made a strange whistling sound whenever he wrote on the board. From the amount she talks she's either lonely, a narcissist or she's testing out new material (she is quite funny to be fair and he would have laughed at her last story if he hadn't been staring out of the window making sure that Vanessa hadn't turned up).

Each time he tries to interject, to ask Charlotte something personal, she changes the subject and goes off on some tangent, launches into another new routine. As she draws breath to imitate her professor's nasal whistle for the third time, River touches her hand.

'Charlotte, I'm really sorry to interrupt you, but what's your surname?'

She looks at him, confused. 'McBeth; why? That's my stage surname. My real surname is Smith – not very showbiz.'

329

'So it's not White?'

She shakes her head. 'No . . .'

Bridget lied about Charlotte's surname too. That's why he couldn't find anything on her when he googled her.

'There's something else I need to ask,' he says, 'about the text you sent me. You said we had a lot in common. What did you mean by that?'

She looks at him over the rim of her wine glass. 'I'd say that was obvious. We've both got stalkers, haven't we? I saw your face when that woman turned up in the pub.'

She's talking about Vanessa, and what happened in the salsa bar.

'I know I was drunk,' she continues, 'and with good reason, but even I could see how horrified you were.'

'I shouldn't have grabbed her,' River glances away, shame coursing through him. 'I shouldn't have grabbed her by the throat.'

'No,' Charlotte says curtly, 'you shouldn't. Not least because she could have had *you* locked up instead of the other way round.'

River looks at her in surprise. He'd expected to be chastised, to be told (as he already knows) that it's never okay to lay your hands on a woman. He hadn't expected her to understand.

'Oh, I'm no angel, darling,' Charlotte takes a sip of her water. 'There was a moment when I confronted my own stalker when I was *this* close,' she holds her index fingers an inch apart, 'to stabbing her in the heart with her own bloody scissors.'

'In the florists?'

A frown creases her brow. 'How do you know that?'

'I'll tell you in a minute.' He reaches for his coffee, his throat suddenly dry, and takes a long, welcome gulp. 'Tell me about your stalker; who she is, what you know.'

Charlotte sits back in her seat. 'I don't know what was worse, the messages or stepping on stage and seeing her gawping up at me every night.'

'What kind of messages?'

'Oh, the normal vile troll stuff – comments about my appearance, how talentless I am, how karma will catch up with me, how I'll die bitter and alone,' she rolls her eyes, 'all that kind of stuff.'

'Did you tell the police?'

'No, because I couldn't prove it was her. I'm on social media all the time because of my job, and you wouldn't believe the amount of abuse I get. I had no way of proving which messages were hers.'

'She turned up to all your shows though?'

'And just sat there, staring at me. She'd wait in the alley too, after the show was over, and wait for me to leave. She'd never actually say anything, she'd just watch as I walked to my car.'

'Creepy.'

'Quite. At first, I thought she was building up the nerve to ask for an autograph, but when I actually approached her she scuttled away. She was there the next night though, and the next. I mean, it's not unusual for fans to get obsessed. There are a few who'll follow me round the country when I go on tour and give me little presents and things they think I'll find funny. I mean, I'm hardly Sarah Millican, but there are a handful of fans who are a bit . . .' she pulls a face, '. . . too keen.'

'So, what makes the one in the alleyway a stalker? If you're used to being followed around, I mean.'

'The flowers.'

He nods, prompting her to continue.

'The bouquet that was sent to the theatre after my notebook was stolen.'

'Notebook?'

'It went missing. It's got like, ten years' worth of jokes and ideas in it. It means more to me than my cat.' She laughs. 'Apologies, Dorothy Parker – that's the cat. I love her really when she's not being a pain in the arse. Anyway, I was desperate to get it back. I put a post and a photo on social media, posters up in nearby streets, offered a reward, all that stuff. Then, after about a week since I'd last seen it, I returned home from my show and found a shoebox on my doorstep. When I opened it my notebook was inside, ripped to pieces, and when I say pieces, they were tiny. There was no way I could tape it back together. It was a fucking piss-take.

'Anyway, I was so pissed off, so heartbroken – all those years of work GONE – that I couldn't bring myself to post anything about it on social media. I didn't tell anyone apart from a couple of close friends. I went to work the next day – still in bits but I needed to distract myself – and I found a bunch of flowers in my dressing room. There was a note scrawled on the florist's card – *Sorry about your book* – but no name. I knew it had to be from the person who'd put that fucking shoebox on my doorstep. No one else knew, apart from a handful of friends as I said.'

'So, you went to the shop . . .' River says, 'to the florists?'

'Yeah. I rang the number on the card and this guy

answered. I asked him if he could tell me who'd sent me the flowers and he said he couldn't, that it was confidential, so I stormed up there, hoping to talk to the manager; and when I went in, I saw her . . . the woman behind the counter, she was the freaky woman who waited for me to leave the theatre each night, the one who went to all my shows.'

River gawps at her. Bridget is Charlotte's stalker, not the other way round. She was the one who'd sent her hideous messages, turned up to every show and, presumably when she didn't get the reaction she was after, stole her joke notebook and ripped it up? He can't believe it. Even as Charlotte was speaking, and all his suspicions were falling into place, he still couldn't equate the middle-aged woman he knows with someone so cold, unhinged, and cruel.

She's been masquerading as a victim when she's a stalker all along. She'd played him; played all of them. He'd *helped her* stalk Charlotte when he'd dropped a tracker inside her bag.

'Your bag,' he says to Charlotte now, 'I need to look inside.'

'Why?' She snatches the handbag closer.

'Something's been placed inside it; a tracker.'

Charlotte looks at him like he's crazy. 'Is this a wind-up?'

'No, unfortunately not. The person who's been stalking you is called Bridget Hopkins. At least I think that's her name, and she's tracking your movements. She knows where you are every minute of every day.'

'How do you . . .' Charlotte delves into her bag and drops handfuls of the contents – tampons, lipsticks, notepads, tissues and receipts – onto the table. The pile gets bigger, and bigger, and bigger, then Charlotte's jaw drops. 'Is this it?' She holds out the tracker. 'How did it get in there?'

River swallows. 'I put it there.'

She shifts away from him, suddenly fearful. 'What the . . . what the actual fuck?'

'I thought she was a stalking victim,' he says, 'like me.'

'What's that got to do with me? And this?'

Charlotte's eyes don't leave his face as he tells her about the WhatsApp group, the meeting in Highgate Woods, and the plan. As he wraps up the story, she shoves everything, apart from the tracker, back into her bag.

'How do I know a single word of what you've said is true?' There's a flintiness to her eyes.

'Because I've got no reason to lie.'

'And I've got no reason to believe you.'

They stare at each other across the table. They've reached an impasse River doesn't know how to cross.

'I'm sorry,' he says. 'I really am. I screwed up. I was just trying to do the right thing.'

Charlotte's eyes narrow. 'I think you should go.'

River has always loved Primrose Hill, with its wide open stretches of grass, its phenomenal views of the city, and its relaxed and airy vibe. He took Meg to Primrose Hill on their first date and laid out a picnic blanket, snacks and a cold bottle of wine. They'd talked and laughed for hours then, after the sun set on their first kiss, lay intertwined on the blanket, looking out at the lights of London sparkling against a black backdrop, its skyscrapers reaching into a star-free sky. It's always been his plan to propose here, in the same spot as their very first date.

He isn't looking at the view now though. He's walking slowly up the path that winds its way through the trees, looking this way and that, seeking out lone females with long dark hair, beanies or purple coats.

As he keeps an eye out for Vanessa, he sorts through what Charlotte told him about Bridget. There's something that still doesn't make sense. Why would a stalker join a stalking support group? Did Bridget get a sick thrill when she read their messages? Did she feed off their fear? Why did she bother going with Alex to rescue Lucy then disappear into the night? Was that for kicks and thrills too?

He reaches into his pocket for his phone. He's got to warn Alex and Lucy about her, to remind Alex to go somewhere Colin Sutherland doesn't know about, to—

He stiffens, hearing footsteps behind him. Someone's running, breathing heavily, getting closer and closer. Is it Charlotte? Running after him to tell him something important? Is it Vanessa? Was she hiding somewhere he couldn't see? He twists to look behind him, but something stops him. It tears into his right shoulder blade – sharp and piercing – then jabs at him again, in his ribs this time, in his spine, in his left shoulder, in his side. He tries to turn, to raise his hands, to stop the pain, but another blow lands, then another and another and now he's on his knees and he's being stabbed again and again. His clothes are wet and sticky, and something warm is oozing down his back. It's clogging up his lungs and he's struggling to breathe.

He swims in and out of consciousness, the cold tarmac of the path pressed against his cheek. As he closes his eyes, he hears a woman's voice, but his brain is so muddled and his back hurts so much he can't understand what's being

335

said. Her voice is discordant music: syllables clashing together, a whisper of vowels. His lips move as he tries to respond but there's no air in his lungs to form words. He's so tired. So, so very tired. He hopes that it's Meg.

Chapter 51

Bridget

FRIDAY 20TH OCTOBER

The day someone dies . . .

There is blood on the soles of Bridget's boots, on the carpet, on the kitchen floor, on her coat and her sweatshirt, on her hands, in her hair, on her face.

'Why does no one listen to me?' she asks the empty flat as she yanks off her boots then pulls off her coat and her sweatshirt and dunks everything into a sink full of soapy water. She carries a smaller bowl of suds into the hallway, drops to her knees and scrubs so vigorously at the blood spots on the carpet that the loose skin on the underside of her arms sways to and fro.

'I told him. I warned him.' Blood stain obliterated, she gets back up, empties the bowl into the toilet, then returns it to the kitchen and puts it next to the sink.

'No one tells me anything!' She shouts at the suitcase as

she drags it off the top of her wardrobe. 'No. One. Tells. Me. Anything!'

She moves from room to room, selecting items she might need, piling them into her arms before she returns to the suitcase and drops them inside.

'Did you tell me you were going to meet up with Charlotte, River? No, you didn't!' She zips the laptop into the laptop bag. 'You stupid, stupid, stupid man!'

'What is it about me?' she screams down the hallway as she returns to the kitchen to check her phone. 'No one listens and no one ever tells me the truth.'

Chapter 52

Lucy

The day someone dies . . .

It isn't until Alex exits the M25 that Lucy remembers her phone. Since they swapped seats in a layby in Devon, they've either chatted or lapsed into companionable, thoughtful silence for most of the journey home.

Alex put the radio on briefly, then turned it off saying the DJ's voice was annoying. Lucy agreed. It wasn't just her body that was battered and bruised; her mind and spirit were too. Her world had imploded and everyone else was just carrying on.

Notification after notification pings up on the screen, so many that she immediately regrets switching on her phone. There are concerned texts from Helen Corry (who was obviously contacted by the police when she disappeared), dozens of messages from other teachers asking why she's

339

not at work, several photos of the Lake District from her mum alongside questions about her girly holiday (*I hope you're having fun!*).

'Alex—' she says, then the hairs on her arms prickle into goosebumps as she spots a new message.

'What?' Alex keeps her eyes on the road. 'What is it?'

'It's River. He's messaged to say that someone else should have died.'

'What?' Now she glances at her, fear in her eyes. 'Read it out. Exactly as he's written it.'

'*Someone else should have died.* That's it. That's all he's written. No one's replied.'

'But we're . . . Oh god, not Bridget? He doesn't mean her, surely? I assumed—'

'Hang on. I'm just checking something.' Lucy scans the messages again, then clicks on Bridget's name. 'River sent his text at 12.59 p.m. and he hasn't used WhatsApp since. And Bridget was on . . . a few minutes ago. She's read the text but hasn't replied. It's not her.' She presses a hand to her chest. 'Oh, thank god.'

'Wait, hang on. If River and Bridget are alive, then who's dead?'

'I don't know.' Lucy looks back down at her phone, as though the answer might magically have appeared on the screen. 'Vanessa? Charlotte? Oh god I hope it's not Meg.'

'Ring River!' Alex suggests as Lucy says, 'I'll ring Bridget now.'

She uses the call option on WhatsApp to ring Bridget and listens as the tone chimes in her ear. The dashboard clock registers one minute passing, then two. 'She's not answering.'

'Hang up and try River.'

340

She taps on his name and turns on the speaker function so Alex can hear what he says. 'It's not working. The call won't connect.'

'Try ringing him normally. Maybe WhatsApp is down?'

The call goes straight through to voicemail. 'River, it's Lucy,' she says after the beep. 'I just got your message. I'm in the car with Alex. What's happened? We're worried. Please call me back as soon as you can.'

'What do you want to do?' Alex asks as a sign appears for Edgware. 'Do you still want to go back to yours to grab your passport?'

Lucy deliberates. There's a huge, terrified part of her that's desperate to buy a plane ticket to somewhere – anywhere – as soon as she can. A part of her knows that as long as Marcus isn't dead she'll never truly be safe. But she can't just leave the country when her friends are in trouble. Someone's died and Bridget and River aren't answering their phones. She can't let Alex deal with that alone, not when she's already shouldering so much.

'River went to meet up with Charlotte near Primrose Hill earlier,' Alex says, 'What if . . . what if Vanessa turned up, there was some kind of altercation and she ended up dead?'

'It's a possibility but . . .' Lucy lets the thought sink in. 'But why would that be the wrong person?'

'Because one of us was supposed to die?' There's doubt in Alex's voice. She can't make sense of what's going on either. 'And would River really text us something like that after he'd killed her? If it was Meg, he'd be too distraught to pick up the phone.'

'So maybe Bridget killed Charlotte?'

They share a look.

341

'Shit,' Lucy breathes.

'Yeah.'

The bright lights of London stream past as Lucy lets Alex's suggestion sink in. Bridget's been nothing but supportive, but everyone has their limits, god knows she knows that. She feels a dark twinge of envy; Bridget killed her tormentor while she couldn't even squeeze the trigger of the gun.

'Before I left London,' Alex's voice cuts through her thoughts. 'River told me that a lot of Bridget's stories weren't adding up. He said she'd lied when the wreath was delivered to the church – about her birthday. And Charlotte's not a florist. She's a comedian. Bridget claims she was working as a stagehand in a comedy club, and that's how they met.'

'What?'

'Exactly.' Alex turns the knob on the dashboard to turn down the heating. Hot air's been blasting through the vents ever since they left Devon. 'I asked her about it when we were driving to Devon, and she claimed she'd done all kinds of jobs over the years.'

'Was she lying?'

'Possibly.'

'But didn't Charlotte turn up at her shop and cause a massive scene?'

'We've only got Bridget's word for that.'

'Why would she make that up? What would be the point?'

'Attention?'

'Pretty twisted if so. I mean, if you want attention get up on stage at a holiday camp and do a bit of karaoke or . . .' she trails off, thinking. It's not sitting right with her, that Bridget isn't who she says she is. She trailed Alex everywhere to try and find her stalker, gave up loads more of her time than the rest of them.

'So . . . your house, River's or Bridget's?' Alex asks.

'River's – he's the one that sent the text.'

'Remind me where he lives again.'

'Chaplin Road, Willesden.'

'Can you put that in Google Maps.' Alex gestures at her phone, still charging on the dashboard. 'And let me know if I've had a message from Sam.'

'You're not worried that—'

'No. River wouldn't have texted something so vague if . . . if something like that had happened but . . .' she tails off and Lucy fills in the blanks. For someone desperate *not* to let herself love anyone Alex cares more about Sam than she'll admit to herself.

'Yep. He's messaged you.' Lucy navigates to WhatsApp and her finger hovers over Sam's name. 'Want me to read them to you?'

'Yes. No. Fuck I don't know. Just let me know if he's okay.'

'He's fine, but he's worried about you. He thinks you're in Birmingham for some reason. Do you want me to text him back?'

'Can you tell him I'm on my way back to London and I'll ring him later?'

As Lucy taps out the message another text from Sam flashes up on the screen.

Just saw on Twitter that a tall, thin man in his twenties with curly hair and glasses has been stabbed multiple times on Primrose Hill. Happened at lunchtime. I don't want to worry you – all this stalking stuff's got me nervy – but your

343

friend River's fine, right? Because that description sounded a lot like him. Hopefully I'm stressing about nothing – there must be hundreds of thousands of blokes in London who look like that. Ring me! Please. xx

Lucy's choked gasp makes Alex look at her sharply. 'What is it?'

She reads the message again, more slowly this time, her heart thundering. Sam's got to be wrong. It's got to be a coincidence. 'Where did you say River went to meet Charlotte?'

'Primrose Hill, why?'

'Oh shit, oh shit.' Tears fill her eyes, and she presses her hand over her mouth, smothering the terrified sobs that shake her body.

'What is it? Lucy what is it?' She can hear the panic in Alex's voice but she can't speak. There's no mention in the text of whether the stabbed man survived or not; but River can't be dead, not after everything they've been fighting for.

'Lucy!' Alex snatches the phone from her hand, glances at it, then swears under her breath as a car cuts in front of them and tosses the phone back at her. 'I can't read that. It's too long. For fuck's sake, just tell me what's happened. I'm freaking out here.'

Between juddering breaths Lucy tells her, watching the colour drain from her friend's face.

'No,' Alex's grip tightens on the steering wheel. 'It's not true. It can't be. River's fine, he's fine. He sent us a message saying that the wrong person died. Someone else is dead. He's fine.'

'Yes, yes,' Lucy says, desperately wishing she'd texted Sam back, or googled the stabbing, before she'd burst into tears.

'Maybe there was a fight and . . . and . . . he killed Vanessa. It must have been in self-defence, because she stabbed him and then he texted us to . . .' She tails off as her explanation falls apart. Why would Vanessa dying be the wrong person? And how could River kill her if he'd been stabbed multiple times? Is he even alive? They can't have lost him, they just can't.

Beside her Alex has become still and rigid, barely breathing, her glassy eyes fixed on the road.

'We need to get in touch with Meg,' Lucy says. 'She'll know what's happened. Do you know where she works?'

Alex doesn't reply. She looks deep in thought. Or locked in a memory. Lucy isn't sure which but the atmosphere in the car's become so charged and loaded that she just wants to get out.

'Bridget,' Alex says suddenly, making Lucy jump, and there's a chorus of angry beeps from behind them as the car swerves into the right-hand lane.

'Pull over!' Lucy cries. 'I think we should ring Sam and—'

'Something's not adding up,' Alex says softly, as though she's talking to herself. 'The lies, Charlotte, her disappearance last night, the message saying that the wrong person died, the fact she isn't answering her phone.'

'But . . . but what about River?'

'He's the reason we're going to Bridget's.' Alex gives her a look loaded with meaning. 'Whatever happened in Primrose Hill, she was involved.'

'You think she stabbed him!' Lucy stares at her incredulously. Bridget? Stab River? Not possible. Even if River was digging around in her life. Alex has put two and two together and come up with six.

345

'Yes. No. I don't know. Maybe Bridget attacked Charlotte and River got in the way. Maybe it was Vanessa. I don't fucking know, Lucy, but I'd bet my life that Bridget does.' There's a frenzied tone to her voice now that makes Lucy want to cry. Their friend has been stabbed and, instead of acknowledging that, Alex is bouncing between denial and recrimination. She's freaking out.

'You don't have to come,' Alex glances at her. 'I can drop you off somewhere safe.'

'No.' Lucy shakes her head decisively. 'I'm coming with you.'

Whatever Alex is planning on doing or saying when they get to Bridget's, she's not going to let her do it alone.

Chapter 53

Alexandra

FRIDAY 20TH OCTOBER

The day someone dies . . .

Alex pounds on Bridget's front door with her fist, rage building within her. 'Bridget! Open the door!'

She's been banging intermittently for several minutes, with no sign of life inside the flat.

'Here, let me try something.' Lucy drops to her knees and opens the letterbox. 'Bridget! It's Lucy and Alex. We're worried about you and we want to make sure you're okay.' She waits, listening, then adds, 'We've got some bad news about River. Please Bridget! Open the door.'

'She's in there!' she says in a whisper as she gets to her feet. 'She's coming.'

A harried-looking Bridget, in an unbuttoned coat and boots, opens the door, a key in her hand. 'What's all the noise? Oh god Lucy—' she throws her arms wide and pulls her into a tight hug. 'Alex, you got her out, thank god.'

No thanks to you, Alex thinks but doesn't say. She looks past her to the hallway and spots a full suitcase and a laptop bag, propped up against one wall. Have they turned up just as Bridget was planning to leave? More reason to be suspicious of her.

'Going somewhere?' she asks.

Bridget follows her line of sight. 'Oh those. Yes. Alex, I'm so sorry I disappeared. I got a text saying that my father's been taken ill, up in Hull, and he hasn't got much time left.'

Alex stares at her, incredulous that she could tell such a bare-faced lie without even blinking. She doesn't know *why* Bridget left in the dead of night, but she'd put money on the fact there aren't any dying fathers involved. And she still hasn't asked about River. 'We were supposed to be rescuing Lucy. She could have died.'

'You didn't though, did you?' Bridget gives Lucy a strange, twisted smile; but Alex isn't done with her yet. She's not letting her take one step out of the front door until she's told her the truth.

'Why didn't you come and find me?' she asks. 'Or send a text?'

'I did text.' Bridget looks indignant. 'I suggested you walk to Chagford and get a cab to Exeter Central from there.'

'Well, I didn't receive it. Show me your phone.'

Bridget glances at her watch. 'Oh dear. Is that the time. I need to leave soon, to get my train.'

'Did you hear about River?' Lucy asks, her eyes filling with tears.

Bridget touches a hand to her throat, as though clutching

a string of imaginary pearls. 'No. What's happened? Is he okay?'

'Sam sent a text saying that someone matching River's description was stabbed in Primrose Hill earlier,' Alex says as Lucy asks, 'Did you see the text, saying that the wrong person died?'

'Died? River is dead?' Bridget's gaze swings wildly from Lucy to Alex.

There's real emotion on her face now, Alex notes grimly. Bridget wasn't surprised to hear that River had been stabbed, but she's genuinely shocked that he may have died. Which means either she stabbed him or she saw it happen.

'Can I use your loo?' she asks. 'I haven't been since we left Devon.' She moves to step into her flat, but Bridget blocks her way.

'Sorry, I really need to get going. I told my . . . told my sister that I'd get up there as soon as I could.'

'And I'm going to have a really nasty accident if you don't let me go for a wee.'

Bridget doesn't move and Lucy looks worried and confused.

'I'm so sorry to hear about your dad,' Lucy says after a pause. She clutches Bridget's hands in sympathy, giving Alex just enough space to slip past Bridget, into the flat.

'Second door on the left!' Bridget calls after her. 'Don't take too long.'

Alex mouths 'Keep her talking!' from behind Bridget's back which makes Lucy frown.

On the left of the hallway is a closed door with a wet patch on the carpet outside, on the right is the open door to the living room. Alex slows her pace as she passes it but

349

there's nothing of interest inside. She passes another closed door (presumably the bathroom) and continues on to two bedrooms at the far side of the hall.

There's a cough as she approaches the bedroom on the right. Lucy's warning her that she and Bridget have joined her inside. She hears the front door click shut, but no sound of a key being turned in the lock. Bridget really is planning on leaving as soon as she can. Alex darts into the bedroom, taking in the minutiae of Bridget's life: double bed, floral duvet, wardrobe, bookcase (mostly true crime, a couple of novels), several plants, a framed print of *The Greatest Showman*, a packet of paracetamol and a reading light on the bedside table. There isn't much else. She opens the wardrobe, scans the row of clothes and the shoes beneath them. Nothing out of order, nothing weird. All very feminine and pretty. No sign of Gary's stuff though – where does he keep his things?

'You can't go in there,' she hears Bridget say. 'The kitchen's flooded. If you wait in the living room, I'll get you some water. No point both of us getting wet feet.'

Alex continues her search. She rummages through the chest of drawers, aware that time is ticking, and finds nothing other than underwear, jumpers, t-shirts and various jewellery boxes hidden under piles of socks. Bridget's obviously nervous about being burgled, not that that's a crime. She looks around the room again and her gaze latches onto the wicker bin at the end of the bed. It's full of rubbish, piled high, but that's not what caught her eye. There are two tracker boxes poking out from the used tissues and make-up packaging. Two? She takes a closer look and plucks out a receipt.

The Spy Shop, it says at the top, then there's an itemised tracker and the date – the fourteenth of October. That was the day River gave them each a tracker in Highgate Woods. Why would Bridget go and buy a second one? What did she need it for?

She tucks the receipt into her pocket and darts across the hall and into the second bedroom. It's a man's room, she can tell that immediately from the smell, and from the few items in the room. There aren't any pictures on the wall and the only decorative items are a hairbrush, a can of deodorant and a handful of loose change. Like Bridget's room there's a wardrobe, a chest of drawers, and a laundry bag full of clothes. Bridget and Gary might be husband and wife but theirs isn't a traditional marriage setup from the look of things. They sleep in separate rooms.

'Alex!' Bridget calls, her voice worryingly close. 'I really have to go.'

She's further up the hallway, outside the bathroom. Alex deliberates, unsure what to do. She can't call out that she's nearly done because her voice will give away her location. But if she doesn't reply, Bridget will become suspicious. Who *doesn't* shout out, 'There's someone in here!' if there's a knock on the bathroom door?

Maybe she should just stroll out of the bedroom and pretend she took a wrong turn? But she's been in the flat for three or four minutes; no one gets lost in a two-bedroom flat for that long.

'Bridget!' Lucy's voice rings out. 'Can you tell me what this plant is?'

'What plant?'

'The one with the wide leaves. I want to get one for my flat.'

Their voices grow quieter. Lucy's leading Bridget back to the living room, thank god. There are only two rooms left to search – the bathroom and the kitchen – and Alex's gut instinct is telling her to head for the kitchen first. Is it really flooded or was there another reason Bridget didn't want Lucy to go in?

As she draws closer to the kitchen she hears Bridget, in the living room, describing to Lucy the importance of watering a prayer plant with rainwater. The door's open. She can see the profile of Bridget's face.

Slowly, quietly, Alex turns the kitchen door handle and steps into the small, white room. She stands very still, looking around her, her heart thudding as her mind tries to make sense of the scene in front of her. The floor isn't flooded but it's damp, water and blood mixing in pools on the tiles. There are bloody splotches on the surfaces too, pink-stained bubbles on the washing-up sponge, and there's an item of clothing in the sink, swimming in water and blood. Alex just stares, her brain stunned into silence, not a single thought in her head.

'No! Alex. Stop!' She's tipped sideways as Bridget charges past her, pushing her out of the way. 'Out! Get out! Get out!'

'What the hell?' Alex feels Lucy's hand on her shoulder, then hears her gasp as she looks into the room. 'Oh my god. Bridget, were you attacked too? Why is there so much blood?'

Alex takes a step backwards, nudging Lucy into the hall. 'She wasn't attacked. Were you, Bridget?'

'I um . . . I . . .' Bridget's eyes are wild and desperate; her gaze darts from Alex to the sink full of blood to a knife rack beside the oven. 'I . . . this isn't how it looks.'

'How does it look?' Alex asks. A strange stillness has settled inside her. It's as though she's trapped in a dream.

'Like . . . like . . .' Bridget inches closer to the knife rack, her hands gripping the countertop behind her. She's stopped staring around wildly; her attention is solely focused on Alex. 'Like there's been an accident.'

'What kind?' Alex asks. There's no way she can get to the knife rack before Bridget, and there are no other weapons within reaching distance. If Bridget comes at her with the knife, she'll have to get out of the way – fast.

'One that wasn't supposed to happen.'

'Why was that, Bridget?' She gives Lucy a small push, urging her to leave the flat. Lucy shakes her head sharply. She's not going anywhere. 'Because River discovered that you're a fraud? Because you needed to shut him up?'

'I'm not a fraud. I'm not hiding anything.'

'You sent the text, didn't you? From River's phone, right after you stabbed him? Did you send the wreath to Natalie's funeral too? Who was it that was supposed to die?'

'I don't know what you mean.' Bridget takes another step closer to the knife rack. At the same moment Lucy says, 'I'm calling the police.'

Bridget moves in a blur, leaping towards the knife rack and pulling out a six-inch blade.

'Move.' She wields the knife, jabbing it at Alex, forcing her to take a step back.

'Bridget,' Lucy grabs Alex's arm and pulls her back into the hall, then stands in front of her, shielding her. 'You don't have to do this. We can . . . we can help you.'

Alex tries to shift her out of the way, but Lucy stands firm.

'How?' There's sweat in Bridget's hairline and her face has flushed a deep pink. 'How can either of you possibly help me? You don't know the first thing about me. Neither of you do.'

'That's not—'

'Fair?' Bridget barks. 'What's not fair is being called *creepy* when you're trying to help someone, being sworn at, being thrown out of someone's house, being ignored when you make overtures at friendship. What's not fair is River treating me like a child and Lucy rejecting my hospitality.'

'Blame me,' Alex moves so she's standing alongside Lucy. 'If you're angry with someone then be angry with me.'

'I do blame you!' Bridget screams. 'I didn't deserve to be treated like that. I—' She notices the mobile in Lucy's hand. 'Give that to me! Slide it, across the floor.'

Lucy glances at Alex, who nods, then tosses her phone across the carpet.

'No police.' Bridget stamps on the screen, then grinds at the broken glass with her heel. 'That's what you two have said all along isn't it?'

Phone destroyed, she moves backwards towards the front door, the knife outstretched, not taking her eyes off them. She dips to grab the laptop bag, straps it across her body, then reaches for the suitcase. She drags it alongside her as she continues to walk backwards until her heel clips the front door, then she steps outside.

'Bridget!' Alex calls after her. 'Who was supposed to die?'

Bridget stops walking.

'Who was it?' Alex shouts again. 'Tell me!'

Bridget zips up her coat then looks across at her, the

strangest expression on her face. 'It was you, Alex. It was always you.'

A cold breeze whistles through the flat as Bridget clicks the front door shut and Alex shivers.

'No,' Lucy grabs her arm as she moves to go after Bridget, 'not when she's got a knife, not when you heard what she said. We still need to ring the police; my mobile call didn't go through. There's a landline in there,' she gestures towards the living room.

Alex remains in the hallway, staring at the damp patch on the carpet outside the kitchen, listening to Lucy frantically explaining to the operator what had just happened. Bridget wanted her dead. The damp patch swims in and out of her vision as she tries to process what she just heard. Why? For what possible reason? She claimed she'd never even watched *Southern Lights*. Was that a lie? Or is there another reason she wanted to kill her? There has to be something in Bridget's bedroom that explains it. There was a suitcase on top of the wardrobe that she didn't have time to examine, and she didn't look under the bed.

She shivers again as another gust of cold air lifts the hair on her arms. Someone's opened the front door. She turns slowly, expecting to see Bridget framed in the doorway, and looks into Marcus's eyes instead.

He dangles a keyring from his fingers. 'Good job Granny's car was still in the garage, eh? And you thought you'd left me behind.'

Chapter 54

Lucy

FRIDAY 20TH OCTOBER

The day someone dies . . .

Lucy is on the phone to the police, telling them about Bridget, when Alex shouts her name. It's a shrill warning cry, so full of fear, that she throws down the phone and runs from the room, straight into Marcus's path. Time slows and she blinks rapidly as she tries to make sense of what she's seeing. There's no way Marcus can be at Bridget's front door. He's in Devon, injured. There's still blood all over his face.

Her body reacts before her mind does and she ducks low to avoid his outstretched hand. She stumbles as she turns, touches a hand to the wall to regain her balance, then takes off on quivering legs. She speeds towards Alex, standing at the far end of the hall.

'The gun.' She grabs Alex's arm. 'Where is it?'

'Not here. It's in my bag, in the car.'

Lucy's fear is reflected in the other woman's eyes. Marcus has shut the door behind him and he's walking towards them, fists clenched, the side of his face splattered with blood. Lucy looks from Bridget's bedroom to Gary's, seeking out weapons, but all she can see are soft furnishings, books and clothes. There's no way to escape: the hallway's a dead-end and the flat's on the fifth floor. They need to find a room with a lock.

She grabs Alex's hand and pulls her towards the bathroom. 'Quickly!' she says, as Marcus roars in anger.

Realising her plan, he's started to run. She gives a shriek of terror and lengthens her stride, speeding across the narrow stretch of carpet, Alex behind her, gasping with fear. Three feet, two feet, one. She reaches for the handle to the bathroom and turns it. Marcus is less than two feet away.

'In!' She shoves Alex into the bathroom then hurls herself through the gap in the door, twists, and slams her hands against the painted wood. The door closes a couple of inches then hits resistance. Marcus is on the other side, pushing back. The door swings towards her, smashing into her nose. For a split second it's as though her brain has short-circuited – all thoughts gone – then her vision becomes blurry as her eyes fill with tears, her face throbs violently and blood streams from her nostrils, sliding over her lips and her chin.

'Push!' Alex screams in her ear and Lucy blindly shoulders the door. Her feet scrabble against the bathroom tiles as she leans her weight into the wood, thighs tensing, teeth gritted. Beside her, Alex alternately grunts and growls. She's giving it everything she's got too but the door isn't closing. Marcus is too strong.

357

'I've called the police!' Lucy shouts. 'They'll be here any minute.'

The door gives, ever so slightly. Marcus has stopped pushing so hard. She can almost hear him thinking – *is she worth it? Or should I just run?*

'Go!' Lucy shouts. 'Leave, before they get here.'

It all happens so quickly. One minute Lucy is looking at Alex, the next she's being thrown backwards as the door slams open as though it's been knocked off its hinges. Her calves hit something hard, and she topples backwards into the bath. With the door wide open her view of the bathroom – and of Marcus – is obscured, but she can see one of Alex's hands resting against the toilet seat; she can hear her groaning in pain. There is a thwack – as powerful as a cricket bat hitting a ball – and Alex cries out again.

'No! No!' Lucy tries to move, to pull her legs into the bath so she can get up, but her ankles, calves and knees are pinioned between the door and the side of the tub. Marcus must be resting his weight into it.

'You fucking bitch,' he roars as another blow fills the air, then another, and Alex's cry becomes a scream.

'Marcus stop!' Lucy shouts, her voice raspy and thick, her face coated with blood. 'Stop!' She puts her hands behind her onto the side of the tub and tries to lift herself up, but without the use of her legs she can't get high or straight enough to push at the door.

More thuds, more thumps, and Alex stops crying out. The silence is more terrifying than the screams.

'Just take me!' Lucy begs. 'Just take me and leave her alone.'

The bathroom grows quiet. Marcus is listening.

358

'Take me back to the cottage,' Lucy says. 'Anywhere. Just please . . . please, please just leave her alone.'

From behind the door Alex whimpers, warning her not to go, but there's no choice to make. Either she goes with Marcus, or she listens to her friend getting beaten to death.

She holds her breath, waiting for him to act, and for the longest time nothing happens; then the pressure on her legs eases as he opens the door.

'Up.' He grabs her by the wrists and yanks her so forcefully out of the bathtub that she falls against him. His arms close around her and he pulls her into his body like they're lovers, locked in a passionate embrace. She tries to turn her head, to look for Alex, but Marcus lays a heavy hand on her cheek, forcing her to look towards the hall. He moves her to the doorway then shoves her towards the front door.

'No!' Alex's plaintive cry follows her as Marcus marches her along the hallway. 'No! No!'

Lucy falters at the front door, terror overwhelming her – will Alex die? Will she? – then her mind empties as Marcus yanks her by the hair so violently that the bones in her neck crack.

'Where's your phone?' he asks her.

She gestures towards the carpet, where Bridget ground her heel into her mobile's screen. 'Broke . . . broken.'

'You shouldn't have brought it with you,' Marcus says. 'There's tracking software on it. I put it on there days ago, just in case you tried to escape. You should have killed me while you had the chance. You stupid fucking bitch.'

Chapter 55

Bridget

FRIDAY 20TH OCTOBER

The day someone dies . . .

Bridget climbs into the driver's side seat of her van, having just hurled the suitcase and the laptop bag into the back. The laptop's probably broken but she doesn't care, she'll have to destroy it at some point anyway; sooner rather than later suits her just fine.

What the hell has happened to her life?

She thumps the steering wheel with her clenched fists then screams at the top of her lungs. A young man, walking past the van, shoots her a startled look and quickens his pace. There's half her life in that flat. No, her *whole* life is up there, and she's going to have to leave it behind.

She dials Gary's number, tapping her foot as she waits for him to pick up. They'll probably have to change their names.

He could be Jacob; she's always liked that name. And she could be . . . Susan? She considers it as a possibility. Amanda? Melissa? Star? That name makes her laugh. Star Starling, a fifty-eight-year-old stripper who gave up a career in LA to move to the UK and feign an English accent. She laughs again, imagining her flabby old body swinging round a pole. She struggles to tense and lift her pelvic floor muscles, never mind anything else.

Sighing, she glances back at the flat. No sign of Alex or Lucy. She should probably get a move on if she wants to avoid the police; that's if Gary *ever* gets round to answering his phone. She knows where he is – that's not the issue – but she needs to tell him what's going on before she picks him up. She can't just rock up and say, 'Hop in! We're going to the Outer Hebrides to start a new life.'

'Ring me back as soon as possible,' she hisses into the phone as it goes to voicemail. 'It's important. Whatever you do, do *not* go back to the flat.'

He's not perfect, and there are multiple reasons why she should just drive off alone, but he's all she's got. Gary's her world and she couldn't live without him. They both need a new start, somewhere a long, long way from London where they can put their mistakes behind them.

She drums her fingers on the steering wheel. She'd better go *somewhere* if she's going to avoid the police. She starts the engine, puts the van into gear, then hesitates. Lucy's coming out of the main door of the apartment block and there's someone with her; someone with long fair hair and a full-length coat. Bridget leans forward, squinting, then gasps in shock.

Marcus? What the hell is Marcus doing, coming out of her flat? Did he go up in the lift as she was running down the stairs?

His arm's around Lucy's shoulders, pinning her to his side. Bridget touches her foot to the accelerator, nudging the van forward as Marcus and Lucy turn left out of the apartment block and head down the street. It's a long road and, with most of London asleep, no one else is around. How the hell did Marcus get from Devon to London if Lucy took the car? And how did he know where she was?

Bridget taps at the brake as Lucy suddenly stops walking; she's trying to get out from under Marcus's arm. She's wriggling and fighting, desperately struggling to escape.

'Go, Lucy!' Bridget cries as the young woman breaks free and runs into the road, leaving Marcus on the pavement, nursing his hand as police sirens wail in the distance.

'Run, Lucy!' Bridget shouts. 'Run!'

But now Marcus is off and running too, covering the same ground as Lucy but in half the time. Bridget presses on the accelerator. The van's engine hums as she picks up speed and moves the clutch into second. She's only metres away from Marcus now and he's closing in on Lucy. In a matter of seconds, he'll catch up with her. Lucy glances over her shoulder and sees how close he is. There's terror written all over her face.

The sirens are louder now. The police will be here within minutes. Bridget panics, suddenly unsure. She's got two choices: reverse or accelerate, escape or kill? She thinks about Lucy – her drawn face at Natalie's funeral, the anguished cry that filled the church. Lucy in Highgate Woods, desperate for River to give them the trackers so she could go back to the job that she loved, to the school. Lucy in the back room of the newsagent's, crouched and desperate, shaking with fear. Lucy in Bridget's living room, sobbing with regret.

Bridget slams her foot down and the van leaps forward. She's about to be arrested for killing River, she may as well take another murder rap too. In for a penny, in for a pound.

There's a dull meaty thump as two tons of metal smash against a fourteen stone man. The van judders as the wheels mount Marcus's body. The force of the impact throws Bridget back in her seat.

She gives herself a little shake then puts the van into reverse and drives over Marcus again. An injured Marcus could heal and continue his stalking campaign. Dead Marcus would have a hard time doing that.

As she moves the gear stick into first to pull away, an eerie blue light surrounds her and the single whoop of a siren fills the air. A police car has pulled up behind her van and the doors are opening. Bridget looks from the wing mirror to the windscreen, to Lucy, standing in the middle of the road, just metres from the van. The lower half of her face is dark with blood, and she's hugging herself. She's so small and slight she looks like a teenager, but she's strong; so much stronger than she knows.

If I'd had a daughter, Bridget thinks to herself, I'd want her to be as resilient and determined as that girl.

Sensing she's being watched, Lucy raises her chin. Her lips move and Bridget frowns, trying to work out what she's trying to say.

'Police!' A grim-faced officer has appeared beside the van. He looks Bridget up and down.

'Hands where I can see them!' He pulls on the door handle

then takes a step back, his hand moving to his radio. 'Slowly, get out of the van.'

Holding her hands palms out, Bridget twists the upper half of her body towards the door. She swings her legs out of the van, a smile playing on her lips. She's worked out what Lucy was trying to say to her.

It was thank you.

Chapter 56

River

Six days later

River stares at the whitewashed ceiling of the hospital ward, listening to the soft bleeps of machines and the groans of the other patients. He's dosed up on morphine, disorientated and tired, but relieved to be alive. He remembers the attack and the searing pain in his shoulder blades, but very little afterwards. He can't remember being rushed to surgery or his first few days in hospital, but he knows that he lost a lot of blood in the attack, a stab wound had pierced his liver and his pulse was weak. He's lucky to be alive.

He turns his head at the sound of the curtain being pulled back, grimacing as the muscles in his neck and back tense. It'll be a nurse or his mum or his dad; they've barely left his side in the last few days.

Joy sparks in his chest as his girlfriend appears around the curtain. They've exchanged dozens of texts since he was hospitalised, but it's the first time he's seen her face.

'Hi my love.' Meg perches on the edge of his bed and gently strokes his fingers, being careful not to dislodge the IV in the back of his hand. Her gaze sweeps the length of his body, to the machines surrounding him, and rests on his face.

'How are you feeling?' The expression in her eyes is soft; so tender that River's heart swells with love and regret.

'Better for seeing you.'

'Don't try and talk,' she says gently. 'Save your strength. I'm just . . . I'm so glad to see you . . . I'm glad you're alive.' As her eyes fill with tears, River feels like his heart might break. 'I never should have left you. If I hadn't, I might have talked you out of going to see Charlotte. You never would have gone to Primrose Hill; you wouldn't have been stabbed.'

'You don't know that.'

She looks away, her face crumpled with guilt, her chest heaving as she sobs.

'It's not your fault,' River says, wishing he had the strength to sit up and pull her into his arms. 'Please don't do this to yourself.'

'I just . . .' She wipes the sleeve of her cardigan over her face. 'I was so scared when I heard the news. I thought . . . I thought you were going to die.'

She wasn't the only one. The anguish he saw in his mother's eyes as she looked down at him in his hospital bed would haunt him for years.

'I'm sorry. I'll pull myself together in a minute.' Meg takes a tissue out of her pocket and noisily blows her nose. 'This isn't going to help your obs.' The nurse in her kicks in and she glances across at the machine to his right, then, seemingly

366

reassured by whatever she sees there, pulls a chair closer and moves off the bed.

'Anyway,' she says, touching his hand again. 'I'm sorry I wasn't here sooner. I wasn't allowed to visit you until the police had ruled me out as a suspect – close family only, I was told.'

'As if you did this.'

'I know,' she says. 'But they had to do their job.'

Two detectives had paid him a visit a couple of days ago and, as best he could, given his morphine haze, he had talked them through the events of Friday night: his phone call to Alex, his suspicions about Bridget and the drink he'd had with Charlotte. He'd seen disappointment in the female detective's eyes when he'd admitted that he couldn't name his attacker; it had all happened so quickly, so silently – so fast that he never saw their face. One minute he was standing on the path in Primrose Hill and the next he was dropping to his knees. 'Is there anything you can remember hearing?' the detective had asked him, and when he mentioned a woman's voice, he'd seen the light return to her eyes.

'Bridget's been arrested,' Meg says. 'Did you know?'

River nods. He'd found out yesterday. The police had found the knife in her kitchen, in a washing-up bowl with bloodied clothes. They'd also found multiple Twitter and email accounts on her laptop. She'd admitted to his attack, and to stalking Alex and Charlotte. The social media messages were vile and relentless; she'd been an adoring fan originally, forming bonds with both women over the deaths of their fathers (Bridget's dad had died a year earlier). Then, as Alex and Charlotte had pulled away and stopped replying, Bridget became frustrated, then vengeful. The police were working on the theory that she'd stabbed River to prevent him from sharing her secret once Charlotte had told him the truth.

'She sent the wreath,' he says. 'And pretended to see Sutherland outside the police station. She got a kick out of seeing how scared Alex was, and the whole time she pretended that she was a victim too.'

'Did you know she ran over someone multiple times, the same night she stabbed you?' Meg says. 'The papers said he died.'

'Lucy's ex,' River says. He didn't know whether to be pleased or horrified when his dad showed him the article. Pleased that Marcus was out of Lucy's life forever but appalled at how cold-heartedly Bridget could kill – if he needed a reminder of how lucky he was to be alive, that was it.

'I'm sorry I called you obsessive.' Meg touches a hand to his cheek. 'It all got too much. I didn't know how to deal with it on top of everything that was going on at work. And your ex—'

'She's not going to be a problem any more.'

Vanessa was the first person the police arrested. Apparently when someone gets stabbed the Met suddenly deploys a whole load of officers to track a stalker down. Her alibi for his attempted murder – she was on CCTV at a pub near her parents' house – was rock solid, but she was charged with stalking and harassment. River had been told that she might get a five-year jail term, given how serious the charges were.

'Have Alex and Lucy been in touch?' he asks Meg, changing the subject. Neither of them wants to give Vanessa another moment's thought.

'Yeah,' she says. 'Thanks for giving them my number.

We've exchanged a few messages and we're going to meet up soon.'

Alex and Lucy had visited him yesterday, Alex walking gingerly, clutching her side, and Lucy with a splint across her nose. They'd both spent time in hospital – Alex for a fractured rib and facial and abdominal bruising, Lucy for a broken nose. He'd cried out in shock when he saw them.

'Don't!' Alex had admonished; one side of her face was a riot of different colours, her right eye swollen shut. 'It hurts when I cry.'

Lucy and Alex had settled themselves either side of his bed and, for the next hour, they'd taken it in turns to tell him what had happened – the escape from Devon, the discovery in Bridget's kitchen, Marcus turning up, the attack and his death. Neither of them could believe what Bridget had done and Lucy had apologised for falling for Vanessa's lies. She'd cried as she told him how terrible she'd felt for misleading him about the tracker. She'd admitted she'd dropped it into the taxi driver's coat pocket on the way home; it was hanging on the back of his chair.

River had forgiven her immediately. If his neighbours, and several of his and Vanessa's mutual friends, had fallen for her bullshit, then what hope did Lucy have? His ex was a master manipulator. She'd done everything she could to isolate him and try and destroy his life.

A lot of tears had been shed in the two hours that Lucy and Alex visited him. There was laughter too: jokes were a panacea to his pain; inappropriate comments washed away tension and silly stories reminded them all that, despite everything, they were battered but not broken; they were all still alive.

'That's good,' River says now, in response to Meg's comment about meeting up with Lucy and Alex. It makes sense that the three most important women in his life spend time together. 'I think you'll like them.'

'If you like them,' Meg says, 'then I'm sure I'll . . .' the rest of the sentence falls away.

'What is it?' he asks. 'What's the matter?'

'You. Me. I was so obsessed with how hard I was finding everything that I didn't really consider what it was like for you. I abandoned you when you needed me most, when we should have stuck together. How can you ever forgive that? How can you ever trust me again?'

'Meg,' he moves his hand over hers, 'I love you, and there's nothing to forgive.'

As she gently drapes herself over him and presses her face to his he closes his eyes, drinking in the scent of her, allowing the morphine and the feeling of her skin on his to numb the edges of his pain. His mind drifts and wanders, out of the ward and hospital, to Primrose Hill, to his flat, to Highgate Wood. As a thought surfaces from the swirling cloud of memories his breath catches in his throat, and he gasps.

'Sorry, did I hurt you?' Meg pulls away from him, startled, her worried eyes scanning his body, then his face. 'Was I pressing down too hard?'

'No.' River shakes his head. 'No, it's not that.' He blinks, trying to bring the thought into focus, to explore it logically, but the drugs are kicking in again and he's not sure if it will make any sense. 'If Bridget was behind all this . . . if she was behind the wreath . . . then who threw the rock with the six?'

Chapter 57

Alexandra

Two weeks later

Alex is sitting on a bench inside Wood Green police station, her damp umbrella on the floor beside her feet. It's a drizzly November morning and she clutches her phone, hoping Sam isn't still waiting for her outside.

Find a café or something, she types. *I might be here for hours.*

He responds instantly. *You sure you don't want me to come in?*

I spoke to the desk sergeant. Just waiting for someone to come and talk to me. I'm okay, you can go. I'll call you when I leave.

The part about being okay is a lie – the heels of her boots are tap-tapping on the industrial lino, and her stomach is churning – but she has to do this alone. Just walking into the building without turning around and walking out again is a huge improvement on the last time she visited the station. Her bravery, in part, is down to the kindness of the officers who discovered her, bruised and bleeding on the floor of Bridget's bathroom. Relief at being discovered had given way to fresh terror when she realised that Lucy had gone.

'It's okay,' one of the female officers had said gently. 'We've got her, she's safe.'

'And Marcus?'

The officer had looked at her blankly.

'Tall man,' Alex had said. 'Young, muscly, long hair. He's the one who attacked me.'

Several of the officers had exchanged looks but said nothing.

'What is it?' she'd asked. 'What's happened?'

'There's been a road traffic incident outside,' the female officer said. 'It's not looking good.'

Fear coursed through her. 'Who's been hurt?'

'The victim is male. Paramedics are working on him. I can't tell you more than that, I'm afraid.'

'You're safe now,' a male officer had said. 'A paramedic will be up here to see you very soon.'

She'd been carried out of the flat and down the stairs on a stretcher. As they'd ferried her past the first of two ambulances, she'd caught a glimpse of a male figure strapped to a gurney inside. There weren't any paramedics bent over him, shocking his heart or pushing IVs into his veins. He lay, still as death, alone.

'Miss Raynor.' A tall, brunette woman with a jaw-length bob and side fringe pokes her head out from around a door. 'I'm Detective Sergeant Alice Hawking. Come through.'

Alex follows her through a narrow corridor to a small,

boxy room furnished with a sofa and very little else. She hesitates in the doorway, heart racing; she's been in one of these rooms before, a long time ago.

'Sorry to keep you waiting so long,' DS Hawking says, gesturing for her to take a seat on the sofa. 'Your phone query a couple of days ago, about a DC Ian McGowan? It was passed on to me.'

'Yes,' Alex takes a seat. 'I tried ringing New Scotland Yard but the number on the website connected me to 101. The person I spoke to said they couldn't transfer me to him, and I didn't know what else to do so I rang this station instead.'

'And you wanted to speak to this person because . . .' the detective glances at her notepad, '. . . he contacted you to arrange a restorative justice meeting with a . . . Colin Sutherland.'

'Yeah, to confront . . .' Alex's throat is so dry the words catch in her throat. '. . . to talk to him about the crime he committed. Sorry, this is hard for me. Is there any water at all?'

The detective glances around the near-empty room. 'I'm sorry. I could get some for you if—'

'It's fine. Don't worry.' Alex presses her hands under her thighs. If she lets the detective leave the room, there's a good chance it'll be empty by the time she returns. She's on stage later – her first performance as Hedda Gabler in the West End – and she'd been *this* close to staying at home. Sam had talked her out of it. He'd said if she didn't sort this out now, she never would.

'The thing is,' Alex says, 'DC McGowan caught me off-guard when he called, and I was . . . I was quite rude. I said I wasn't interested but I've changed my mind. I was

373

a victim of another crime recently, one that could have killed me, and I've realised that I'm not scared any more. Not of Sutherland, or what he might say.'

'Right.' There's a sigh in the detective's voice as she shifts in her chair. 'So, the thing is, Alexandra, there isn't actually a DC Ian McGowan in the Metropolitan Police Force.'

Alex stares at her, open-mouthed.

'I'm afraid so.' DS Hawking looks back at her notepad. 'The other thing is that Colin Sutherland didn't make a restorative justice request. He's still in prison, in a medical wing. Terminal cancer, apparently, unlikely to see out the month.'

Alex presses her hands to her mouth, trying to make sense of what she's hearing. Someone calling themselves DC Ian McGowan had called her a few weeks ago. She'd been on a Zoom with the others; they'd heard every word she said. Maybe she should bring River and Lucy in with her, to prove she's not going mad.

'He's definitely still in prison?'

'Yes. Medical wing, like I said.'

She wrestles with the information. She'd got herself all hyped up to meet him, to confront him, to look him in the eye and tell him how murdering her parents had destroyed her life. But he's dying . . . and he doesn't want a meeting? She's conflicted: glad that he's dying, but now she'll never get to tell him how she feels.

A new thought strikes her, one that makes her sit up taller in her seat and her heart race.

'Why did no one tell me this?'

'About Sutherland?'

'Yes! My victim support officer told me that Bridget

admitted she didn't see him outside the police station, but she never mentioned that he was still in prison.'

The detective shifts in her seat. 'Sorry, I'm not following. Bridget . . .'

'Hopkins, my stalker. She's awaiting trial. She also killed Marcus Wordsworth and tried to kill my friend, River Scott-Tyler.'

'Right.' The detective looks thoughtful. 'Well, I can only apologise for the oversight. What's the name of the officer?'

She tells her and a cold shiver works its way up Alex's spine as she writes it down. If a detective didn't call her – then who did? One of the trolls who's been harassing her for years on Twitter? One of the many men who think it's fine to send her dick pics, rape threats and lascivious comments? Some bastard who tracked down her phone number and thought it would be funny to taunt her about the most traumatic event of her life? She feels sick. Someone that wasn't Bridget threw a rock at them, inscribed with the number six. She's been chatting about it with River and Lucy, throwing possibilities back and forth over the last two weeks. The only plausible explanation they've come up with is that Bridget paid someone to throw it at them, to make them more fearful, to take any suspicion off her. But no rock was found in Bridget's house – she must have thrown it away – and the detectives involved in her case are no closer to discovering the truth.

'If you hear from this person again,' DC Hawking says, 'do please get in touch. We don't take impersonating a police officer lightly and obviously we're concerned for your welfare too.'

'Okay.' Sensing the discussion is over, Alex gets to her

feet. She's going to have to change her phone number again. Maybe even move house. She's definitely going to have to leave social media for good; there are far too many weirdos around.

She follows the detective out of the room, down the corridor and back into the reception area. She shakes her hand, says thank you, and heads outside.

She spots Samuel, sitting on a bench under an umbrella and laughs. 'I thought I told you to go somewhere dry.'

He returns her smile and stands up. 'What can I say, I'm lazy. How did it go?'

She considers lying. It'll stress him out if she tells him the truth. Besides, it's the first night of the play and he'll worry if he thinks there's another stalker out there; she's worried about that herself. But maybe Lucy was right; maybe she doesn't have to shoulder everything alone.

'The call was bullshit,' she says. 'There's no one in the Metropolitan Police called DC Ian McGowan, and Colin Sutherland's still in jail. Dying of cancer apparently. There was no request for restorative justice. The whole thing was one massive wind-up.'

'You're kidding?' Samuel's eyes widen. 'Are you okay?'

She shrugs, then pushes her hands deep into her pockets. 'Who knows? I haven't got the headspace to try and figure it out. Want to grab a drink? I would say lunch but I'm so nervous about tonight I think that I'd puke.'

'You sure you're okay?' He knows her too well to accept a brush-off about something so massive.

'I've got to be, haven't I?' She kisses him on the mouth then links her arm through his. 'It's the first night of the play.'

*

Alexandra is dead; sprawled on the ground, her cheek against the cold, wooden floor, one arm stretched above her head, the other wrapped around her body, her eyes closed, her lips parted.

A man stands over her, 'She's dead.'

'People don't do such things,' another man says.

She gets up slowly, walks to the front of the stage with the rest of the cast and, as the audience breaks into rapturous applause, she bows. She leaves by a side door, pauses for a moment then returns to the stage and, as the audience continues to clap and whoop, bows again. People – hundreds of them – are on their feet, clapping wildly, smiling, delighted; so many eyes on her, so much energy in the room. She looks at her fellow actors and they all – even Conrad – return her smile. The rest of the cast have done multiple performances with her understudy over the last few weeks, but this is special. This is something she's dreamed of for so long.

She feels as though she's floating as they all file off the stage again. Floating, exhilarated, exhausted and the most joyful that she's felt in years. She was *so* afraid before she walked on stage just two hours earlier – and not just because of the pressure of the role. The wreath at Natalie's funeral was meant for her; Bridget had said as much. The plan must have been to kill her on the opening night of the play, and it makes her shiver, thinking about Bridget sitting out in the audience – watching her intently, with hatred in her heart. How was she going to do it? Was she going to leap onto the stage and stab her like she stabbed River? Would the audience have watched, open-mouthed, thinking it was fake blood – a part of the play?

What about her troll? The man who pretended to be a

detective. Was he in the audience tonight? The thought makes her shiver as she heads back to her dressing room, cast members slapping her on the back, clapping and shouting well done.

'Superb!' Liz says, pulling her into a hug. 'Absolutely phenomenal. I couldn't tell you this before, but we had reviewers from the *Evening Standard*, *The Times* and *The Guardian* in tonight and I know they'll be as blown away as the audience.'

'Do you think?' Her chest tightens at the thought of a scathing review. That's something else she's been trying not to think about all day.

'I *know*, darling.' Liz hugs her again. 'Now go and get yourself showered and changed. Champagne on me backstage in half an hour. Don't be late or I'll finish the lot.' She cackles uproariously then catches sight of someone behind Alex and raises her hand. 'Sonya, darling! Could I please bend your ear?'

Alex slips into her dressing room and puts the gun on the dressing table – she'd walked past the stagehand without giving it to him again – then rests against the closed door and pulls long, deep breaths into her lungs. She did it. She fucking did it. She cups her face with her hands, closes her eyes and lets out a squeal of excitement. Right now, she doesn't care if the critics rip her performance to shreds. She's fulfilled a long-held dream and every moment on stage was terrifying, wonderful, madness. She gets to do it all over again tomorrow, and the day after that, and the day after that. She moves around the room, smelling the bouquets that have been arriving all day. There's one from River and Meg saying they can't wait to see the play at the weekend, another from Lucy saying she's incredibly proud. There are flowers from ex-cast mates, friends from drama school, from her Auntie Genevieve and her cousin Kate:

Sorry we can't be there tonight but hope to see you soon. Your mum and dad would be so proud of you, Lexie. xx

A wave of grief, so powerful that she grips the edge of the dressing table, passes through her. No one's called her Lexie for years. It's a name her family called her – her mum, her dad and Ben. She called herself Alex went she went to drama school and locked ten-year-old Lexie away in a box like she'd never existed at all.

She steadies herself, staring at her reflection in the mirror, then dips her fingers into the pot of stage make-up remover and rubs the greasy goo all over her face. She uses a cloth to remove the worst of it then heads into the en-suite to wash off what's left. As she splashes her face with water her mind returns to something that's been bothering her for a while. The first time she went to Wood Green station Bridget had waved at her from the park. At the time she'd assumed it was a wave of hello, but it wasn't, was it? It was a warning gesture, telling someone to stay away. But who?

As pounding music rattles the walls of the theatre Alex dabs at her face with a towel. There's a loud knock at the door. Sam! Her stomach flutters in excitement. He had complimentary tickets for the performance and she's dying to find out what he thought.

'Come in!' she calls, stepping back into the dressing room, wishing she'd had time to take a shower.

Her excitement levels plummet as someone short and stocky steps into the room; a man with a youngish face and a receding hairline. It's the stagehand . . . she racks her brain for a name. He started during rehearsals, before her whole world fell apart. A name pops into her head and she smiles.

'Hi Jerry. I'm so sorry, I completely forgot to give you the gun. Again.' She hurries to the dressing table. 'Only this time it was because I was buzzing so much I completely—'

'It's Gary.' He closes the door behind him.

Alex hesitates, her hand resting on the gun.

Gary. She turns to look at him, her mind whirring. 'Bridget's husband, Gary?'

He turns the key in the lock and tucks it into his pocket. 'Wrong, I'm her son.'

She can see it now, in the shape of his face, the colour of his eyes and the length of his nose. He's taller and plumper than Bridget but there are echoes of her face in his. She'd never have noticed them if she hadn't been looking but now they're all that she can see.

'You were supposed to die,' Gary says, taking a step towards her, 'Didn't you get the message I sent on River's phone?'

Alex closes her hand around the gun and backs away from him. 'That was you?'

'Who did you think it was, my mum?' As he moves closer, she catches a whiff of his aftershave: musky, peppery and dry. 'I couldn't get rid of her. Always hanging around like a bad smell, getting in the way.' His dark eyes spark with something that isn't humour. 'She took the rap though, for that fucking dick. River, what kind of name is that?' His left hand is open and relaxed, but his right hand is clenched, closed over something. He's tried to pull the sleeve of his jumper down, but it rides up as he gesticulates. There's a flash of silver. He's holding a knife.

'You tried to kill him,' Alex says.

380

'He was sniffing around, asking questions. I heard him talking to Charlotte, in the café. He thought he was better than me, better than mum. He was going to go after her, ask her questions, get her to talk. He thought he was clever, that he could catch me out.'

'He didn't know who you were.' Alex glances at the door. There's no way she can get across the room to unlock it without him catching her. 'Help!' she screams instead. 'Somebody help!'

Gary grins. 'They're not gonna hear you. There's a proper little party going on backstage – beer, nibbles, music, the works. Liz is already halfway to forgetting her own name. Your big night, Alex. The one that was supposed to happen fucking weeks ago. Do you know how long I've waited for this? How patiently I've had to wait?'

'For what?'

He stares at her through narrowing eyes, mulling over the question. 'For this. For your opening night. To wipe that smug smile off your face. It's about loyalty, Alex; about not fucking people over.'

'But I don't know you. We've never talked.'

Something changes in his eyes, and he charges at her, shoving her shoulders so hard that she topples backward. Her head hits the wall, the gun flies out of her hand, and she drops to the floor. He looms over her, sliding the knife from beneath his sleeve.

'Oh yes you have, but you forgot about me . . .' he taps the side of his head so hard it makes Alex wince, '. . . the moment you met your boyfriend. One minute it was yes, Gary, I understand, Gary, thank you for sharing that with me, Gary, now it's Gary-fucking-who?'

She prays that Samuel's still at home, that he never made the show. 'Remind me. Was it online that we talked? I've had a lot of conversations with a lot of different—'

Gary's boot connects with her diaphragm, and she gasps.

'You fucking people.' His top lip retracts to reveal the gap between his teeth. 'This is why I *hate* you. You and Charlotte, and all the other celebrity bitches, you're all so fucking fake. You *pretend* to like people. You'll talk to your social media followers if you think you can sell them a ticket or book or a whatever the fuck it is that you're peddling but if they're lonely, if they're nice, normal people who just want to talk to someone, then fuck them.'

'Was it . . . was it . . .' she scrabbles around in the only memories she's got of memorable social media conversations, too terrified to pick one in case she's wrong. 'What was your Twitter name?'

'GZ4752. Photo was a McLaren MCL36.'

The letters and numbers mean nothing, but she's got a vague memory of a Formula 1 car. 'Your dad died,' she says, bracing herself for the next kick.

'Oh, so you do remember.' He raises his eyebrows. 'Well, I'm glad it made such a big fucking impression on you.'

'He killed himself,' Alex says. 'I'm so—'

His kick lands square in her chest; a searing pain spreads out to her back, neck and jaw, making her howl in agony. 'Don't say you're sorry. Don't you fucking dare. I thought you might care, once upon a time. I thought the fact your parents were murdered would make you a little bit fucking empathetic. But no! You're all fucking narcissists, play-acting and pretending, just out for what you can get. You don't care about normal people, do you? I don't think you know

382

half the names of the crew because you're so fucking wrapped up in your precious fucking—'

A knock at the door makes him drop to his knees. He presses a hand to Alex's mouth then manhandles her to her feet. 'It's him,' he whispers. 'I put a note on your door before I came in – Do Not Disturb – then in brackets (unless you're Sam). Cute, don't you think?'

She writhes and twists beneath his hand, then, as he presses the knife to her throat, she holds herself very still. She's struggling to breathe now; each time she inhales something crunches under her skin, near her ribs, but she doesn't care what happens to her. As long as the door stays locked, Sam will be safe.

There's another knock and in the gap between songs she hears Sam shout, 'It's me! Open up.'

She wriggles desperately, gritting her teeth against the pain as she tries to drive her elbow into Gary's side so he'll release her mouth, but he's holding her too tightly.

'Open the door,' he hisses in her ear.

She shakes her head. She'd rather he slit her throat. Gary's body stiffens behind her then he throws her away from him and she hits the floor chin first. Her teeth clatter together, and a shooting pain radiates through her jaw. She tries to shout Samuel's name to warn him but it hurts to open her mouth. She grabs for the gun, lying inches from her outstretched hand. Grunting, she inches herself closer, and curling her finger over the trigger, rolls onto her back and looks up, just as Sam walks into the room. At his feet is a bouquet of flowers, his palm open as though he just let them go. Gary is behind him, one arm hooked around his midriff, the other holding a knife to his throat.

'Let him go.' Alex straightens her arm and lines up the target. She can only see half of Gary's face, but that's all she needs. 'Let him go or I'll shoot.'

His laughter fills the room. 'Think it's a real gun, do you? Think you're Hedda Gabler? Are you going to shoot yourself too?' His laughter stops as quickly as it started. 'It's a fake gun you stupid bitch.'

Remembering what Lucy told her, she adjusts her aim so the sight's trained on his eye.

He yawns, feigning boredom, and tightens his grip on the knife. 'I'm going to kill him, then I'm going to kill—'

It's a ping, a pfft, the softest sound as a single pellet leaves the air pistol, travels across the dressing room and buries itself into the skin, the fat and the muscle above Gary's left eyebrow, then continues its journey into his brain.

Chapter 58

Lucy

Three months later

Lucy tries not to stare as she follows Alex and River into the visiting area of HMP Bronzefield. She's never set foot in a prison before and the whole experience – from showing her passport at the visitor centre and putting her belongings into a locker, to entering airport-style security and being frisked – makes her feel as though she's entering another world. She'd expected the visiting area to be cold and austere, like the one in Happy Valley when Ryan goes to visit Tommy Lee Royce, but it's more like a nice play centre, with toys for children, posters on the walls and a tea and snack bar.

She helps River and Alex arrange four chairs around one of the low tables then sits down and tries to keep still. She's been nervous about visiting Bridget for days – partly because she's worried about how it will affect River and Alex, partly because she's scared. She thought she knew Bridget when she didn't really know her at all. The look in the other woman's eyes when she reversed over Marcus still haunts her. It was as though a part of her had disconnected, like she was no longer there.

Lucy places her hand on River's knee. 'Are you okay? Sure you still want to do this?'

He nods stoically but she knows that he's worried. Meg tells them everything that River won't share – that he barely sleeps and when he does, he has vivid nightmares; that he won't leave the house after dark, that he's in near constant pain.

'Alex?' Lucy asks. 'How are you?'

'I'm fine, Lucy, thanks.' She pulls her coat tighter around her even though it's warm in the visitor's room.

Alex's leopard-print jacket is either in Devon, or in a police evidence bag somewhere. They've both spent hours in police interview rooms being asked about their relationships with Bridget, with each other, about the trackers, their stalkers and whether they'd gone too far in seeking revenge. A squat, balding detective had suggested to Lucy that maybe she'd conspired with Bridget to have Marcus killed. She'd lost her temper then. 'Was that before he abducted and tried to strangle me, or when I was running away after he'd beaten up my friend and left her for dead?'

Alex also faced intense questioning about the air pistol she'd used to shoot Gary. Whose was it? Why did she have it? Had she known it was loaded when she'd pointed it at Gary and fired?

Only Lucy, River and Sam know the truth: that Alex had secretly switched the fake gun and pistol before the performance began. Aware that her troll might be in the audience, she'd used the pistol on stage for the duration of

386

the play. She knew there was only one pellet inside, but it made her feel powerful, holding its weight in her hand. She'd mimed pulling the trigger, reacting as the sound engineer played a gunshot – just as she had with the fake gun.

The version of the truth Alex told the police was that Gary had placed the air pistol on stage and she'd used it throughout the performance unaware that it was real. She'd reached for it instinctively when he'd threatened her and Sam with a knife. It was self-defence; no one was more surprised than her when a pellet lodged itself in his brain.

The pellet caused life-changing injuries, but it didn't kill him, and they'd all taken the stand in court, first for Gary's trial and then for Bridget's. Lucy cried in the gallery as she watched River gingerly approach the witness box, resting his weight onto a stick. He was so brave, the way he answered the barristers' questions; Alex was too. It was an honour to count two such strong people as her friends.

Now, as Bridget walks towards them in a grey sweatshirt and grey jogging bottoms with her hair pulled back into a ponytail, River and Alex visibly tense.

'Hi!' There's fear in Bridget's eyes as she sits down on the empty chair and presses her hands between her knees. 'Thank you all for coming.'

'This isn't a restorative justice meeting you know,' Alex crosses her arms and sits back in her chair, putting as much distance as she can between her and Bridget. River glances longingly over towards the tea and snacks bar.

'I know.' Bridget's tone is light and pleasant, but she can't bring herself to smile. Her gaze drifts towards River. 'How are you?'

'Scarred,' Alex says. 'Having nightmares, in pain. How do

387

you think he feels after being stabbed in the back by your son?'

'Alex.' River shoots her a look. 'It's okay. I've got this. I'm getting better, Bridget, with Meg's help; day by day. But I miss the person I used to be. I miss feeling like there was nothing I couldn't do.'

Bridget bows her head, her hands trembling. 'When I saw River's WhatsApp message saying he was meeting Charlotte for lunch at a café in Primrose Hill I rushed back from Devon as fast as I could.' She glances at Alex, who's staring at the floor, then returns her gaze to River. 'I knew Gary would trail her there but I never dreamed for one second that he'd hurt you. I thought it was Charlotte he was after, so when I saw him trailing you as you left the café, I tried my best to catch up with him, but I was too far away and he was walking too quickly, and he wouldn't answer his phone. As I said at my trial, I did try to help you. I tried . . . I tried to stop the bleeding with my hands but . . . there was so much blood and then other people started pointing and walking towards us and I panicked. I rang an ambulance, when I was far enough away.'

'That was big of you,' Alex says under her breath. 'Someone give that woman an OBE.'

'What I don't understand,' Lucy says, 'is why you didn't report Gary to the police? Not just then but months earlier, when you saw his laptop and all those awful messages he'd been sending on Twitter under different names: the abuse, the body shaming, calling women liars and sluts and whores, making disgusting comments about their family members and all the vicious, nasty threats.' Dozens of the tweets he'd sent were read out in his trials and each one made her shudder. It was terrifying, how quickly he went from pleasant and respectful to obsessive and vengeful.

'He's been unwell,' Bridget looks at her beseechingly, as though she's the one member of the group who might possibly understand, 'since his dad took his own life.'

'That's no excuse, and you know it. You saw what I went through with Marcus. I told you the excuses he made for his behaviour and you're using almost identical ones for your son.'

'It's not the same,' Bridget says. 'What Gary did – it was just words.'

'Just words?' Alex sits forward in her chair, the base of her throat flushed red. 'Are you fucking kidding me? He stabbed River! He nearly killed Sam.'

'I was . . . I was talking about the tweets,' Bridget began. 'He—'

'He tormented me online for months. He texted me and called me a whore then, when he didn't get a reaction, he called pretending to be a police officer, taunting me about Colin Sutherland. He wrote in lipstick on my dressing room mirror that it was my fault that my parents died. He photographed me in the restaurant and sent me that hideous photo. He followed me to Covent Garden and sent me texts, telling me he was watching me. He did similar things to Charlotte, and god knows how many other women as well.'

'I know . . . I know he did, and that's when I realised that things might be getting out of control. That's why I bought a tracker for him, so I'd know where he was.'

'Out of control? You continually lied and misled me, when you knew exactly where he was, the whole time. How was that supposed to protect me? Are you as nuts as he—'

389

'Don't call him that!'

'I don't understand how you can possibly justify this. Any of this.' Alex rests her elbows on her knees and cradles her head in her hands. 'Your behaviour, or his.'

'I was trying to understand him, to stop him, to keep him out of prison. That's why I joined the forum.' Bridget's jiggling so violently on the edge of her seat that a prison officer drifts closer, concerned. 'I googled "How to stop a stalker" and found the group. That's what I was trying to do, stop him. I never wanted any of this. I thought there might be some tips for someone out there like me . . . someone who was trying to stop someone they love making bad decisions . . .'

'And you found us, instead,' River says. 'And pretended you were a victim too, even if that meant making Charlotte the bad guy. Surely, Bridget, you've got to acknowledge how screwed up that was?'

Alex looks up from her hands. 'How long was it until you realised I was one of his victims?'

'I recognised you in the Zoom, from *Southern Lights*, obviously, but I'd seen your Twitter profile on Gary's computer. I'd read the messages he'd sent you.'

'Bit of a coincidence, wasn't it?' River says, his eyes narrowed in suspicion. 'That you just happened to connect with Alex in a stalking support group?'

'Yes!' Bridget sits up taller, gripping the sides of her chair. 'Yes it was, that's why I was so shocked when I saw her on Zoom. But there were dozens, maybe hundreds of women he was trolling, not just Alex and Charlotte: newsreaders, TV presenters, authors, scientists, politicians and musicians. Some of them would just like his reply and then he'd reply to every tweet they sent. Some of them, like Alex, took pity on him and talked to him; properly talked to him. They were the ones he got angriest with, when they stopped interacting with him.'

'Did you know he sent the wreath?' Lucy asks.

'Not straight away, but I recognised the description of the woman who'd brought it to Nat's funeral. Dark-haired, nose ring, neck tattoo, strong accent. She sounded like his Polish friend Agata. I couldn't be sure, of course.'

'And you didn't confront him?' River says. 'You pocketed the rock at Highgate Woods too, didn't you? So we couldn't show it to the police?'

'You saw how scared we were!' Alex says. 'Have you got no empathy?'

Lucy shakes her head in bewilderment. 'How many people did he need to kill before you told the police?'

The barrage of questions seems to floor Bridget and she stares into space, gawping, until Alex says, 'I need a break. Anyone want some tea?'

Everyone but Bridget nods and, as Alex weaves in and out of the tables towards the snack bar, Bridget starts to cry.

'It's been so hard, dealing with all this by myself. Gary was twenty-nine when his dad died, and it hit him hard. He and Charlie were best mates. They were obsessed with Formula 1, always jetting off here, there and everywhere to watch the races. I used to love it; I'd get the flat to myself for a change. Then Charlie lost his job, and everything changed. It was like he'd lost a part of himself, not being able to work. It really knocked his pride, and . . .' she waves a hand through the air as though pushing the memory away.

391

'Anyway, Gary struggled after Charlie died, he rarely left his room. I thought he might be depressed but then he told me there were people on the internet who were helping him, that he'd made some new friends.

'I went into his room one day to get his laundry basket when he was having a shower, and his laptop was open on his bed. Because he'd been so secretive about these new friends, I snuck a look. There were so many browser windows open – Twitter, email, Instagram – different accounts, hundreds of messages to celebrities, some of them nice but most of them . . .' she pulls a face. 'I only got a glimpse at the laptop that once. He logged out every other time, like he knew that I knew. Only a handful of names stuck in my head – Alex's, obviously, and Charlotte McBeth, a comedian at the comedy store where he worked.'

'As a stagehand,' River says.

'Yes.' She glances away, unable to meet his eyes. 'I started going along to her shows, because I'd seen some of those horrible threats Gary had posted on Twitter, and I thought if I was there, it would stop him from doing anything awful. I went so many times, heard the same jokes over and over again. It used to really annoy him but that was what I wanted. I thought maybe he'd leave her alone or leave the job. Then I started finding things hidden away in his room – underwear, lipstick, photographs of random people with bits of sellotape on the back. I didn't realise they were hers until about two weeks after he left the comedy club to start at the theatre. I was emptying the bins and I found a writing notebook all ripped up in Gary's bin. I'd seen Charlotte's social media posts about it – saying it had gone missing and begging for it to be returned – so I put all the bits in a shoebox, hoping that she could piece it together, and left it outside her house. I felt so bad about what Gary had done, destroying all the jokes and the stories she'd worked so hard on, that I sent her some flowers – anonymously of course. I put a handwritten note in an envelope and tucked it amongst the stems, then left the bouquet at the back of the shop for the delivery driver to pick it up. Mark must have noticed that the shop's business card hadn't been stapled to the cellophane, and attached one. When I realised what he'd done I knew it was only a matter of time until she found me.'

'She turned up at the shop,' Lucy says. 'Because of the address on the back of the card.'

'She was so angry.' Bridget flushes at the memory. 'I was convinced she was going to stab me with my own secateurs.'

'When did you realise Gary wasn't just trolling Charlotte? That he was stalking me too?' Alex sets three plastic cups of tea on the table. Bridget flinches at her proximity and the wary expression returns to her eyes.

'When you told us someone had written something horrible on your mirror in lipstick.' She picks at a food stain on the hem of her sweatshirt. 'I googled the name of your play and found the name of the theatre. I knew then. It was where Gary had just started work. I wasn't helping him, Alex; I was trying to protect you. I thought that if I put trackers on you, and Gary, and Charlotte then I could stop something bad from happening. I could turn up and stop him. And it worked, didn't it? Nothing happened to you, but I . . . I didn't . . . I never in a million years thought he'd go after River. And I thought he'd stop after that happened, so I pleaded guilty. I made him promise that he'd leave you alone.'

Lucy watches Alex as she sips at her tea. Whatever mental talking-to she gave herself over at the snack bar seems to have worked. She looks calmer than she has all day, more in control of her emotions, but not detached. Not like she was at Natalie's funeral, where she had a strange, absent look in her eyes.

'I could have died,' Alex says, taking another sip of her drink. 'So could Sam. Your son held a knife to his neck. If I hadn't shot him, he would have slit his throat.'

'He's not well.' Bridget continues to scrape at her sweatshirt with her fingernail. 'He's getting psychiatric help. He's all I've got.'

'I don't blame Gary.' Alex raises her gaze. 'I blame you. You terrorised me by pretending that Sutherland was out of jail. You knew how fucked up I was by what he'd done and you lied anyway. You could have done the right thing, Bridget. You could have told the police the truth and taken a dangerous person off the streets.'

'He's not just a person!' Bridget stares at her defiantly. 'He's my son.'

'And what price love?'

Neither of them speaks. As the silence becomes increasingly uncomfortable Lucy searches for something – anything – she could say to mend the atmosphere, then mutes the thought. She doesn't have to be a peacemaker or an apologist. Now Marcus is dead she doesn't have to fear tense situations, cold silences or hostile standoffs anymore.

She's not sure how she feels about Bridget. She hates her for what she did to River and Alex, but she never did anything that put her own life in danger. Bridget whisked her away from Marcus once, attempted to help her escape a second time then, when saving her was no longer an option, she did the only thing she could – she took his life. Was that what she'd been trying to do all along – save everyone, including her son? Had she muddled along, trying her best, until she was faced with an impossible choice – choose him, or choose them?

River shifts in his seat. His meds are shut away in a locker and she can see the pain on his face.

'I'm sorry!' Bridget says suddenly. 'River, Alex. I'm sorry. Really I am. I never wanted any of this to happen, you have to believe that. I went about everything the wrong way, but I didn't want any of you to get hurt. I swear. You're right, Alex. This is all my fault.'

No one speaks and a loaded silence descends on the group. Lucy shifts in her seat, desperate to break it, but it's not her forgiveness that Bridget wants. When the tension becomes so unbearable that she can't stand it for another second, River clears his throat and speaks.

'I accept your apology Bridget and I forgive you. It's not a decision I've reached easily. Believe you me, I've battled with anger for months and I've had the . . .' he shakes his head, '. . . the darkest thoughts. But I'm not going to let them consume me, not like I did with Vanessa. I nearly lost Meg and that's never happening again.'

'Thank you.' Bridget bows her head as her eyes fill with tears.

Alex leans back in her chair, tensing her arms as she stares at the ceiling. Whatever she's about to say, she's not finding it easy.

'I've spent half my life carrying the weight of hatred.' She rocks forwards and looks Bridget in the eyes, 'and I'm not going to let you or Gary steal a second from the life I've got left. I came here today to get answers: answers I never got from Colin Sutherland because I was too scared to confront him. And now he's dead and I'll never find out the truth. But I've made my peace with that now. I've said what I came here to say, and I've listened to what you said. I don't like it and I certainly don't understand it – I probably never will – but I forgive you, Bridget.' She reaches for River and Lucy's hands and gives them a squeeze. 'I think maybe it's time to go.'

River gets to his feet, his right hand floundering against his thigh as though he's trying to make up his mind whether or not to shake Bridget's hand. He settles for a nod instead. 'Goodbye then, Bridget. I'm glad we had this conversation.'

'I am too.' Alex's gaze is softer than it was when they entered the prison half an hour ago. Her voice is too.

Lucy hangs back as her friends head towards the exit. 'Are you okay?' she asks Bridget, who's watching them go. She looks broken. 'Is it really awful in here?'

'It was nicer at home,' Bridget gives a small laugh, 'but I'm getting used to it. Gary writes to me twice a week and my cellmate's nice, if a little emotional. I've been teaching her how to make flowers out of crepe paper. She's been sending them home to her kids.'

'That's nice,' Lucy says, even though the thought of sharing a cell with a stranger terrifies her. One decision – that's all that had stopped her from wearing a grey sweatshirt of her own. If she'd pulled the trigger instead of losing her nerve . . . if the bullet had entered Marcus's eye . . . then her fate – and Bridget's – would be swapped.

'I've got a little cleaning job that keeps me busy,' Bridget continues, 'and I've asked the officers if I could lead a floristry class. They've told me to ask again in six months' time.' She gives a little shrug. 'That's something to look forward to, I guess.'

'You gave up your freedom,' Lucy says, 'so I could have mine.'

'I'm not so sure about that.' Bridget gives a dry little snort. 'You know I got time for aiding and abetting too.'

'I do, yeah. The thing is . . . and I couldn't say this in front of River and Alex . . .' Lucy takes her hands in hers, '. . . but I'll always be grateful to you for saving me from Marcus.'

'I'm not all bad then.' Bridget's eyes crinkle as she smiles. 'Just forty or fifty per cent.'

Chapter 59

Alexandra

With her arm linked through Sam's, Alex follows Lucy and River as they make their way through the garden of remembrance in north-west London. It's a bright and sunny February afternoon with clusters of snowdrops peeping from beneath rosemary bushes and the green noses of eager hyacinths pushing through the earth.

'I've found her,' Lucy says softly as she pauses by a memorial vase, the plaque glistening in the sunshine and a bunch of yellow daffodils, blue irises and white tulips bursting from the vase.

Alex lets go of Sam's arm. He nods at her, his eyes solemn. 'I'll give you guys some space. I'll wait in the car.'

As he heads back down the path Alex crouches beside the memorial and touches her fingers to the plaque. 'Hi Natalie.'

'It feels like so long ago,' Lucy breathes, 'and yesterday, all at the same time.'

River crouches down too. 'I still feel like we could have saved her.'

Alex looks at him. 'We barely saved ourselves.'

'I suppose. I just . . .'

'I know,' she says softly. 'Me too.'

'When is it going to end?' Lucy asks. 'She was just walking home from work.'

None of them have an answer, and the question hangs in the air.

Wordlessly, they take turns tucking a single white rose in amongst the daffodils then stand, shoulder to shoulder in front of the memorial to their friend, Natalie, whose life was taken too soon.

Alex closes her eyes. She was so angry when the vicar used that phrase. She'd wanted him to say it as it was – to use the word murder – but that wouldn't have been right. That would have put the focus on the crime, and not on the baby, the girl, the woman that Natalie had been. That she is remembered is what's important; not how she died.

She tilts her face towards the sun, feels its rays warming her skin, then pulls the cool February air deep into her lungs. She feels as though she's spent the last twenty-five years of her life living underground and someone's shown her the sky.

'Lexie?'

She opens her eyes and turns her head towards the source of the sound, shielding her eyes from the sun. She blinks, trying to make sense of what she's seeing. It's been organised for weeks, this meeting, but she's never really believed that it would happen. She thought he'd change his mind, or she would, or the world would conspire to keep them apart. Now that he's here, now that she can see all six foot two of him with his deep brown eyes, his

399

broad shoulders and his lopsided smile, she can't believe that he's real.

She walks towards her brother, feeling as though she's in a dream. When he opens his arms, she runs.

Author's Note

Fifteen years ago, I was stalked for several months by my controlling and coercive ex-boyfriend. After four years together, and multiple attempts to extricate myself from the relationship, I'd decided that enough was enough, it was over, and I was never going back. My ex was intelligent, eloquent and manipulative and every other time I'd tried to leave him, he'd managed to talk me back. This time I decided he wouldn't get that opportunity. There would be no communication – no replies to phone calls, emails or texts. That lack of control was something he just couldn't deal with, and so the stalking began.

At first there were calls – dozens of them, my phone ringing all day and all night. I'd turn it off only to discover multiple voicemails and text messages when I turned it back on – some loving, some accusatory, so many telling me that I'd never find love again. It felt like an assault, like I was being bombarded with words. Then he started ringing my landline, which I had to unplug from the wall. Letters through the post followed and cards, with photos of the two of us (in 'happier times') pasted inside. Flowers too and presents, all consigned to the bin. Then he started turning up, travelling down from London to my flat in Brighton, standing outside in the rain, his finger pressed to the bell. I'd sit in darkness in my living room, curtains drawn, too scared to move, with my hands pressed over my ears. *I know you're in there*, he'd text me. *I heard you moving around.*

After four years together he knew all my insecurities and fears and I found it increasingly hard to ignore certain messages that were designed to press my buttons, to make me respond. He'd driven away so many of my friends over the course of our relationship but my friend Lisa had refused to abandon me. She kept me strong during his onslaught, urging me to text her, not him. My sister and her then girlfriend offered me refuge. He knew where I lived but he'd never been to their flat. I moved into their spare room, but I still wasn't safe. My ex knew where I worked in London, and what days I went in. I told my boss I had to change my schedule, but I was still terrified each time I stepped on the tube.

At no point during this time did I think about going to the police. Back then they only got involved if victims of stalking were being openly threatened and my ex was too clever to do that, he preferred to mentally torture me instead. As weeks ticked into months, each day brought with it new fear – what tactic would he try next? He sent me multiple emails, creating new accounts every time I blocked one. He used the contact form on my website and sent me so many messages I had to take it down. When loneliness drove me to join two online dating services, he tracked down my profiles and messaged me. When I clicked on his profile he'd copied what I'd written, making his profile a male version of mine. He found my secret Twitter account, he found blog posts I'd commented on and he tried to hack my Facebook account. I was no safer online than I was in real life.

He was an IT professional, and he knew every technological trick to trace my digital footprint, but there was one thing he didn't know about. I had a hidden statcounter on my website which provided me with statistics: how many people visited my website each day, how many times they'd visited, what country they were from, and details of their IP address. Because I'd logged onto my website from my ex's flat I knew his IP address, and his work IP address showed up with the company's name. Some days I'd log into the statcounter and see that he was looking at my website *right now.* Unnerving, but also strangely reassuring. If he was checking out my website from London, then I was safe to leave my Brighton flat, knowing he wasn't waiting for me nearby. It was the only control I had.

Control is something I wanted to give back to the stalking victims in *Every Move You Make,* but I chose to give them a different kind of technology. I gave them trackers to place on each other's stalkers. I gave them hope. But just like real life, even the best-laid plans can go wrong.

I was lucky. My ex stopped stalking me when I finally admitted to my parents what was going on, and my father rang him and threatened to report him to the police. But there are many, many stalkers who can't and won't stop, regardless of cautions, restraining orders, or even a prison term. According to a study by the University of Gloucester stalking was present in 94 per cent of the 358 cases of criminal homicides they examined. Surveillance activity, including covert watching, was recorded 63 per cent of the time. The Office of National Statistics state that there were 709,388 stalking and harassment offences in the UK, in the year ending March 2023. Stalking and harassment legislation has become more stringent since I was a victim of stalking but that doesn't make the experience any less terrifying.

If you, or someone you love, are being stalked or harassed please *tell someone*. Keep a record of every form of contact and get in touch with the police. You can also get advice from various charities and organisations include the Susy Lamplugh Trust, and the National Stalking Helpline.

https://www.suzylamplugh.org/

National Stalking Helpline: 0808 802 0300

Acknowledgements

Huge thanks to my always brilliant editor Helen Huthwaite whose insightful and thoughtful editorial suggestions helped bring this book to life. To Elisha Lundin and Raphaella Demetris thanks so much for everything you did for this book. I hugely appreciate the work and time you all put in.

Maddie Dunne-Kirby, Ella Young and Gabriella Drinkald, you went above and beyond with marketing and publicity. Thank you for all your hard work. Big love to Tom Dunstan and Samantha Luton who work their sales magic book after book, and to Anna Derkacz for being her brilliant self. My grateful thanks to Toby James whose superb skills created the amazing cover for this book.

To my agent Madeleine Milburn, and her brilliant team, thank you so much for your continued support. August 2024 will be sixteen years since I signed on the dotted line. Where has the time gone?

Thank you to River Scott-Tyler for his generous bid in

the Books for Ukraine auction so his name would be featured in this book. Julia Kerruish, one of my Facebook page followers, suggested Southern Lights as the name of the soap opera that Alex used to work for. A brilliant suggestion, thank you so much. Neil Lancaster and Imran Mahmood – I'm so grateful for all the help you gave me with the policing and legal research in this book. Drinks are on me, next time we meet. Thank you, Claire Douglas and Kate Gray for doing word races with me (Claire won by a mile this time. In fact, she's already lapped me). Thank you Kate Harrison for being my go-to person to chat through plot issues, you're the best.

All my love to my wonderful family – my parents Jenny and Reg who are my biggest supporters, my brother David who isn't the biggest fan of reading but reads my books (that's brotherly love right there) and my sister Bec who has been bugging me to dedicate a book just to her since she shared a dedication with Dave back in 2011. You've been very patient Bec, here it is! To Sami Eaton, Louise Foley, Ana Hall and Angela Hall, thank you for being the best sisters-in-law that I could wish for. Frazer, Sophie, Oliver, Rose and Mia, the best nieces and nephews in the world. Steve and Guinevere Hall, and James Loach, you're pretty damned cool. To my crime family – thank you for making me laugh and keeping me sane. The biggest part of my heart is shared between Chris and Seth Hall, you're my everything, thank you for loving and supporting me the way you do.

Finally, a huge thank you to all the readers, booksellers, librarians and reviewers who continue to read, stock and champion my books. Your support means the world.

If this is your first C.L. Taylor book, or your tenth, thank you so much for picking up *Every Move You Make*. If you want to know when I've got a new book out, do sign up to my newsletter. You'll be sent a free ebook as a thank you from me. https://cltaylorauthor.com/newsletter/

To keep in touch with me on social media follow me on:
X: @callytaylor
Facebook: @CallyTaylorAuthor
Instagram: @cltaylorauthor

Every Move You Make
Book Club Questions

May contain spoilers

1. Lucy's actions in the book are driven by her dark secret. Did you judge her when you discovered what she'd done?

2. River takes charge of the situation after the wreath is delivered and buys the trackers and tells the others what to do. Vanessa tells Lucy that he's controlling and coercive and that makes Lucy doubt him. How suspicious of him were you?

3. Alexandra is mistrustful of the police, because the man who murdered her parents was an ex-police officer. Did her unwillingness to go to the police frustrate you or were you sympathetic to her fear?

4. Bridget never mentions any friends or family and says that Gary is her whole world. How much do you think her loneliness drove her to do what she did?

5. If you have a child, how would you approach it if they did something illegal? Would you be tempted to cover for them so they could avoid going to jail?

6. River makes a decision to stay in London and protect Meg, rather than go to Devon to protect Lucy. Did you agree with his decision?

7. For you, what was the most terrifying moment in the book?

8. Who did you think sent the wreath? Why?

9. How satisfying was the ending? Did what you hoped would happen play out?

10. Which books would you recommend to readers who enjoyed *Every Move You Make*?

What would you do if your husband framed you for murder?

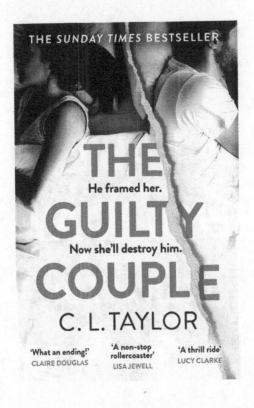

THE *SUNDAY TIMES* BESTSELLER

He framed her.

THE GUILTY

Now she'll destroy him.

COUPLE

C. L. TAYLOR

'What an ending!'
CLAIRE DOUGLAS

'A non-stop rollercoaster'
LISA JEWELL

'A thrill ride'
LUCY CLARKE

The smash-hit Richard & Judy Book Club pick from the multi million-copy crime thriller bestseller.

You come to Soul Shrink to be healed.
You don't expect to die.

The addictive and suspenseful
psychological thriller.

Three strangers. Two secrets.
One terrifying evening.

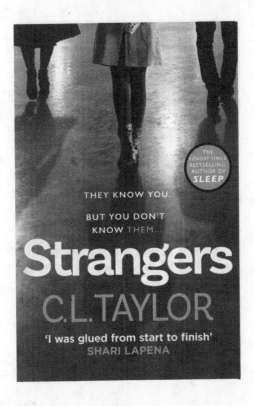

THE SUNDAY TIMES BESTSELLING AUTHOR OF *SLEEP*

THEY KNOW YOU.

BUT YOU DON'T
KNOW THEM...

Strangers

C.L. TAYLOR

'I was glued from start to finish'
SHARI LAPENA

A gripping novel that will keep you
guessing until the end.

Seven guests. Seven secrets.
One killer.

The addictive Richard & Judy Book Club pick from
the psychological thriller bestseller.

Sometimes your first love won't let you go ...

Sometimes your first love
won't let you go...

THE
FEAR

'Claustrophobic and compelling'
KARIN SLAUGHTER

C.L. TAYLOR
The *Sunday Times* bestseller

The sensational thriller from the
Sunday Times bestseller.

What do you do when no one
believes you . . .?

The nail-biting, twisty thriller from the
Sunday Times bestseller.

You love your family. They make you feel
safe. You trust them. Or do you . . .?

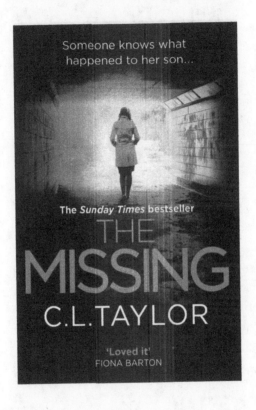

Someone knows what
happened to her son...

The *Sunday Times* bestseller

THE
MISSING

C.L. TAYLOR

'Loved it'
FIONA BARTON

The unputdownable psychological thriller to leave you on
the edge of your seat.

She trusted her friends with
her life . . .

A haunting, compelling psychological thriller
to have you hooked.

Keeping this secret was killing her . . .

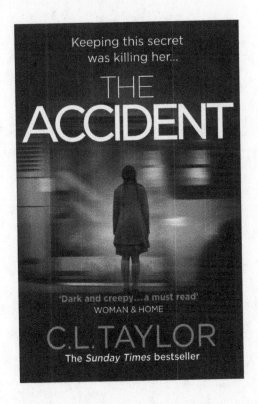

A riveting psychological thriller from the
Sunday Times bestseller.